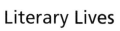

Literary Lives

This classic and longstanding series has established itself making a major contribution to literary biography. The books in the series are thoroughly researched and comprehensive, covering the writer's complete oeuvre. The latest volumes trace the literary, professional, publishing, and social contexts that shaped influential authors—exploring the "why" behind writers' greatest works. In its thirtieth year, the series aims to publish on a diverse set of writers—both canonical and rediscovered—in an accessible and engaging way.

More information about this series at
http://www.palgrave.com/gp/series/14010

Patricia Laurence

Elizabeth Bowen

A Literary Life

Second Edition

Patricia Laurence
City University of New York
New York, NY, USA

Literary Lives
ISBN 978-3-030-71359-1   ISBN 978-3-030-71360-7   (eBook)
https://doi.org/10.1007/978-3-030-71360-7

This Palgrave Macmillan imprint is published by the registered company Springer Nature Switzerland AG.
The registered company address is: Gewerbestrasse 11, 6330 Cham, Switzerland

To my grandchildren, Noah, Zach, Salomé, Limor, and Solal

Acknowledgments

Writing a biography almost half a century after Elizabeth Bowen's death leaves few of the living to consult. Biography then becomes an itinerary—to libraries, universities, museums, and institutes that contain writings about her life and times in Ireland, England, and America—but also a journey to the landscapes that Bowen loved. Beneath the physical archive is the "psychic archive"[1] contained in letters, memories, people, and places—varied and unexpected—created by Bowen herself, family members, friends, literary agents, past biographers, historians, and critics. There are many to thank along the way.

First, heartfelt thanks to Phyllis Lassner, Professor Emerita, Northwestern University, for her early belief in and encouragement of this biography and her expert reading—given her own early and prescient Bowen publications—of the manuscript in its early stages. I also owe a particular debt to Laetitia Lefroy, Bowen's first cousin, for generously offering an interview and patiently providing family information as well as photos of the Colley family in endless e-mails over the course of several years. Judith Robertson, niece of Charles Ritchie and editor with Victoria Glendinning of Bowen and Ritchie's correspondence and journals, *Love's Civil War*—deserves special thanks for graciously offering letters, notes, and information about Charles Ritchie and his Canadian colleagues. I am grateful also for the generosity of Professor Allan Hepburn, McGill University who shared information in the early stages of this project, and, importantly, brought Bowen's life as a public intellectual and cultural and political agent out of the shadows for Bowen studies through publication of her unpublished writings and talks, Edinburgh University Press.

And thanks to my editor, Allie Troyanos, for her belief in my work, and Rachel Jacobs for her patience with the preparation of this book for the press.

Biographers and Critics: "Books are built upon books," states Virginia Woolf. Mine is no exception, and I have learned much from Victoria Glendinning's portrait, *Elizabeth Bowen: A Biography* (1977) published four years after Bowen's death, and her recent co-edited collection of letters and journals of Bowen and Charles Ritchie. Invaluable early writing on Bowen includes Hermione Lee, *Estimations* (1981, 1999); Patricia Craig, *Biography* (1986); Phyllis Lassner, *Elizabeth Bowen* (1990), and *The Short Fiction of Elizabeth Bowen* (1991); Heather Bryant Jordan, *How Will the Heart Endure: Elizabeth Bowen and the Landscape of War* (1992); and Andrew Bennett and Nicholas Royle, *Elizabeth Bowen and the Dissolution of the Novel* (1995). The 1999 Bowen centenary spurred numerous publications, including Alan Hepburn's collection of Bowen's unpublished writings and talks (2005–2010) and Glendinning and Robertson's *Love's Civil War: Elizabeth Bowen & Charles Ritchie, Letters and Diaries, 1941–1973* (2008). Influential critical studies followed, including Maude Ellmann's psychological exploration, *Elizabeth Bowen: The Shadow Across the Page* (2003); Neil Corcoran's prescient exploration of Bowen's writing on childhood, war, and Ireland, *Elizabeth Bowen: The Enforced Return* (2004); and Clair Wills' *That Neutral Island: A History of Ireland During the Second World War* (2007), an invaluable resource for revelations about how life was lived under neutrality as well as the political reasoning behind Ireland's policy.

Librarians: The pursuit of letters has taken me on several trips to libraries where I have met remarkable librarians, caryatids of archives. In America: for early encouragement, guidance, and a fellowship award for research, gratitude to Thomas S. Staley, retired director of the Ransom Center, University of Texas at Austin, Molly Schwartzenburg, librarian, and Pat; Gayle Richardson and Sue Horton, Huntington Library, CA.; Jennifer Tobias, MOMA Library, NYC; John Tofanelli, Coordinator of British and American Collections, Columbia University; Bob Scott, Columbia University Technical Lab; and Shelley B. Barber and Justine E. Sundaram, John J. Burns Library, Boston College. In England: for generous, timely and expert guidance through the labyrinth of the British National Archives, Kew, Neill Cobbett, Modern Overseas Records Specialist, SOE and Propaganda Modern Overseas Records; Colin Harris, Bodleian, Oxford; Rod Hamilton, David Sharp, BBC Archives, British National Library; Janet Adamson, Folkstone Family and Oral History Society, Hythe for early and generous assistance with Hythe family records and the census; Andrew J.P. Gray, archivist, Durham Library, Durham; Patricia McGuire, King's College Library, Cambridge University; Alison Smith, Archivist, Oxfordshire History Centre, Oxford; Andrew Melcher, Chair of Hythe Civic Society; Andrew Hudson, Heritage Room Folkestone Library; and Sue Kewer, Hythe. In Ireland: thanks to Ms. Sam Coade and

Frances Clarke, Division of Ms., National Library of Ireland; and Ruth Potterton and Estelle Gittins, Trinity College Library, Dublin.

For Interviews and Correspondence: In Ireland: Colley family members, Laetitia Lefroy, Lady Jessica Rathdonnell, Christopher and Mary Hone, and Finlay Colley; Declan Kiberd, eminent critic of Irish literature; Bruce Arnold, writer, art critic, and journalist; Brenda Hennessy, Keeper of the Keys of St. Colman's Church, Farahy and Arthur Hennessy; Mary Dwane; Professor Nicholas Grene, Trinity College; and Billy Coman, Director of Housing, Social and Community Development, Dublin. In America: Ann Berthoff, Professor Emerita, University of MA at Boston; Cynthia Lovelace Sears; and Professor Sam Mintz, CUNY (deceased). In Canada: Judith Robertson, Edie Jane Eaton.

Fellowships. Gratitude for support of travel and research: a Mellon Grant from the Ransom Center, University of Texas Austin, 2007–2008; the Fulbright Foundation for support at UC College Cork, Ireland, 2011; Huntington Library, CA., Research Grant, 2014; and the generosity of the Schoff Fund at University Seminars of Columbia University, 2018–2019, where some of the material in this work was presented in the Modern Irish Seminar, led by Professors McGlynn and Burke.

Special thanks also to Holly Gibson and Derek Gottlieb for the excellent index.

Information and Support from Friends and Colleagues

In Ireland: Professor Eibhear Walshe, UC Cork, for early support, enlightened conversation, and travel to Farahy and Bowen's Court; Patricia Coughlan, James Knowles, and Lee Jenkins for interviews and hospitality at UC Cork; Irene Furlong for assistance with Dublin records; Emily Murphy; Moses Freedman; Danny Morrison; Sally Phipps; and Donna Mulcahy. In England: Howard Moss, friend and colleague of Bowen; Brinsley Hughes, Churchwarden of St. Leonard's Church, Hythe, and Vicar, Reverend Tony Windross; Jean and Cecil Woolf (deceased) for savvy, timely advice about publishing and unfailing hospitality; Deidre Toomey; Ann Rowe and Avril Horner; and Joe McCann. In gratitude also to John House (deceased) who generously shared his private collection of his father's, Humphrey House, correspondence with Elizabeth Bowen in 2011. In America: Professor Mary Ann Caws for inspiration, and Professor Rachel Brownstein, for encouragement; Regis Zaleman for technical support; and Arlene Shaner of The De Witt Wallace Institute for the History of Psychiatry. And, not least, my research assistant, Raya Dimitrova, John Jay College, who has patiently and expertly searched for sources, books, and photos over the course of many years.

Experience in seminars has enriched my thinking and writing: foremost, the Women Writing Women's Lives Seminar, CUNY, with its rich presentations and lively discussion of the genres of biography and memoir, and the encouragement and support of its members—particularly Professors Deirdre Bair (deceased), Kathy Chamberlain, Belle Chevigny, Evelyn Barish and Dorothy O. Helly, Dee Shapiro—over the years; the Modern Irish Seminar, Columbia University; the James Joyce *Ulysses* reading group led by Professor Nick Fargnoli; and the Proust Reading Group formerly of the Mercantile Library. For encouragement and/or reading parts of the manuscript along the way: Professors Belle Chevigny, Bella Halsted, Roberta Matthews, and my faithful friend and supporter, Professor Marylea Meyersohn; and friends, Nili and Alberto Baider, Terese and Michael Goldman, Jeremy Mack and Elizabeth Laderer, Sandy and Rabbi Jim Rosenberg and Allen Tobias. Special gratitude to Henry Hardy, expert custodian of the words and works of Isaiah Berlin.

Last, but always first, my gratitude to my adventurous, accomplished, and independent son and daughter, Jonathan and Ilana, to my spirited grandchildren, and to my husband, Stuart, who countenanced long periods of silence while I completed this biography.

Note

1. Derrida, "Archive Fever."

Praise for *Elizabeth Bowen*

"Book of the day: Patricia Laurence's refreshing interpretation of Bowen's life captures her as a rule-maker and a risk-taker in both love and letters."

—The Irish Times

"With its rigorous new archival research and sensitive, detailed, and astute analysis, this new literary and cultural biography of Elizabeth Bowen is bound to become a crucial resource for Bowen scholars as well as British and Irish culture and modernist Studies. Through newly discovered correspondence and a widened cultural and historical sphere, Patricia Laurence offers a new perspective that establishes Bowen's significant place among the most prominent intellectuals and writers of her day."

—Phyllis Lassner, *Professor Emerita, Northwestern University, USA, and author of* Elizabeth Bowen *(Women Writers Series, 1990) and* The Short Fiction of Elizabeth Bowen *(1991)*

"Linearity does not tally with Elizabeth Bowen's style of writing, living, or remembering, and this engaging critical biography presents what Laurence ably demonstrates to be Bowen's 'kaleidoscopic life' as private woman, public intellectual, spy, propagandist, and author in a style and format that does her intriguing and contradictory subject justice."

—Mary Burke, *Associate Professor of English, University of Connecticut, USA, and author of* 'Tinkers': Synge and the Culture History of the Irish Traveller *(2010)*

"Laurence integrates important new material in her resulting mosaic concerning Elizabeth Bowen's active anti-fascism in World War Two Eire and in London under the Blitz. She advocates persuasively for a new 'placing' of Bowen in the context of *transnational* twentieth-century women's writing that includes Somerville and Ross, Virginia Woolf, Eudora Welty, and Christa Wolf."

—Sybil Oldfield, *Emeritus Reader, University of Sussex, UK, and biographer of* Spinsters of this Parish: the life and times of F. M. Mayor and Mary Sheepshanks *(1984) and* Women Against the Iron Fist: Alternatives to Militarism 1900–1989 *(1989)*

"Bowen is a difficult writer who attracts complex arguments and sophisticated theorising. The great asset of this biography, however, is its readability. Laurence writes clearly and accessibly, sharing a great amount of often complex material in a way that easily engages the reader: this is a real plus, especially for those new to Bowen's work. … *Elizabeth Bowen: A Literary Life* is a timely, readable book, which will create added interest in Bowen's life and work."

—Nick Turner, The Elizabeth Bowen Society, *bowensociety.com,*
Vol. 3, September, 2020

"This biography of Elizabeth Bowen draws upon rich and varied archival material. Patricia Laurence has been intrepid in tracking down correspondence, interviewing scholars and surviving relatives, and visiting locations that inform Bowen's fiction."

—Allan Hepburn, Modernism/modernity, *November 2020 Vol.27:4*

Contents

List of Figures

1

Introduction

Two Paths

The day Elizabeth Bowen began her late-life memoir, she took a walk around Hythe, England, looking for a road she had known 60 years earlier. It was there. Not a soul was on it. "Nothing of its character was gone. The May Saturday morning was transiently, slightly hysterically sunny, with a chill undertone."[1] Such scenes "cast themselves on the screen as a silent film: I have a wonderful visual memory," said Bowen, "but I remember the conversations […] hardly at all."[2]

This biography will recover some of those conversations, but begins on *terra firma*, two paths that reveal terrains of her imagination and aspects of her personality. First, the path by her ancestral estate, Bowen's Court in Kildorrery, Ireland, that both imprinted the past and immersed her in Anglo-Irish traditions; then, a path along a row of seaside villas on the coast of Hythe, England, a landscape that nurtured the *farouche*, her untamed qualities. She loved Hythe's "villas with white balconies, bow-windows so rotund that they stuck out like towers, steps up the garden, rustic arbours and Dorothy Perkins roses bright in the sea glare."[3] This was Kent's dramatic coastline, which stood in contrast to the green, sprawling expanse of Bowen's Court: here Bowen was not in the shadow of the mountains of Kildorrery, but rather on bald downs that "showed exciting great gashes of white chalk."[4] On a clear day," she said of Hythe, "the whole of this area meets the eye: there are no secrets"(Figs. 1.1, 1.2, 1.3, 1.4).

© The Author(s), under exclusive license to Springer Nature Switzerland AG 2021
P. Laurence, *Elizabeth Bowen*, Literary Lives, https://doi.org/10.1007/978-3-030-71360-7_1

Fig. 1.1 Hythe Seaside Villas, England. Rights holder and Courtesy of P. Laurence

Fig. 1.2 Hythe Seaside. Rights holder and Courtesy of P. Laurence

Bowen's Court, however, had its secrets. The grand house, with its history of ten generations of Bowens, grounded her itinerant childhood, but also revealed her Anglo-Irish family's infatuation with a "will to power" as well as the taint of Bowen family "madness." It stood there, a place of peace beneath the low-hanging clouds, amidst acres of green, surrounded by woods and the purple of the Ballyhoura, Kilworth, and Blackwater Mountains. Bowen allowed few doubts about the solidity of these childhood places in her early

Fig. 1.3 Surrounding grounds, Bowen's Court Rights holder and Courtesy of P. Laurence

Fig. 1.4 Bowen's Court, Kildorrery Ireland. Rights holder and Courtesy of P. Laurence

memoir, *Seven Winters*: "No years, subsequently, are so acute. … The happenings […] are those that I shall remain certain of till I die."[5] Yet she cautioned that this early memoir was "as much of my life story as I intend to write—that is, to write directly."

Though these paths mark Bowen's girlhood, they do not fix her. She, often in flight from these places—her self shifting—remains elusive. "Who am I?" queries a character in a Virginia Woolf novel, "it depends so much upon the room." In Bowen's case, many rooms, people and places created her, and as she grew into a writer, she fiercely compartmentalized her finely wrought self. It led to her rejection of the genre of autobiography and biography. "Most people do better to keep their traps shut," she warned after reading the autobiographies of her friends Stephen Spender and John Lehmann.[6] As for biographers she asserted that they are "misguided by the notion of a fixed or coherent life [, that] generally falsifies."[7] People can never be fully known, she reflected, an observation that transferred to her characters. In an interview with Jocelyn Brooke, Bowen confessed that she also found it somewhat boring to remember childhood facts or chronologies—the voluntary recall and smooth timeline upon which a traditional autobiography or biography relies. Life is full of irresolution, and memory comes only in patches, she said, remembering Proust. Consequently, a biographer or autobiographer resorts to producing a "synthetic experience […] only half true," and is unable to come up with the valued "nugget of pure truth."[8]

Biography is an unruly venture. A linear or coherent telling of a life, then, does not accord with Bowen's philosophy and style of being, living, and writing. Following her lead, this biography presents a life that spotlights scenes or offers glimpses of her hidden faces and unexplained aspects of her life. It presents her flickering "I"s—a modernist stance—rather than a conventional story. She was a public intellectual, spy, air-raid warden, ambassador, essayist, scriptwriter, and journalist and writer of split Anglo-Irish identity. Like Lois, a young woman coming of age in 1920s Ireland in *The Last September*, "she was fitted for […] being twice as complex" as someone from an earlier generation, "for she must be double[,] as many people having gone into the making of her."[9] Her life then as a writer was a companion spirit to her life as a woman.

Preserving Silences

In the last years of her life, Bowen was provoked to write parts of her autobiography when she found some accounts "wildly off the mark." She thought, "[I]f anybody *must* write a book about Elizabeth Bowen, why should not Elizabeth Bowen," and she began *Pictures and Conversations*, a fragmentary work, published posthumously.[10] Bowen remained, nevertheless, jealous of her privacy, and wrote to her friend Francis King at the end of her life that "as a succession of experiences, and my reaction to them, it clearly must have some connection with the stories I write but that is a connection I should find damagingly public to explore."[11]

Bowen's observations about biography emerged in 1950s England, a time when the genre seemingly demanded an orderly and chronological story but allowing, however, unacknowledged gaps about a subject's sexuality. The topic was taboo. This was before Michael Holroyd radicalized the genre by exposing the sex life of Lytton Strachey in a groundbreaking biography that appeared in 1967, the same year as the passage of the Sexual Offenses Act that decriminalized homosexuality in England. At that time, the cult of personality, which prevails today when authors become celebrities, had not yet surfaced in interviews and public presentations in the media. Bowen famously rejected a PEN interview with the remark, "Even to my friends, I do not find that I talk much, often or easily about my writing. As for the outside world, I never can see why I should. Why can't they just read my books if they care to—and leave it at that."

Having little faith in the genre, Bowen controlled her archive, ensuring private gaps about her life. The major collection that she sold to the Ransom Center at the University of Texas preserves mainly correspondence and manuscripts relating to her work, eclipsing personal information and details of romantic relationships. It is a product that, as Beckett said in another context, is "complete with missing parts."[12] We have, for example, only half of the correspondence with her friend and lover, Charles Ritchie: the passionate letters she wrote to him; much of his side is lost as he destroyed the intimate passages he wrote when his letters were returned to him. Also missing is what she wrote to him after the death of her husband, her depression after the sale of Bowen's Court, her expression of her wish to live there with Ritchie, and increasing resentment of his married life. All remain undocumented and only hinted at. That is as she wished it to be.

And so there are various kinds of silence: those that she privately kept; the cultural taboos of the time; and the censorship of her agent and literary estate—perhaps governed by family wishes. In the valuable collection of Bowen and Ritchie's private correspondence and journals, *Love's Civil War*, edited by Judith Robertson and Victoria Glendinning, ellipses, at times, are inserted by the editors for reasons of clarity, length, or tact; at other times, Bowen or Ritchie inserted them in their own letters and journals in the interest of privacy. Literary agents in Bowen's time also influenced what information was publishable. Even though some taboos were dismantled in the 1960s, Bowen's first biographer, Victoria Glendinning, was subject to sexual censorship in 1973 by Bowen's agent, Curtis Brown. Thirty-two years later, Glendinning wrote a letter to *The Times'* editor, explaining that the agent had urged her "clean up" the Sapphism—that is, omit Bowen's relationships with women—and threatened to withdraw all permissions if Glendinning did not.[13]

Historical forces also played a role in silencing aspects of Bowen's life and writings. We have only snippets of information about her activities and reports for the British Ministry of Information (MOI), or her role as a propagandist during and after World War II, or as a cultural ambassador for the British Council in the 1950s during the Cold War. This missing dimension is the result of the violent ruptures of the Civil War in Ireland, the loss of archives during the London blitz, and the deliberate destruction of certain documents by individuals, political groups, or governments in England and Ireland. Some documents in London were "destroyed under statute," according to Robert Fisk.[14] None of Bowen's wartime MOI reports, Fisk states, has been uncovered, as far as is known, in Ireland, since "in 1945 Irish authorities shredded 70 tons of documents considered too sensitive for scrutiny," and in Northern Ireland, records were weeded. Even Bowen's Court, the grand house that framed her visits to Ireland, disappeared, sold by Bowen in 1959 and razed by its new owner in 1960. Given these witting and unwitting concealments, and the disappearance of parts of her archive, she remains an elusive figure despite the fact that she is the author of 10 novels, 13 collections of short stories, and 16 works of non-fiction.

Concealment extends from her archive to her evolving modernist narrative style. John Bayley, friend and critic, credited her with the invention of new narrative conventions for concealment or not saying things in the modern novel. She preserves varying kinds of silence leaving much unsaid because of her sense of the "unknowability" of people and, therefore, characters. She plots silence and stillness into her writing, receptive to modernist skepticism about the adequacy of language and its ability to capture human experience, given the irrationality of world events in the buildup to and aftermath of World War II. "Not knowing" her characters fully is a modernist and philosophical stance, and invites the reader to restore wholeness.

Though she may artfully describe period furniture, the graceful folds in a dress, or the "ravening" beauty of a young woman, internal lives are only suggested. Max in *The House in Paris*, for example, is only half known, "like a road running into a dark tunnel." His inner turbulence and the reasons for his violent suicide are left to the reader's imagination. The adolescent Portia in *The Death of the Heart* and Leopold in *The House in Paris* suffer with secret grievances about hypocritical adults, saying nothing but taking up their pens in fragmentary letters or diaries. In a course she taught at Vassar, she told her students, "there is a touch of the sphinx in many human beings, and this 'sphinx' quality is one which—quite often—the [short story] legitimately exploits." Not all dialogue in a novel is verbal. Bowen's belief in the "unknowability" of character continued to deepen during and after the war as many people emerged capable of unspeakable crimes against humanity in the name of Fascism and Nazism. Hidden, demonic forces in people's psyches were unleashed—as in the partially sketched, willfully blind German spy, Robert Kelway, in *The Heat of the Day*—as armies swept across Europe. And fine words spoken before the war were somehow lacking and not to be trusted: public and national declarations rang hollow. As a result, Bowen's novels have an undertone of the unsaid, the hidden. Words, the interruption or fragmentation or lack of them became her underlying theme, as they did for many modernist writers, such as Virginia Woolf and Samuel Beckett.[15] This acknowledgment that language was *manqué* led her to find ways to preserve what was unsaid in narration and enjoin the reader to collaborate with the writer to understand and decipher her hidden ironies and silences. In addition, these associations are deepened by her attention to the elusiveness of the "self"—the multiple "I's"; her affinity for the new media of photography and cinema that inflect her style; her pleasure in speed and new technology; and the hauntings of the gothic that transform into modernist surrealism.

Bowen was a writer of her time, surrounded by people of talent and outstanding intelligence and personality who were engaged, at various times, in propaganda, spying, and, even treason during World War II and the Cold War. It was a climate in which much was unsaid—"loose lips sink ships" was one of the popular slogans of the day—and her literary voice, style, and themes embodied this historical and cultural concealment. From the 1930s on, clandestine political conversations swirled around her and eased her movement into the British Ministry of Information and other propaganda activities. As Roderick, the returning soldier in *The Heat of the Day*, says to his mother when questioned about his taking notes on a conversation, "[R]eally, Mother […] conversations are the leading thing in this war!" Everyone is watchful: Stella, his mother, is a spy, and he, a dislocated soldier at the front, takes notes at home.

This biography spotlights such still scenes, memories, faces, and places. But it also brings forward some conversations—ones Bowen could barely remember—with friends, writers, and editors, to bring her out of the shadows. The conversations are gathered from letters and documents—a "polyphony," as M.M. Bakhtin might term it—that preserve her voices—"her flashes of insight like summer lightening" as well as her funniness, brutality, and poetry, observed by her friend and lover, Charles Ritchie. Her voice is part of a chorus of voices that reveal the traces of society in her times that can be found in the language of friends, intellectuals, and writers.[16]

Reinventing Bowen

The complexity of Bowen's life as a woman—its puzzling and untamed aspects—as well as a writer of her time, has been neglected in some earlier biographical and critical studies. We do not read her for a simply told story, as John Banville observed; we go to her for a good story, usually laced with complexity and keen irony—or sometimes "a trap for the unwary."[17] Penelope Lively asserts that Bowen is one of the great writers of the early twentieth century, marrying style and content in "setting up an atmosphere […] and producing the unexpected word that makes you sit up and be startled, the arresting phrase."[18] *A World of Love* deploys such surprises, with Maud, one of the daughters, "thoughtfully *gimleting* through her inquisitor's eye" or Antonia asking "in a *charnel* note, 'What is it?'" or Jane, whose beauty "had *ravened* nothing but fairness out of her mother"[19] (emphasis added). We go to her for the poetry that weaves in and out of her style. Sean O'Faolain rated her among the best English novelists (though she would chafe at the "English" category) in the first three-quarters of the twentieth century, as did Kingsley Amis. She was a poetic chronicler of her times who forged new visual and sensory paths. She is now, almost half a century after her death, primed to be read by "a jury of her peers," as Elaine Showalter proposes for women writers. Bowen's reputation has changed in the last decade from that of a little-read author to that of a central figure in midcentury "intermodernism" which is a way, both aesthetic and social, of reading authors whose writing after or between the wars is embedded in history; in addition, she is also classified, at times, as a late Modernist. Though her reputation faltered in the leftist 1960s–1970s, given her political conservatism, and, generally, her depiction of the affluent, upper-middle class and stance toward the feminist movement, now, there is renewed interest in shades of conservatism, exploration of imperial pasts, and, importantly, feminine sensibility. She is now illuminated as readers discover her interest in independent modern women who share her passionate and poetic temperament behind a worldly exterior. And she is engaged with her times as history sits at her writing table and is an unsettling presence as she writes between the wars and the cultural and national spaces of England, Ireland, and Europe. She is also an experimental writer aesthetically poised between poetry and prose, the seen and the unseen, as well as the sounds and silences of the modern age. Part of the reinvention of Bowen here is to remove her from local contexts in Ireland and Irish and English literature and catapult her into the transnational acknowledging that traditional genre, literary, political and national categories do not fit. The attention and more extensive research into her work as an informant for England during the war, for example, is viewed in the context of other women writers like Christa Wolf who briefly collaborated with the Stasi in East Germany. Wolf's inability to honestly confront her participation—as with Bowen—breathes new life and complexity into an outworn Irish debate about Bowen's loyalty. In juxtaposing Bowen with German Wolf who also lives in a partitioned nation, as well as other women writers—British Virginia Woolf, American Eudora Welty, and Irish Somerville-Ross, for example, we rethink her narrative issues and literary context in relation to women writers in different nations.

This biography moves in new directions. Chapter 1, "Introduction," presents two paths in Bowen's life and divisions in her personality—in Ireland and England—and rejects the notion of a rooted life. Bowen herself opposed the coherence and smooth line of traditional biography—or life—as a "falsification" and urged the preservation of a mosaic or kaleidoscopic pattern in the telling. It proceeds chronologically and is divided into sections on key themes that emerge in her life and writing during those years.

Chapter 2, "Change," presents Bowen's early sense of being a "born foreigner," a sense of dislocation shared by her generation and the declining Anglo-Irish ascendancy. Flux is her métier as she travels from Dublin to Kent after her father's breakdown, and endures her mother's death, itinerant schooling, and the emergence of a stutter. Mad little girl stories and *The Death of the Heart* reverberate with her childhood and adolescent feelings of not being "located" anywhere.

Chapter 3, "Terrains of the Imagination," presents contrasting paths—the seaside of Hythe, England, and the green expanse of Bowen's Court, Kildorrery, Ireland. She also traveled away from these places to Italy, France, and the United States, leading a modern unsettled cosmopolitan life.

Chapter 4, "Outsiders," focuses the importance of Bowen's friendship and conversations with cultural outsiders: Isaiah Berlin, brilliant historian and raconteur, and William Plomer, talented writer and editor on the fringes of Bloomsbury. Having settled in Oxford after marriage to Alan Cameron, she met Berlin and an impressive group of left-wing intellectuals, scholars, and writers in the Oxford Circle who contributed to her informal education; her relationship with Plomer, an unconventional and talented writer and Cape editor highlights important aspects of her narrative style debated by critics today.

Chapter 5, "Love and Lovers," presents cameos of her marriage and loves outside of marriage, "loves without a home": Humphrey House, Goronwy Rees, Sean O'Faolain, May Sarton and, most importantly, Charles Ritchie. Traces of these romantic experiences enter her novels, *The House in Paris, The Heat of the Day*, and *To the North*.

Chapter 6, "Snapshots of War," highlights Bowen's wartime experiences. Being as old as the century, she lived through World War I and the Irish War of Independence as an adolescent, and World War II and the Cold War, when mature. The turbulence of the wars and the times enters her writing, particularly in *The Last September, The House in Paris*, and *The Heat of the Day*. "Art and Intelligence" continues to describe her experiences and writing during World War II.

Chapter 7, "Art and Intelligence," exposes Bowen as a spy in neutral Ireland, 1940–1941, writing reports for the British Ministry of Information. Her documentary writing, and life as a cultural figure and ambassador emerges during this period and brings to light her liminal personality as she easily crosses borders between nations, loyalties, and gender roles. Her life of personal and national concealment and silences enters into the texture of her writing in *The Heat of the Day* and her wartime stories.

Chapter 8, "The Roving Eye," focuses on Bowen's visual imagination that led to her progressive interest in the new media. Still shots of photography, filmic montage and the shadows, dreams and collage of the new art movement of surrealism—as well as attention to radio—contribute to her practice of new narrative modes.

Chapter 9, "Reading Backwards," reveals Bowen's fiction to be an original amalgam, hewing to no specific aesthetic or place in conventional literary history. Portraits of Bowen's literary friendships with Virginia Woolf, Rosamond Lehmann, and Eudora Welty are highlighted as well as her relation to women's movements of the time. Other admired English, Irish, and European writers from the eighteenth to the twentieth centuries are Jane Austen, Charles Dickens, Jonathan Swift, Maria Edgeworth, Somerville & Ross, and Marcel Proust, among others.

Chapter 10, "Late Life Collage," presents fragments of Bowen's life between her husband's death and the sale of Bowen's Court. Lecturing in America, traveling to Rome, serving on the Royal Commission on Capital Punishment, she nevertheless, completed *A Time in Rome* and *A World of Love*.

Chapter 11, "A Frightened Heart," deepens a period of disappointed love, homelessness, serious illness, and continued writing in her life. Having abandoned the fantasy that Bowen's Court would shelter her and Charles Ritchie,

Bowen bought a modest house in Hythe, a return to her childhood landscape, a comfort, and completed the novels, *The Little Girls* and *Eva Trout*.

Kaleidoscope

Bowen's life is viewed in this biography through a kaleidoscope of faces, places, feelings, countries, and loyalties. The kaleidoscope—sometimes viewed as a playful toy—casts her life and writing as a changing pattern of places, moods, atmospheres, textures, and colors. It was the object she said she would want with her if she were stranded on a desert isle. This instrument of flux as well as the opening doors of a doll house (another playful image interspersed in her writing) reveal, perhaps, the key to Bowen's vision: stability and flux. So many "houses" are revealed—emotionally sheltering and stable places—and are viewed through the flickering kaleidoscope of the times and her art. She uses the terms "mosaic" and "collage" at various times to to suggest the random patterning of her writing, and such terms might equally apply to the telling of her life. Valuing the fragment, the incomplete and the unsaid is a modernist gesture that invites the reader to imagine and supply what is missing. Her life, which spanned the years from 1899 to 1973, reveals patterns of relationships with friends, family, fellow writers, editors, intellectuals, and lovers. Bowen as a subject remains free to wander amidst these figures, elusive.

We can, nevertheless, follow her to some degree along the forked paths of her life and her writing. The light of research hits mirrors and releases loose bits of imagery, color, and experience into biographical narration: a scene, a landscape, a conversation, a book, a moment, a memory, or a face is highlighted in each chapter or section of this book, illuminating something larger. Bowen confirms this spotlighting as a part of her own narrative method: "I have isolated—I have made the particular spotlighting faces or cutting out of gestures." The turn of a page or chapter—like the turn of the cylinder of a kaleidoscope—reconfigures what patterns emerge.

Notes

1. *PC*, 3.
2. Bowen, "Coming to London," 79.
3. *BC*, 419.
4. *PC*, 24–25, 3, 4.
5. *SW*, 9.
6. EB to WP, May 6, 1958, DUR 19. Also, Spender, *World Within World*. Lehmann, *Whispering Gallery*.

7. *Out of a Book*, 48.
8. Bowen, "Out of a Book," 48; Woolf, *A Room of One's Own*, 3.
9. *LS*, 36.
10. Curtis Brown, foreword to *PC*.
11. EB to Francis King, August 25, 1971, HRC.
12. Beckett, *Proust and Three Dialogues*, 101.
13. Victoria Glendinning, "The S Word," *Times* (London), March 27, 2005.
14. Fisk, *In Time of War*, ix.
15. See "The Narration of Interiority," Laurence, *Reading of Silence*, 13–35.
16. The theories of M.M. Bakhtin, Ferdinand de Saussure, and genetic criticism underpin this biography. Bakhtin asserts the multiplicity of voice, the "polyphony" dramatized in this biography's many voices; Saussure's principle of "interdependence" in creating any "value" is demonstrated in presenting not only Bowen's work but what exists outside of it; and genetic criticism's broad process that includes historical and literary documents and others' letters and writings as undercurrents in a writer's final text is observed.
17. Banville, "Sunday Feature, Centennial Program, 1999," BBC, NSA.
18. Lee & Lively, "Woman's Hour," December 8, 2008, BBC, NSA.
19. *WL*, 14, 101, 137.

2

Change (1899–1925)

On Not Reading

Bowen was not allowed to learn to read until the age of seven. Until then she idly turned the pages of picture books under her mother's fearful eye. Concluding that her husband had overworked his brain as a lawyer, straining his constitution and precipitating a breakdown in 1906, Florence Colley wanted to prevent her daughter from "burning out her eyes." Bowen recalled that picture books then were her "only clues to a mystery […] on my walks through familiar quarters of Dublin I looked at everything as a spy."[1] There is curiosity and excitement in these first scenes of watchfulness—perusing picture books and walking with her governess in St. Stephen's Green—but her father's illness shadows her life of books from the start. She begins then as Kierkegaard claims of observers as a "secret agent" to expose what is hidden in books and family life on Herbert Street.

When she was seven, a sharp-edged governess was introduced at Bowen's Court. She announced to Elizabeth that with her mother's approval she would begin to learn to read. The initiation was tense as the governess "like a witch […] slowly tapped her pencil along the impregnable lines of print."[2] Gone were the enchanted readings of *Perseus* and *Jungle Jinks* by a previous governess; instead the "print smells […] of metal and ink" threw "a lonely coldness over [her] senses" and effaced the pleasure she had in looking at illustrations and being read aloud to.[3] This same anxiety colors a scene of reading in *The Death of the Heart*. The adolescent Portia dreams that she is sitting high up in a window sharing a book with a friend, Anna. She becomes alarmed when she discovers that she can no longer read and the forest under the window "was

© The Author(s), under exclusive license to Springer Nature Switzerland AG 2021
P. Laurence, *Elizabeth Bowen*, Literary Lives, https://doi.org/10.1007/978-3-030-71360-7_2

being varnished all over: it left no way of escape."[4] The words on the page became as incomprehensible as they were in Bowen's young life. Her introduction to reading then not only reveals family anxieties but her early exposure to and fascination with pictures and images that sustained her and, later, streamed into her writing.

Eventually, she did develop into a reader and from then on, she said, her life "was haunted by fiction." She wrote that if she could read her way back through the books of her childhood, "the clues to everything could be found." Books were "power-testing athletics" for her imagination.[5] She discovered what she could feel by "successively 'being' a character in every book" and that "doubled the meaning of everything that happened in [her] otherwise constricted Life."[6] Writing would stimulate the same doubleness and "return." Bowen once observed that what makes the writer is the part of her that never grows up, the earlier patterns brought to light by the vigilant writing eye.

"As a little girl," Bowen said, "I was precocious in my drawing and painting in an Edwardian way. I thought I would be a painter."[7] This activity piqued her visual sensibility as had picture books. She attended classes in Dublin held by Elizabeth Yeats, W.B. Yeats' sister, and remembered "the excitement of that free brushwork, the children's heads bent, all round the big table, over crocuses springing alive, with each stroke, on the different pieces of white paper."[8] Her days then were taken up not only with drawing lessons in the home of Mainie Jellett—a childhood friend from a prominent Anglo-Irish family who later became a cosmopolitan and innovative Cubist painter in Ireland—but also with pleasant walks in Dublin and dancing classes in Molesworth Hall.[9] She had a privileged childhood during her first seven years, and was brought up by a succession of governesses, part of whose job was to "discipline" her as her mother could not bear to do it herself. Always sensitive to images, she remembered two threatening paintings in her Herbert Place bedroom: one of a burning Casablanca and another of a baby in a cradle floating smilingly in a rushing flood. The paintings signaled alarm.

Family Life

Initially, Bowen was born into a peaceful family in Dublin in 1899, a long-awaited child born nine years after her parents married. She lived with her mother's family, the Colleys, at Mount Temple, Clontarf, overlooking Dublin Bay, until she was two or three. The census records her father, Henry Bowen, as a resident there with the family in 1901. During that period her mother, Florence Isabella Pomeroy Colley, was ill. A few years later they moved to 15

Herbert Street, and spent the next four years there except for summers at Bowen's Court, her father's family estate in Kildorrery in the northeast corner of County Cork. She was the only child of Henry and Florence. Fussed over and guarded, Elizabeth resembled Geraldine, a character in "The Little Girl's Room": "each young tendril put out found a wire waiting, she clung and blossomed."[10]

Though Bowen said she had fewer early memories than anyone she knew, she relates some in *Seven Winters*. She described her mother and father as rebels, and imagined her mother as a "mad" little girl. Florence was a misfit in Colley family surroundings generally recognized as idyllic. She had visions, and her days were punctuated by stormy naughtiness. She sometimes locked herself up in a room and wept. There was something ecstatic about her good and bad behavior, and Florence may have had, Bowen speculated, the makeup of a complex saint. It took years for her to acquire calm. She also had "flame-like quality" as Florence was always reading and full of ideas.[11] But she was not, said Bowen, like the bluestockings of the day, self-consciously literary and intellectual. And though unconcerned with dress, refusing even to shop with her own mother for her wedding dress, Florence was "lovely to look at, with a pointed and curved face over which expressions [ran] like light from quick-running water." She had a flickering quality, "for she could be disconcertingly subtle, which was veiled by vagueness, or if not vagueness, something gentler than nonchalance." Subtlety and "vagueness," part of her charm, were peculiarly Victorian qualities that fed the feminine mystique cultivated by young Irish women of a certain class who were disengaged from the world and its so-called "masculine" logic. In 1847, the word was used to differentiate women from men: "The sharp practice of the world drives some logic into the most vague of men: women are not so schooled."[12] Did Florence Colley's otherworldly, spiritual, and flame-like temperament stream into Bowen's? Did Bowen recall her mother's vagueness and eccentricity as she, schooled and disciplined, evolved into a sharp-edged public intellectual and hard-working writer whose prose in certain genres sparkles with clarity. She, unlike her mother, was grounded in the actual.

Bowen's parents relished being independent and ruled "their private kingdoms of thought, not always in communication with the other."[13] Henry was engaged in the practice of law; Florence, in running the household. As many in the Anglo-Irish culture in Dublin, they lived apart from Catholics, socializing with a small circle from Trinity College, the Bar, the Church of Ireland, and those who lived in the big houses. They were curiously removed from important cultural movements like the Irish literary revival or the Gaelic League that promoted pride in the Irish language and theater. They were not drawn to the Abbey Theatre founded in 1904 with plays by John Millington Synge who, though coming from a privileged Anglo-Irish family, often wrote about Catholic peasants; or to Lady Gregory or Sean O'Casey; or to the popular William Butler Yeats who separated himself from the traditions of the Anglo-Irish and the Protestant and Catholic religions to find refuge in a mythic ancient Ireland. Elizabeth too began to separate early to set up her own world, taking refuge in rooms, books, pictures and conversation.

The Breakdown

But "the blow fell" when Bowen was six. Her father's mental state—his bipolar pattern of chaotic shouting and apprehensive silences—had created alarming moods in her home. Her mother's brother George, then unmarried and disabled by deafness, lived around the corner, and they moved in and out of each other's homes in support. Laetitia Lefroy, George's granddaughter, said that the family considered him a source of protection as they feared for Elizabeth and Florence's safety, at times. He called upon them regularly during this unstable period, and enjoyed their companionship.[14] Eventually, doctors ordered Elizabeth and Florence to leave, as they were not only victims of Henry's rages but their presence provoked him. When she was six years old, mayhem erupted and she was rushed from her home in the middle of the night. Her father was shouting and raging, and rescued by relatives, she sped away in the dark, never to return to Herbert Place. She was taken to her mother's family estate and then to Bowen's Court, family homes that would shelter her that night and throughout her life (Fig. 2.1).

This scene emerged from a history of melancholy and gloom that surrounded her father's family. When reading a terrible account of her paternal grandfather, Robert Cole Bowen, she confided to a friend that he eventually went mad at Bowen's Court: "an undercurrent is [...] always here in this place."[15] The current was passed that night to her home on Herbert Place. Though Bowen's father and grandfather were largely absent from her life, their specters silently shaped her childhood, and traces of their "madness" drift into her stories of little girls and women.

His illness encircled her as a child, but she asserted with characteristic pluck in her early memoir that she escaped from the "apprehensive silence or chaotic shouting" of her father's "agonizing mental illness [...] with nothing more disastrous than a stammer."[16] This explanation though emotionally comforting, at the time, is conjecture in the light of recent medical research that

Fig. 2.1 Elizabeth, six years old. Rights holder and Courtesy of The Beneficiaries of the Estate of Elizabeth Bowen, 2019

attributes stammering to genetic origins. Nevertheless, she experienced and coped with this disability throughout her life. She concedes in The *Heat of the Day* that Robert's limp, his wound from the war, "like a stammer has a psychic center."[17]

Her father's illness began in 1905, and it precipitated her and her mother's flight from Dublin in 1906 to live with Colley relatives in Kent. She was the only Bowen child to grow up in England. Like one of the little girls she would write about in her fiction, Elizabeth was "often and quickly shaken," during these years, "like a kaleidoscope."[18] She was expert, however, at rearranging the colored bits of glass, and obscured this difficult time in her life in her fragmented memoirs whose gaps mark the painful moments in her life. She was a watchful and sometimes shy child who did not realize fully what these changes meant but sensed that an emotional abyss could open at any time. She understood later what a heartbreaking decision it was for her mother to leave her father alone in Ireland when he had his breakdown. She went back and forth to Dublin to tend to her husband in the first year away, but it was finally decided that he would be hospitalized and they would give up the Herbert Place house and move across the sea to Kent. Each time Bowen and her mother moved to a new place, their Dublin furniture traveled with them; it contained the past, as the servant, Matchett, observes in *The Death of the Heart*. After Folkestone, they lived in Erin Cottage, Lyminge, and then returned to Hythe, the town that her mother loved.

She marveled that her mother showed no signs of stress as she struggled to meet the financial obligations at Bowen's Court and their expenses in England. Charlie, her father's brother, and George, a Colley uncle, financially supported them as Florence had to handle the expenses of both Bowen's Court and Henry's hospital care.[19] Nor, according to Bowen, did her mother show signs of inner turmoil or loneliness, though as a pretty young mother alone she probably aroused some gossip. She learned, like her mother, to restrain emotion. Often transplanted, taken care of by one aunt or another, Bowen developed a diplomatic manner, a habit of "not noticing" things—and a stammer.

The Stammer

An angel, she said, pressed her hand to her lips in sorrow, secrecy, or anxiety at times. She had a stammer, a hesitancy, and always distinguished it from a stutter, the rapid-fire arrest at the beginning of words that was, in her view, a more serious disorder. The emotional distress of her father's sometimes violent outbursts, or his silences—now viewed in medical hindsight as a bipolar disorder—left her, she said, not knowing when to speak or be silent. She recounted painful experiences related to her stammer when she was being schooled in Kent after leaving her father in Dublin. Though she was demonstrative and, seemingly, an extrovert, there were cracks in her defenses. When being home-schooled with the Salmon girls in Old Cheriton at the age of eight or nine, she expressed her dislike of their governess, Miss Clarke, "when she was sarcastic, or when she picked on me about my stammer which in her view was due largely to faults of character, over impatience, self-importance," a punitive, popular view of stuttering at the time.[20] Some viewed a stammer, like mental illness, as a willed infirmity. "You try," said Miss Clark, to "get too much out at the same time [...] Concentrate on one thing, draw a deep breath, then say it slowly." A few years later, when Bowen's mother died, a period of "stupidity" descended, and in a rare moment of self-analysis, something she generally avoided, she offered that this period of silence might have been due to "denied sorrow."[21] Bowen also acknowledged that her shyness as an adolescent was prolonged by her stammer, admitting that she later "became truculent and was inclined to bully [...] My aunts, on their visits to Hythe, commented on my increasing bumptiousness."[22]

Her mother and nurturing aunts, nevertheless, encouraged a healthy outdoor life in Hythe, and according to her cousin Audrey Fiennes, Bowen was physically daring and always spoke her mind. John Bayley, a later friend in the

1960s, was sympathetic to Bowen, and confided his own childhood tensions about stammering relating that between the ages of four and eight he "took it so badly—worse than ever when my dear father, from the best motives, became possessively and obsessively preoccupied with it."[23] Bowen never mentioned a family concern with her stammer.

Her carefree days in Hythe and, later socialization into conversation as an adolescent at the Downe House School mitigated her impediment. The progressive school cultivated the art of conversation pitting students against each other in conversation teams vying with chatter and charm. Gaining practice in the weekly program of social talk bolstered self-confidence and prepared Bowen and her classmates to be skilled conversationalists and hostesses as adults. Shyness was also considered to be a deformity, according to Bowen, in Anglo-Irish culture.

Bowen felt more embarrassment than she expressed about her impediment. As an adult, her stammer seemingly did not interfere with her social or erotic life or with her impulse toward conversation as a public intellectual: she sailed on the wings of talent and a strong personality. The men in the Oxford circle with whom she conversed appreciated her strong intellect, social graces, and scintillating conversation, and scant mention was made of her stammer. Perhaps it was considered a part of the style of Oxonians at the time. She had a rather patrician, British-sounding voice, and her stammer may have recalled the speech of Evelyn Waugh's characters—their stuttering a kind of upper-class affectation. She liked to talk and did it well. According to her friend, Rosamond Lehmann, her voice was low and musical and the stammer was part of her charm giving "an edge at once comical and endearing to the marvelous wit, irony and incisiveness of her conversation."[24] Eudora Welty noted the modulation in her voice, relating to William Maxwell that when Bowen mentioned that she did not have any time for him, she said it "with a shadow across her voice, you know how she modulates according to feeling."[25]

Leo Marx, critic and friend, remembered Bowen at a conference he attended in 1957 in Nottingham, part of a series on academic topics held in country houses. He and Bowen discussed the English and American novel and became good friends. He admired her work and found her serious commitment to the art of the novel inspiring, but, "even more, her courageous struggle with a serious speech impediment. The weekend was extremely taxing for her—we talked with the assembled group around the clock—but her enthusiasm never flagged. She inspired respect for her distinctive sense of intellectual responsibility to the novel."[26]

Despite her strong ego, however, she could not help noticing the stammer's effect on different listeners and audiences. Some friends noted that they found it "charming"; others, "distracting"; some said, "humorous"; and some reported looking around in "embarrassment" at her public lectures. Virginia Woolf, cutting, observed Bowen on one occasion, sitting "rayed like a zebra, silent and stuttering."[27] Nevertheless, Bowen often gave talks for the British Council, and a memo in the Council's files noted that her "stammer was not at all disturbing" but "endearing," and it typed her "a most successful lecturer with a most successful stammer."[28] In the context of later, more despairing and honest letters to her friend, Charles Ritchie, she labeled her stammer a "deformity," and he noted that in 1942 she sought the help of an Austrian psychologist who had a new approach to the problem. After the visit, Bowen related to Ritchie that the specialist was drawn to her, confided his personal problems, and neglected to address her needs, an amusing but unconvincing story in which she again denies or diminishes the importance of the stammer.

Speech-correction clinics in the 1940s advocated simple methods of treatment devised by specialists such as Dr. Lee Edward Travis of the University of Southern California. Among the methods employed were lip-training, the manipulation of facial muscles, the use of phonograph recordings of speech, and electric brain-wave measurements: all to observe and address what was then termed "static" in the brain or a "nervous condition."[29] In 1938, the stutter became a national issue in Britain when George VI, who also suffered from a speech impediment, unexpectedly became king when his brother, Edward VIII, abdicated the throne.[30] While Bowen did not share the king's shy personality, one suspects that she did experience his travail, as a child and an adolescent. Victoria Glendinning, her early biographer, reported that if Bowen were alone and talking to herself, a habit she developed later in life, she did not stammer, and in the last few days of her life, though she was weak, "her stammer disappeared completely."[31]

Professor Ann Berthoff when teaching at Bryn Mawr invited Bowen, then Donnell Visiting Professor, to give a talk in her "Experimental Writing" class. She noted that Bowen would sometimes start stammering on her second or third sentence, and "her arm would arc outwards as she rode through the stutter," the gesture arresting it.[32] Others noted that when Bowen gave a formal talk, the stammer diminished after awhile. When she read her own work, *The Little Girls*, aloud on the BBC in the 1950s, her stammer was stimulated on the first syllables of words, while freer conversation on a broadcast literary panel, "The Artist in Society" with Graham Greene and V.S. Pritchett, led to more fluent speech. It is not known, however, if BBC technology was employed to erase the hesitations, and it might be noted that the other panelists spoke twice as long as she did.

Bowen also had bouts with bronchitis stimulated by her smoking that complicated her stammer. Laryngitis or loss of voice is mentioned as early as 1934, and again in a 1936 letter to Stephen Spender when she was 37 relating that she was feeling rather disconnected as she had "stopped smoking—altogether for life. As I've been chain-smoking for years this is having a bad effect: half one's faculties seem to be gone."[33] Her dancer friend, Agnes De Mille wrote to her mother in November 1936, "Elizabeth Bowen has lost her voice. Literally. Hasn't spoken in a month and has been told she must never smoke again. All nerves have gone under the double deprivation and she sees few guests. I'm trying to get in touch with her now. The trouble seems to be some sort of chronic laryngitis."[34] Though Bowen resolved to give up heavy smoking, the habit continued throughout her life. According to Mary Dwane, a young Irish servant at Bowen's Court, Bowen requested that 100 cigarettes be purchased at a Mitchelstown shop about every three days.[35] Scenes in Bowen's novels often feature a modern woman with a cigarette burning between her fingers.

Despite these issues of voice, Bowen gave talks on the BBC and lectured for the British Council in Hungary and Czechoslovakia in the late 1940s, and all over America in the 1950s. She had one of the longest and best visits with Eudora Welty, in February 1961 at Bryn Mawr College, where, according to Welty, they had "a fine rowdy" time in the Deanery, a 46-room, elaborately decorated mansion then used for entertaining important guests.[36]

Critic and friend, John Bayley wondered in a letter to Bowen "if stammerers don't get a special pleasure from style and the written word. I still regard speech," he said, "as a tedious business."[37] Though Bowen enjoyed social relations and was not prone to remarks like this, she also took special pleasure in experimenting with written words, spending most of her days writing in isolation. "My writing," she said in an essay, "may be a substitute for something I have been born without, so-called normal relations with society."[38] She remained largely silent about her impediment which was present her whole life.

The Bowen Family "Madness"

Another issue about which there was silence was the undercurrent of "madness" in her father's family. Like her mother's family, the Colleys, they belonged to the Irish-Protestant Ascendancy, and were Unionist identified. Hubert Butler, a relative, noted that, in general, the Bowens were "unliterary and unintellectual," rather focused on the acquisition of land.[39] Her father, Henry, broke with tradition and became a lawyer, a choice that enraged her grandfather, and incited his black moods. Bowen relates how he "died in the throes of a violent mania brought on by a continuous quarrel" with his son and heir about his vocation. The neighbors thought him mad.

This early period marked the beginning of a long silence about her father, who though absent during her childhood, remained a haunting presence in her life and writing. At the first signs of his mental illness, noted by relatives in the summer of 1905, he committed himself to a hospital in England. Here the treatment was believed to be more enlightened than in Ireland, with an emphasis on the comfort and understanding of patients instead of the previous century's notion of "chains, darkness and anodynes."[40] During that summer, Bowen was at Bowen's Court with a governess and a little girl named Gerty who was boarding with them, and her mother stayed by her father's side, according to Victoria Glendinning. In the winter, her father, back from England, had violent spells that landed him again in a hospital, this time outside Dublin. In her family history, Bowen records how he stayed with a relative in Mitchelstown and then some friends, praising his "will" to get well. But she is silent about the fact that he was institutionalized. In the spring of 1908, he returned to Dublin and doctors ordered him into St. Patrick's Hospital, a private psychiatric hospital where he spent a year and a half, from March 1908 to September 1909.[41] The entry in the patient register at this hospital reads:

> No. 55 Bowen, Henry Cole
> Age 46 Male Protestant
> Admission 20 March 1908
> Barrister 15 Herbert Place, Dublin
> Lord Chancellor's Order (By inquisition)
> Probable cause of illness: Heredity
> Species of disease: Subacute mania (?) [sic]
> Recovered 23 September 1909
> Transferred by order of Lord Chancellor to his home.[42]

The hospital was founded by Jonathan Swift, one of Bowen's favorite Anglo-Irish authors, who contributed £11,000 of his £12,000 estate to its building. Swift wrote in his satiric "Verses on the Death of Dr. Swift":

> He gave the wealth he had
> To build a house for Fools and Mad
> And shew'd by one satiric Touch
> No nation wanted it so much.

Ireland was a nation that indeed needed to modernize its hospitals and methods for dealing with mental illness, according to Joseph Robins in his study of Irish working houses (early places of treatment) and asylums. "By 1901, there were about 17,000 inmates in asylums originally planned for less than 5000, and the total insane population then in institutions or at large was calculated at 25,000."[43] Doctors lacked scientific knowledge about mental illness or care of patients, it being a pre-drug, pre-Freudian, and pre-therapeutic era, and the common medical vocabulary for describing mental illness was "mad," "fool," and "lunatic." Laetitia Lefroy noted that people in Ireland, in general, were afraid of those who behaved differently, and mental illness (even stammering) was generally believed a sign of moral weakness or character defect.

In September 1908, Henry had been vaguely diagnosed with "anemia of the brain," and "subacute mania" with the probable cause being "heredity." Like other diagnoses of the time, the terms "mania, monomania, dementia, melancholia, imbecility, and general paralysis of the insane" had no scientific basis. But his state of raging frenzy with alternating silence and depression, as confirmed in Bowen's recollections, point toward a bipolar illness. St. Patrick's Hospital, like others of the time, practiced coercion through the use of instruments of restraint, shock treatments, bloodlettings, cold baths, swinging chairs, and straitjackets. A visiting committee in 1906, two years before Henry Bowen entered, observed a bath for 150 patients out of order for several months, inadequate heating, and poor ventilation. Florence and other members of Henry's family were seemingly afraid of his state, and ignorant of or helpless before the conditions he undoubtedly endured in his six-year fight against mental illness.

The irony of Henry Bowen's residence in Swift's crumbling eighteenth-century hospital cannot be ignored, given his literary daughter's lifelong admiration of Swift and the homage she paid him at Trinity College when receiving an honorary degree in 1949. Bowen heard the knockings of lunacy early in her own home, and as a six-year-old, she was confounded. She and her mother did not rejoin her father after his release from the hospital, and the exact date of his dismissal is unknown, though St. Patrick's records indicate that he was released to his "home" from the institution in September 1909. He battled his illness in various ways in isolation until 1911, when the census records his address in a boarding house in Leeson Street, central Dublin, a street divided by the Canal.

Bowen came to understand her father through the eyes of three people: her mother; Stephen Gwynn, a schoolmate at St. Columba's; and Sarah Cartey, a housemaid at Bowen's Court. According to Florence, Henry was "innocent and noble." His family, particularly his father, took exception and judged him as obstinate as he had reacted against his father's "success regime" since childhood. Early on, he detached from "the usages of the world" and the family plan to take on the business of estates. Melancholy and guilt descended upon him in 1882, when his mother, to whom he had been close, died after having nursed him through smallpox that he had contracted on a trip abroad. A cousin remembers that Henry and the other young Bowens were "black as crows" in the year after her death.[44]

In spite of the family's tempestuous quarrels, Bowen's father returned to the study of law, defying his father's dictates, and was called to the Irish bar in 1887. Henry was drawn to the law, and at the beginning of his career, he developed a large practice in chamber work, and later, the Land Commission. His contrariness gave him, according to his daughter, "a lasting bent against horses, men servants, social discrimination, ideas about farming, and display in any form." Bowen, of similar forthright character, shared her father's aversion to display and flattery. His independent and democratic stance brought him into conflict not only with his own father but with his class; perhaps as a defense, he developed into "a solitary moral being," as perceived by both Bowen and Gwynn. His independence and the consequences he suffered are marked in her family history.

Her father's Anglo-Irish school, St. Columba's, "the Eton of Ireland," brought more solace in memory than in experience to Henry, according to Stephen Gwynn. Later an accomplished journalist, poet, and nationalist politician, Gwynn remembered Henry as a "tall, shambling, untidy, red-haired youth of fifteen," a runner-up for best scholar in the school.[45] Henry never attempted cricket or football and evidenced a streak of gloom and asocial behavior that many found puzzling, given all the privileges of coming from a wealthy, landowning family. He was six feet two inches, and according to Bowen, had a "great shock of springy red-gold hair."[46] Gwynn noted Henry's clumsiness; he was often dropping or losing things and his daughter found that "the constant comedies of his vagueness kept him from ever being a prig." Though he was slow, and clumsy with his hands, he was not so with people, according to Bowen, and possessed the qualities of fairness and charity. Though Gwynn saw a feeble sportsman and a "slow mind" without spark or power of improvisation, Bowen saw her father as an accomplished man of ideas who "by the design of his own nature" was not fit to play the role his own father had demanded as landlord and manager of Bowen's Court and Camira, another family estate. Perhaps his gloominess was an early sign of a serious depression and incipient mental illness.

At St. Columba's College, Henry was one of the prefects and won prizes for his learning in the 1880s (Fig. 2.2). Enrollment declined at the time he attended because of the prevailing Anglo-Irish response to the economic

Fig. 2.2 H.C. Cole Bowen, Bowen's father, at St. Columba's College, the "Eton" of Ireland. Prefects: (far left) H.C. Cole Bowen (1874); his friend, C.W. Gwyn (1882), second from left, et al. Rights holder and Courtesy of St. Columba's College, Dublin

impact of the Land War of 1879–82 on their estates and the demoralizing effect of the Home Rule Bill of 1886. The Anglo-Irish were becoming less certain of their place in Ireland and instead of sending their sons to St. Columba's, they began choosing schools in Britain where young men could study for careers there and throughout the empire. Even before then it was a natural progression for boys of the Ascendancy to go to public school in England, Cambridge University, and sometimes, as with Uncle Winkie, a theological college. Nevertheless, Bowen's father distinguished himself at Trinity College in ethics, Latin, and Greek, but avoided societies and clubs. Gwynn noted his disengagement from politics during a turbulent time in Ireland when Parnell's leadership was challenged; Henry rather was engaged in local causes, remaining loyal to St. Columba's as a fellow from 1910 to 1930. Henry's contributions were reported by Richard Brett, a senior tutor, librarian, and teacher of Greek and Latin who noted that Henry's "grieving friends" dedicated a monument to him on the campus in homage to his qualities of learning and kindliness in 1932, two years after his death.

After six years of treatment in hospitals, and with the support of his sister, Sarah, and devoted friends such as Gwynn, Henry was well enough to leave institutions and return to work in 1910. He became a land-purchase lawyer in Dublin around 1910, and in 1918, six years after his wife's death, married Gwynn's sister, Mary Katherine: he had always been welcomed and warmly supported by the Gwynn family. In his work, he championed the Land Reform Acts, measures to transfer the ownership of land in Ireland from British landlords to Irish tenants, sometimes with the economic aid of the government beginning in 1870. It is an irony, and a reflection of the Anglo-Irish strand from which Bowen emerged, that he worked to dismantle the inherited estates that his father had worked all his life to preserve, and illustrates an independence of mind and spirit that Bowen shared.

A few years before his death, he completed an exhaustive 803-page, leather-bound book, *Statutory Land Purchase in Ireland Prior to 1923*. The preface explains that the main object of the treatise was "to trace the orderly development of the legal principles underlying and conditioning the growth of the system of Statutory Land Purchase in Ireland."[47] His tome included sections on ancient monuments, arrears of rents, bankruptcy, disused mills, estate duty, heirs, the Irish Land Purchase Fund, sales of estates of lunatics or persons of unsound mind, married women, sand and gravel, seaweed, stone, clay, tenants, and trees. One of Bowen's lovers in the 1930s, received her father's book from Blackwell's and praised it writing that he had a clearer vision of the Land Acts: "it is a terrific work […] really a book for [a] practicing lawyer."[48]

Henry Bowen also handled the Pembroke estates on the south side of Dublin, the largest family-owned estate in County Dublin.[49] He became a prominent member of the Church of Ireland and a respected judge in the Court of General Synod, Dublin Diocese.[50] He was an accomplished man with a prodigious intelligence that was passed on to Bowen. Nelly Gates, a Bowen's Court neighbor, summed him up as a "gentle giant of a man."[51] After his recovery, Gwynn noted, Henry's chief interests were the growing talent and increased recognition of his daughter, Elizabeth "as a novelist of the newest flight." His obituary in the *Irish Times*, May 30, 1930, emphasized his prominence in the Church of Ireland, and this commitment remained an influence on Bowen who was a churchgoing member all her life, attending chapels when living Oxford, Farahy Chapel near Bowen's Court and, later, St. Leonard's Church, Hythe, according to Laetitia Lefroy, her cousin.

Bowen also saw her father's life through the eyes of Sarah Cartey, the main housemaid at Bowen's Court, who knew him when he was a child and had seen "the red headed schoolboy, the anxious young head of the house, the proud bridegroom, and the lonely man fighting breakdown for many years."[52] She conveyed, without a word spoken, as Bowen gratefully acknowledged to her family, her sense of Henry's "triumphant dignity." According to Bowen, he lapsed into mental illness again in 1930, and died shortly after. Sarah Cartey prepared his body and called for Bowen. "You must come and see him," she said proudly. "He looks lovely." Bowen bowed her head in assent, noting that Sarah's "fingers had fluted the linen over his body into a marble like pattern, a work of art," reminiscent of the image of Marcel's grandmother in death in Proust's *Swann's Way*. The description of her father's body and funereal linen reflects Bowen's and Proust's aesthetic that life or death is heightened by art. In Gwynn's account, Henry was loved by his tenants at Bowen's Court and referred to them as "my neighbours."[53] Protestants and Catholics alike appreciated how he ministered to them with helpfulness, generosity, and a sense of justice and hundreds formed his funeral cortege. They carried him on their shoulders from the room where he died in Bowen's Court to St. Colman's Church, Farahy, where he and Bowen worshipped, and buried him in the little churchyard there.

Henry's mental illness was believed to be a genetic disorder inherited from his father, who lived at high pressure as the manager of two estates, Bowen's Court and Camira. People lived in dread of her grandfather, as he "liked[,] in fact, to see things done properly, and signalized any lapse by a sharp yell."[54] This "lunatic self" that lurked in her childhood later emerged in some of her fictional characters. St. Quentin, the worldly novelist in *The Death of the Heart*, observes of human nature that "each of us keeps, battened down inside himself, a sort of lunatic giant, impossible socially, but full-scale—and that it's the knockings and batterings we sometimes hear in each other that keep our intercourse from utter banality."[55] The "lunatic giant" driven by irrepressible needs is another aspect of the madness Bowen explores in a female character, Eva Trout, the lumbering, monstrous heiress and neglected orphan who turns everyone's life into a nightmare. Though Eva is generously taken into the home of her teacher, Iseult, Eva conspires against her and destroys her marriage, provoking Iseult's cry, "I have murdered my life." Eva's broken relationships litter the novel. Her will, "the patient encircling will of a monster," destroys homes much like the bomb that is the primary metaphor of the novel.[56] Bowen's home as a child was also disordered by her father's and grandfather's manic behavior.

The Colley's Sanity

Though the Colleys were cut from similar Anglo-Irish cloth as the Bowens, they were different. They did not share the Bowen's preoccupation with land or their dark moods, unpredictable behavior, "madness," and volatility.[57] The

Bowens were a propertied family, a patriarchy, preoccupied with the acquisition and maintenance of estates; the Colley family, on the other hand, a matriarchy run by strong women who, though they loved their homes and gardens, were not attached to any particular place. Bowen described the Colleys as "undeviatingly sane" with a flair for family life. The Colley's Victorian house at the time overlooked Dublin Bay, and Bowen remembered "that house as being under a magic glass." She also recalled the Sunday visits and the warm and close-knit family she had visited as a young child. Henry Fitz George Colley married Elizabeth Isabella in 1852 and had a family of six boys and four girls: Florence (Bowen's mother), Bessie, Maud, George (looked after Florence and Elizabeth during the early days of Henry's mental illness), Laura (took care of Bowen with Wingfield after Florence's death), Wingfield, Gerald, Constance, Gertrude, and Edward (Fig. 2.3). Her grandmother ruled like a Victorian matriarch, with "wicked" domineering gifts, according to Bowen, but her grandfather, Henry Fitz-George Colley, was ill, silent, and sad. Bowen, who spent some time growing up among them, noted that "in their love of the present, in their power of storing up memories, they were ruled by an innocent sensuousness."[58] Friends said that Bowen shared this gift

Fig. 2.3 The Colley Family. Florence Colley, Bowen's mother (front row, far right). Colley Family Rights holder and Courtesy of Laetitia Lefroy

of high spirits and flair for living in the moment, qualities that countered the Bowen family melancholy that emerged with the early death of the mother, and a "proud fine-strung place-bound nervousness."[59] Spontaneity and witty talk sparkled among the Colleys, while the Bowens' monomaniacal passions seemed to spread gloom. Henry, her father, was drawn to the Colley high spirits and chose for his wife the lively Florence from a group of vivacious sisters. Bowen observed of Florence that "she was the unusual one—capricious, elusive and gently intent on her own thoughts."[60] In addition, she was not a local girl, but the educated daughter of wealthy landowners from Castle Carbury. Today, all that is left of the Colley house near Mount Temple, occupied by them from 1860 to 1904, is a building dating from 1863. Its iconic clock tower, designed by the architect of the campanile in Trinity College, resembles the school tower, and was immortalized in Christy Nolan's novel *Under the Eye of the Clock*.[61]

They traced their lineage to Walter Cowley (or Colley), an English solicitor general for Ireland in 1537. The family was granted land and a manor in County Kildare in return for loyal service to the crown during Queen Elizabeth's reign. They acquired other lands, built a house near a castle in Carbury (Carbery), created orchards and gardens, and leased out farms to and collected rents from Irish tenants: the Anglo-Irish pattern. These possessions made the Colleys—at one time—the most extensive and powerful owners in the northwest region of the country.[62] Colley ancestors are buried in the graveyard on Carbury Hill. Florence, however, was born with her siblings in Lucan Lodge and the family retained some lands in Carbury that were let. In spite of this history, Bowen viewed the Colleys as unlike most Anglo-Irish families in not being tied to any one place.[63] She would follow this pattern of movement in her own life though rooted, at times, in Bowen's Court.

Bowen barely mentions the calamitous events of her childhood that interrupted the peaceful times with the Colleys and at Bowen's Court. She says little in her memoirs about her father's departure from their Herbert Place home in 1906 to a mental hospital; his absence and struggle in institutions in England and Dublin over the course of six years; and "the unbearable year" after her mother's death in Hythe in 1912, when she was 13. What is withheld, however, reappears in the varying colors, patterns, and feelings of her fiction. The reflections of her emotional and sensory past, and her sympathy with the feelings and thoughts of lonely, orphaned, or "mad" little girls and women (and, sometimes, boys), pervade her work. The specter of inherited madness to which she might fall victim shaded her in her mother's worried gaze, and according to Laetitia Lefroy, the Colley family viewed her as "scarred" by the early loss of her father and her mother's death; however, Victoria Glendinning, Bowen's early biographer, disagrees: "It is easy to see Elizabeth Bowen as scarred," but this was not the case.[64]

Throughout Bowen's topsy-turvy childhood, the Colleys provided stability when she was in Dublin and, later, in England. They nurtured her composure. As she shifted in and out of various family groups between Ireland and England, "her manner took on a touch of clear-sighted good sense, like Alice's throughout Wonderland."[65] But unlike Alice, who has good sense but cannot control her mad world, Bowen took control, as would the strong female adolescents and adult women in her novels who express their discontent with women's roles. There were times when she felt she had fallen down an emotional well, as when she was uprooted from her home in Ireland. But she was primarily "like someone in a new element, a conjurer's little girl" who levitated above disturbing experiences. Her imagination transformed her rootless life in other people's homes: no place in particular was home, so she carried her stability and sturdy sense of self within.

Bowen described the physical and emotional shift from the peaceful Ballyhouras Mountains surrounding Bowen's Court to the "white chalk, thunderbolt and tidal waves" of Folkestone and Hythe. She rejoiced upon her arrival: "On a clear day, the whole of this area meets the eyes: there are no secrets."[66] She described herself as a "social extrovert," "a tomboy," *farouche* and uninhibited in her play and exploration in the open, sunny spaces. Two of her favorite cousins who joined in were Noreen Colley, ten years younger than Bowen, and Audrey Fiennes, about the same age. Bowen described their gang and the game of "I dare you" that involved tree and roof climbing to great heights, blindfold acrobatics on bicycles, one-leg hopping on walls, and bravely balancing on parapets over railways.[67] Her robust upbringing shaped her later boldness in bicycling and fast-driving cars. When she moved to Folkestone a year later, she found a more "law abiding" atmosphere, but she was never a retiring child. Like that "conjurer's little girl," she rose to challenges, yet she masked a vulnerability.

Bowen noted that her Colley grandmother was quick-minded but "sturdily anti-intellectual: she denounced reading as a selfish and useless habit. 'Whoever's is this?' she would say with ringing contempt, if she found a book in the downstairs part of the house."[68] Her daughters read upstairs in their rooms. Christopher Hone, son of Valerie Colley, observed that there were writers in the family. Joseph (Maunsel) Hone, the distinguished biographer of Yeats and George Moore, was in both Yeats' circle, and, at times, in James Joyce's. Bowen wrote a review of Hone's history, *The Moores of Moore Hall*, in 1939, in which he maps the fate of an Irish landed family of both Catholic and Anglo-Irish strains, and the dilemma of descendants inheriting family estates. Inheritance here was viewed as something between a *raison d'etre* and a burden, a view that Bowen shared. Moore Hall, built in 1792, was burned by the IRA in 1923.[69] According to Richard Ellmann, Joseph Hone visited James Joyce along with other young writers like "Dermot" Chenevix Trench (a cousin who championed the Gaelic League) in Martello Tower suggesting crossovers between Anglo-Irish and Catholic writers. Hone, coincidentally, was a partner, mostly in a financial role, with George Roberts, the Dublin publisher of drama and literary works, Maunsel and Co. The firm considered publishing *Dubliners* and dangled Joyce for years, eventually rejecting it, some said, under the influence of the Vigilance League and for fear of libel.[70] Other writers in the Colley-Bowen family were Hubert Butler, a well-known and accomplished essayist, and, today, Turtle Bunbury, a historian and travel writer, the son of Jessica Rathdonnell, Bowen's cousin.[71]

The Colleys maintained an estate outside Dublin that Bowen's Aunt Edie inherited in 1936 after her father died, all male heirs having died in wars (her brothers Robert and Guy, in World War I). Bowen used to stay at Corkagh with Edie and George: theirs, an unconventional marriage given that George was deaf from a childhood illness and interpreted people through slight lip reading and body language. Nevertheless, he was able to communicate enough to run the farm, do house accounts and tinker with machines and cars when they moved to Corkagh. Laetitia Lefroy, the granddaughter of Edie and George, remembers living at Corkagh as a child until she was ten, and then later when she returned to go to Alexandra College (that Bowen's mother also attended) and, later, Trinity College. Though some described it as physically uncomfortable—worn furniture and cold rooms—it was an emotionally nurturing place, and Bowen spent time there after her mother's death as well as others of her generation who sometimes needed a temporary home. Aunt Edie was an active figure, a "character" attuned to gardening, neighborhood news, and an incorrigible matchmaker and Elizabeth and her generation provided much material, according to Laetitia. She was always concerned with Elizabeth, and teased and chastised her as she did all in her family. It was she who swept Bowen away from an "inappropriate" suitor in 1921 to accompany her, her husband, and children, to Italy.[72] Bowen's cousins saw more of her in the 1960s, after the death of Alan Cameron. Ritchie, Bowen's lover after 1941, visited Corkagh and Kilmatead, a sign of her comfort with the family. The Colleys did not know much about Bowen's intimacies but were accepting as few of their age and social standing would have been. Her aunt passed on Corkagh to her son, Dudley Colley who died prematurely and it was then sold; later Bowen would stay at the Mill House, nearby. Here she had a close relationship with Finlay's maternal aunt, Noreen Burns ("Toddy"), a good cook and caterer by profession and treasured by the family for her helpfulness, loyalty, and unobtrusiveness. She sometimes assisted Bowen in entertaining at Bowen's Court; Bowen helped her move into her holiday house in Valentia Island, off the coast of Ireland, with Finlay and his mother. Bowen's friendship with this extended family was a retreat from her frenetic professional life, according to Christopher Hone, and "epitomized the ease with which she related to people […] she wore her great literary prowess and intellect lightly."[73]

The Colley family was matriarchal and progressive about educating women. Bowen's mother studied at Alexandra College founded in 1866 to educate girls in a Church of Ireland (Anglican) ethos. Here she studied English language and literature, natural science, holy scripture, arithmetic, and philosophy (mental and moral) and probably some Latin, Greek, and French. The school was based on the ideals of Queens College in London, the first college of higher education for women in England in 1848. The founder and principal of Alexandra, Anne Jellicoe, was guided in its development by Richard Chenevix-Trench, Bowen's great-uncle. Florence attended the school from its opening as did other women in the Colley family, an elite private education typical for Anglo-Irish girls of a certain class.[74]

The Unbearable Year

In the summer of 1912, Bowen wrote, "Florence, my mother, was told by a Dublin doctor, to her delight that she would be in Heaven six months hence." "Delight" expresses Florence's relief, she then 47 years old, after her many operations for a cancer that had worn her out. The Colley family encircled Bowen, then 13, when her mother died. "An unbearable year," she wrote, "I could not remember her, think of her, speak of her or suffer to hear her spoken of."[75] She never forgot the closeness, the physical intimacy with her mother, but no longer feeling "her mother's cheek on her own," like Portia in *The Death of the Heart*, said that she learned to live without her.[76] This rent in her emotional life and world was comparable only to her flight from Dublin in 1906 after the eruption of her father's mental illness. Her mother's death was also the same year that her aunt Constance died of consumption and her uncle Edward died on the *Titanic*.[77] Maude Ellmann, wrote that Bowen was barely able to utter the word "mother" after her death,[78] a state confirmed by Curtis Brown, Bowen's agent and editor, who noted that the death was "a loss so devastating that to the end of her life she would not willingly refer to it."[79]

It was a depressing year for her father also as he was beginning to feel quite well and had discussed reuniting the family again when released from the hospital. According to Laetitia Lefroy, the Colley family viewed this reunion favorably, but Florence did drag her feet, having grown to love Hythe, and then reluctant to return to Dublin after the discovery of her cancer. They were reunited briefly in her last days, and Bowen described these evenings as "stuffy and bodeful […] thrummings of a bomber, circling, coming brutally nearer each time," imbuing the personal with the violence of the times.[80] Her cousin Audrey often heard Bowen sobbing in the night; Bowen did not attend her mother's funeral. In a state that she called "stupidity," with her inability to express sorrow, Bowen wore a black tie to mark the event when attending Harpenden Hall. She adopted a pose of being lazy in school, "a dunce girl," as a defense against her sadness. Nevertheless, she found comfort in a visit from her father and then in the Harpenden home of Uncle Winkie, Reverend Wingfield Colley, because of his "understanding speechlessness" and his sister, Aunt Laura. In Bowen's fairy tale for young people, "The Unromantic Princess," a young princess, Angelica, who has just lost her mother is given the gifts of common sense and punctuality by fairy godmothers that enable her to become independent of godmothers and responsible for her own life: much like Bowen who possessed the same gifts plus others.[81] Illustrations in this tale depict a young woman on horseback with bobbed hair in conversation and pursuit of a boy she had met at a party, making her own destiny.

She wrote little about her mother, though this was the central relationship in her life, not only because of the devastation of this loss but also because she mistrusted the genre of autobiography. In her family history, *Bowen's Court*, she focused mainly on her father and his family. She could approach her mother only through fiction, where she distanced and transformed the emotional state of motherlessness. Children in her novels—Portia, Leopold, Henrietta, and Theodora, among others—experience, as she did, moments of sudden tragic importance. Young Henrietta feels "as though a great dark plumed hat had been clapped aslant on her head" in *The House in Paris* after being exposed to Leopold's dark secrets and reminded of her own.[82] In a quiet conversation, Leopold cruelly confronts Henrietta with her own mother's death though she has treated his loss sympathetically. "Are you still unhappy about your mother?" Leopold asks. Henrietta turns her face to the wall, demurs, "I'm not thinking about her," and tries to distract him with conversation about a train. His taunting confirms the narrator's observation: "there is no end to the violations committed by children on children." Leopold then announces that he does not remember his mother, but he "will" see her again. Henrietta, expert in hiding her feelings, "turned down her eyes, smoothed her dress," walking to the other side of the room, examining nothing, exhibiting only boredom.

Contemporaries of Bowen point to other ways of dealing with the death of a mother. William Maxwell, a good friend of Bowen's who solicited her stories for the *New Yorker*, also experienced the early death of his mother when he was ten, but, unlike Bowen who worked by indirection, sought to articulate the void that he felt in his autobiography: "the worst that could happen had happened, and the shine went out of life." At the time, he was desperate, made a suicide attempt, and it shaped his writing career. Though "other children could have borne it," he notes, "somehow I couldn't."[83] He remained an admiring and loving friend of Bowen's often joining Eudora Welty in meetings in Ireland and New York with his wife, Emmy, until the mid-sixties when she told Welty she had no time for him and he was dropped summarily, as Bowen sometimes did with friends.

Virginia Woolf, who also lost her mother early, when she was 13, confessed to being haunted by her death from that time until she was 42, when she finally laid her to rest in creating the character of Mrs. Ramsay in *To the Lighthouse*. Bowen also indirectly poured her mournful feelings into characters in some of her stories: the children in "The Little Girl's Room," Portia in *The Death of the Heart* and Leopold in *The House in Paris* learn to live without their mothers. In one of her few autobiographical pieces, Bowen describes the intimacies she and her mother shared in their itinerant life in Kent, longing to live in a white balconied seaside villa but unable to afford it. When not living with relatives, they would squeeze into a hotel or manage to get the agent's key to a villa and have a game within the fantasy residence, "a pavilion of love." Yet "in the last of these villas in which it came about that we did actually live, she died."[84]

Just before this "unspeakable event," her father came out of a mental hospital in Ireland. Though she would then visit him at Bowen's Court in the summers, Bowen was brought up mainly by her aunts and cousins in England and Ireland. She first went to live with Lilia Chichester, a childless dowager; then with the widowed Isabel-Chenevix Trench. After her mother's death, she was greatly comforted by her aunt Laura, her mother's sister, and "uncle Winkie"— Wingfield Colley, her mother's unmarried, much-loved gentle and shy brother—in Harpenden, Southview, Kent. After staying with them for a while, Bowen entered the school, Harpenden Hall, Hertfordshire, which was housed in a romantic seventeenth-century building. But she was "in a state of shock and the less said the better: total bereavement, disfigurement, mortification, disgrace." This strange vocabulary of martyrdom conveys her sense of that "unbearable year" and the way it influenced her temperament. Afterward, there were times that she wanted to be a "nonentity"; at other phases, a "celebrity." She attended Harpenden Hall for two years, and her father visited during the holidays. Finally, preferring not to be fussed over by the committee of hovering aunts, she was sent to the Downe House boarding school in 1914, a fine progressive school for girls. Uncle Winkie married Helen Brownlow in 1915 and remained involved with Bowen throughout her adolescence. Laetitia related that Winkie was much loved in the family, "gentle and quiet and shy."[85] Bowen also often stayed with her mother's brother, George, and his wife Edie when they lived in Faunnaugh, Rathgar, a suburb of Dublin, until 1916, and then later when they moved to Corkagh. And in the summer of 1916, she was overseen by her Uncle Henry and Aunt Sarah at Bowen's Court. As Laetitia observed, "Elizabeth was passed around. Children didn't have parents."

Bowen did not go to college as some women in her class did, but she read a great deal and traveled abroad, mostly to Italy. She tried to write poetry and paint, but experiencing failure at art school, she moved on to writing stories. Her youthful courage, a quality that would bolster her throughout her life, belies the sharpness of feeling that her mother's death caused.

An Itinerant Education

As a result of her mother's death as well as her father's absence and their move to Kent, Bowen had an itinerant education. She attended various schools in the triangle formed by Folkestone, Lyminge, and Hythe when she first traveled to Kent with her mother. According to the 1909 census, she lived with the widowed Isabel Chevenix-Trench at 9 Radnor Place; in 1911, she moved and was listed as living with her mother: Florence Colley (age 46); Elizabeth Dorothea Cole (11) [Bowen herself—her father was a Cole]; and Ellen Graham, domestic (40), at 1 Church Villas, Lyminge, Folkestone. Bowen attended Lindum School, but eventually her mother considered it too demanding, harking back to her fear of overworking Bowen and evoking the family "madness." She then sent her for home schooling with the Salmon girls, beautiful daughters, Bowen said, of the rector Robert Cecil Salmon of St. Martin's Church in Seabrook, Old Cheriton (now a part of Folkestone).[86] But Bowen's jealousy was aroused when observing the ideal family life of the girls, Veronica and Maisie, feeling that she "was not yet fit to intake sweetness and light." She began acting "like a yahoo" in this conventional family, exhibiting the toughness of the character Anna in *Friends and Relations*: "vigorous as a crocus" in "her little sheath of assurance."[87] She boldly explored the outdoors with her cousin, Audrey Fiennes, who visited Hythe twice a year, and with whom she wrote and acted out stories or played "imaginary family."[88] She also liked to sketch clothes, hinting at her lifelong interest in fashion. And she loved to dance, though she did not have a strong musical sense; she and Fiennes later held a makeshift dance at Bowen's Court.

The Downe House School in Kent, that Bowen entered in September 1914, a year after her mother's death, strengthened her confidence and shaped her literary interests. The school was small, about 40–50 girls, and was considered one of the finest boarding schools in the region for the well-to-do, founded in 1906 by the progressive Olive Willis, a pioneer in women's education. "The school was operated with discriminating literary and academic parents."[89] Olive Willis' anger about being locked out of libraries and educational institutions motivated her to act and found a school, and other such schools began to arise in the 1870s, encouraged by Gladstone's act for universal elementary education. It opened about 20 years before Woolf spoke with indignation of her exclusion from the Oxbridge library in her talk "A Room of One's Own" at Newnham College, Cambridge. The establishment of girls' schools and women's colleges such as Girton and Newnham took prodigious effort, and financial resources that women often lacked.[90] Woolf, born 17 years before Bowen into an elite literary family, was schooled at home with tutors and in her father's library, but Bowen, of the next generation, attended a public school that encouraged women to think, go to college, and seek careers. The rallying cry of the Downe House School was that girls should not be "L.O.P. H." (Left on Pa's Hands)[91] (Fig. 2.4).

Bowen entered the school at 15 as the war mounted. She was not part of the conversation of girls in her school with brothers in the war or attentive to news reports. Removed from the war, deadened to its effects, she like Stella in *The Heat of the Day* "had grown up just after the first world war with the generation which, as a generation, was to come to be made to feel it had muffed the catch. The times, she had in her youth been told on all sides, were without precedent."[92]

Bowen recorded early impressions in the 1957 *Downe House Scrapbook*. All the girls "seemed very sure of themselves—and for some reason, to the comer-in from the outside, this was not alarming but reassuring." It was an atmosphere in which everyone was absorbed and "one was plunged straight, deep, into the middle of something." The only nightmare in adolescence is "a shifting universe," and Bowen was still reeling from the death of her mother and her father's absence. The school provided her with stability and direction in a transitional period.[93] She sketches a picture that reveals her early preoccupation with place, landscape, and architecture. The school was a white Georgian building, three stories high and its shallow front lawn,

Downe House. 1915.

E.Richards. E.Cobb. M.Olton. A.Blackwood. M. to introll. D.Voyle. S.PG. A.Barns. B.Foyle. A.Lucas. K.Shiel. E.B. Reynardson. C. Manders. D. wallace. K. Fanken.

P. Jones Hon. B. Wallace. E.Sanders. B.Bowen. J. L. Grover. P. Erskine. D.Sedgwick. G.Cotton. S.Cobb. J.Sand. wilk. B.Wilson. J.Whilby. A.Richards.E.Broadbent. S. B. Carter.

Fig. 2.4 1915 Bowen at Downe House School. B. Bowen (the "B" is for Bitha, a nick-name Bowen did not like) [second row from the top, fourth from the left]. Rights holder and Courtesy of Jennifer Kingsland, Archivist, Downe House Archives

swagged in July with Dorothy Perkins roses [and which] stood back from the tarmac road outside the Kentish village of Downe [...] A bed of azaleas outside the senior study French window made the summer term exotic. Features of this lawn landscape were an old mulberry tree with an iron belt and a mound with a large ilex [...] on which Shakespeare plays were acted.[94]

It was the former home of Charles Darwin, 14 miles south of London's Charing Cross.

Willis brought an unusual spirit of gaiety to the school reflected in her way of addressing students: "Need you?" rather than "Don't." Willis had, according to Bowen, a power to motivate, but did not overly "manage." Instead, she introduced freedom into the atmosphere, encouraged easy conversation among teachers and students, and showed respect for the girls' individual personalities. She outlawed exams and instead focused on nurturing a love of learning. Bowen wrote three poems for the school magazine in 1916, and, later, an essay on the school for the *Jubilee Scrapbook* in 1957. In one poem, "Spring," we read a parody, a sign of her lifelong humor:

Alas, all vanity yet let us not bemoan
The passing of sere winter when the spring
Smiles on us showering forth her welcome gifts
Of primroses, and—er—primroses—and—well
You know the sort of thing that season brings.

Archaisms such as "alas" and "ye" and "ho" sprinkle another poem, "Pastoral Symphony, or a Reminiscence of the Cudham Entertainment," but in "The Enchanted Garden," fresh and clichéd language intermix:

In the arbour down the alleys by the fountain's sparkling rim
Broods the spirit of the garden where the long leaves listless lie,
In the everlasting twilight when the evening beam grows dim,
And the little branches quiver as the noiseless feet go by.

Bowen absorbed the literary atmosphere of the school, known also for its music instruction. Willis taught literature and French, and as head of the literary society she encouraged the girls to read aloud and introduced the tradition of acting plays in French. One may assume that Bowen gained her French skills at the school as well as later travels to Paris; this later blossomed into her love of Proust and her essay on Bergotte, a literary character from *In Search of Lost Time*, and her love of Flaubert, Maupassant, and Henry de Motherlant. But Bowen was also taught here "how not, if possible, to behave and how not to exhibit feeling."[95] Her restraint of emotion during this period of vulnerability after her mother's death was nurtured in the school. Family, culture, class, and temperament contributed to this habit of "withheld emotion."

Willis allowed the girls to wear their own clothes, not uniforms, and, "our hair was so skinned back that our eyes would hardly shut"—though judging from a 1915 photo, this was not the case at all times. Willis encouraged independence of mind and seriously attempted to prepare the girls for schools such as Somerville, Oxford, which she had attended. In the 1930s, 16 percent of the Downe House students reportedly went on to careers outside marriage. When Bowen graduated in 1918, she did not go to college. She wrote to Ritchie that she "felt a solid resistance to the idea when I was student age. I've a theory—at any rate in 'some' natures, for one, mine—only having <u>had</u> experience makes learning acceptable…. It's really only quite late in life that I've begun to have a <u>desire</u> for knowledge."[96] When she was 19, the year that her father remarried, she enrolled in the London County Council School of Art. Secretly, however, she had a desire to be a writer, and said in an early essay that attending the art school was a sort of disguise. When her father married

Mary Gwynn, she met Mary's brother Stephen, a poet and journalist. He confirmed her belief that authors generally lived in London and that may have influenced her decision to move there in 1918.[97]

Bowen remembered that Willis had kindly exhorted the girls to "grow up" and stop being "girlish," and never once addressed them as "future mothers." She was bred to independence in the school, and life had thrown her upon her own emotional resources given the absence of her parents. She noted that few of her friends anticipated maternity. When, in 1934, 11 years after she married Cameron, she wrote her account of Downe House, she observed that though some of her friends had "since become mothers, it still seems inappropriate." She could not remember discussing men with the other girls; "possibly the whole sex had gloomy associations" because of the war. Bowen was the product of a school of which the principal might confide to a prospective parent, "I feel it my duty to tell you, dear Mrs. X, that our girls do not marry well." Nevertheless, Bowen did want to marry; many in her class felt they could not do anything else in their lives till this was done. In her novels, Bowen's characters voiced a variety of views of marriage. Lady Naylor, in advising young Lois against an unsuitable liaison in *The Last September*, asserts the progressive idea: "There is a future for girls nowadays without marriage." The British Mrs. Michaelis, Karen's middle-class mother, however, remarks in *The House in Paris*, "a woman's real life only began with marriage [...] girlhood amounts to no more than privileged looking on."[98] Bowen married Alan Cameron, then director of education for the city of Oxford, in 1923, when she was 24 and he was 30, perhaps to have a perch and "to have it done." She once told Molly Keane, according to Sally Phipps, that when you are young, you think of marriage as a train that you simply have to catch. You run and run, then sit back and look out the window and realize you are bored.[99]

Bowen captures the mannerisms, affections, innocent fetishes, sexualities, and boredom of schoolgirls in her essay on Downe House, as well as in her descriptions of St. Agatha's School in her novel *The Little Girls*. She does not neglect the damage that children sometimes do. Portia, the watchful, diary-keeping innocent in *The Death of the Heart*, is perceived as a disruptive force in the home of her half-brother as she records hypocritical, bourgeois lives. Anna, his wife, asserts, "either I or she is a monster."[100] And in observing the precocious adolescents Leopold and Henrietta in *The House in Paris*, the narrator notes the insensitivity of children to children. Though Bowen's days at Downe House appear to have been benign, her descriptions of earlier schools—for example, feeling out of place in home study with the perfectly mannered Salmon children, or when dealing with the pressures at Harpenden Hall—suggest childhood wounds and bewilderment.

Bowen wrote that she could not imagine a girls' school without war, its sounds issuing from the Biggin Hill Aerodrome near her school. She remembered that on her first evening, Willis addressed them on the outbreak of the war, and it went on for a year after she left. The girls observed Zeppelins circling, and one wrote of how she could hear the "dull boom of the barrage in Flanders" on summer nights.[101] Bowen wrote, "The moral stress was appalling. We grew up under the intolerable obligation of being fought for, and could not fall short in character without recollecting that men were dying for us."[102] Her generation matured, she said, "with a horror of being *bouche inutiles*," useless mouths to feed, a warning Bowen carried into her active service during the blitz.[103] Her experience of war when a schoolgirl, piqued by her earlier affinity with violent adventure stories, would mount to a fugue during World War II.

Bowen also put on "grateful record" that at the Downe House School, the headmistress, Olive Willis, "did definitely teach me how not to write." Not only did she read much and write poetry but was given early and important encouragement from a friend of the headmistress, Rose Macaulay, in 1923. She read her stories, recognized her talent, and invited her to tea at the University Women's Club, to introduce her to Naomi Royce-Smith, editor of the *Saturday Westminster*, who published her first story. Macaulay wrote often and admiringly in later years of Bowen's "exquisite" poetic style. Of *A World of Love*, she wrote, "I adore its texture, its light, its color, its climate, its landscape—it is like watching naiads in a translucent pale-green stream [...] the way you make one feel the water, the heat, the whole setting: and oh your prose!"[104] She personally responded to her books in perceptive letters and publicly through BBC's "The Critic" up to *The Heat of the Day* (1949). Though Bowen, in kind, wrote flattering reviews of Macaulay's novels, she was not as faithful a friend.

Bowen was an uninhibited child. Going her own way, she valued and created stories about wild little girls like herself over the course of her writing career: "I became farouche in the solitary unrestricted [society and] movement of little girls" in the in the fields of Kent "I was let to run wild [...] I was a tough child."[105] This touchiness and air of delinquency matured as she became a woman and entered into her female characters like Emma, a married woman who travels through a threatening wartime night to an affair in her story "Summer Night." She describes Emma who enters her lover's living room, "Farouche, with her tentative little swagger and childish, pleading art of delinquency." It was a quality, salient in her life and her female characters, that she later explained as helping her to work off her early sense of being solitary... unrelatable.[106] Because nonconforming little girls in Bowen's stories can find no language in which to express themselves aloud or be understood, they act out—or they write in their diaries or letters or even on the body. In "Summer Night," in a millennial gesture, a child tattoos her feelings on her body. Di, the daughter of Emma, acts out the "anarchy" she feels one threatening night when her mother has gone off to an assignation with a lover and violent wartime air battles are taking place overhead. Di steals out of bed, strips her nightgown and "got out a box of chalks and began to tattoo her chest, belly and thighs with stars and snakes, red, yellow and blue."[107] Both the terror of the war surrounding her and her mother's absence—the national and the personal—are expressed in her disturbing and knowing message written on her body.

As a child, Bowen also sought expression and wrote and acted out stories with her cousin Audrey; she even composed alternate chapters of a novel about Bonnie Prince Charlie with her next-door friend, Hilary. From an early age, she experimented with unusual vocabulary, often incorrectly according to Audrey, a sign of her early interest in startling words, reading and play acting.[108] Howard Moss speculated that her lifelong interest in odd vocabulary and synonyms may have been a strategy for circumventing her stutter.

Reading

When she finally learned, Bowen was bolstered in her young life by reading. She read voraciously, and when she had absorbed one author, she went on to another. Her early reading of Lewis Carroll's *Alice in Wonderland* evoked her admiration for the pluck and resourcefulness of a young girl when challenged by an adult world of rules that made no sense. This understanding would illuminate her later sketches of adolescent girls like Portia in *The Death of the Heart*. A no-nonsense, forthright approach to life was one that Bowen shared, and she highlighted its value in her feminist fairy tale, "The Unromantic Princess." The queen at the princess' birth invited fairy godmothers to the christening to grant her gifts, but to the queen's disappointment, they arrived in a workaday mood and gave her the qualities of "commonsense" and "punctuality." The princess longed for beauty—"curls" and "bright blue eyes"—recognizing that her "commonsense eyes" did not attract suitors. After her mother's death, the princess realizes that "fairy Godmothers may do much to spoil … your chances, but they cannot really interfere with the nice character you have inherited from your father and mother and the right way you are brought up." She becomes responsible for her own life and takes the initiative in searching for a boy poet that she once knew. When they meet and he, in fairy tale fashion, asks to marry her, she decides to make him a court poet. He says, however, that he would rather run a kingdom with common sense and punctuality. They marry and decide in no-nonsense fashion that their children will not have fairy godmothers.

Bowen also shared Alice in Wonderland's query, "What's the use of a book without pictures and conversations?" This thought was provoked when Alice, sitting by her sister on the riverbank, became bored and peeped into the book her sister was reading. It had no pictures or conversations in it and so did not interest Alice. When she was a writer, Bowen would be sure to evoke "pictures"—vivid descriptions of landscapes, houses, places, atmospheres and images—guided by her strong visual imagination. And she appreciated Tenniel's illustrations, and recalled Alice's warning in titling her unfinished autobiography, *Pictures and Conversations*, at the end of her life.

At the age of 12, Bowen became discontented with Alice's dull, trim back garden and world. Outside the Downe House boarding school, she observed "the thunder clouds which were to burst in 1914 were […] mounting on the horizon—but unobserved by me. Hemmed in by what seemed to be too much safety, I felt bored and hampered-ungrateful, but there you are: I still can distinctly remember the sensation. Worse still, I had exhausted the myths of childhood."[109] Then, one of the most formative stories of her childhood, Rider Haggard's *She*, took hold. In this tale she entered a mythic and violent world, awakened to a parable of female power and daring adventure: a dominatrix capable of incredible physical feats that left baffled male adventurers in her wake. She was also captivated by Gefenhagn's illustrations and noted a favorite, a violent one of a lion and crocodile locked in a death grip. She, the character, was totally in control of her world unlike the hapless Alice who played, according to Bowen, trivial games in her garden. Not only was Bowen awakened to feminine force in this bloodcurdling tale—a force that she would later unleash in strong women characters—but the power of the word to move readers. She had given up on childhood tales and admired now adventurous female characters.

She was caught between plucky Alice and the superwoman, She, drawn to violent and thrilling tales, but also enchanted by mystery. She read classic Celtic tales about strange spirits that lived in rocks, a force that would re-emerge in her own inspiriting of objects in her writing. Often considered "wild" by her aunts, rambunctious and physically hardy, Elizabeth was also attracted to contemporary stories such as Susan Coolidge's *What Katy Did*: about a "boyish" girl in 1860s America who also wished to be beautiful and loved (like the "unromantic" princess). She liked female characters who showed brains and common sense—like Alice and the "unromantic princess"—and bravery like She, as well as the boy characters in Henty's *The Boy Knight* who face trials during the Crusades and *By Sheer Pluck*, about a young student who travels to Africa with a well-known naturalist. She also mentioned Emma Orczy's *The Scarlet Pimpernel*, a spy thriller about the French Revolution that, she said, made her a Tory for life: a spirit that infused some of her own later writing in *The Heat of the Day*.

She also read Louisa May Alcott, Arnold Bennett, and Charles Dickens. Her love of Dickens was nurtured at the Downe House School where the debate and literary war cry one term was to choose Dickens or Scott as a favorite author. She read him throughout her life and confessed that Dickens was really at the root of so many things she saw and felt. Like Dickens, she threads her stories with vivid feelings of abandonment of children and adolescents. And she read history, geography, and natural history to feed her common sense. Not long after her eighth birthday, still living in Hythe, she said "I entered upon a long voluptuous phase in which I saw life as a non-stop historical novel, disguised only thinly (in my day) by modern dress."[110]

Experiencing what a book could do when she was a child and adolescent, stimulated her later writing. Through these early books and stories, she developed a habit of imagination—perceiving the world through visual and literary images—that, she said, remained with her throughout her life as a writer.[111]

Resurrecting Rooms

From these early experiences, Bowen would sketch scenes or revisit various childhood rooms in her memoirs and stories like Marcel Proust, one of her favorite authors. She embraced these experiences and acknowledged the difficulty of "resurrecting" the rooms and places, yet there was a lifelong pleasure in retreating into these rooms through writing. "In the end," Proust's Marcel announces, "I would revisit them all in the long course of my waking dreams [...] I would enjoy the satisfaction of being shut in from the outer world."[112] Bowen too enjoyed this feeling of being shut in a familiar room, a retreat from her itinerant childhood. One of her gifts as a writer is to enter the secret room of a lonely girl in her early stories and novels, a girl without a mother or away at school or one who is drawn to a mulberry tree where little girls are sharing secrets. In reading these scenes, we are given a glimpse of her childhood personality as she brings together two times of life in different places: an adult with associative feelings from childhood.

Bowen's fiction originated in recalled places: "the bricks used to build the story," she said, "must arise from experiences and observations only obtainable from the lives you have led."[113] A visual writer, she remembered and conjured rooms in her family history, *Bowen's Court*, homes with their expressive objects, furniture, and paintings, as well as the outside landscapes.[114] The views, the sensual atmosphere, and the architecture of places and rooms each carries an emotional and psychological residue. In her novel, *The Little Girls*, beloved objects bring back the past to a trio of adult friends: a coffer, a painting in a remembered room, a swing. In her own rooms, Bowen accustomed herself to solitude. Nevertheless, she was a physically hardy child, often running wild in the fields, and found the physical spaces outside these rooms magical. *Terra firma*, the tangible, the actual, would always be the foreground, stimulating her writing, unlike Virginia Woolf, whose imagination could be piqued by an abstract mark on a wall.[115]

One of her first visual memories in her autobiography, *Seven Winters*, is of the Herbert Street row house in Dublin where she lived until she was seven. She describes the rooms as an Impressionist painting, having "had a watery quality in their lightness from the upcast reflection of the canal."[116] The emotions in the house, were similarly shifting and uncertain, "unique and intensive, gently phenomenal," given her parents' solitary and independent ways. She sketched the home as happy, at times, and claustrophobic, at others. Until she was about five, half the year was spent on Herbert Street, and from May to mid-October and then Christmas, at Bowen's Court. Every Sunday afternoon was passed with the Colleys at Mount Temple, Clontarf. In her later recollections in *Pictures and Conversations*, the Dublin house becomes "dark and dreary," the same rooms colored by the memory of her father's illness at another time. She felt oppressed, she said, not only by his sickness but also by the pity that was visited upon her and her mother because of their ordeal. Bowen wrote that the eighteenth-century rooms in the house repelled the imagination with "rational proportions and faultless mouldings, evenly daylit, without shadow, curiousness or cranny."[117] Writing in her late 1960s memoir, she projected a gloom and paralysis upon the rooms and the house on a street lined by geometry.

Misunderstood girls often retreat to their rooms to write about a hypocritical or insensitive adult world. Secret thoughts and angers surface in dreams, diaries and letters. In the story "The Little Girl's Room," a mother's death haunts a preadolescent girl living in a prettified room where she confronts the death through dreams. Fawned over by her grandmother, the room is a retreat, enclosed "by volutions of delicacy and sweet living shadows: the inner whorls of a shell, the heart of a flower."[118] An image reminiscent of Georgia O'Keeffe, conveys the physical delicacy, femininity, and intimacy of an actual room that is also a metaphor for the whorls of the inner life of a little girl. The room is "enclosed by more than material walls," and in the mind of the child is "the secret form of little girlhood." It is only in a room in which a little girl has learned to be lonely that she can find "solicitude for things": a bed, lamp, chest, rugs. Time flutters its "little moth wings" in the room, and the shadow of mortality enters in the form of mad dreams and conversations with her dead mother that generate tumultuous feelings of love and anger. "Imaginary Furious People" emerge in a dream. She shouts out "Enemies" to the angry women she imagines surrounding her, and a "nightly session of the red passion" suggests the anger of another orphan in *Jane Eyre*. She is "in a conspiracy," not with other little girls, but with herself, as she defies the loss of her mother. Imprisoned by her grandmother's artful arrangements of her life, her reflection "flits out of the looking glass," her identity somehow mislaid by her grandmother. She is a girl before a mirror with a night self and a day self, as well as a girl transforming into a woman. "It's all up," her mother tells her in the dream, and Geraldine falls asleep in her "narrow bed," that "was innocent as an early grave ... like a little girl in an epitaph." Over the bed of this sleeping innocent is a damask panel picturing Carpaccio's *The Dream of St. Ursula*, an angel hovering near the sleeping future martyr, later to be pierced by arrows.

As a child, Bowen felt that a protective angel hovered in the gilt frame over her bed and Eudora Welty claimed that both she and Bowen believed in such angels as adults. Bowen's mother encouraged her belief as a child, but warned against fairies and the Irish lore surrounding them, anxious always about "will-o'-the-wisp" qualities that might draw Bowen from rational paths into the perceived Bowen family madness. In her fiction, an angel appears in *The House in Paris*, when Henrietta tries to comfort Leopold, troubled and in despair about his absent mother:

> Henrietta let her forehead rest on the marble too: her face bent forward, so that the tears she began shedding fell on the front of her dress. An angel stood up inside her with its hands to its lip, and Henrietta did not attempt to speak.[119]

Guardian angels stand up for parentless children in Bowen's stories, having a bodily as well as spiritual presence, as in Milton's *Paradise Lost*, "with hands to its lips."

But she also places a pen in the hand of some of her adolescent girls and signals the dangers of adolescent expression. Writing gives some of the girls in her stories—Portia, Theodora, Maria, Vivie—another self, crafted from within, other than the familial role plotted by their families—as it did in Bowen's life. The diabolical 13-year-old Maria is provoked to write a fraudulent letter about the curate, Mr. Hammond. In doing so, she incites a hellcat scene, creating an uproar in the Dosley house where she is being cared for like Eva in *Eva Trout*. Theodora in *Friends and Relations* similarly casts a suspicious eye upon a household—two couples, the Studdarts and the Tilneys—when she is away at boarding school. Seeing into the truth of things, she writes gossipy letters filled with suspicions about Janet Tilney's secret love for Edward Stoddard, her sister's husband. Theodora, like Maria, detects the boredom and hypocrisy of the English middle class. Similarly, Vivie in "Summer Night" forces the wartime tensions and erotic disruptions in her home to the surface of her body by drawing threatening images in chalk. These girls force secrets into the open through what they write. Unwittingly, perhaps, this is a feminist gesture on Bowen's part; she awards the power of the pen to female adolescents who gain voice through writing. They cast an innocent but sharp, "truthful" eye upon the middle-class scenes from which they feel displaced, and cause mayhem through their writing. Watchful Portia does the same.

In *The Death of the Heart*, which many consider Bowen's finest novel, Portia, an orphaned adolescent, inspires fear in her adopted family because she records her acute feelings in a secret diary. When her diary is discovered and read, the household is driven to hysteria by her "monstrous" observations. Her half-brother Thomas and his wife, Anna, have taken in the 16-year-old Portia, child of a second marriage of Thomas' father. Portia is described as having "those eyes that seem to be welcome nowhere that learn shyness from the alarm they precipitate." The novel opens with Anna's indignation about being subjected to the "misconstructions" of an adolescent girl whose diary writing is "not like writing at all." Portia conspires not with other girls but against the cold adult world. Woolf asks, when "the self speaks to the self, who is speaking?" In this novel, Bowen is in dialogue with her girlhood self, another "I," in her fiction.

Anna's writer friend St. Quentin counters Anna's sense of persecution and presciently observes of the diary, "Nothing arrives on paper as it started, and so much arrives that never started at all."[120] This passage heralds Derrida's dictum that words are "manqué," lacking, and often misconstrued inviting us into the writing and textuality puzzles that the critics, Bennett and Royle expertly explore. St. Quentin and Anna agree that there is something "monstrous" about an adolescent girl with little life experience daring to write about them at all. Portia writes accusingly, and Anna reads defensively: "Then we sat in the drawing-room, and they wished I was not there. This house makes a smell of feeling." Bowen unleashes a discontented female adolescent voice in literature in this novel and alerts us to the glories and dangers of writing. That we have access to a girl's voice in writing is a gift, but we may not want to hear what she has to say. St. Quentin, the sophisticated, successful writer in the novel, ironically advises Portia not to keep a diary; "It is madness to write things down." He remarks, "You hide, God's spy." When Portia rejoins, "I write what has happened. I don't invent," St. Quentin corrects her: "You put constructions on things. You are a most dangerous girl." He suggests that she is misinterpreting the adult world around her, or that it is not her place to watch and judge those who have taken her in. When Portia enters an immaculate, empty room in Windsor Terrace, she looks all around "with her reflecting dark eyes, glancing at each clock, eyeing each telephone"—objects that had just been subjected to a spring cleaning. The mirrors contain more "reality" about her situation in the Quayne household than does the actuality: "Blue spirit had removed the winter film from the mirrors: now their jet sharp reflections hurt the eye: they seemed to contain reality." What is written similarly takes the film from the adults' eyes. Portia's "reflections" in writing, as in the mirror, contain "reality" and "hurt the eyes" of the adults as in Bowen's art about life.

For Bowen, what matters is not the reality of childhood or adolescent events, the recollection of which Bowen defines as autobiography or biography, but the transformation of those events into fiction. Bowen invents Portia and turns the actual feelings of adolescence into art. The girls she writes about are often perceived as "monstrous" or "mad" as they expose the betrayals or hypocrisies of the adult world. Writing and madness were associated early in Bowen's life, in relation not only to fictional little girls but also to women who choose to become writers. At times she felt or was perceived as "mad" because of her unusual choice of a writing career, or the Bowen strain in her family. Until she received affirmation through the publication of her first book of short stories, *Encounters*, she underwent the usual discouragements after rejection of her early stories reflecting, "I could not have been further out of the movement. I had not gone to a university, I had no part in any intellectual life. I had read widely, but wildly."[121] During this time of struggle, she thought that her choice of a writing career was "mad." She could sense the suspicion of "scribbling women," who in the early twentieth century were perceived as wild, foolish, absurd, and "mad" because they broke the female mold.[122] She opposed the conventional order of things with ardor.

Bowen was writing amidst modernist skepticism about the adequacy of language and its ability to capture human experience and the irrationality of world events in the buildup to and aftermath of World War II. And though there was a female literary subculture in the early part of the twentieth century, it did not escape Bowen that there was still prejudice against women writers. When she received public recognition upon the publication of *Encounters* in 1923, she felt it was a sign that she was not a "mad" misfit, working so intensely and in isolation from a literary culture. Enclosed "in the architecture of an overwhelmingly male-dominated society," as Sandra Gilbert and Susan Gubar tell it, Bowen, like other women writers, was "trapped in the specifically literary constructs of what Gertrude Stein was to call 'patriarchal poetry.'"[123] And though the social position of women writers had progressed since the nineteenth century, women who "attempted the pen" still struggled to redefine expectations and norms. It could not have escaped Bowen's notice that in 1937, just across the Irish Sea, the Irish constitution affirmed that the place of women was "in the home." She struggled to live an independent life and self-conscious comments surface in her letters about her effort to free herself from social constrictions as a woman and as a writer.

In *The Death of the Heart*, Bowen not only hands the pen to adolescent Portia to express herself by writing in her diary, she poses the important question of who the "real" writer in the novel is and who is to represent women's point of view. Is it the prominent career writer, St. Quentin or the "innocent," querying adolescent, Portia, writing in her diary? The novel suggests that St. Quentin, like other established male writers, pretended to understand the experience of the Portias of the world, but Portia pens her own judgment of the world in her journal—like the Portia of Shakespeare's play. St. Quentin betrays Portia, misrepresenting her, as Bowen says, with the touch of "malice" that colored his view of women. In this novel, Bowen breaks a young girl's heart with adult betrayals. Portia begs for an understanding of the role of writing in her life: an acknowledgment of its dangers for those around her who are alarmed at her honest assessments and its comforts for her as she is unable to express aloud her judgment of the hypocritical adult world. Portia's struggle reflects Bowen's own story of writing: the art that helped her as a sometimes angry and bewildered child and adolescent adjusting to the instability of her father's mental illness and the sorrow of her mother's early death.

Bowen shares Proust's view that "adolescence is the only period in which we learn anything," and her writing presents myriad adolescents—Portia, Leopold, Henrietta, and Theodora—in the process of learning.[124] She was labeled combative and arrogant by her aunts, and she shared Portia's adolescent confusions about her place in other people's homes as she moved, an orphan, from household to household and school to school. Writing was, she said, her "relation" to society and people. In writing she recreates a "gladness of vision" that she asserts is her own.[125]

William Trevor shared Bowen's interest in observant and "mad" little girls, and writes of one who sits in judgment of her parents in "The Story of Lucy Gault." Lucy acts in strange ways that are labeled "mad" by those around her, but in Trevor's work, the girl's thoughts and feelings are not articulated as they are in Bowen's. Lucy lives with her parents and two sisters in a big Anglo-Irish house that is attacked by IRA rebels. When her parents decide to leave, Lucy asserts, "I won't go […] why must we go?" Her father responds, "They don't want us here," signaling the hostility toward the Anglo-Irish and prefiguring their eventual flight from Ireland.[126] One night her father shoots a Roman Catholic intruder; Lucy, horrified, runs away in rage. After long, fruitless searches for Lucy, her parents leave and travel to Europe to escape the Troubles. Lucy remains alone in the house, a "mad" little girl as defined by people who sit in judgment of her and her parents. The narrator critically notes that "the Gaults had held on too long" in their big house, ignoring the aspirations of the dispossessed in Ireland. Lucy rejects their position, stays and cultivates the "emptiness" of her existence. Trevor represents Lucy from the outside, through other people's views; Bowen, on the other hand, uses the device of the diary in *The Death of the Heart* to express Portia's secret thoughts and give her voice.

Bowen is unique in amplifying the muffled voices of adolescent girls yearning to be heard in the adult world—sending a feminist alert in handing the pen to Portia to write her own version of reality. Portia and other adolescents mirror Bowen's preoccupation with the power of writing and reading that enable them to imagine other ways of being as a girl and as a woman.[127]

Notes

1. SW, 10–11, 18.
2. BC, 417.
3. BC, 417.
4. DH, 140–141.
5. PC, 51.
6. "Out of a Book," 51.
7. Bowen, "Frankly Speaking."
8. Bowen, "Mainie Jellett," 115.
9. Bowen, "We Write Novels," 26.
10. Bowen, "Little Girl's Room," 125.
11. *BC*, 389, 391.
12. *Oxford English Dictionary*, "vague" in discussion with Victorian specialist, Kathy Chamberlain.
13. *SW*, 9.

14. Laetitia Lefroy, interview by PL, Dublin, June 2011. Bowen's first cousin, once removed.
15. *PC*, 12, 10, 12.
16. *PC*, 12.
17. *HD*, 97.
18. *HP*, 48, 46.
19. *BC*, 415.
20. *PC*, 15–16.
21. According to Carol Gilligan, a girl's stammering or loss of voice may relate to the authority of the father. Bowen, under stress of her father's illness could be seen as not knowing when to speak, leading to the stammer. Gaining voice then becomes a lifelong quest.
22. *BC*, 420.
23. John Bayley to EB, n.d. (ca. 1968), HRC 10.6.
24. Lehmann, EB Obituary.
25. Welty to Maxwell, *What There is to Say* …, October 30, 1968, 248–249.
26. Leo Marx, e-mail to PL, March 26, 2008.
27. April 19, 1934. *D* 4, 208.
28. British Council Report, 1954, HRC 10.4.24.
29. See DeWitt-Miller, "Cure for Stammering."
30. Movie version of his struggle, *The King's Speech*.
31. Glendinning, *Elizabeth Bowen*, 240.
32. Ann Berthoff, interview by PL, Concord, MA, February 10, 2008.
33. EB to SS, May 20, 1936, BOD, MS. Spender 39.
34. Agnes de Mille to Anna George de Mille, November 17, 1936, SC.
35. Mary Dwane, interview by PL, Farahy, Ireland, May 2011.
36. Welty, *What There is to Say* …, June 1951.
37. John Bayley to EB, n.d. (ca. 1968), HRC 10.6.
38. Bowen, "Artist in Society."
39. Butler, *Independent Spirit*, 155.
40. Robins, *Madman and the Fool*, 63.
41. Information from Veronica, Bowen's cousin, 2011: queried by Lefroy.
42. Medical record, Andrew Whiteside, archivist, St. Patrick's University Hospital, October 15, 2013.
43. See Robins, *Madman and the Fool*, 77, 112.
44. *BC*, 373.
45. "Stephen Gwynn, Obituary."
46. *BC*, 367.
47. Bowen, *Statutory Land Purchase*.
48. HH to EB, June 1933, HHC. With permission from the Literary Estate of Humphry House.
49. The Pembroke estates, one of the most valuable in Ireland.
50. Persons can qualify for election as a lay judge of the Court of the General Synod or a solicitor of ten years' practice in any part of Ireland. See The

Constitution of the Church of Ireland, section 3c, Diocesan Courts. https://www.ireland.anglican.org/cmsfiles/pdf/Information/Constitution/constitution.pdf (accessed 9/16/20).

51. Glendinning, *Elizabeth Bowen*, 26.
52. Bowen, "Most Unforgettable Character," *MT*, 26.
53. "Stephen Gwynn—Obituary."
54. *BC*, 345.
55. *DH*, 407.
56. *ET*, 91, 95.
57. *PC*, 10–11.
58. *BC*, 384.
59. *BC*, 384–385.
60. *SW*, 8.
61. Ruth Potterton, librarian, Trinity College, Dublin.
62. Kelly, "Last Days of the Colleys," 96.
63. *BC*, 384.
64. Glendinning, *Elizabeth Bowen*, 23.
65. *HP*, 16.
66. *PC*, 3–4.
67. Bowen, "On Not Rising to the Occasion" in Hepburn, *LI*, 109.
68. *BC*, 387.
69. Bowen, review, *The Moores of Moore Hall*, *SIW*, 42ff.
70. See Ellmann 276–277, 288, 290, 321, 335.
71. Butler, *The Children of Drancy, Independent Spirit*; Chenevix-Trench, "What Is the Use of Reviving Irish?"; Bunbury, historian, *Vanishing Ireland: Recollections of our Changing Times*.
72. Lefroy interview.
73. Christopher Hone to PL, April 6, 2011.
74. Alexandra College 1860s curriculum, Aileen Ivory, college librarian, Dublin, October 2013.
75. *MT*, 290.
76. *DH*, 191.
77. Melchers, *Hythe Civic Society Newsletter* 99, December 1999–January 2000. Edward Pomeroy Colley died, age 37, aboard the *Titanic*, traveling first class. The letter to his Aunt Edie aboard ship was auctioned for £6000–£8000 in 1999.
78. See Maud Ellmann, 218ff.
79. Curtis Brown, *PC*, xx.
80. *PC*, 48–49, 50, 52.
81. Bowen, "Unromantic Princess."
82. *HP*, 46.
83. Maxwell, *So Long, See You Tomorrow*, 7, 130.
84. *PC*, 28–29, 57.
85. Lefroy interview.

86. Information offered by Anne Charlier to Janet Adamson, archivist. In the 1911 census, the rector had two daughters, Mary, 10 years, and Lucy, 13 years (not Veronica and Maisie, as Bowen named them in *BC*).
87. *FR*, 61.
88. Glendinning, *Elizabeth Bowen*, 119.
89. *Dictionary of National Biography*, 384.
90. See Woolf, *Room of One's Own* and *Three Guineas*.
91. Information from Diana Williams (née Temple), Downe House alumna, 1960–1965, e-mail to PL, April 2015.
92. *HD*, 24.
93. Essay, *Downe House Scrapbook*, 1957.
94. *MT*, 15.
95. *MT*, 21.
96. EB to CR, June 29, 1958, *LCW*, 297.
97. Bowen, "Coming to London," 77.
98. *HP*, 68.
99. Sally Kean Phipps, *Molly Keane*.
100. *DH*, 7.
101. *Downe House Scrapbook*, 1957.
102. *MT*, 17.
103. *Downe House Scrapbook*, 1957.
104. RM to EB, undated, possibly late 30s, HRC.
105. *P&C*, 9–12.
106. Bowen, "Artist in Society."
107. "Summer Night," CS 596.
108. Glendinning, *Elizabeth Bowen*, 25.
109. "She," broadcast February 28, 1947. In *MT*, 246–250.
110. Kenney, 25.
111. "We Write Novels," 26.
112. Proust, *Swann's Way*, 7.
113. Curtis Brown, Introduction, *PC*, xlii.
114. Discussed in Ellmann, 8.
115. Woolf, "Mark on the Wall," *Complete Shorter Fiction*, 77–83.
116. *SW*, 10–11.
117. *PC*, 28.
118. Bowen, "Little Girl's Room," 131.
119. *HP*, 219–220.
120. *DH*, 10, 111, 113, 248, 328, 201, 302.
121. *ES*, viii.
122. See Gilbert and Gubar.
123. Gilbert and Gubar, *Madwoman in the Attic*, xii.
124. Proust, *Within a Budding Grove*, 423.
125. Bowen, "Out of a Book," 53.
126. Trevor, "Story of Lucy Gault," 17, 22.
127. Corcoran, Ellmann, Bennett-Royle focus upon the importance of letters and writing.

3

Terrains of the Imagination

Bowen's Court

Eudora Welty placed Bowen's portrait of her family and its estate in *Bowen's Court* at the heart of her work. Her history of the house—its landscape and the Anglo-Irish ascendancy recovered through her research in books, letters, diaries, wills, and family portraits—is a history of family feeling about a place. It was a house that contained her childhood, her memories of family "madness," her writing self, her life as a hostess, her romantic dreams, and anxieties about its preservation. Every time she had to shut up the house Bowen felt that something died in her to be renewed when she returned to its "emptiness." She lived with a fear that she might die in England and never come back to the house.

If landscape is a language, as Bowen believed, then she and Eudora Welty, her friend during the 1950s, spoke the same language. Bowen confided to Charles Ritchie, "I think she's like me in preferring places to people ... Nothing can happen nowhere."[1] Welty shared her view that "places" furnished a concrete and credible "gathering spot" for feeling, history, and writing.[2] Bowen added that places also have magic.

A portrait of Oliver Cromwell to whom the Bowens owed this estate and its position was once at the top of the front stairs of the house. As head of the English campaign in Ireland, 1649–50, he brutally invaded and confiscated land. Bowen unscrolled the history of feeling in the house beginning with the first Welsh Bowen, Henry III who set foot on the land in 1776 with a mythic hawk that marked the perimeters of awarded land where the austere Georgian house would be built. Bowen resources continued to expand and in the 1870s,

© The Author(s), under exclusive license to Springer Nature Switzerland AG 2021
P. Laurence, *Elizabeth Bowen*, Literary Lives, https://doi.org/10.1007/978-3-030-71360-7_3

they owned 1680 acres in County Cork and over 5000 acres in County Tipperary upon which their estates were built.[3] She records Henry III's fanciful decision to beget a child to look out every window of Bowen's Court, and describes as well Henry Cole Bowen's marriage to the beautiful Jane Cole, fabled to be related to Old King Cole of nursery fame. Welty praised Bowen's fair-mindedness about "the stretches of the past [...] that have been, on the whole, painful," revealing "an inherent wrong" in the family's land grabbing.[4] Bowen conceded that "the structure of the Anglo-Irish society was raised over a country in martyrdom." In self-defense, she speculated, they protected themselves by numbing their feeling for the Irish people.

In comparing her childhood Dublin home, 15 Herbert Place, to Bowen's Court, she said "winter lived always in Dublin, while summer always lived in County Cork."[5] She was released from the melancholy Herbert Street atmosphere after her father's breakdown, and, as an adult in the midst of her life of movement and change, she would often recall the estate of silence and peace where she could write without interruption. Christmas, spring, and summer were generally spent there and she grew up "accustomed to seeing out of [...] windows nothing but grass, sky, trees enclosed in a ring of almost complete silence." She remarked on its "glassily magic moods" and reflected in 1962 that "the only thing I really loved in Ireland was Bowen's Court."[6] She wrote, "It is not our exalted feelings, it is our sentiments that build the necessary home."[7] After her husband's death in 1952, work became synonymous with Bowen's Court where when not travelling she would spend nine months of the year. The Georgian style, three-story house—high and bare—was set among 300 acres of lawns, fields, and trees with the Ballyhouras and Galtee Mountains in the distance, and ever-changing skies above. One could not only see the purple mountains but a forest of trees, limestone cliffs, watchtowers, mills, kilns, quarries, stone bridges, farmhouses, castles, and church spires. The groves, overseen and loved by her father, were always special. They both loved the feeling of emptiness looking out at the open space of the lawn toward the view. This was a childhood landscape that entered later, powerfully, into her writing. Its beauty grounded her, and it had a history of sheltering ten generations of Bowens.

The atmosphere of Bowen's Court in her childhood was created by the presence of her mother and the housekeeper, Sarah Cartey. Her mother, dreamy and unobservant, lacked the pragmatic skills to run Bowen's Court during the summers the family spent there. Bowen related that her grandmother had tried to teach her mother and her sisters housekeeping skills. In rotation, the girls would each keep house for a week at their Mount Temple home; three days after Florence's turn began, others in the family begged that she be taken off duty. At Bowen's Court, Elizabeth's delight was to escape to one of her favorite rooms downstairs, the laundry room, with Sarah, a young Tipperary girl, who assumed the housekeeping chores that overwhelmed her mother. "Happiness stays for me, about the warm smell of soapsuds. I remember her short strong arms red from the heat of water, and the hilarious energy with which she turned the wringer."[8] And she enjoyed Sarah's wit. The house was a magical place with its memory of Sarah and remembered sensations of "rattling down the main staircase on a tin tray convinced that I was negotiating Niagara Falls."[9] She was happy there in the summers.

The house had its comforting rituals. Visitors reported on the bounty of fruit to greet her after an absence, "peaches ok, raspberries good, 75 lbs. sent to Fermoy, 300 lbs. before, everyone is polishing the house for your return."[10] Molly O'Brien, her faithful cook, also recalled this self-subsistence, how the fruit was bottled—raspberries, especially—and abundant fresh vegetables came from the garden. Bowen relished the menu of potatoes done in their jackets cooked with peas, beans, and spinach. Outside there were acres of grazing land.

But the house also contained an anxious history. Bowen knew that the land on which it was built was "ignobly gained," through British colonialism, and this still was a provocation to the Irish.[11] Bowen would acknowledge that

> like all pictures, it does not quite correspond with any reality. Or you may call the country a magic mirror, reflecting something that could not really exist [...] I suppose that everyone, fighting or just enduring, now carries one private image—one peaceful scene—in his heart. Mine is Bowen's Court. War has made me this image out of a house built of anxious history.[12]

The anxious history emerges from its colonial origins and traces of the Bowen family madness. According to Bowen, Eudora Welty captured this haunted quality in a photo she sent after a visit. Bowen noted its oddness to Charles Ritchie having "never seen, visualized or remembered the house from this particular angle. It looks more like a house in a dream or in a story"[13] (Fig. 3.1).

These historical, economic, and psychological assaults coursed beneath its vaunted tranquility. William Plomer, her friend, an outsider, reminded her of this after his visit stressing the underlying violence, the "ignorance, prejudice, intolerance, injustice, folly, famine accompanying the English occupation of Ireland."[14] He wondered why the British "labeled them rebels or terrorists" instead of trying to understand their feelings. Bowen wrote little about postcolonial struggles or the devastating Irish famine and emigration in the mid-nineteenth century. Cork victims of the famine lie buried in a corner of

Fig. 3.1 Bowen's Court, photo by Eudora Welty. Rights holder and Courtesy of Mississippi Department of Archives and History

St. Colman's churchyard where Bowen, her father, and husband also lie, slightly elevated, dividing the two groups who inhabited Cork: the inheritors, the Anglo-Irish, and the local Catholic farmers and servants. In the corner of the cemetery is a tombstone honoring the million victims of the 1845–52 Irish famine, recalling also the deportation of 50,000 indentured Irish to England during that period (Fig. 3.2). The evolving relationship between the two worlds was a subject Bowen took up in *The Last September, A World of Love*, a few short stories, and in the setting for her *Nativity Play*. But her style of telling would follow Emily Dickinson's, "tell all the truth but tell it slant / Success in Circuit lies."

Yet she also valorized the big Anglo-Irish house driven by her "cloven-heart"—her divided English-Irish identity—as Sean O'Faolain observed. In *Bowen's Court*, she noted that the new settlers wished to enhance their lives

Fig. 3.2 Irish Famine Victims Gravestone, 1845–47, Farahy Churchyard. Rights holder and Courtesy of P. Laurence

with an aesthetic, and "the security that they had, by the eighteenth century ignobly gained, they did not use quite ignobly. They began to feel, and exert, the European idea—to seek what was humanistic and disciplined."[15] If this big house in acres of green, like others in the neighborhood, seemed somewhat culturally staged, it is because these houses were, as Vera Kreilkamp astutely notes, a "staging of intent."[16] These Anglo-Irish houses stood alone, separate from the majority Catholic community surrounding them, and connected with one another socially and in spirit with an aesthetic and manner derived from England and Europe. Bowen compared the isolation of these houses to only children like herself who "do not know how much they miss [...] singular, independent and secretive."[17] The Anglo-Irish houses that survived the Civil War, 1922–23, including Bowen's Court, were a beleaguered minority shoring up ruins while violence raged around them. In the 25 years following independence, from 1921 to 1946, the Anglo-Irish population fled and their numbers shrank from 10 percent to 6 percent.

In Bowen's view, these grand houses despite their origins had much to teach. The occupants were sociable and hospitable, at least to one another. The house, she said, like the *domus* in Rome, nurtured character, good manners and behavior, and politeness that radiated to the larger society. "Well why not be polite—are not humane manners the crown of being human at all? Politeness is not a constriction: it is a grace: it is really no worse than an exercise of the imagination on other people's behalf."[18] Bowen defended these values—preserved, she said, within the houses—from the attacks of the neighboring Irish, the young, the rebellious, the dispossessed, and the uncultured. She asserted that "a barrier has two sides": the beleaguered Anglo-Irish house kept negative forces out and positive ones within. Yet she was too wise to embrace this legend uncritically, too clear-sighted to enter into a cult of nostalgia, and too intelligent not to have registered the Anglo-Irish violation of Ireland.[19] Bowen, though attached to certain traditions that were preserved in her writing, was a self-critical inhabitant of a big house, acknowledging that her class failed to balance privilege with service and responsibility in Ireland.

The Cost of Ownership

Bowen became the only female Bowen to inherit Bowen's Court. Though her father, Henry, had chafed at being an estate manager, he maintained Bowen's Court economically until his death in 1930. Again she was an anomaly as the transmission of property to women was very unusual in Ireland. Mary Dwane, a former servant, said that when Cameron, Bowen's husband, managed the estate, he was "shrewd," unlike Bowen. After his death in 1952, Bowen lost his pension and struggled economically. For six years, she attempted to support the estate through intense lecture tours in America, the only country, she said, in which she could make money rather than spend it. Yet she still entertained lavishly after Cameron's death: costs rose, and to generate income, she wrote hasty reviews, gave lectures, and agreed to reprints of her stories in American journals. Welty worried about Bowen's state of mind and health at this time, lecturing all over and not producing much writing. She urged her to submit a story to the *New Yorker* to earn a better rate, as Welty had recently earned $2760 for "The Bride of the Innisfallen."[20] Bowen's financial crisis worsened in the late fifties. She plaintively wrote to Ritchie, "Can you possibly send me $100?" It was June 1958, a year before she sold the estate, and she noted in the same letter that she was in Cork to sell a great deal of silver and some pieces of good jewelry.[21] The house's "virtue" to her, she said, in those last years while Ritchie was in Europe and could hop over, was that it was "our home." Ritchie expressed distress in his diary about her fantasy; the question for him was "whether I can contribute money to keep it going. The trouble is that it IS my home but that I get the pleasure of it at her expense in money and worry." He then cryptically adds, "If we were married …" and worries that he is doing her "harm." He reflects that he wants her to keep the house, but what is the solution? "To offer $10,000 pounds? Does she want it? Have I got it?"[22] Waves of guilt about the loss of Bowen's Court swept across Ritchie, but he never assumed any financial responsibility or offered—to general knowledge—to spend his life with her.

When she inherited the house, it was in decline. Virginia Woolf visiting with Leonard in April 1934 uncharitably described it: "pompous & pretentious & imitative and ruined—a great barrack of grey stone, 4 stories & basements, like a town house, high empty rooms and a scattering of Italian plasterwork […] the wake sofa on which the dead lay, carpets shrunk in the great rooms, tattered farm girls waiting […] the old man of 90 in his cabin who wouldn't let us go."[23] It was the antithesis of the avant-garde style of decorating by Vanessa Bell and Duncan Grant in Bloomsbury and Charleston that Woolf valued. Also, it was uncomfortable: it had primitive plumbing, and the small staff that assisted visitors carried water up and down for baths, and then tossed it out the window into the garden. Though the house had its detractors, they offended loyal Molly O'Brien, the cook at Bowen's Court from the time she was 15 until the day it was sold. With ghosts in her eyes, Molly recalled the beautiful hospitality Bowen offered: "footpaths by the bedroom fires before dinner—yes, and carry the slops down in the morning. Cold? How cold they were? A hot stone jar put in the beds late, and a fire blazing in every room. And the silver candlesticks and the brass candlesticks laid out at the foot of the staircase for them to take up to bed."[24] She recalled the traditions, the brown buns made early every morning, the salmon mousse for parties, the big silver sauce boats with the special horseradish sauce, and the small potato cakes "the size of a two-shilling piece." In the late forties, when Bowen received a large royalty check for *The Heat of the Day*, she thought of luxuries and said to her husband, "It won't buy a Jaguar, but we can throw out the wooden tub, and have baths at Bowen's Court."[25]

Bowen struggled to keep up appearances; however, the expense of repairs and support of a small staff were overwhelming. She wrote, "I think everyone knows that life is not all jam in the big house," and many wondered why she struggled.[26] The house always remained unfinished, and she opened only a few rooms. She sold her grandfather's Victorian furniture and furnished the house with a few elegant pieces, including a piano in the drawing room. She brought color to the airy halls, lobbies, and rooms, describing the drawing room to a visitor as "flamingo- and oyster-colored; it was one of the few completely furnished rooms in the house. The second-floor Victorian guest room was decorated in rose and white, and led to an unfinished ballroom—in which the workmen "lost interest," said Bowen—with rough flooring.[27]

After almost three decades of struggling ownership, and being perceived as one of the "heartless rich," Bowen gave up and sold Bowen's Court to a neighbor, Cornelius O'Keefe, in 1959 for £12,000 (the equivalent of approximately £360,000 today) through her lawyer, John Carroll.[28] The decision was wrenching. When asked who was her next of kin by a lawyer, she realized that only 2 or 3 of her 15 cousins were close. Really, she told him, my next of kin is Bowen's Court. And then there was the fantasy of living there with Charles Ritchie. In August 1945, early in their relationship, she had written, "this house was built by that long-ago unconscious Bowen for you and me to be happy in. That July when you and I were here it reached its height. It will again when you're back."[29] Bowen told few in her family of her plans to sell the estate, and when her cousin Noreen and her husband, Gilbert, heard, they went to Kildorrery to consider purchasing the house. It was reported that they went to the lawyer's office and "he showed them the door": it was already sold to O'Keefe. Bowen believed he would sustain it; Reverend R.B. MacCarthy, however, cast doubt on O'Keefe's character in a letter to Derek Hill, a painter friend of Bowen's: "I heard to-day that the ruffian called O'Keefe to whom E.B. sold the place is an illegitimate son of a St. Leger and rather specializes in getting country house (& their timber) presumably at least partly out of spite. What disastrous judgment she seems to have had in practical matters or was it a sort of death-wish."[30] Patrick Hennessey painted a portrait of a somewhat tense Bowen—in an uncharacteristically diaphanous dress—standing in front of a window revealing a surrealist sky at Bowen's Court, and captured perhaps her final unease in that cultural landscape (Fig. 3.3). Though she had to sell the house and land, she resolved that what was lost in life could be preserved in art. "Nothing stays; all changes" reflects the painter Lily Briscoe in Woolf's *To the Lighthouse*, "but not words, not paint."[31] Bowen's Court—still green and surrounded by beautiful mountains on three sides as well as its troubled history—is alive in her family history *Bowen's Court*; Derek Hill's commissioned painting; her novel *The Last September*; and the imaginations of those who read her novels or visit the now empty demesne.

Fig. 3.3 Elizabeth Bowen at Bowen's Court, Patrick Hennessy, 1957. Rights holder and Courtesy of Royal Hibernian Academy, Dublin

Outside the Walls

If one walks up the cobbled road—once a grand avenue—to Bowen's Court, the ruined demesne walls emerge, leading nowhere except to a beautiful expanse of field and trees. Formerly eight feet high, the walls were built by the Anglo-Irish to keep the local Irish out. Catholic Irish society lived outside and some locals did not love the walls, the house, or the Bowens; others worked for and admired the family. Bowen no doubt felt affection for certain servants in the house and on the estate, particularly Sarah Barry and, later, Molly O'Brien, who was trained by Barry. Molly ruled and kept the house running efficiently in her absence, along with local Farahy families, the Barrys and the Gateses. However, she wrote little of her relations with servants, except for Barry, who became "The Most Unforgettable Character I Ever Met," and, occasionally, O'Brien, who followed Barry. In her fiction, Bowen's trust and reverence for the servant is revealed in the character of Matchett in *The Death of the Heart*: "Kneeling to turn on bedroom fires, stooping to slip bottles between sheets, she seemed to absent herself to the overcoming night. The impassive solemnity of her preparations made a sort of altar of each bed: in big houses in which things are done properly, there is always the religious element. The diurnal cycle is observed with more feeling when there are servants to do the work."[32] Traces of an aesthetic and holy element are here in the rituals of the maintenance of a big house sustained by its votaries, the servants. Molly Keane noted in an interview that servants were an important part of the Irish big house—their personalities respected—not silent and distant like English servants. Though Anna would admonish Portia in *The Death of the Heart*, "you ought not to listen to servants," targeting Matchett, Portia would respond with the candor of innocence, "Why. When she's the person who sees really what happened."

Molly O'Brien, the main cook, was the heart and fiber of the house, said Brenda Hennessy, who became her friend when she moved to Kildorrery in 1983. "She is a marvelous person, Molly" wrote a frequent visitor to Bowen's Court, "pretty and ageless and able; her service to Elizabeth was given with deep affection, pride and a lot of enjoyment. Leisure was there too—and fun." Molly would plan the menu with Bowen every morning, and took pride in making a tasty chop for Alan for over 30 years "without once using Worcestershire sauce." Molly said that Bowen treated people well, and "was high spirited but could take things in her stride." She lived in a lovely white cottage given by the Bowens upon her marriage and kept greyhounds. When Mary Dwane, a Farahy resident, was 13, she entered service to be trained by O'Brien, "excited to cross the bridge and go up the wide avenue to Bowen's Court."[33] Alan, Dwane remembered, was "stern and quiet," respected because he had been at the Battle of the Somme in World War I, and a "stay-at-home man," unlike Bowen, who was often traveling. He died three months after Dwane's arrival and during that period of illness stayed in his room. When asked about Ritchie's visits to the house, Dwane said that the servants knew "something was going on," and described him as "the Canadian ambassador, a fine man, tall and dark with a longish face." Bowen had a strong personality, she said, and was not "stand-offish." During the day, Dwane made the beds, polished the timber floors, served, and helped O'Brien in the kitchen along with two other girls, Hannah Hanley and Kathleen Shannon, the parlor maid. Every three days, Dwane would go to a shop in Farahy to buy 100 cigarettes for Bowen. When interviewed by Mary Murphy in 1994, O'Brien said that the neighbors "felt great affection" for Bowen who often—with an element of noblesse oblige—donated flowers to the local Catholic church, distributed Christmas candles among neighbors at the holiday, and kept one burning in the window.[34] In addition, a bell would be rung every week, and those outside the walls would buy or be given fruits and vegetables from the farm. And on Fox Hunt Ball evenings, Bowen would keep all the windows open so the community could hear the music. The Bowens, however, were a different strain of the Anglo-Irish, not horsy or fox-hunting Protestants like Molly Keane, Bowen's writer friend. Neither Bowen or her father was interested in the sport. Keane's life was closer to the style of the waning Anglo-Irish in Ireland: she rode superbly, relished races and hunting, parties and amusements, all of which entered her sharp-edged depiction of the class in *Good Behavior*. Bowen's trajectory growing up and living in England—isolated from Irish culture except for biannual visits to Bowen's Court—was different. She was serious about writing in her twenties: a published author at 24, married without children, a hard-working writer, and part of the intellectual Oxford circle; Molly Keane led a more rakish life in her twenties. When Bowen wrote *The Last September*, she captured the graces as well as the impending doom of big house culture but a more acerbic Keane bitterly pinioned the negligent adults and corrupt relationships within those houses. Nevertheless, Molly was quick-witted (often considered ruthless) and entertaining, and Bowen welcomed an Anglo-Irish friend who knew about writing. Molly had famous friends like Fred Astaire, Peggy Ashcroft, and John Gielgud having written for the theater at one time under the name of M. J. Farrell. And she loved receiving an invitation to Bowen's Christmas at Bowen's Court with its decorations and roaring fires with her two daughters, Virginia and Sally, after her husband's early death in 1946. According to Virginia Brownlowe, Molly's daughter, they were drawn together by their engagement with people and "loved beauty, humor, drink and conversation."

While the house staff of four and a gardener and handyman kept the house running, Bowen would write in her study or in the library all day, with short breaks for meals. She lived mainly on the middle floor of the house in three rooms: the bedroom she had slept in since she was a child, the study attached to it and the dressing room. The many dinner parties and the occasional ball that Bowen sponsored were held in the front hall; a table and sideboard would be set up for the guests, and after meals, they would retire to the living room (called the library) for dessert or drinks (Fig. 3.4). The drawing room was not used, and the top floor had bedrooms for staff painted blue, green, and yellow. In her letters, she discusses curtains, rugs, décor, and furniture with friends like Plomer and Woolf, a preoccupation reflected in a collection of essays she edited, *These Simple Things: Some Small Joys Rediscovered*. In this volume

Fig. 3.4 Lady Ursula Vernon, daughter of the 2nd Duke of Westminster; Major James Egan; Mary Clarisse, Lady Delamere; Elizabeth Bowen; Major Stephen Vernon; Iris Murdoch, 1950. Rights holder and Courtesy of Finlay Colley

Marianne Moore contributed "The Knife," Rumer Godden "Bread," and Alan Pryce-Jones "Glass." In the same volume, Bowen wrote "The Teakettle" about "the noble, necessary kettle slight."[35] Though her friends would exclaim "you mean teapot," she insisted she meant teakettle, without which there can be no tea. The teapot, she explains, is dependent upon the kettle for tea-water. She does, however, describe a rich array: "the homey brown teapot with its realist farmhouse ancestry; the fragile porcelain; the antique silver variation, Queen Anne; the curved Georgian, fluted Regency or rotund Victorian." And the tea table in the drawing room was, Bowen noted, the apt location for talk and gossip.

Though her employees were generally appreciative, it was rumored that some of those who were hired "used" Bowen. She often mentions driving, dining, or socializing with Jim Gates, a second-generation local who helped manage the estate. Michael Collins, a neighbor who knew Gates, questioned her choice of companionship in later years, as Gates was rumored to have led an unsavory and profligate life. Other locals found the Bowens and Bowen's Court a provocation. Jack Maume, once a Farahy neighbor whose father went to prison for his principles in the Land League, was brought up, he said, to detest the Bowens and their ilk. They were associated, he said, with "the curse of Cromwell." Emily Murphy, a researcher in Cork, remarked that her grandfather would frequently tell her bedtime stories in which Cromwell figured "as a diabolical creature with horns and a forked tail."[36] To this day, "the curse of Cromwell on you" is an insult in Cork, a hated figure in myth and folklore. Maume diminished the status of the Bowens in the neighborhood, claiming that they served as a buffer between the Kingstons and St. Legers (also big houses), asserting that they were looked down upon "as only Cromwell's stable boys."[37] Though Maume dismissed Bowen's Court and all it represented, Mike Gould, another Farahy resident, praised it and experienced its demolition as a sad day.[38] When Bowen's Court was razed, Brenda Hennessy said, "they tied a band around it, pulled it, and it fell into itself. When we arrived there it was a big heap."[39] At the end, Mary Dwane said, much was burned—letters and papers—and other belongings were thrown down a well on the property. The stone from Bowen's Court was excavated and sold.

Down the road from Bowen's Court is the Farahy St. Colman's churchyard where Bowen, her husband, and her father are buried. The church now serves as a memorial to her and her writings. Molly Keane remembered that Bowen had "a strongly disciplined religious side," and described her coming into the hall at Bowen's Court at 11 o'clock on Sunday morning, dressed in country clothes, and walking down the drive to the little church built by the family at the estate gates. "She never pressed anyone to go with her. She prayed. She sang. She listened to any sermon."[40]

The Fictional House

Danielstown, the big house in her novel, *The Last September*, captures the historical narrative of the beleaguered Anglo-Irish gentry. Bowen was the child of such a house, and anachronistically, attempts to shore up its ruins against the historical tide in 1928, writing her novel eight years after the frenzy of IRA house burnings in Cork. In the novel, the Naylor family supports the British troops that patrol the countryside outside their home, ready for reprisals against the IRA; yet they are also sympathetic to the defiant local people, the Catholic farmers, among whom they live. It was her favorite novel, she said, built around the atmosphere of a place.[41] There is a premonition of its destruction in its setting: "The house seemed to be pressing down low in apprehension, hiding its face … It seemed to gather its trees close in fright and amazement at the wide light lovely unloving country, the unwilling bosom where it was set."[42] There is an "unstated" violence beneath the decorous description that John Banville intuits and that informs his film version.[43] In the end, the sky turns a fearful scarlet, "in February, before those leaves had visibly budded, the death—the execution, rather—of the three houses, Danielstown, Castle Trent, Mount Isabel, occurred in the same night … The door stood open hospitable upon a furnace."[44] As Sir Richard and Lady Naylor look in distress at the conflagration in the sky, the burning of the big house relieves the next generation, Lois, Laurence, and Laura, of the moribund dream of the ascendancy. As Phyllis Lassner observes, they realize their own capacity for life in another place.[45] In Banville's dramatic adaptation, the violence surfaces not only in the "execution" of the big house but in Lady Naylor's savage dismissal of the penurious British soldier in pursuit of Lois. Bowen draws parallels: a young woman grows up during the birth of the Irish Free State. She and the other characters, under the spell of history in a big house in the Irish countryside are being carried along toward a violent fate, Irish rebels hidden within. Inside, claustrophobically, the family is "sealed in lamplight, secure and bright like flowers in a paperweight."[46] Premonitions of the dying house surface, "High above a bird shrieked and stumbled down through dark, tearing the leaves. Silence healed, but kept a scar of horror." Lois is unaware of the political implications of the big house, the IRA rebels she encounters, and her romance with a British soldier, just as Bowen was when she dated British Colonel Anderson as a young woman.

Ill adapted for survival like the earlier Anglo-Irish Gore family in Brian Friel's *Home Place*, the Naylors maintain shadowy traditions. Bowen's father lived amidst the horror of this dying and the burning houses: he wrote to Bowen in the early 1920s: "You must be prepared for the next news and be brave. I will write at once."[47] Bowen too lived with fears: "So often in my mind's eye," she said, "did I see [Bowen's Court] burned that the terrible last event in *The Last September* is more real than anything I have lived through."[48]

Anglo-Irish families were drawn by culture and tradition to bond in those beleaguered times. Bowen wrote of a gathering at one of the big houses,

Mitchelstown Castle, at the outbreak of World War I, owned by Cyril Connolly's aunt, Anna Brinkley. Anglo-Irish from all over northeast County Cork assembled to affirm their standing in Ireland, according to Bruce Arnold who attended. Threatened, the families spoke of the tensions in Europe and the loyalty of their military brothers serving in the war in England. "If the Anglo-Irish live on and for a myth," Bowen said, "for that myth they constantly shed their blood." Anglo-Irish heirs of the big houses died in that war, as well as some Irish who fought with the promise that their participation might lead to the end of partition, a promise that was, nevertheless, betrayed. In 1921, Ireland was divided into Northern and Southern Ireland. The larger Southern part was the self-declared Irish Republic and left the United Kingdom, later becoming the Irish Free State, and now, the Republic of Ireland; Northern Ireland remains a part of the United Kingdom.

Bowen's father, then the inheritor of Bowen's Court, was not a loyalist or anti-Irish: Bowen said that she "never heard in this house—why should I?—any remark about 'the Irish' prompted either by panic or the wish to insult. Not only was there no context for such a remark but my father would never have uttered it—nor, I believe, for all their aberrations, would any ruling Bowen before him."[49] In the years following his release from St. Patrick's Hospital, he focused his energy on the Church of Ireland, becoming a judge in the General Synod, and wrote a voluminous history of the Land Acts in Ireland. How much did Bowen know of her father's progressive Land Acts research? Humphry House read and praised it for its progressive legal thinking and research that reflected his concern for an evolving Irish society, culture, and environment. Unlike other Anglo-Irish families, Bowen and her father had a different feeling for the land and never cut down trees for profit. Mary Dwane, one of the maids, said, "Bowen would never touch a tree. If a tree fell down or was struck by lightning in a storm, she would go to bed and be upset for the rest of the day."[50]

Land and Trees

Henry not only loved trees but recorded in his weighty legal volume the historical opinions and restrictions on the cutting of trees in Ireland as well as the common-law meaning of "timber" under the extension of the Land Purchase Act of 1903. The extension was designed to oppose the deforestation of Ireland by the English occupiers. There were regional objections not only to the sites deforested to build the big houses but to the damage done to the landscape by the additional cutting of timber on estates for profit.[51] Reforestation became a dream of the Irish nationalists.

Bowen's grandfather Robert, however, took exception to this policy of pres-ervation. When he passed down Bowen's Court to Henry, his eldest son, he entailed on his younger son, Robert, his will to interfere in Henry's succes-sion. He ordered the destruction of the trees that he had planted and loved, in revenge against Henry for not having agreed to be an estate manager. Bowen wrote that in his dark will, "he determined that Henry should not enjoy his trees, so wood after wood began to fall to the axe." Robert, the younger son, carrying out orders attempted to destroy the trees, grove after grove, until Henry took out an injunction against him. Bowen's history describes Robert as "a Giotto figure of Anger, the figure tearing, clawing his own breast."[52] In this scene, we can see the destructive family pathology from which Henry emerged and the fear of madness from earlier incidents that this inspired in her mother. He did, nevertheless, go on to care for the estate after coming out of the hospital in 1910 until his death in 1930. Bowen said of her father, "he saw men as trees walking, he bowed to the trees." "Above all," she said, "Bowen's Court was the abiding thing in his life—for Henry V's feeling for Bowen's Court, I can find no word that he would have countenanced." The word "countenance," with its old French trace of "demeanor" and "bearing," suggests the tone of her father's dutiful love of the estate, the place he had once refused to manage in favor of a career in the law. His protection of the trees and the landscape from his father's rage explains why even when Bowen's Court was failing economically, Bowen also did not sell timber from the estate that might have saved it. Declan Kiberd, the critic, said that cutting a tree was probably like a "death" to Bowen.[53] He said that "apart from perhaps being more Gaelic than she's given credit for, she is also incredibly culturally sensi-tive in understanding that one of the hated things about the Anglo-Irish [...] was the removal of the trees." The sound of timber being axed by the English to make way for the big estates or to sell timber for profit echoes throughout Irish history. Kiberd recalled that in Gaelic poetry of the 1600s and 1700s, "there's a constant lament about the felling of the woods by the English occu-pier. And literally they are accused of huckstering off the woods at sixpence a tree. That was the price. And the Celtic poets would have felt the way Bowen did." Kiberd remembered a nineteenth-century poem that Irish children recited in school: "What shall we do without timber? The last of the woods has been felled." Through many phases of Irish history, under James I, Elizabeth I, and Henry VIII, this destruction was part of the colonization policy. Along with this came the imposition of English law, language, and culture, and the expulsion of the Gaelic language and culture. The land was cleared not only to build Anglo-Irish estates for the colonizers but to create farmland that English absentee landlords would manage and profit from abroad, and that the Irish would work.

Trees in Bowen's writing sometimes "embrace" the viewer or are part of an "impoverished" space: their presence can enrich or comfort; their absence is a scar on the landscape, revealing that economic motives prevailed over environmental, aesthetic, and historical values. The trees offer Lois the comfort of an encircling arm in *The Last September*. As she leans out a window of the big house in Danielstown, "The screen of trees that reached like an arm from behind the house—embracing the lawns, banks and terraces in mild ascent—had darkened, deepening into a forest. Like splintered darkness, branches pierced the faltering dusk of leaves. Evening drenched the trees."[54] The trees in the landscape enfold Lois and transform into a forest, a metaphor for her deepening consciousness. The trees are not innocent of history; they reveal the ravages of war and divisions of society. In *A World of Love*, a small, crumbling mansion is described as having "an air of having gone down: for one thing, trees had been felled around it, leaving space and the long low roofline framed by too much sky."[55] The landscape, the state of disrepair of the mansion, and the demise of big house culture are of a piece: place in Bowen pertains simultaneously to feeling, politics, and history.

Bowen's landscape subtly bears the trace of political events. The ruined landscape surrounding the mansion in *A World of Love* has been destroyed by IRA marauders who deforested areas around the big houses. During the War of Independence, the IRA guerilla war against the Anglo-Irish was also an "invasion" of their confiscated land, the burning of crops, the cutting down or burning of timber, and the torching of big houses like the one Lois lives in: "Evening drenched the trees; the beeches were soundless cataracts. Behind the trees, pressing in from the open and empty country like an invasion, the orange bright sky crept and smoldered."[56]

Bowen, in her descriptions of settings in her stories and her observations about trees, joins the landscape tradition of Irish writers. Seamus Heaney, in his translation of the medieval Irish stories of Sweeney, "Sweeney Astray," animates the wild, mad figure driven to the tops of trees.[57] Bowen is drawn to the fields, hills, mountains, and glens that Sweeney praises, but also to the haunting "darkness" of the forest that points to the repressed and untamed parts of the cultural and political psyche of Ireland. Joyce laments the destruction of trees in Ireland in the Cyclops chapter of *Ulysses*, describing an Irish wedding that includes a plea to "save the trees of Ireland for the future men of Ireland on the fair hills of Eire, O," and the wedding guest list is composed entirely of trees: Miss Fit Conifer of Pine Valley, Miss Poll Ash, Miss Barbara Lovebirch.[58] In Yeats' poetry too, trees are in harmony with culture. But his poem "Two Trees," 1893, already points to the barrenness in the landscape of Ireland as a symbol of his heart. Bowen reveals impoverished landscapes but metaphorically preserves trees, refusing to be complicit in their removal. She is firmly against the English devastation of Irish land, and a modern preservationist to boot.[59] In noting the harmonious relationship between trees and big-house values, she and her father reveal the organic nature of Anglo-Irish culture: the preservation of trees as part of a Celtic tradition of kinship of spirit between people, houses, and nature.

Hospitality

Hospitality and grace, another vaunted value in the big house is highlighted in *The Last September*. Here Bowen describes the ascendancy style, graces, and pleasures—family rituals of parties, tennis, dances, flirtation, and squabbles—and plots the relationship between the big house and the Irish people surrounding it. Bowen held on to a modified version of this way of life until the mid-1950s, when she realized the futility of her sacrifices to maintain its graces. Outside, a new, democratic Ireland cast a cold eye upon its style and class hierarchy. The old order collapsed: estates began to disappear because of the high cost of taxes and upkeep, and a new society based on more egalitarian values would replace it.

Stuart Hampshire, one of Bowen's Oxford friends, nevertheless, confirmed that one thing she did for Ireland was to preserve and introduce many English and American literary friends to Bowen's Court and its beauty. Her hospitality blossomed in the 1930s when she inherited the house and continued into the late fifties, seeking to share the house, the grounds, and the glory of the surrounding Irish landscape with her usual generosity. Her warning: "We are 80 years behind the times, 30 miles from the nearest station and responsibly superstitious."[60] She was a stellar hostess. Her animation and love of Bowen's Court is reflected in the letters of invited guests, often exhilarated and happy after a lavish weekend of indulging in good food and her favorite elegant dessert, Pavlova, lathered in ice cream, strawberries, and whipped cream. Painstaking in arranging her parties, she consulted with Molly O'Brien the cook, Mr. Barry, her assistant, and expected formal dress and ladies retiring to the drawing room after brandy. Log fires were brightly lit during the winter months and each guest was given his own oil stove. But her talent went beyond style.

L.P. Hartley, in a thank you note, praised her "wonderful gift" of interpreting her guests to each other. "It is as though you furnished each with a passport to the others' personalities, and a unique sense of fusion comes of it."[61] Bowen always admired people who had a fully developed "social instinct": "one of the most attractive and even virtuous things in life; it almost seems to me," she said, "like the modern version of Christianity."[62] Howard Moss remembered a visit to Bowen's Court with Elizabeth at the center noting she "gave it a special charm by seeming just as delighted to be there as we did. There was a library—silhouettes on the mantelpiece, shining glass cases of books, a brown velvet sofa in front of the fireplace—a room which was Elizabeth Bowen's, the writer's, room. I remember one day looking through the bookcases and finding the typed ms. of *The Death of the Heart*. My heart turned over."

Critic, Declan Kiberd, however, likens Bowen's attempts to shore up such hospitality to a "performance" of Anglo-Irish manners "when style was all they had left—those takers of toast and tea at the Shelbourne Hotel."[63] But to many of her friends, visitors, and fellow writers, she was preserving disappearing forms and manners, the beauty of which she believed in, and to her this was not a cultural irrelevance. In writing of the passing of this Anglo-Irish class and its forms, she participated in both its annihilation and preservation. The imprints of her ancestors remained vivid and present to her, and she bravely asserted this relationship against the cultural tide, defending the presence of the past in the big house—though knowing it had had its day. Her ancestors' "extinct senses were present in light and forms," she said. "The land outside Bowen's Court windows left prints on my ancestors' eyes that looked out: perhaps their eyes left, also, prints on the scene? If so, those prints were part of the scene to me."[64]

Yet the Bowen's Court windows through which she gazed at the landscape separated her from the past and her ancestors, and created the necessary distance for art. As the Belgian critic, Georges Poulet notes, "The dream exists only by reason of the glass, that is to say, the distance [that] is not simply the obstacle which forbids us from approaching it. It is also the protective medium—make-up, veil, or windowpane—which shields us from mortal contact."[65] Bowen spent most of her life in England, and Bowen's Court was a peaceful retreat, a dream, shielded by distance and time from mortal contact in the way that Mount Morris is removed from the war in *The Heat of the Day*.

To her, the view from Bowen's Court was a breathless scene—the circle of trees, the 300 acres of fields, the mountains surrounding the estate. But she moved with modern currents in the city of London during and after the war, and class boundaries eased as democratic winds swept the country. Nevertheless, her friend, William Plomer observed, "Bowen belonged to a class, Anglo-Irish gentry that was already anachronistic, made up of old eccentrics still living in their walled demesnes and extravagantly built county houses, but rapidly dying out" and he wondered why she struggled to keep her house in Ireland.[66]

Yet on a visit, he described the weekend guests—David Cecil; Noreen, Bowen's cousin; Cameron coming up from London; Derek Verschoyld his South African friend; and the planned visits of John Lehmann and Roger Senhouse.[67] Bowen was a barometer of the atmosphere of the summer days:

> A sort of belated June is going on here, and owing to the fine summer the hay is only now being cut. They are haymaking in the intervals of showers. In the field in front of the house between those clumps of trees, with clankings, voices and very nice smells. Not only the hay but the lime trees smell very strong at night, which used to be because of the damp and steaming heat then sudden morning chills. At intervals colour and sun break over the country, then the summer goes on being wet again. The sweet peas are very late and the peaches only just ripening.[68]

She loved the seasonal rituals of Bowen's Court, but it was the staff of servants who kept Bowen's Court running, whether Bowen was there or in America, as she increasingly was in the 1950s.

The subject of welcome or unwelcome guests frequently enters her stories and novels. After the death of her parents, Portia in *The Death of the Heart* is received with a chill into the home of her half-brother and sister-in-law, in contrast with the warmth of Mrs. Heccomb's welcome in her home by the sea. Other characters become unwelcome guests in other homes. Confident and scheming Davina introduces her shy friend, Marianne, into a party of strangers occupying someone's house in "The Disinherited." Marianne appears "as though she had been a refugee, her coming in had seemed to constitute some kind of emergency."[69] The personal state is fringed with the alarming politics of the day, not only the dispossessed Anglo-Irish but "refugees" in Europe, and Ireland's "emergency." In one of her last pieces, the frightening fragment "Moving On," Bowen depicts a group of young people invading and terrorizing the home of elderly, vulnerable people. The alienated youth in this story prompt "the fear of the dispossessed" that she notes in *Bowen's Court*,[70] prefiguring the contemporary cultural issue of homelessness. The houses that Bowen depicts that one might expect to be shelters against the turbulence of history contain both domestic and national terrors. It is her narrative gift to capture in a stroke the interiority of characters in the houses in which they live in tune with Ireland's changing history.

Seaside Villas: Kent, England

After her father's breakdown in 1906, she left 15 Herbert Place in Dublin and Bowen's Court for the light, sunny rooms of Kent, England. She and her mother stayed with relatives or in rented seaside homes, like Portia in *The Death of the Heart* who trailed up and down the French coast with her parents. They first moved to Oak Park Villa in Hythe, then in the spring of 1907 to Folkestone, where they stayed with her widowed aunt, Isabel Chenevix-Trench and her two daughters, Cesca and Margot. Isabel was the daughter-in-law of Richard Chenevix-Trench, the archbishop of Dublin.[71] Here, a surprising connection emerges between the Colley-Chenevix-Trench branch of her family and James Joyce. When living with her Irish cousins in Folkestone, Bowen uncomfortably observed that "nationality showed itself" as they went about the town in "Celtic robes of scarlet or green, with Tara brooches clamped to their shoulders." They were encouraged in this identification by their cousin, Dermot-Chenevix-Trench, the link to Joyce.[72] "Dermot" was an Irish name that "Samuel" legally adopted after graduating from Oxford with a passion for the Gaelic League founded for the preservation of the Irish language and culture. In 1907, the same year that Bowen moved into her aunt's house, Dermot was there teaching his cousins Gaelic as well as preparing the pamphlet, "What is the Use of Reviving Irish."[73] Dermot met Joyce, and may have served as the model for the provocative Englishman, Haines, in *Ulysses* described by Joyce as "a ponderous Saxon [...] God, these bloody English bursting with money and indigestion."[74] According to Richard Ellmann, Dermot was "insufferable," and Joyce disliked him upon meeting. Whether he became part of Joyce's composite of Haines is speculation, but Bowen's mother tartly observed of these cousins that "no Trenches were ever so Irish as all that."[75] Nevertheless, her English cousins' identification with Ireland, and hers with England, "wishing at times to out-English the English by being impossibly fashionable and correct," reveal the conflicted identities of the Anglo-Irish living in England before Irish independence.

In Kent with her mother, she ran freely in the open terrain, released from Dublin and its family troubles. She became a demonstrative, social, and extroverted child. Her cousin, Veronica noted that Bowen "was always very untidy when she was growing up … her hair falling down, her blouse hanging out of her skirt, that sort of thing."[76] Part of the disorder arose from her itinerant life. In Bowen's *Friends and Relations*, the difficult 15-year-old Theodora complains that her unsettled family often sat on a suitcase in a railway station. When someone at a Swiss boarding school says to Theodora, "I hope you are not homesick?" Theodora replies, "I have no home at present."[77] Bowen, a child trained to movement, change, silence, and observation, asked no questions as she moved from house to house. There were secrets to be kept: one did not talk about father's mental illness or mother's death. The frequent moves brought her, she said, to the "first comprehension of life being other than mine."[78]

Bowen was an "intaker," as Eudora Welty once said, and was always watching adults, much like Portia in *The Death of the Heart*. Once she moved to England, Bowen divided her visual past: Dublin and Hythe were opposed places in her mind. She often remarked that she saw England more than the English did because of her fresh impressions when she arrived as a child: she had a migrant's sense of unfamiliarity. Only the fresh seaside outdoors at Hythe and the embrace of the Colley aunts saved her from anxious confinement as her mother continued to hover over her activities. Bowen later related to Ritchie, "all the Bowens who went round the bend (and there were many of them) did so on account of continuous unchecked brooding. So my mother always warned me against it."[79] Though an only child, she was not forlorn, and spent most her time with fun-loving young companions, cousins, school friends, or holiday acquaintances. In Folkestone, she had "a sense that the air lightened: the whole scene might have been the work of an artist with much white on his brush."[80] "On a clear day," she notes, "the whole of this area meets the eye: there are no secrets."[81] Folkestone evoked not only delirium with its open sea views but her admiration of Italianate villas with her litany of things:

> I found myself in a paradise of white balconies, ornate porches, verandahs, festooned with Dorothy Perkins roses, bow-window protuberant as balloons, dream-childish attic bedrooms with tent-like ceilings, sublimated ivory-fretwork inglenooks inset with jujubes of tinted glass, built-in over mantels with flight upon flight of brackets round oval mirrors, oxidized bronze door handles with floral motifs.

Elizabeth Hardwick dubs such detail her "theology of objects," and there is a sense of the sacred in the familiar object, traces of another world in words like "paradise," "dream" etc. In her postwar story, "Ivy Gripped the Steps" and her novel, *The Little Girls*—both set in fictional Southstone, a shadow of Folkestone—we find her roving eyes often resting upon such things.

Life in Kent, however, was framed not only by these visual scenes, but by reading and, eventually, by writing. As an adolescent, she became dizzy with the awareness that for years she had been living in the same Hythe and Folkestone that she found in H.G. Wells' *Kipps: The Story of a Simple Soul*, where Artie Kipps is raised by an aunt on the southern coast of Kent. Her growth into a writer is marked then not only by places but her discovery that reading and writing would bring her back to these earlier places, landscapes, and feelings.

It was in England in these open landscapes, that she first tried to find words to match her impressions that, she later said, made her into a novelist. Hythe also looked across the sea to France, and Bowen wrote to Woolf in 1935 about her love of the gala town of Dieppe on the English Channel: "The joyousness of the steamers with many colored flags, the ladies in large white hats and officers in bright uniforms."[82] Sleeping in a room that faced the sea, she said, reminded her of her seaside childhood. In Hythe, her rooms were full of light.

Encountering the contrasting landscapes in Folkestone and Hythe, so different from Kildorrery, stimulated, Bowen said, her visual imagination: the sea and the chalk white cliffs on the coastline of Kent contrasted with her memories of urban Dublin and the acres of green surrounding Bowen's Court. All entered into a visual reservoir, along with the images and paths of Rome where she often traveled as an adult. Both Kent and Rome stimulated her visual and historical imagination. In Hythe she was awakened to the discovery of monuments where the British navy patrolled the coast. English history burst upon her, she said, as "a gigantic musical, everyone figured including the Ancient Romans," whereas history in Ireland, because of the experience of British colonialism and oppression, tended to be played down.[83] History "inebriated" Bowen. Hythe, Bowen's Court, and Rome became texts as she recreated and preserved scenes in her writing, along with an undercurrent of history in her novels, *The Last September*, *The House in Paris*, and *The Heat of the Day*.

She did acknowledge that she lived through contemporary Irish history, the early 1920s without much awareness: "they were a placid decade of my own existence. I recall a succession of parties."[84] Like the young woman, Lois in *The Last September*, she was removed from the conflicts in the movement toward Irish independence, preoccupied with her own life and future having spent 1918–1919 in London, and part of 1921 in Italy. Yet the violence reverberated in the threats to Bowen's Court. Houses in the neighborhood were being burned daily by the IRA.

Bowen returned to Hythe near the end of her life, 1966, when she purchased a modest brick house on Church Hill, overlooking St. Leonard's Church that she and her mother had attended. The house, a modern structure with two floors and three small bedrooms, was built in the 1950s, and nestled among larger and older homes on the hill. Her vaunted hospitality continued but since the house was small, friends were entertained at the White Hart Hotel on High Street in town, and she left, according to rumor, a pile of coins in guests' rooms to feed the gas meters. Hythe street directories listed her in residence on Church Street in 1966, 1968, and 1970 and then in the years before her death, 1971–1973.[85] She named her home after her mother's family estate, "Carbery," and upon her death, Alice Birdwood, a Colley cousin, inherited the house. A small blue plaque affixed in 1988 commemorates this place. A few of her mother's relatives had dispersed to England for an education, military service, or a career, but most stayed in Ireland. Bowen and her mother were anomalies though Hubert Butler who entered the family through marriage, noted the later flight of the younger generation of Anglo-Irish: "For our parents of the ascendancy it was easy and obvious to live in Ireland, but we of the 'descendancy' were surrounded in the 1920s by burnt out houses [...] England beckoned us and only an odd obstinate young person would wish to stay at home."[86]

London and Paris

Other places beckoned Bowen throughout her life. She grew up in seaside Kent, and as a young woman dreamed of living in London, Though she spent a year there as an art student in 1918–1919, she did not experience the city fully until she moved there when her husband got a job with the BBC in 1935. Here, in her new residence at 2 Clarence Terrace, her literary personality began to flourish and she blossomed as a hostess. Regent's Park struck her immediately like something out of a book: the elegant stucco terraces designed by John Nash, the glorious rose garden. Her townhouse on the Royal Park entered her books and stories over the 17 years that she lived there. The surrounding trees, grass, and lake created for Bowen the illusion of being in the country. People entering the apartment might ask, "Am I still in London?" The Camerons rented an upstairs room to their friend Billy Buchan, who was then working with Alfred Hitchcock. "In a bare plain way," she said, it was "very lovely with green reflections inside from the trees such as I have only seen otherwise in a country house." Though Bowen preferred the country, where she could write in peace, London was often the fictional center of her novels.[87]

In *The Death of the Heart*, the toney Windsor Terrace apartment and way of life of the Quaynes is juxtaposed with the raggle-taggle seaside life at Mrs. Heccomb's bungalow, Waikiki, in Southstone. Hythe and the Clarence Terrace apartment loom in the background of the visually detailed descriptions of the two worlds that Portia enters.[88] The pristine and gleaming apartment sets the tone for the heartless treatment of the orphaned Portia:

> The spring cleaning had been thorough. Each washed and polished object stood roundly in the unseeing air. The marbles glittered like white sugar; the ivory paint was smoother than ivory. Blue spirit had removed the sooty rockery through the bars of the window.[89]

The Regent's Park Terraces maintained an elegance, separating itself from the alienating flats springing up all over London, such as Stella's bleak wartime apartment in *The Heat of the Day*. Bowen railed against such flats in the same collection of essays in which Leonard Woolf protested the ugly blocks of flats materializing in Bloomsbury. She supported the efforts of architects like John Summerson to preserve "politer" London, like the layout of her apartment with a terrace on three sides overlooking the park.[90] Her memory, always architecturally precise, outlines the four gateways into the park; the boat-house; a children's pool; a tea garden; and the Inner Circle with its famous rose beds where she and Charles Ritchie had their idyllic walks. Her roving eye in wandering around St. John's Woods, spies the stucco, ironwork detail, and moldings around the doors, and the alternation of classical and romantic styles. But she astonishes the reader with her observation of the "time-colour" of the villas coming out of the "early nineteenth century: Laburnum, lilac, acacia appear indigenous."[91]

The terraces were considered the most daring feature of the "Metropolitan Improvements town planning project," and in the early nineteenth century, Nash completed 8 of the 26 houses envisioning "a private garden city for the aristocracy." But Nash's vision, said Bowen, was "the swan song of an age in which culture was linked with wealth, taste with breeding."[92] Bowen notes social change in the new residents of these terraces, actors, painters, singers, theatrical promoters, critics, editors, poets, and writers like her, who had known good wine, reflection, and talk in these large spacious rooms. Like Bowen's Court, these houses were stagey and showy, yet bathed, said Bowen, in northern light.

Both her Regent's Park townhouse and Bowen's Court grounded her, yet she wrote about people who were restless. When the Watsons move into a semi-detached house, no sooner are they settled than Mrs. Watson is "overcome by melancholy."[93] She feels like an "utter stranger" in the new estate that is filling up with workers. "An estate," she says, "is not like a village, it has no heart." Bowen true to her elite values and aesthetics was horrified by the municipal decisions about housing and architecture in the 1940s—as the city of London expanded into suburbs for the working class after the war. The Watsons live "entombed" in a house on a newly developed suburban "estate," not a "village" that has community. She hints at their alienation and bewails the blocks of twentieth-century flats replacing the beautiful Victorian houses on Albert Road in her neighborhood.[94] They bred, she said, disaffected, rootless people who committed strange crimes, revealing her insulation from as well as prejudice and indifference towards the needs of poor, dislocated Londoners after the war. In such a house on Rose Hill, the Bentley murder occurs in her story, "The Cat Jumps." It opens with the guests at a party of the Wrights, the new owners of a house, discussing a ghastly murder that has occurred there: their voices coming out "from some dark interiority ... each personality attacked by some decomposition."[95] The past of the house would determine character as in other stories and novels.

The city of Paris would also heighten her romantic imagination in remembered rooms. Her memory of the city is intertwined with her intense relationship with Charles Ritchie and she wrote in October 1947 before his marriage, "I don't think I'll ever love any place, I mean any interior on earth as much as I've loved 218 Bd. St. Germain ... I have been working very hard ... a great rush of work is exhilarating ... Most of all, because of you I am happier than I've ever been in my life." She remembers the days and places in France with him—Fontainebleau, Senlis, Chartres—and exhorts him to remember them as clearly as she does. Ritchie does remember but differently. He wrote a humorous letter to a Canadian colleague, Lester Pearson, about his adventures in hunting for this St. Germain apartment that involve him in strange transactions with a Hungarian duchess and a Chinese ambassador. He concludes, "I have, however, found a flat, too expensive for me, too large for me, too cold for me, but all the same a very attractive flat on the left bank in the Boulevard St. Germain."[96]

Paris, when it entered her writing in *The House in Paris*, became an abstract of small, quiet streets that run uphill from the Seine to the Boulevard Montparnasse. When Henrietta, the young girl en route to Mentone, approaches the Fisher house in such a neighborhood where she is to stay overnight, the material and emotional ambiance of the neighborhood emerges:

> The Fishers' house, opposite which the taxi stopped, looked miniature, like a doll's house: it stood clapped to the flank of a six-storied building with balconies [...]. Up and down the narrow uphill street the houses were all heights: none so small as the Fishers ... Unbright light struck between the flanks of the houses, making their inequality odder still: some were trim and bright, some faded, crazy or sad.[97]

When she enters and is led upstairs by Naomi, they creep up like "thieves": the inside reflects the eeriness of the neighborhood outside. "No story," says Bowen, "gains absolute hold on me ... if its background—the ambiance of its happenings—be indefinite, abstract or generalized." Characters operating in such a vacuum, she asserts are "bodiless": consequently, her characters will always emerge bearing the emotional and physical traces of a particular place.[98] Actual rooms, apartments, houses, landscapes, and places in Ireland, England, and Europe became the visual terrain of Bowen's imagination and writing.

Notes

1. Bowen, "Notes on Writing a Novel," 177.
2. Welty, "Place in Fiction," 117, 122.
3. National University of Ireland, Galway, Landed Estates Database, http://landedestates.nuigalway.ie/LandedEstates/jsp/family-show.jsp?id=2664. Accessed December 15, 2015.
4. *BC*, 453, 248.
5. *SW*, 4.
6. EB to CR, May 7, 1962, *LCW*, 231.
7. *DH*, 140.
8. Bowen, "Most Unforgettable Character," *MT*, 258–259.
9. Bennett, "House," 173.
10. HH to EB, June (ca.1933), HHC. With permission from the Literary Estate of Humphry House.
11. *BC*, 27.
12. *BC*, 457.
13. EB to CR, May 14, 1950. *LCW* 173.
14. Plomer, *At Home*, 138.

15. Bowen, "The Big House," *P&C*, 27.
16. Kreilkamp, 17.
17. *PC*, 25.
18. Bowen, "The Big House," *PC*, 29.
19. *BC*, 453.
20. EW to EB, August 5, 1951, HRC 12.3.
21. EB to CR, June 16, 1958, *LCW*, 30.
22. CR journal, July 2, 1958, *LCW*, 311–312.
23. Woolf, April 30, 1934, *Diary* 4, 210. The "old man," Patsy Hennessy, St. Geoffrey's Well.
24. Keane, "Elizabeth of Bowen's Court."
25. Bennett, "House," 177.
26. Bowen, "The Big House," *PC*, 28.
27. Bennett, "House," 172.
28. Donnelly, "Big House Burnings," 147–148. Donnelly cites methods for estimating values in today's money; one recommends multiplying the British sterling values of 1920–1921 by 30. He also recommends consulting http://www.measuring worth.com/ukcompare/. Accessed May 6, 2011.
29. EB to CR, August 24, 1945, *LCW*, 57.
30. R.B. MacCarthy to DH, April 1, 1973, PRONI D/4400/C/2/28.
31. Woolf, *To the Lighthouse*, 267.
32. *DH*, 90, 291.
33. Dwane interview.
34. Molly O'Brien: see Murphy, "Regionalism and Nationalism," 146ff.
35. *TST*, 11–17.
36. Brenda Hennessy's reported remarks on Michael Collins and Molly O'Brien, in Murphy, "Regionalism and Nationalism," 32ff.
37. In the Act of Settlement of Farahy Townlands, eighteenth-century records reveal that Lord Kingston was allotted 1227 acres, compared with John Bowen's 655 acres, and thus Maume's assessment. Farahy Parish history: http://www.corkpastandpresent.ie/places/northcorkcounty/grovewhitenotes/fairyhilltokanturkcastle/gw3_103_119.pdf. Accessed November 2015.
38. Interview with Mike Gould, January 24, 1993, Murphy, "Regionalism and Nationalism."
39. Brenda Hennessy, interview by PL, Farahy, Ireland, May 2011.
40. Keane, "Elizabeth of Bowen's Court."
41. "Elizabeth Bowen and Jocelyn Brooke."
42. *LS*, 60.
43. Banville, BBC Sunday Feature: Radio 3, 1999, NSA.
44. *LS*, 302–303.
45. Lassner, *Elizabeth Bowen*, 46.
46. *LS*, 41–42.

47. Padraig O Maiden, "The End of Bowen's Court," September 28 (ca. 1959), in Hennessy's Miscellaneous Files.
48. Preface, second edition of *LS*, 204.
49. *BC*, 278.
50. Mary Dwane interview.
51. As reported in Donnelly, "Big House Burnings," 149.
52. *BC*, 376, 365, 371.
53. Kiberd interview.
54. *LS*, 26.
55. *WL*, 11.
56. *LS*, 25–26.
57. Heaney, *Sweeney Astray*.
58. Joyce, *Ulysses*, 268.
59. An affinity between Bowen's view of trees and recent environmental studies: Wohlleben, *Hidden Life of Trees*.
60. Bennett, "House," 2.
61. L.P. Hartley to EB, March 12, 1934, HRC 11.5.
62. EB to CR, September 7, 1948, *LCW*, 134.
63. Kiberd, *Inventing Ireland*, 367.
64. Bowen, "Culture of Nostalgia," 451.
65. Poulet, *Interior Distance*, 244.
66. Alexander, September 10–18, 1935, from "Notes on a Visit to Ireland," 197–198.
67. WP to EB, August 17, n.d., HRC 11.8.
68. EB to WP, August 17, n.d., DUR 19.
69. "The Disinherited," *CS*, 387.
70. *BC*, 172.
71. Janet Adamson, archivist, Folkestone, England, 1909 Irish census.
72. *BC*, 420.
73. Trench, "Dermot Chenevix Trench," 39ff.
74. Reference by Peter Reichenberg, member of *Ulysses* reading group.
75. *BC*, 420.
76. Documentary, *The Death of the Heart*.
77. *FR*, 41.
78. *SW*, 55.
79. EB to CR, January 29, 1957, *LCW*, 260.
80. *SW*, 20.
81. *PC*, 3, 28.
82. EB to VW, August 26, 1935, SU.
83. *P C*, 26.
84. Bowen, "Coming to London," 80.

85. Janet Adamson, archivist for the Folkestone Historical Society England, information from local street directories listing Mrs. E. Cameron residing in "Wayside" on Church Hill, Carbury ("Carbery") in 1966, 1968, 1970, and 1971–1973.
86. Hubert Butler, 85.
87. Bowen, "Autobiographical Note."
88. Correspondence, Miss Beckett, *Harper's Bazaar*, Grosvenor Square, July 1, 1945, HL, 52742–52813.
89. *DH*, 303–304, 34.
90. John Summerson, visitor to Bowen's Court and Regent's Park, wrote about Nash's architecture in Georgian London.
91. Bowen, "Regent's Park and St. John's Wood," 156, 152.
92. Ibid., 152.
93. "Attractive Modern Homes," *CS*, 525.
94. Bowen, "Regent's Park and St. Johns Wood," 154.
95. Bowen, "The Cat Jumps," *CS*, 367.
96. CR to McIntosh, Feb. 27, 1947, Robertson personal collection.
97. *HP*, 9.
98. *PC*, 26–35.

4

Outsiders (1925–1935)

A Born Foreigner

Attached to Dublin, Kildorrery, and Hythe, Bowen felt, nevertheless, culturally adrift in both England and Ireland. She relished the feeling of traveling
from one place to another, and wrote to her friend Isaiah Berlin from America
in 1933: "I should like to move constantly and live in many places. Be part of
them, I mean, for a time," adding "I must be a born foreigner."[1] Bowen's restlessness and desire to move is counterpoised always with her need for a still
point, a home. Upon her marriage to Cameron in 1923, she wrote, "To his
belief in my work," and to his "patience with a writer wife, I owe everything."[2]
It was her marriage to Cameron, an intelligent, kind, and educated man, that
created the first stable home for her writing.

In the years after her marriage, the feeling of being a foreigner remained not
only when traveling but as a socially untutored young Anglo-Irish woman living with her older, English, educated, veteran husband in Oxford. She had felt
the same, at times, growing up in Ireland, where she and her family were viewed
as outsiders, Anglo-Irish Protestant gentry in a Catholic country. Yet they considered themselves Irish and insiders, though acknowledging they "had been
hybrids from the start in Ireland" given their Welsh roots.[3] Like Stella in *The
Heat of the Day*, Bowen felt "the uncertainties of the hybrid."[4] In a familiar pattern of preserving what she is at the same time undoing, she asserted in 1937,
"I never have even pretended to *love* England, she has nothing to do with me,
after all"; earlier, she had credited England with making her into a novelist.[5]
And Ireland? Throughout her writing life it gave her, she said, a base, a landscape, and "a terrain of the imagination" though she only wrote two novels

© The Author(s), under exclusive license to Springer Nature Switzerland AG 2021
P. Laurence, *Elizabeth Bowen*, Literary Lives, https://doi.org/10.1007/978-3-030-71360-7_4

clearly set in Ireland, *The Last September and A World of Love*; another with a house in Ireland in the background, *The Heat of the Day*; and seven stories.[6] She is best understood as being outside of or on the borders of different cultures, places, and nations beginning with her Anglo-Irish identity that made her feel a "foreigner," as she said, in both English and Irish society.

Bowen always said she was most fired up by being an outsider: her temperament and writing were stimulated by change, chance, contrast, or "dislocations" in a positive sense, Derrida's "defamiliarization." Her way of dealing with dislocations was to lock herself in as "a nonentity, in some ideal no-place, perfect and clear as a bubble," like Lois in *The Last September*. The no-place for Bowen was writing. Feelings of restlessness or irresolution in love or life were dispelled as she moved toward the writing table, away from those who demanded conventional relationships, unwavering attachments, fixed selves, sharp borders, clear gender roles, and unchanging national loyalties. She was an original writer, idiosyncratically Irish, and an uncommon woman.

Her movement reflected the age of the refugee, as her friend, William Plomer, had recognized. He expanded on the despair and suspense of their generation, reminiscent of today:

> the fate of more people, it appears, in the twentieth century than in previous times to move about, to live in exile, and to share the material advantages of some community with which they have little in common and little or no sense of community—particularly in urban or suburban surrounds. Persons with no strong religious or political adhesions, without assessable property, or children, or even a settled family life, and either self employment, casually employed or unemployment.

Populations shifted and boundaries of countries were redrawn, leaving many feeling bitter and uprooted. The conflicting goals of the Allied powers after World War I resulted in a harsh peace treaty that left Germany neither pacified nor stable. Bowen observed that writers like Anthony Powell, Evelyn Waugh, Cyril Connolly, and Henry Green "fully entered upon creative life in the dense, packed decades" between the wars: all were at Oxford following World War I, ready to play their role in the next war and write about the space between.[7]

In Bowen's story "The Disinherited," written in Oxford, she explores the movement of different classes in the 1920s and 1930s. It captures a cross-section of feelings: the economic and social depression of the working class; the bitterness of characters like Davina who were "disinherited" from a "grand manner" of living under the old order. It also reflects the naivety and unease of those who moved to suburban villas, like Marianne and her civil servant husband, and the desperation of those on the run, like the ruthless servant Prothero.

Davina and Oliver are the unvirtuous elite who have become the "enemy of society, having been led to expect what [they] did not get." Though Oliver has "birth," he has little income, no ability, and expensive tastes. Like Davina, his past lover, and many of Bowen's friends, "the old order left him stranded, the new offered him no place." He got on as he could, grappling for money and living in the house of a lord, cataloguing his library: "Not having been born for nothing into a privileged class, he was, like Davina, entirely unscrupulous."[8] Davina, living in the home of her aunt, Mrs. Archworth, is similarly bitter, haughty, unable to support herself, and resentful that she is expected to do so.

Bowen observed the decline of this class growing up. She registered a feeling of emotional "disinheritance" long before the burning of Anglo-Irish big houses in Ireland or the dislocation of the English after the war. The empty feelings she experienced after leaving Ireland as a child returned after the death of her husband in 1952 and then when visiting Rome in 1959 after the sale of Bowen's Court.

> I shrink from the feeling of being foreign—who does not. Mine may be a generation with an extra wish to acclimatize, to identify anywhere, at any time, with anyone, one may be seized by the suspicion of being alien—ease is therefore to be found in a place which nominally is foreign: this shifts the weight. Rome is the ideal environment for a born stranger.[9]

Bowen sidesteps the debate among critics about her identity complicated by English, Irish, Anglo-Irish, Welsh, American, and European loyalties and loves. She lives on borders. When traveling in America in 1933, she wrote to Berlin that she felt Anglophobic; though before and during the war, she identified with the British; after it, experiencing political change and deprivations in London, she felt more comfortable living in Ireland. Her lover Sean O'Faolain described her as "heart-cloven and split-minded"—born and raised Irish, residing mostly in England, and creating her literary style from a patchwork of traditions, Anglo-Irish, Irish, English, and European. Otherness descended the moment Bowen went to England as a child, never to leave, and despite many critical assertions, the dislocations and movement were not temperamentally jarring, but a part of her being modern, modernist and on the move. The move to England as a child created, she said, "a cleft between my heredity and my environment—the former remaining, in my case, the more powerful." She did not share, however, her characters' sense of entitlement. In England she became an active agent making up her own life.

She returned twice a year to Bowen's Court to visit her father, and to Italy almost every spring, identifying with its style and spirit. She also frequently traveled to Paris to be with Charles Ritchie, and to America for teaching and lecturing. After the sale of Bowen's Court, she traveled to Rome to "center" herself, confirming Declan Kiberd's observation that Bowen's "truest sense of herself may have come when she was in motion, crossing from one country to another."[10] This fluidity of personality, identity, and suspension of place—what she once labeled "unstuck"—was a part of her self-invention as a woman and writer. She remains elusive to those who try to place her in a narrow nationalist, gender or literary bed.

In the 1930s, she was attracted to friends who were, like her, "between" England and their birthplace culture. Bowen—born in Ireland and living most of her life in England—often expressed her alternations of identity, reflected visually perhaps in a mobius strip, a band that is unorientable. Among her important friends who shared this ambivalent identity with different cultural nuances were Isaiah Berlin and William Plomer. Isaiah Berlin was a Jewish exile from Russia, who became a renowned Oxford historian, fiery thinker, and raconteur; William Plomer, a radical South African poet, short-story writer, novelist, librettist, and editor at Jonathan Cape. Both remained lifelong friends. Berlin, the only surviving child of a wealthy Jewish timber merchant from Riga, emigrated to London in 1920 at age 11 with his parents, who had suffered under Bolshevik rule and encounters with anti-Semitism; Plomer arrived in 1926 in retreat from the turbulent South African climate of apartheid after Leonard and Virginia Woolf's Hogarth Press published his first novel, *Turbott Wolfe*, about an interracial romance. Both friends left their native countries and emigrated to England, identifying with dispossessed people they left behind. Berlin identified with the Jews, particularly during the period of rising anti-Semitism that began before World War II, and, later, with the establishment of the state of Israel. Plomer identified with the outrages against black South Africans, writing journalism and fiction about the interface of cultures and cross-cultural romance. In the 1940–1950s, his interest in South Africa was rejuvenated and he returned to support writers like Nadine Gordimer.

Bowen also became friends with Lady Ottoline Morrell, a society hostess and patron who loved to entertain and had a passion for literature and the arts and a liberated love life. She created salons for creative individuals. A staunch individualist, she also had a gift for conversation, gossip, friendship, and creating literary salons at Garsington Manor near Oxford and Gower Street in London. Morrell, along with Berlin and Plomer, outsiders, brought aspects of Bowen's personality and talents into relief. Morrell recognized her originality and introduced her to a literary and artistic circle, but the first circle Bowen encountered was the Oxford circle after her arrival in Oxford in 1925 with her husband, Alan Cameron, who was then assistant secretary of education for Northamptonshire and Oxford.

The Oxford Circle

Bowen was introduced to the sociable Oxford circle by Eric Gillett, a friend of her husband's. She was welcomed into the brilliant circle and Eudora Welty confirmed her caliber:

> I think she had the best analytical mind of a writer, about writing, that I've ever come across. She had a marvelous mind, you know, all aside from the imagination and sensibility you need to write fiction. I know they felt that in Oxford, where she and her husband lived for a time. She was such marvelous company in the evening for those Oxford people. She was not in the least academic, but their minds could play together.[11]

Those in the circle would recognize, as later Charles Ritchie did, that Bowen had a pleasant "hardness" about her, a fine-edged mind. David Cecil, then an eminent critic and fellow at Wadham College, received her as an exciting new novelist and welcomed her attendance at his lectures on Victorian literature; he introduced her to Cyril Connolly, another respected critic. He mentored her reading, and noted in *Enemies of Promise* that certain Mandarin writers preoccupied him during those years, figures that may have entered his conversations: Lytton Strachey, Woolf, Proust, D.H. Lawrence, Aldous Huxley, George Moore, James Joyce, and Yeats.[12] Later Bowen would become a professional reviewer of such writers in the *Tatler*, the *Spectator*, *TLS*, the *Observer*, the *New Statesman*, *The Listener*, *Cornhill*, and *The Cork Examiner* among others.[13]

Bowen and Connolly had common ancestry in Cork; his family was associated with the eighteenth-century Gothic Mitchelstown Castle, burned down by the Republican army in 1921. Eight miles away, Bowen's Court was left standing, perhaps because the Bowens had fed famine victims, according to rumor. They shared an Anglo-Irish heritage, though Connolly had "surrendered most traces of his youth and Irish upbringing" after attending Eton and Oxford, according to journalist and art collector Bruce Arnold. Connolly, like Bowen, lived most of his life in England pursuing a literary career: he founded *Horizon* during the war, became literary editor for the *Observer* and a reviewer for the *Sunday Times*.[14] The Connollys moved next door to Bowen in London's Regent's Park in 1945, and she considered them among "the nicest" of her lifelong friends though when Virginia Woolf met them at Bowen's Court in 1934, she snobbily remarked on "the reek of Chelsea."[15] Though the Connollys were bohemian in manner and dress, Bowen's friends generally appeared more staid and mannered, observing a decorum that Bloomsbury mocked.

The most important member of the Oxford Circle to Bowen was the brilliant thinker and historian Isaiah Berlin, who was at All Souls College. He welcomed her into this formidable circle of intellectuals from which women were generally excluded. She entered as a young writer with only a boarding school education though she had already published a well-received book of short stories, *Encounters*, in 1923. It was an accomplishment as there was little interest then in the short stories of anyone except Katherine Mansfield, a writer whom Bowen admired. Despite this success, many of Bowen's early stories were rejected, and she felt "further out of the movement" as she had not formally participated in intellectual life.[16] Three years after *Encounters*, however, she published another book of short stories, *Ann Lee's and Other Stories*, and a year later, her novel *The Hotel*, 1927. Then in 1929, *The Last September* appeared, her most Irish novel, portraying British and Irish violence during the War of Independence. Her writing blossomed in Oxford.

She became a part of the Oxford scene, and her perceived "masculinity" of mind, élan, and habits of discipline during her ten-year residence, fit the mold. Maurice Bowra welcomed her as a remarkable young writer, and noted the vivid part she played in their lives. He, at the time, was a budding Greek scholar, then a fellow of Wadham College and, later, its Warden, 1938–1970. He was widely admired as a wit, a scholar, and a conversationalist. Berlin described him as "rebellious by temperament and [...] the natural leader of a group of intellectually gifted contemporaries, passionately opposed to the conventional wisdom and moral code of those who formed pre-war Oxford opinion."[17] Bowen was drawn to nonconformity and liked "intensity" in people: Bowra possessed both. He embraced not only Bowen's intelligence but her dignified manner, the hauteur of the Anglo-Irish, and his biographer Leslie Mitchell noted that he "always showed great sympathy for men and women who had been born into aristocratic values and security, but who then were dispossessed by historical floods."[18] Bowen was one, but being a writer surrounded by brilliant young men at Oxford provided an intellectual and social grounding. He described her as "handsome in an unusual way with a face that indicated both mind and character," complimented her quick perceptions and ready responses as a creative writer who was not an academic. The circle offered her an informal education among some of the best minds of her generation talking of ideas, literature, morals, civilization, personalities, and private life. Emancipated by this erudite and freethinking conversation in male society, Bowen began to challenge accepted positions in intellectual domains and continued to question the social roles of women. She grew more confident in her intellectual style, and her modern self-assurance and hauteur are reflected in a character like Marda Norton in *The Last September*. "Bright and hard-looking in her coat and skirt," she reacted to things with "cool and somber amusement."

When she published *The Hotel* in 1927, Leslie Hartley praised it and it was followed by other books "written with a fine, forceful feeling for words and flashes of disturbing insight."[19] Bowra noted the force of Bowen's "masculine intelligence [...] fully at home in large subjects and general ideas," revealing, as others in the circle, their gender biases and, unwittingly, her challenge to gender norms. But he also noticed her interest in décor, hospitality, and history. "She often spoke of Rome and her affection for Oxford's past, fitted uncommonly well into Oxford because she believed in it and had a historical insight lacking in many historians. The ancient buildings and the relics of a traditional way of life there confirmed her conviction that learning was founded in a fundamental human need."[20] And though she felt more "English" in the Oxford circle, Bowen was discernibly Irish and members often complimented her generous Irish hospitality at Bowen's Court.

Bowen also became more politically aware among this network where some came in contact with or engaged in Communist espionage and counterespionage. Isaiah Berlin, Cyril Connolly, and Goronwy Rees were friends at that time with Guy Burgess, who invited Rees to be a double agent and enlisted Berlin to go on a trip to Russia with him: they were unaware until 1951 that he was part of a Communist spy ring. An atmosphere of intrigue overshadowed this group, but there is little evidence that Bowen's political positions moved to the left with some in this circle.

Bowen introduced herself to this circle as "Mrs. Cameron," though she never brought her husband along. At this stage in her life, most of her friends found Cameron only "tolerable"—overweight and garrulous—but Bowen was committed to the relationship. When Bowra introduced her to another in the circle, the handsome Goronwy Rees, in 1931, however, she was attracted. She admired his soft manners, quick mind, and good looks. Rees, like Bowen, was an outsider in Oxford, the first Welshman to become a fellow at All Souls College; Bowen brought up by her father to respect her heritage, was part Welsh, and felt an affinity with Rees and his temperament.

Berlin also introduced her to Humphry House, one of her first lovers who became a renowned Dickens critic. He was a chaplain at Wadham College preparing to be an Anglican priest when they met, but then lost his faith and relinquished his position. Bowen saw him through this period of spiritual doubt and entered his romantic turmoil. She was also a friend of Stuart Hampshire, a colleague of Berlin's at All Souls, with whom she engaged in spirited conversation about philosophy, literature, and music, sometimes at

Bowen's Court. All were lively scholars finishing their degrees at Oxford, later to become influential public intellectuals, scholars, literary critics, writers, wardens, diplomats, and journalists.

She fit into this British academic and social group, yet there were skeptics like the novelist Margaret Kennedy, who admired Bowen's intelligence but viewed her as having "an amateurish foundation" for a literary career. Bowen's cousin Christopher Hone remarked that she once asked her husband if she had a good education. He answered, "No, but you have the makings to get one."[21] Bowen wrote admiringly of her father's prolonged education at Trinity College and his unworldly accomplishments, distinguishing himself in classics and ethics as well as the law, and was drawn to the intellectual life, ripe to learn. Maurice Bowra noted that unlike some Irish, Bowen "did not talk for effect but kept the conversation at a high level and gave her full attention to it," and even though "she had the fine style of a great lady [...] she came from a society where the decorum of the nineteenth century had been tempered by an Irish frankness."[22] The men in this circle liked this frankness, and it enhanced her acceptance.

Accounts of Oxford in the 1920s expose traces of hostility toward women and acceptance of homosexuality. According to Rees, then a student at All Souls, homosexuals formed a group that identified with the arts, unlike the athletic public school boys, who sometimes shunned aesthetic and intellectual values. Rees summed up the general stance that what men love and admire most at Oxford "is found in the male image."[23] The self-taught stammer— such as the aesthete Anthony Blanche affects in *Brideshead Revisited*—was considered attractive. Perhaps Bowen's own unaffected stammer and stylishness fit the fashion. Though some found the stammer distracting, Bowra and Rosamond Lehmann believed that it added force to her conversation. This group in Oxford was a prelude to other literary circles that Bowen would sometimes frequent as her reputation grew in in the 1930s: Ottoline Morell's soirées and Woolf's evenings at Monk's House. And though she was accepted into the male Oxford circle, relished it, and achieved success as an author in a male-dominated context in 1940s–1950s, there was another aspect of her experience as a woman that was reserved in her thinking and writing.

Isaiah Berlin

Three years after Bowen met Berlin in the Oxford circle, she wrote, "I can think of so few things that have any permanent value for me, or that (objectively) seem to me real: I know knowing you is one of them."[24] Their relationship, more intense from 1925 to 1940, before they both became engaged with the war, attests to the caliber of her intelligence. One of the most brilliant men in Oxford, he remained prominent in her field of friendship, from which many were dismissed. Friends like May Sarton and Eddy Sackville-West complained that she cut them off without warning. Berlin wrote to his friend Marion Frankfurter, the wife of the Supreme Court Justice, in 1936 that in his own relationship Bowen "continues to be a delightful person, understands everything one says, and loves low life, toughs, blood, and anything violent."[25] He intuited an aspect of Bowen that many missed in her personality and writing: the *farouche* quality: the untamable, forthright, frank, and unconventional under a veneer of propriety. Berlin shared this quality. Virginia Woolf talked of arguing "with Isaiah, who is a very clever, much too clever, like Maynard [Keynes] in his youth, don: a violent Jew."[26] Similarly, Goronwy Rees confirmed an inner turbulence in Bowen in a letter to Berlin: "the goodness in her comes out of a strange welter of desires and emotions: there is in her very little which corresponds to the calm & peace she creates at Bowen's Court—only this unerring sense of style & perfection & instinctive aversion from all vulgarity."[27] Her turbulence arose from a nervous temperament, a demanding writing career, her life as a public intellectual, and intense and sometimes frustrating romances.

She was tall, about 5′8″, and Bowra described her manner as that of "someone who has lived in the country and knows its habits."[28] May Sarton compared her to a drawing by Holbein: "Hers was a handsome face, handsome rather than beautiful, with its bold nose, high cheekbones, and tall forehead; but the coloring was as delicate as the structure was strong—fine red-gold hair pulled straight back into a loose knot at her neck, faint eyebrows over pale-blue eyes."[29] 'Handsome' was the descriptive word used: never 'pretty'. Molly Keane remarked that she had "the look of an Elizabethan, not beautiful, but dressed with distinction, a presence when she walked into a room, men would turn around and look, a certain enchantment."[30] She did not evoke traditional femininity, a quality sometimes derided by the men in the Oxford circle. Rather, they remarked upon her energetic manner, her compassion, her wit, and generous hospitality at Bowen's Court.

Engaging in good talk was all, and Bowen was drawn to Berlin and Bowra, both witty raconteurs in the circle. Berlin was said to talk at four times the normal speed—a "gabble" perhaps modeled after Bowra, with an Oxonian accent overlaying his native Russian.[31] Bowen and Berlin were an unconventional pair: she, a stammerer from an early age, attracted to this brilliant man's torrents, his verbal felicity and humor; he, to her sharp intelligence, responsiveness, and ability to listen. He remarked in an interview that she was "a wonderful talker, highly intelligent, very sympathetic, charming and interesting and agreeable […]. Full of life […]. And we talked about books, talked about people": it "just worked chemically."[32] They became friends.

What people remembered about Berlin's conversations, according to Michael Ignatieff, his biographer, "is not what he said […] but the experience of having been drawn into the salon of his mind."[33] Berlin did not suffer fools and Bowen, Berlin said, "makes one feel cleverer, more sympathetic, more nicely poised than one is, one cannot talk about nothing, one is kept up to the mark, & she never does not respond at all, but always reacts in some way to all one does or says."[34] He appreciated her intellect, "tough shrewdness and aristocratic elan."[35] She shared his recognition of "the necessity of keeping up standards against the ocean of mediocrity."[36] One of the important functions of philosophy, according to Berlin, was to defend against cultural barbarians. Yet they were different: she, politically conservative and sexually adventurous with no particular interest in abstraction and philosophy; he, a left-wing Jew, timid with women, and not drawn to her writing. He observed in an interview with Michael Ignatieff that "she was Christian, she was religious, she liked mainly men, she liked joking and voted conservative and wanted people to be masculine and no nonsense, hated pacifists and vegetarians and that kind of thing."

She liked joking and they had fun together. He loved her playful side—she reveled in gossip and intrigue—and, he confessed, "life is not worth living unless one is indiscreet to intimate friends."[37] Bowen and Berlin enjoyed each other's humor, talk, company, values, and storytelling. Berlin described his years at All Souls College as among his happiest when Bowen was a part of his life. Their correspondence, most intense from 1932 to 1938, attests to their close relationship. After Bowen left Oxford for London in 1935, she and Berlin continued as confidants: they not only discussed intellectual matters but shared confidences about his loves and her intimacies with Humphrey House and Goronwy Rees. After 1940 they became more distant as they plunged into war activities, but drew together again in 1960 when she was homeless after the sale of Bowen's Court, and Berlin rented a house to her near his home in Old Headington. There she became friends with his wife, Aline Hablan, also of Russian Jewish heritage, whom he had married in 1956. In later years, Bowen would say that she never missed London, but, often, Oxford, because it was a place where there was time to talk.

Berlin enjoyed talking more than writing, and admired Bowen's disciplined writing life. He loved *The House in Paris*, but confided that he read a few of her books "with only moderate pleasure: they are like very good conversation, but perfectly motionless, with no direction, and like artificially constructed universes […] & always very unheimlich, almost macabre."[38] Her favorite guests at Bowen's

Court were those who did not interrupt her strict writing schedule, and Berlin when visiting in 1938 was grateful for this discipline. He was struggling with his editor's directive to reduce his voluminous Marx manuscript; Bowen took him captive and locked him in a room. He accomplished the task and wrote afterward that he "never [...] had so much to thank for before in my life."[39] This book, *Karl Marx: His Life and Environment*, 1939, would set him on a new intellectual course. In the mid-1970s, Henry Hardy, a philosophy student at Wolfson, proposed to collect Berlin's writings and talks and entered into a productive 23-year editorial relationship with Berlin. The expertly edited published collections established Berlin's reputation as a leading thinker of the century.

The letters between Bowen and Berlin illuminate cultural selves at play. Bowen appreciated his growing love and respect for England; his engagement with literature, particularly Proust and Jane Austen; his nostalgia for Russia, its language and literature, particularly Tolstoy; and his sense of being Jewish in the Christian world of Oxford. His foreignness was remarked upon by Virginia Woolf, who described him as "the great Isaiah Berlin, a Portuguese Jew by the look of him, Oxford's leading light; a communist, I think, a fire eater."[40] Undaunted by vociferous conversation and debate, Berlin was a lightning rod in intellectual circles, but decidedly anti-Communist.

Refugees and Jews

From the early 1930s onward, Berlin, like most at Oxford, turned his attention to politics. Beginning, however, in 1931, Spender brought home the darkening news from Germany about the daily intimidation and violence toward Jews and the reign of terror of the Nazis. Berlin had always had a strong Jewish identity and an awareness of anti-Semitism even at Oxford where in 1932, at 23, he became the first Jew elected as a fellow at All Souls. But Hitler's success in the German elections and other world events led him to expand his outlook beyond the university to international politics.[41] When war was declared in 1939, he stated that the daily personal engagement with Oxford life and teaching that used to absorb him was pushed back, and politics became more compelling. As Henry Hardy observes in his notes to Berlin's letters, Geoffrey Dawson, Lionel Curtis and other older, nonacademic Fellows at All Souls supported, in the 1930s, appeasing Germany. "They didn't say 'Hurray for Hitler,'" said Berlin, but unlike the younger, more militant dons (except Quintin Hogg), they felt that resistance would likely fail, "and talked in the privacy of their own rooms." As Hardy puts it, Berlin's "response was unequivocal."[42] From 1932 onwards, he was aware of Nazi horrors, acknowledging that these were "unique" in history.

Bowen wrote to him in 1952 remarking how much more he knew about the silences and disappearances of people "thanks to Nazis and Russians."[43]

In May 1940, when France fell to the Germans, Berlin remarked: "The events in France have removed the centre of some peoples' lives—Elizabeth Cameron's for example—who obviously orientated herself by an imaginary Paris."[44] But perhaps Berlin was wrong about Bowen's awareness. In 1933, refugees began flooding the streets of Paris and London because of the boycott of Jewish businesses and professions—the Star of David being painted on windows—as well as book burnings in Berlin. France's long-held Enlightenment stance as a refuge for the dispossessed began to fade as the arriving refugees not only challenged economic resources but also provoked questions about identity, race, and nationhood as well as the idea of liberal democracy that France espoused. Prejudice against Jews was awakened.[45] Plomer wrote to Bowen in 1935 that he hoped things were more soothing in Ireland, where she was visiting, than in England, where Hitler's politics reverberated in the wave of immigrants on the streets of London.[46] Berlin, observing the refugees, felt they "cast a certain gloom."[47] Bowen too sensed the gloom and captured it in her writing.

Ireland was anti-Semitic in the early part of the war, according to Robert Fisk, but no more so than any other country at the time.[48] Fisk said the Irish government had refused a Vatican request to give refuge to a number of Jewish doctors, and Sinn Fein had distributed anti-Semitic, pro-German pamphlets in Dublin. The Nazi Wannsee Conference in January 1942 listed 4000 Jews to be exterminated in a projected invasion of Ireland. Bowen noted in another 1940 MOI report, "anti-Semitism in Eire is considerably on the increase. It is said to arise from business jealousy—plus the inevitable results of the campaigns abroad. It has ugly manifestations in the business world."[49]

An intriguing aspect of *The House in Paris* is Max's French-Anglo-Jewish background. The novel's interwar setting is marked by a search for a home as Max moves between Paris and London, and Leopold, his son, having been adopted by an American family moves between America and Paris hoping to live with his English birth mother. The liminal state and homelessness of both reflect Bowen's subtle interest in the condition of Jews, outsiders, and refugees in 1930s Europe amidst growing anti-immigrant and anti-Semitic sentiment. She was, along with other modern writers like Rebecca West, Phyllis Bottome, Storm Jameson, Naomi Mitchison, and Winifred Holtby engaged in the history and politics of her day. Beginning in 1933, German anti-Jewish legislation and campaigns were initiated by Hitler, particularly for those in the professional classes—businessmen, lawyers, judges, and journalists along with book burnings: consequently, Jewish refugees began entering Paris and London along with others who were being attacked on the streets of Poland and Russia. These cultural dislocations surrounded Bowen as she wrote her novel between 1932 and 1935.

Responsive to the times, she creates a French Jewish character, Max, living in Paris in the 1930s, to introduce new material into the novel that reflects the cultural climate. Traces of anti-Semitism surface in the remarks of the British upper-class matron, Mrs. Michaelis and the French Mme Fisher's remarks upon Naomi's engagement to Max: "He has the ability of his race, though some people do not find him sympathetic." Max's "harsh edge" is noted, and "that touch—Jewish perhaps—of womanliness."[50] This allusion is a reminder of Otto Weininger's anti-Semitic theories—of which Bowen was aware—in which he contrasted notions of German "manliness" to Jewish male weakness and "femininity." His book *Sex and Character* "transmitted the anti-Semitic and anti-feminist discourses of the 1890s to the 1920s and 1930s, from modernist Vienna to modernist London" and Paris.[51] Yet in Bowen's description, Max was devilishly manly and attractive, as "Intellect, feeling, force were written all over him."[52] He is a compelling character who, nevertheless, projects a sense that he is not rooted anywhere. He is not a part of England or France, and, therefore, suspect in both societies. Fears enter on a personal level in the narration of Mrs. Michaelis and Mme Fisher who express the growing alarm about the increasing presence of Jews, DPs, and other outsiders in London and Paris in the 1930s. Bowen turned her roving novelist's eye to this new subject.

History in Fiction: *The House in Paris*

The House in Paris had a powerful effect on Berlin. "I have just read The House in Paris again: it connects with something or other, since it moves & harrows me literally more than anything I've ever read, & is an extremely major event."[53] Berlin wrote to Bowen at least three times, affirming A.S. Byatt's observation that this novel grows in the mind over time. It is not just "a Modernist parable about time," as Jean Radford presciently observes (its structure of Present–Past–Present), but "a novel of its time, a historical novel which reflects upon England and Europe between the wars and on the political character of Paris since 1789."[54] It is a novel about those who make or have choices imposed upon them; those who are orphaned, homeless, emotionally abandoned, and betrayed. It is a novel about being a stranger.

Bowen's characters are often overtly uninvolved in history—they do not read the newspapers—but the climate of personal pain and impersonal history on the streets of Paris and London enters this novel.[55] Bowen herself said that she wrote fiction with the texture of history, though this is often unacknowl-edged by critics. Certain words from the national lexicon surface in her writ-ing suggesting the theme of outsiders: "refugees," "foreign," "enemy," "races," and "Jew." Time acts on the characters and the relation of people to one another is subject to what is happening during changing times. The words create a nimbus of feeling that menaces the novel, "caution," "suspicion," "and "betrayal."[56] There is throughout a leitmotif of the outsider and homelessness. In merging the personal and the national state, Bowen amplifies the times. Mme Fisher's house in Paris, for example, is experienced as oppressive, antago-nistic, crowded, and aggressive by Henrietta, an orphan who spends a day there in transit to her grandmother's in Mentone.[57] Vibrations creep up the spine of the house, it is dark, it is cramped. This squashed-in house on a nar-row street is as unknowable as the public streets and spaces beyond, crowded with refugees who do not know their fate. The claustrophobic house contains its own violence as it is the site for Max's despair and the slitting of his wrists, a gash that registers the shock of the times.

Bowen's preoccupation with the political climate signals her movement as a novelist away from the romance of individual personality, which she felt was now played out in her conception of character in the novel. "People are simply there to conduct something or generate something," she wrote to Stephen Spender in 1936. She announced, "I do dislike particularization, quaintness and vivid little touches. What is unique in any given people does not seem to me interesting (as a matter for books)."[58] She turns the reader away from the psychological to a more philosophical, historical, and poetic plane, and cre-ates characters who embody the general forces of the times. As she said of her wartime stories, "through the particular, [...] I felt the high-voltage current of the general pass."[59]

She had always espoused the idea that any imaginative writing was also inadvertently about history. As observed of Stella and Kelway in *The Heat of the Day*, "Their time sat in the third place at their table. They were the crea-tures of history."[60] The rootlessness and personal pain of characters between the wars permeates *The House in Paris*, just as the "rising tide of hallucination" is infused into her wartime stories *Ivy Gripped the Steps*, and into *The Heat of the Day*,[61] and Irish civil unrest into *The Last September*. In the preface to her wartime stories, she outlines this stance: they are not war stories as tradition-ally understood, as there are no accounts of battles, "action," or even "air raids." Rather, she states, these are "more studies of climate, war-climate, and of the strange growths it raised. I see war (or should I say feel war?) more as a territory than as a page of history; of its impersonal active historic side I have, I find, not written."[62] She reminds us that the narrative of nation found in official histories and newspapers often suppresses the personal narratives of war—the "feeling war" of people that she attempts to capture in her writing.[63] History is not viewed separately as a "character" but imperceptibly intertwined with characters' desires and conflicts.

The romantic dissonance in Bowen's finely drawn characters, Karen Michaelis and Max Ebhardt—one carefully bred, upper-middle-class, English; the other a rootless French English Jew—is imbued with historical tensions as well as personal betrayal. Karen has no quarrels with her comfortable life until she meets Max again. She views her protected "inherited world enough from the outside to see that it might not last," a world that her "hungry or angry friends could not tolerate." But "perhaps for this reason, she obstinately stood by it."[64] Her romantic liaison with Max poses a question about the naivety of lovers of different "races" (Bowen's word) or cultures who ignore history. For Bowen the Third Reich's race theories about Jews were ominous, and her novel was published in 1935, the same year the Germans announced the Nuremberg race laws that reversed emancipation. Jews were henceforth defined by the percentage of Jewish heritage in grandparents. Bowen anachronistically refers to the Jews as a "race" in her novel, implying a genetic identity.[65]

Berlin's powerful first reaction to this novel is not surprising. It awakened aspects of his one-sided romantic relationship with Rachel Walker, a vivid, fashionable student who was infatuated with him. He wrote to Bowen that his experience merged with her novel "with fearful acuteness, so that real events & descriptions in your book became fused into a very heightened but very painful state of consciousness."[66] The conversations between Karen and Max, he said, "are really bloodfreezing & fascinating. My future course with Miss W. is directly & deeply influenced by this book." He sees Max as "a macabre character whom I'm grateful not to resemble, altogether the effect on me is of a play where one identifies oneself with situations & characters, about which one has nightmares & dreams."[67] As with Max, it was Berlin's difference that drew Walker into a romantic relationship. Jews were sometimes perceived as foreign because of a darker skin tone,[68] and Berlin also evoked "the humane sweep of Europe, Don Giovanni, Budapest, Elliot [sic], El Greco—the aristocrat swirling down the marble staircase to the Blue Danube."[69] He tried to extricate himself from Walker's fantasy and in 1935 wrote to Bowen about the failures in their communication, recalling her "remark about the seriousness & literalness of inter-racial conversation [...]. We went on aiming at each other, missing mostly, with desperate gravity. Dear me. I can't possibly marry her."[70] As the narrator in the novel observes, "Talk between people of different

Fig. 4.1 Isaiah Berlin and friends, Commemoration Ball, New College Garden. Berlin: bottom row, far right; Rachel Walker: third from right. Courtesy of the Family of John Ward-Perkins

races is serious; that tender silliness lovers employ falls flat" in naivety without the awareness of history in which it partakes[71] (Fig. 4.1).

Max's charm for Karen was his unlikeness. She rejects her middle-class fiancé, and does not conform to Ray's sister Angela's view: "It's better to inbreed than marry outside one's class. Even in talk, I think. Do let us be particular while we can." Karen's marriage to Ray would have "that touch of inbreeding that makes a marriage so promising."[72] Berlin's personal life fused with the romance of Max and Karen in Bowen's novel.

Presenting the fraught issue of Jewish belonging, Max says to Karen, "I am not English; you know I have no humour to cushion myself with; I am nervous the whole time." He is also not comfortably French. He bears the nervousness of Jews all over Europe, "I cannot live in a love affair," he says, "I am busy and grasping."[73] He crosses other cultural lines as a sexual interloper in his erotic escapade with his fiancée's best friend, Karen. Finally, Max is ambitious and a banker. He bears traces of popular Jewish stereotypes, yet emerges as a strong, attractive character in Bowen's novel.[74] He is a compelling, if haunted figure, and awarded Bowen's favorite compliment: "he did in fact cut ice." But Max destabilizes Karen, who feels "foreign" when with him, "more cut off from her own country than if they had been in Peru." She is emotionally, morally, and culturally adrift after their encounter, "As lovers, Max and she were a couple of refugees, glad to find themselves anywhere." They crossed borders from France to England for their liaison and the personal use of the word "refugees" reflects the climate of the times. When Karen's mother discovers the liaison, she cynically reminds her daughter that Max has seen how much wealthier she is than Naomi, "I do not like saying this [...]. But you have behaved like an infatuated woman, an 'easy' woman, and he is a very astute man. No Jew is unastute."[75] Karen rejects the insinuations and stereotypes that her mother projects.

Leopold, the son of Max and Karen, born after Max's death, is "a dark-eyed, very slight little boy who looked either French or Jewish; his nose had a high, fine bridge." When he meets another child, Henrietta, at Mme Fisher's home, they share the emotional helplessness of many of Bowen's fictional children, alone in the world without parents. In a painful, anguished scene, Leopold waits for his mother to arrive, "Leopold turned round facing the mantelpiece and suddenly ground his forehead against the marble. One shoulder up dragged his sailor collar crooked; his arms were crushed between his chest and the mantelpiece. After a minute, one leg writhed round the other like ivy killing a tree." Leopold is not only an "enemy" in Karen and Ray's relationship—an ever-present reminder of Max who also is an "enemy"[76]— but an emotional and cultural orphan, as Ray reflects toward the end of the novel: "This little brittle Jewish boy [...] was the enemy."[77] It was not unusual to hear Jews spoken of as the "enemy" or "enemy aliens" after the Dreyfus Affair in France at the turn of the century.[78] Leopold's lineage as a *mischling* (a legal term used in Nazi Germany for someone with mixed Aryan and Jewish ancestry) would make him suspect as "a hidden Jew."[79] He introduces the vexed issues of belonging, assimilation, and the "hybrid," a word that surfaces in Bowen's novel. Leopold, having been abandoned, would come back to haunt not only Karen but also England, as the displaced figure of two cultures. Victor Gollancz, the publisher of *The House in Paris*, asked Bowen, "I wonder if you realize how un-English it is. It will be appreciated most by Maxes, Frenchmen and Jews."[80] Bowen thought it her most "European" novel, shot through as it is with *amour fou* and history. The personal relations of Karen and Max here, and of Stella and Robert in *The Heat of the Day*, exist amid the historical tensions of "wars, treaties, persecutions."[81] The wing of history brushes Bowen's characters.

No one in this novel quite belongs where she or he did after encounters with Max and Leopold, the foreigners. The house is oppressive and antagonistic and there is displacement and violence. Henrietta, the motherless eleven-year-old, feels "like a kaleidoscope often and quickly shaken" in the Fisher household; Karen is haunted by her passionate and destructive relationship with Max and the unwanted birth of their child; Leopold becomes a Salinger-like savant, a precocious adolescent emotionally wounded by the acts of his parents; Max is unstable and unhinged by his betrayal of Naomi, his passion for Karen, and his strange attachment to Mme Fisher.[82] The house in Paris where these dislocations occur is silent and still within but shadowed by Max's violence and silent refugees haunting France after Hitler's rise to power.

The novel has no emotional or cultural closure. The home that Bowen leads Leopold toward redefines what is "English," personally, culturally, and politically. Leopold's return will prove once again Homer's insight in the *Odyssey* that home is a dangerous place to which to return. Karen and Ray's tolerant home, indeed England, will abandon the xenophobia of the Fishers and embrace this strange and needy adolescent, Leopold: it will incorporate the "other."[83] Bowen, propelling a serious Jewish character into her 1935 novel, illuminates how uncomfortable and threatening life can be for outsiders.

William Plomer

Bowen was drawn to Berlin as well as William Plomer, as émigrés who engaged her with their differences and intelligence as well as their wit. They were highly talented in their respective fields, and both engaging conversationalists, a *sine qua non* for Bowen's friendship. Though both were unconventional, Berlin led a high-powered intellectual life within a revered institution. Plomer, on the other hand, led a freelance literary life as a writer and editor on the fringes of Bloomsbury—having been published by Leonard and Virginia Woolf's Hogarth Press—as well as a countercultural life in homosexual circles. Never moralistic about sexuality, Plomer was one of Bowen's several literary homosexual friends, and she was drawn to his amusing stories, bawdy poetry and sharp wit that perhaps animated the wild side of her personality. They both loved being in stimulating cultural and literary circles, and his store of cultural experience from South Africa, his travel and experiences in Japan and Greece, and his passion for literature infused his conversation. He was a political firebrand in South Africa in his youth and a nonconformist, and such self-styling and intensity often attracted Bowen. If Bowen's voice had an inhibition or stammer, in Plomer's there was always a chuckle, according to Peter Alexander, his biographer. E.M. Forster, a close friend of Plomer's, remarked that people loved his gaiety, wit, and endless flow of stories. Bowen did too.

Fig. 4.2 William Plomer and Virginia Woolf, Monks House, Rodmell, August 1934. Rights holder and Courtesy, Reproduced by Durham University Library, (PLO/Ph/A5/11)

They met after Bowen wrote Plomer a letter praising his novel *The Invaders*, in 1934, nine years after he had emigrated from South Africa. The "invaders" in the novel are working-class characters and homosexuals.[84] His friendship with her was quite separate from his other literary and personal relationships, and they met for tea or dinner, museum or gallery visits, movies, sallies to the Caledonian flea market or, alone, for private conversation. Their delightful letters to one another from 1935 to 1963 teem with literary gossip, barbs about royalty, conversation about books, and responses to each other's writing. Tales and gossip about their friends became part of the tapestry of their friendship. Plomer initially saw Bowen as "sensitive, wise and charming" and having literary gifts; he was also drawn to her gentility and manners and recognized his own nonconformist spirit in her. Bowen reveled in his amusing stories and naughty-boy satiric edge: she treasured his amiability, kindness, and conversational sparkle as well as his literary talent. (Fig. 4.2).

Other Lives

Bowen and Plomer were linked not only in the enjoyment of their literary lives in London but also their private erotic friendships and relationships. There is a Japanese saying: if someone wants to tell a secret, he must open wide the sliding doors and screens of his paper house to allow the wind to blow through and air them out. Bowen and Plomer did not open all their doors, both having guarded temperaments. They did, however, allow the winds of change, the years between the wars, to sift through their correspondence. Both projected into their writing their unsettled childhood backgrounds and the social and cultural currents swirling around them. Plomer was glad to return to England in 1926, having been entangled in relationships abroad. He lived for a few years with a lover in Japan; then had a tortuous love affair with a handsome sailor in Greece; spent time in France; then returned to Greece with Tony Butts, a talented painter who provided him with a luxurious lifestyle. Though a private person, like Bowen, he confided his "life of pleasure," as he termed it, to her. Over time, pleasure became a driving and, at times, dissolute force in his life. When he met Bowen, he had recently recovered from a period of illness during which he received treatment for syphilis. She in turn confided her relationship with her married lover, House, who subsequently became Plomer's friend. Though Plomer was not openly homosexual, he had confronted the subject in his 1931 novel *Sado*. His friend Harold Nicolson wished he had discussed the theme more openly. Plomer, maintaining his reticence, queried in his autobiography, "Am I to blame because it is not possible to be so frank in this country as in France or Germany or China?"[85] Nevertheless, Plomer drew Bowen into a world that she apparently welcomed, sharing stories of his sexual and cultural escapades; she, her affairs with House and Rees, and perhaps her relationships with women as well. In addition, they were both shadowed in intelligence activities during the war.

Plomer had a gift for friendship. Ian Fleming, best known for creating the character of James Bond, recruited him into the Naval Intelligence Division (NID)—the intelligence arm of the British admiralty—where they shared an office as well as vivid intelligence experiences. Fleming created Bond—who later entered blockbuster films—as "a compound of all the secret agents and commando types I met during the war." He poured his experiences into fictional adventures that Plomer relished and later welcomed and edited for Cape.[86] *Goldfinger* was dedicated to Plomer. Bowen and Plomer corresponded during this time, years that she considered "the best," unlike Plomer, who worked under high pressure in NID and felt like a "prisoner" during his six-year stint. Fleming always maintained that Plomer "cared about people." But his views of women were suspect, Bowen excluded.

He often expressed an angry or reticent attitude toward women, according to his biographer Peter Alexander. Bowen was the female exception, "passing" into his male homosexual world as she had in the Oxford circle because of her scintillating conversation, sympathy, manner, and strong intellect. She escaped Plomer's misogyny.[87] She spoke her mind and, like Davina in *The Disinherited*, was a woman "who was born to make herself felt."[88] In a letter to Plomer, Bowen described arriving at Bowen's Court one weekend in September 1945:

> I came out here feeling like death, full of irritations and repugnancies, but am feeling much better now. I have worked like a black out of doors (hewing down nettles and undergrowth, clearing woods) which was just what I wanted & hardly laid pen to paper or finger to typewriter [...]I think I have the makings of a better forester than gardener: plenty of brute strength and aggressive instinct, but the reverse of green fingers—in fact almost anything I plant dies.[89]

Like her father, she was drawn not to gardening like many in the Colley family but to larger landscapes.

A Chronicler of the Times

Bowen considered Plomer a chronicler of the age. After reading his autobiography *At Home*, she touted, "The book is you, as we know and love you (I don't know why I use the first person plural instead of the first person singular). Again and again reading it I felt as though you were in the room; at the same time I remained rightly in awe of that non-personal greatness one recognizes in a friend."[90] She recognized his insight as he described "the bound psyche" of people who had been "transplanted" with a constrained spirit as a mark of their generation.[91] It was a generation "on a furlough from life," as she wrote in *The Heat of the Day*, a time when one became used to impermanence, "when one knew many people well but knew little about them; when everything happened as if by accident."[92]

Bowen and Plomer were not only sensitive witnesses to their times but activists at various points in their lives. Plomer lived in South Africa with his family in his teens and was drawn to journalism and literature to illuminate the "colour question" there in his twenties. To oppose the system of apartheid, he founded the journal *Voorslag* ("Whiplash") with Roy Campbell and Laurens van der Post, a magazine that published only two issues as its proprietor objected to the journal's criticism of the colonial system. At a memorial service for Plomer in 1973, van der Post said, "he had the singular gift of being angry in a classical sense—a passion that does not blur, but makes passion clearer. He became the first person writing in English in South Africa to express this anger in terms of love, and so changed the imagination of a whole age in Africa."[93] Plomer linked an inner struggle, his homosexuality, with an outer struggle, apartheid. This double voice of personal anguish and national outrage gave Plomer's novel "the force of a Scream," according to Alexander—a voice of protest that would never be heard in a Bowen story. She and Plomer would not agree on politics—he, radical; she, conservative—though they were in temperamental accord. He broadcast his anger about British imperial and colonial policy while Bowen favored the propertied, conservative, anti-Labour, Tory class. She nevertheless acknowledged the colonialism behind big houses and actively opposed Fascist forces in World War II. The wrongs of colonialism and the idea of the British empire, however, continued to animate Plomer on a visit to Bowen's Court in September 1935. He presented a sanguine view:

> A heavenly place to visit, but might be less heavenly to live in. It is so melancholy, so full of the ghosts of feuds and famines, the clouds fly low, the trees sag under the incessant rain, and the very air seems charged with a sense of grievance. How could one keep out the climate, how could one keep the Pope and Ulster, Mr. de Valera and Mr. J.H. Thomas, the land annuities, the censorship and the future at a proper distance, except by taking to drink, going over to Rome or London, or cutting one's throat?[94]

Plomer, more overtly censorious of English colonialism than Bowen, wrote of his sympathy with Sinn Fein in his autobiography, and later produced "Empire" for the BBC at E.M. Forster's urging. In *At Home*, he reflected on the feuds, famines, and sense of grievance in Ireland: "As I grew older I wondered [about] the ignorance, prejudice, intolerance, injustice, folly, famine and violence accompanying the English occupation of Ireland [and whether] the English instead of trying to understand the feelings of other peoples, have labeled them 'rebels' or 'terrorists.'"[95] Plomer also presciently targeted another issue: "At school in England the history [of Ireland], this producer of wits, poets, heroes, beauties, and (let us admit it) bores, had not been properly taught to us. It had either been ignored, glossed over, or given an Orange tinge."[96] Bowen was removed from the climate of grievance in Ireland, but she was not always at ease. After the war, she wrote to Plomer that she was feeling more Irish than English because of the passing of Winston Churchill's "stylishness." To her, this meant not only his wealthy, aristocratic background and manner but also his gift of fighting words that inspired the British people during the blitz. It was partly Churchill's style and rhetoric that lured her into engagement with the MOI. She, nevertheless, took a swipe at the women in the Labor movement and the austerity of life in England:

> I have adored England since 1940 because of the stylishness Mr. Churchill gave it, but I've always felt when Mr. Churchill goes, I go. I can't stand all these little middle-class Labourites with their Old London School of Economic ties and their women. Scratch any of those cuties & you find a governess. Or so I have always found.[97]

This amalgam of politics and style provoked Declan Kiberd to label her a "dandy" in the tradition of Oscar Wilde. The style, he said, was part of her need "to maintain an aristocratic hauteur and decorum in the absence of any available court at which to rehearse and play out such gestures."[98]

Her lover, Charles Ritchie shared, at times, her snobbery and conservatism. He too regretted the resurgence of British socialism and what he perceived as the drab, working-class style the Labor Party introduced into London life after the war. Ritchie, entertaining a girlfriend about five months after he met Bowen, noted in his journal that he liked the things that money bought: "smart women, fashionable glitter, all the frivolities that charm the eye."[99] What he really dreaded, he said was the "austere prospect of cotton stockings" replacing the silk. "The sober socialism of the future would mean the eclipse of style, the disappearance of distinction—for mixed and intermingled with the vulgarity of our age is the survival of pleasant, ornamental, amusing people and things [...]. The intellectuals do not mind, because they despise the glitter and speciousness of rich life. But the aesthetes—like myself—have their misgivings."[100] This gives us a clearer picture of Ritchie as a bon vivant possessing elitist qualities that attracted Bowen yet drew him into social and romantic worlds sometimes inimical to her. Though she was stylish, attractive, and passionately in love with him, she did not lead a glittery life, devoted as she was to writing and public issues. Perhaps this is why, even when she was free to marry after her husband's death, she knew that Ritchie, drawn to the varieties of love, did not intend to spend his life with her.

When the Labor government exited in 1960, Bowen noted, "One immensely cheering-up fallout in this country has been the change of government. I always have thought the world of Edward Heath. The idea (up to last June) of a possible further five years of that dreary Labour government had become a nightmare. Though in our own way we're still having heaps of 'unrest.'"[101] During Heath's tenure as a conservative prime minister,

1970–1974, he was popular with Bowen but not the Irish. She belonged to a class with values that were rapidly dying out yet she held on to inheritance, for example. After Cameron's death, friends urged Bowen to sell Bowen's Court, and she acknowledged it was empty but not lonely. She observed in 1957, a few years before she sold it, that she never saw the house's 30 rooms fully furnished over the almost 30 years of her ownership. But, she said, I "turned this to good account: I set pen to paper and describe each room in turn. [...]. The notes make excellent material for my books."[102] Plomer, not fully understanding the complexity of her attachment, wondered why she struggled for so long to keep the actual house, not content with the lyrical "paper houses" she had penned in her works.

Though their bond might seem unlikely, they remained lifelong friends. Politically and socially tamer than Plomer in her writing, Bowen, nevertheless, marks the violence historically simmering beneath the crust of civilization in the early 1920s in *The Last September*, the pre-Vichy historical tensions and dislocations before World War II in London and Paris in *The House in Paris*, and national treason and personal betrayal in World War II in *The Heat of the Day*. She also exposed class conflicts surrounding her in London, insincere relationships between men and women, new kinds of female liaisons, and new alliances between the Irish, Anglo-Irish and English—people of different political and religious stripes—in her war stories and "Nativity Play" at the end of her life.

Plomer as Editor

Plomer also became Bowen's literary advisor and editor. David Garnett, the "acknowledged doyen of all publisher's readers," identified Plomer as one of the most talented writers of the younger generation upon reading his submission, "The Child of Queen Victoria," in 1932. William Maxwell, editor of the *New Yorker* agreed and praised this story, "it is like Conrad if Conrad were William Plomer."[103] What better friend, conversationalist, and editor for the talented young Bowen? Garnett wrote in a report to Cape on that occasion,

> Plomer is certainly about the most original and keenest mind of the younger generation [...]. He is emphatically of the minority—i.e. of the section of writers, the real intelligentsia, the unconventional critical-minded literary artist whom the British Public in general don't like, and therefore only buy in restricted quantities. He is a Left-winger in popularity.

He added, "of course he ought to have gained 'The Book of the Month' years ago, so far as *original* literary excellence goes. But he is too unconventional and keen."[104] With his acumen, Plomer helped smooth the path of Bowen's novels *The Heat of the Day* and *The Little Girls* through Cape's editorial squabbles.

Veronica Wedgwood said of Plomer, "in publishing history there have been readers who were his equal; I am sure there has never been one who was better."[105] He was remembered at Cape for his prescience, wit, and advancement of not only Bowen but the writers Derek Walcott, Arthur Koestler, Alan Paton, John Fowles, Stevie Smith, and Ian Fleming, as well as those the press regretted rejecting, Vladimir Nabokov and John Betjeman. Alan Paton wrote that the best of Plomer was not his novels or poetry but his roles as a publisher's reader, critic, consultant, and reviewer for over 40 years, and Bowen recognized his sustaining critical gift: "Yours is a judgment by which I set grand store." When he considered the ending of *The Little Girls*, which troubled both Knopf and Cape, she wrote:

> what pleasure your letter about my book gave me—not only did it warm my heart but it was a *magnificent* piece of criticism—I entirely see what you mean about the circular saw: I often feel I am humming with nothing to bite on. The only thing to do is to bite larger chunks [...] the letter means more than anything—you get right round to the intentions of the book.[106]

The independence and unconventionality of Plomer's editorial stance appealed to Bowen's originality. He worked part-time as a reader: "My temperament and talent did not impel me to try and make a living by writing books; they impelled me to write books only when I wished and only of whatever kind I wished."[107] He was a versatile writer with an unusual breadth of interest, having published half a dozen volumes of stories, poetry, and autobiography, and later writing plays and librettos.

When Bowen decided to switch publishers from Gollancz to Cape in the early 1940s before publication of *The Heat of the Day* and *The Little Girls*, it prompted a discussion of her writing style by Cape editors, a conversation about the "acrobatics" of her syntax that continues in critical circles today.[108] Plomer, though on the fringes of the firm, became her protector at Cape, at times in opposition to Daniel Bunting (pseudonym: Daniel George), who was appointed chief reader. We hear Plomer's excitement about Bowen's unconventionality in his letters: her new subjects, her ironic edge, her pinioning of the bourgeoisie, her expression of the disappointments of love, women's lives, her ability to capture the elusive atmosphere and historical period of the war, and her stylistic experiments. The novel, he opined, was the medium for women writers in the 1930s and he cynically criticized and misread what he termed, the "unreal chronicles" of rustic life by women who "seemed anxious to show that they were genteel and sophisticated in a 'nice' way who were no doubt expected to appeal to their numerous equals who used the circulating libraries."[109] But Bowen was different.

When Prose Has to Do the Work of Poetry

Bowen's style not only skirted the borders of prose and poetry but the narrative and the visual.[110] When Bowen moved to Jonathan Cape, she was already an established writer, and Cape proposed a uniform edition of her works, carefully choosing the covers, designed by Joan Hassel. This was typical of the craftsmanship of this house, one of the best in England at the time. "They were neat volumes, jewels of production; although their small format mistakenly presupposed popularity," according to Michael Howard, the son of Wren Howard, a business partner of Jonathan Cape. Bowen had published nothing but stories during the war and had begun writing *The Heat of the Day* in 1942. Cape welcomed her, as "the novel was in a poor way," as Wedgwood, once an editor at Cape, had observed.

Despite the accolades, Bowen's reception at Cape initiated critical questions about her writing style. It drew in the outside reader, Plomer, but the chief reader, George, listed "snags in the crystal stream" of her prose in his four pages of notes on *The Heat of the Day* in May 1948. He questioned the oddities of her syntax: for example, the sentence "Ann, rooted halfway across the lounge, fixed on him, one could not say how intuitively, her eyes." Though sensing that Bowen may have wanted to place psychological emphasis on "eyes," George complained, justifiably, that it takes a reader considerable time to work out the meaning of this graceless sentence. Bowen, though appreciative of this careful reading, nevertheless sent a staunch general defense of her style.[111] She wrote that she had corrected all omissions and repeated words "noted by you and William [Plomer] incorporated suggestion and queries as to points." She worked on some phrases in the dialogue that "as you rightly point out, are obscure and misleading." But Bowen's concession to his critique of some offending sentences ended there. Her main defense of her word order and style was that "prose had to do the work of poetry":

> [I am] sticking to my guns about various word orders which you query. I cannot myself bear *fanciful* arrangement of words in sentences. But in this novel, many sentences in which the order is queer are deliberate, because the sentences won't

(as I see it) carry the exact meaning, or still more important make the exact psychological impact that I desire in any other way.

She selected a sentence from the first chapter of *The Heat of the Day* as an example: "And, at the start of the concert, this tarnished bosky theater, in which no plays had been acted for some time, held a feeling of sequestration, of emptiness the music had not had time to fill."[112] The readers questioned the word order of the second part of the clause, "this tarnished open air theater *in which no plays had been acted for some time* [emphasis added]." Bowen replied, "but *I* want the psychological stress to fall on *time* not on *acted, so* therefore I like to give *time* the more *sounding* position of the two." In the final version of the sentence, she added the uncommon word "bosky," meaning "wooded" or "sylvan" suggesting that something promising might occur in the theater's new life, counterbalancing the word, "tarnished," with its trace of "unused" or "spoiled." Her style, dense with meaning, can be difficult.

She acknowledged in the same letter to George that she wanted to "keep the jars, jingles and awkwardness" that "seemed unseemly" or "felt to falter [...]. They do to my mind express something. In some cases, I *want* the rhythm to jerk or jar—to an extent even, which may displease the reader."[113] What she does not say is that the jar, fissures, and cracks embodied in inversions of word order, ellipses, or double and triple negatives that interrupt or subjunctives that suspend meaning is the poetry and music of the modern mind. War and modernity erupt and the instabilities of daily life work their way into the rhythm and syntax of her interrupted sentences. The ring of the telephone "tears talk" in "Summer Night," reminding us that conversations during the war included more interruptions, and, therefore, the pauses, silences, starts, and stops of Bowen and other modern authors' syntax and dialogue becomes a "jar" to modern ears. Her use of the word "rhythm" suggests her concern with the music of the sentence, and leads to her breakthrough to a new kind of sentence that works—most of the time. She wrote:

I *hate* "poetic" prose; but it seems to me that in passages where prose has to do the work of poetry—do more, in fact, than words can achieve *through reason*—a certain poetic license may be taken with prose. It's dangerous, I admit, and should only be done with infinite deliberation, and at one's own risk. So, all these things I'm sticking to. I'm sticking to very much *at* my own risk! If I'm either jumped on or ridiculed by the critics because of them, I shall remember (as you and William will be too nice to remind me) that I *was* warned!

In another letter she states, "I write for sound, rather than for the eye; after saying the sentences aloud, under my breath, as one might test out a line of poetry. Stress and rhythm seems to me as important in prose as in poetry—at any rate, for my purposes."[114] Perhaps during and after the war—this comment made in 1946—she was seeking "new forms for thinking and feeling" and sound surfaced and intertwined with her visual imagination in new ways.[115] She shores up this position in her essay, "The Poetic Element," written in 1950 after the war and these exchanges with George and Plomer about her "style." In the essay she defends the "poetic" dimension of the novel, in tune with Woolf, who announced in a 1927 essay that the modern novel would attempt to embody the attributes of poetry, its ambiguity and intensity.[116] Though the rhythm of their sentences is different—Bowen grounded in *terra firma* and a sense of place, story, and time that distinguishes her from Woolf—they both sought to make the form of the sentence and the genre of the novel more elastic.

George asserts, wrongly, I think, that Bowen "writes so colloquially, so much in the rhythm of speech [...] with her placing a stress on the key word of a sentence." But it is the poetic, the aural or visual effect of word order, rather than the "colloquial" that she reaches for. Bowen justifies another of her sentences from *The Death of the Heart*: "The impersonation had (as Portia noticed) fury behind it." Bowen admits that it is a jarring sentence used to match Eddy's outrageous mood. "I like," she said in a letter to Frank Rouda, "to control style enough to sometimes put all its beauty—potentiality into screeching, hideous reverse."[117]

Such effects are "uncontainable" in conventional syntax and diction, and so she attempts another style.[118] George's judgment of her "willfully tortuous syntax" misses Bowen's experiment in writing to express new meaning: a style and vocabulary that sometimes startles, disrupts word order, places new emphasis, and at times, misses the mark, but hovers always on the border between poetry and prose and something new.[119] She animates this style to counter Robert Kelway and other's assessment that "language is dead currency" as it had become in much wartime propaganda and rhetoric plastered on billboards, touted in newspapers and magazines, and broadcast on the radio. In her wartime collage, her refined word choice, purposeful and odd syntax with its unique emphasis, Bowen directs her editors, readers, and critics to a sentence that begins to disrupt the linear narrative and incorporate the language and sensations and documents of war, the media and poetry. In a 1950 conversation with Jocelyn Brooke about style, she noted that she revised by "snipping away dead wood—anything too cerebral, too confused—anything which fails to convey sensation." Again, she wants to replace analysis with image and sensation—as in poetry; in philosophy, she veers toward postmodernists perspectives—like those of David Foster Wallace who aimed to collapse borders between the literary and the popular, to strip away the cerebral, to engage with the ironies of a TV generation, and to innovate and inject new language and sensation into the novel.[120]

When A.E. Coppard, an editor friend of Bowen's, lent *The House in Paris* "to an elderly dame from San Francisco, a human encyclopedia," she "liked the tale very much but thought it such a pity that you could not write grammatically!"[121] Kingsley Amis, born a generation after Bowen, welcomed the suddenness in the syntax of her sentences, and Penelope Lively suggests that "the startling word" keeps the reader attentive. There are those, however, who did not appreciate the odd word that popped up in her style, and Peter de Vries parodied it in the *New Yorker* in 1952:

"Tennis anyone?" The face thrust in at the library door had the square, animal good looks that are encountered in photographs of men examining niblicks [iron-headed golf clubs] in their underwear.[122]

One of the most vocal criticisms of Bowen's style came from Olivia Manning, who, unlike Bowen, relished being boldly public: "I cannot stand E.B.'s attempts at Style [...] what a tiresome writer she is. The attitudes and grotesqueries of style, all to say nothing much. It is like someone eating bread and milk with their legs crossed over their heads."[123] Though there are misfires, strange words, and opaque sentences, sensitive readers of Bowen respond to the new suddenness and rhythms she infuses into her sentences. Such readers adjust their conventional expectations of a prose sentence to listen to her poetry, sometimes an arresting music, or an odd word.

George, the initially resistant Cape editor, finally recanted on these stylistic matters in *The Heat of the Day*. In March 1948, he asserted that "all the points I raised were either trivial or stupidly pedantic," except for omissions or alterations left obscure. He was responding either to Bowen's strong stance or to other Cape readers, probably Plomer. He mysteriously suggested that he would not have dared make the stylistic points "if I hadn't been, so to speak, instigated." By whom? He goes on to praise *The Heat of the Day* not only as her best novel but also her "best story for the larger public." It was published in February 1949 and sold a record 45,000 copies in spite of the initial editorial brouhaha.

The poet, Stephen Spender embraced her style. He noted a "dissociation" that seems to take place in her characters; when they talk, "one regards their conversation as some *object* extraneous to them." He acknowledged that this is not "character" in the novelist's sense, "but indeed, 'out of character,'" as the critics Bennett and Royle also suggest. Spender said all he cared for in writing was "the touch of light, the turn of observation which makes me think how unexpected, how large, now uncomfortable life is, how little it fits into the roles of character or description."[124] Rose Macaulay in her BBC "Critics" broadcast also found fascination in the "mere texture of the writing (this I suppose I really care for more than any other quality in a book)." She and Spender are responsive here, it seems, to Bowen's ambition to write narrative that would take on, as Virginia Woolf had sought to do, the attributes of poetry. In a 1950 talk, Bowen addressed the limitations and the possibilities of narrative prose. As the novel evolved, she said, "story began to diverge from poetry, lose height, and become entangled with minutiae" or the circumstantial. The novel in taking on the functions of analysis and explanation became, "if not anti-poetic, unpoetic." She sought to preserve poetry and to contain the irrational, the psychological overflow, the "unregimentable elements in mankind and humanity which no hard set form of the classical, of the disciplined story can hope to contain." This spills over into her unusual words and sentences.[125] She is aware that sometimes these sentences "tangle up the reader and obstruct him," but she nevertheless ventures to transform them.[126]

In the same essay, "The Poetic Element," Bowen expresses her admiration for Flaubert, Stendhal, Emily Bronte, Hardy, and then Proust, Henry James, and James Joyce, because they "cracked" the form of the novel, allowing the poetic and the irrational to seep into the genre. Bowen places herself with them on the frontier of the modern novel as she shapes her new sentences to reflect how people think, feel, see, hear, and sense—in her case, with emphasis on sensation and the visual. She will stand by her new language. As she states in her essay, her style "is not purely suppleness and surface for its own sake": she aims for "a muscularity and a strength." The style she aspires to has poetry, "which has a transparency of glass," as well as prose, which, "according to its value, can have anything up from the heavy, unresounding opaqueness of earthen ware."[127] She echoes Emily Dickinson, explaining her experiment "to use the narrative language at white heat." She concedes the risks: "if in our experimentation we bungle or fail, if our language offends and seems incomprehensible [...] a new position, a new forward post for the story must be allowed for." Experimental writing demands an experimental reader and, as she was aware, it can sometimes fall flat.

Style

"Style" was one of Bowen's favorite words, and it surfaces frequently in her correspondence with Plomer, who shared her preoccupation. To have "style" was a compliment, not only the stamp of a writer as discussed above, but a mark of individuality in one's fashion, house decoration, the kind of pen one used (she used a Biro), manner of speaking and living, and even politics. Bowen might take note of a "stylish" person, "stylish" France, a "stylish" Fox Ball, or "stylish" house decorations. She had a personal manner of dress that her friends noted: she shopped at Ohrbach's when in New York and ordered dresses from Irene Gilbert, the Irish dress designer. Plomer was similarly attentive to style, leading some friends to observe a pretentiousness. He was described by one as looking like "a mixture of Puck and Buddha," often donning a hat, then considered eccentric or "shoppy": only shop assistants wore them in the 1930s. Style also extended to handwriting, and Plomer was an amateur graphologist in an age that considered the typewriter indispensable. He exhibited pride in his own controlled script and when Bowen learned to type in the mid-thirties, she wrote apologetically: "After the extraordinarily nice things you've said about my writing—you once said it was *stylish*, which made a great impression on me—it seems rather a pity to type you [a letter]."[128] This was when she was writing *The Death of the Heart*, of which she typed several drafts.

Bowen was also drawn to the "style" of one of Plomer's eccentric and rebellious friends, Anthony Butts, an artist who painted her portrait in 1938. She found him fascinating and admired his wildness and unique way of talking, particularly about his family: he was descended from Thomas Butts, a patron of William Blake. After Woolf's suicide in March 1941, and that of Butts' two months later, Bowen confided to Plomer that they were the only two people she missed. As she embraced their nonconformity, she held fast to her secure life with her husband in London and Bowen's Court. Yet she always reserved her roving eye in friendship and love and for imaginative and actual ventures outside the conventional: her relationships with Berlin, Plomer, and Butts fly in the face of the "proper" Bowen myth. She was an original. She often felt like an outsider and formed friendships with those who felt likewise.

Notes

1. EB to IB, December 18, 1933, BOD, MS. Berlin 245, folio 14.
2. Autobiographical note for *Mademoiselle*, August 17, 1954, HRC 1.5.

3. *BC*, 277.
4. *HD*, 125.
5. EB to IB, August 19, 1937, BOD, MS. Berlin 245.
6. Bowen, "Frankly Speaking."
7. See journal, *The Space Between: Literature and Culture*; also, Bluemel, *Intermodernism*.
8. *FBMS*, 59.
9. *TR*, 19.
10. Kiberd, *Inventing Ireland*, 367.
11. Devlin and Whitman-Prenshaw, *Welty*, 7.
12. Connolly, *Enemies of Promise*, 21.
13. See *WWF*.
14. Arnold interview.
15. Woolf, *Letters* 5, October 18, 1932, 111.
16. *ES*, viii.
17. Lloyd-Jones, *Maurice Bowra*, 16.
18. Mitchell, *Maurice Bowra*, 73.
19. Bowra, *Memories*, 190–191.
20. Ibid.
21. Hone interview.
22. Bowra, *Memories*, 190–191.
23. Rees, *Looking for Mr. Nobody*, 40.
24. EB to IB, shortly after September 23, 1936, BOD, MS. Berlin 245, folio 70r–v.
25. IB to Marion Frankfurter, June 3, 1936, Berlin, *Flourishing*, 170.
26. Woolf, *Letters*, vol. 5, July 3, 1935, 410–411.
27. GR to IB, September 26, 1936, BOD, MS. Berlin 274, folio 27r.
28. Bowra, *Memories*, 190.
29. *World of Light*, 192–193.
30. Keane, in "Life with the Lid Off," September 28, 1983, BBC, NSA.
31. Ignatieff, 65, 51.
32. Interview with IB by Ignatieff, 7 May 1991, MI Tape 13, p. 15.
33. Ignatieff, 4.
34. IB to Marion Frankfurter, June 3, 1936, Berlin, *Flourishing*, 170.
35. Ignatieff, 65.
36. IB to EB, ca. October 3, 1938, Berlin, *Flourishing*, 289.
37. IB to Morton White, May 7, 1970 (copy held by the Isaiah Berlin Literary Trust).
38. IB to Marion Frankfurter, June 3, 1936, Berlin, *Flourishing*, 170.
39. IB to EB, after September 15, 1938, Berlin, *Flourishing*, 282.
40. VW to Quentin Bell, December 3, 1933, *Letters* 5, 255.
41. Ignatieff, 52–53.
42. Berlin, *Flourishing*, 289.

43. EB to IB, October 8, 1952, BOD, MS. Berlin 245, folio 146r.

44. IB to Marion Frankfurter, June 23, 1940, Berlin, *Flourishing*, 304.

45. See Paxton and Marrus, *Vichy France and the Jews*, 34–44. By the end of 1933, France had started imposing restrictions because of its own economic depression as well as prevailing prejudice against the Jews.

46. WP to EB, September 29, 1935, HRC 11.8.

47. IB to Marion Frankfurter, June 23, 1940, Berlin, *Flourishing*, 304.

48. Fisk, *In Time of War*, 431.

49. *SIW*, 60.

50. *HP*, 139, 111, 124.

51. Radford, "Woman and the Jew," 103. Also Cheyette and Marcus, "Some Methodological Anxieties." Otto Weininger, in *Sex and Character*, 1903, first created a link between femininity and the Jewish male in contrast to the image of German manliness and heroism prevalent at the time. This notion fed anti-Semitic views and seeped into thought, rhetoric, and literature: "The most manly Jew is more feminine than the least manly Aryan" (Weininger, *Sex and Character*, 306). Sander Gilman, in *The Jew's Body*, his study of the historical rhetoric surrounding the Jewish male, states that the Jew is perceived as "the hysteric; the Jew is the feminized Other" (76). See the chapter "The Jewish Psyche" in *The Jew's Body* for a fuller discussion of these perceived qualities.

52. *HP*, 111.

53. IB to EB, before August 26, 1936, Berlin, *Flourishing*, 192.

54. Radford, "Late Modernism and the Politics of History," 39.

55. A.S. Byatt, introduction to *HP*, ix; "Foreign faces about the London streets had personal pain and impersonal history behind the eyes." *IGS*, x.

56. *HP*, 31, 94, 27.

57. *HP*, 9–11.

58. EB to SS, May 20, 1936, BOD, MS. Spender 39.

59. *IGS*, xiv.

60. *HD*, 217.

61. *IGS*, ix.

62. *IGS*, viii.

63. See Chatterjee, *The Nation and Its Fragments*, 138ff.

64. *HP*, 69.

65. *HP*, 139, 171, 214.

66. IB to EB, shortly before September 27, 1935, Berlin, *Flourishing*, 133.

67. Ibid.

68. See Gilman.

69. Rachel Walker to Barbara Stancliffe, postmarked March 25, 1935, Berlin, *Flourishing*, 720.

70. IB to EB, shortly before September 27, 1935, Berlin, *Flourishing*, 133.

71. *HP*, 171.

72. *HP*, 134, 69.
73. *HP*, 159.
74. Gilman, *The Jew's Body*, details the historical, medical, and popular rhetoric about the Jewish body and psyche: 63ff. 80.
75. *HP*, 111, 172, 119, 195.
76. *HP*, 150, 167.
77. *HP*, 242.
78. The Dreyfus affair was a legal scandal that polarized French society, when a Jewish captain, Alfred Dreyfus, was falsely accused of treason.
79. See Horowitz, "Lovin' Me, Lovin' Jew."
80. Glendinning, *Elizabeth Bowen*, 97.
81. *HP*, 156.
82. *HP*, 48.
83. See Zadie Smith, *White Teeth & NW: A Novel*; Salman Rushdie, *Midnight's Children*; Chimamanda Ngozi Adichie, *Half of a Yellow Sun*; Jhumpa Lahiri, *Interpreter of Maladies*; Karin Desai, *The Inheritance of Loss*; J.M. Coetzee, *Disgrace*; Caryl Phillips, *Cambridge*.
84. Now viewed as a novel about homosexuality.
85. Simon Nowell Smith, Postscript to Plomer, *Autobiography*, 477.
86. EB to WP, September 24, 1945, DUR 19.
87. Exceptions: Plomer proposed marriage to the aristocratic Lillian Bowes Lyon, 1933; he, fascinated by lineage, aristocracy, and royalty despite his progressive, anti-imperialist views. Alexander, *William Plomer*, 188–189.
88. Bowen, "The Disinherited," *CJ*, 378.
89. EB to WP, September 23, 1945, DUR 19.
90. Ibid., May 6, 1958.
91. Plomer, *Double Lives*, 13.
92. *HD*, [page?].
93. Alexander, *William Plomer*, 320, 83.
94. Plomer, "Notes," 93.
95. Plomer, *Autobiography*, 138–139.
96. Plomer, *At Home*, 137. British literature courses now catching up to Plomer's criticism.
97. EB to WP, September 24, 1945, DUR 19.
98. Ritchie, *Siren Years*, 374.
99. SY or LCW.
100. Ritchie, *Siren Years*, 112.
101. EB to WP, September 1, 1970, DUR 19.
102. Bennett, "House," 177.
103. Maxwell to Welty, "What There is to Say …" January 9, 1983, 375.
104. Alexander, *William Plomer*, 192.
105. Howard, *Jonathan Cape*, 170, 432.
106. EB to WP, October 24, n.d. (ca.1963–1964), DUR 19.

107. Plomer, *At Home*, 154.

108. See Teekell, "Elizabeth Bowen: *Language at War*" and Osborn, "Reconsidering Elizabeth Bowen" and *Elizabeth Bowen: New Critical Perspectives*.

109. Howard, *Jonathan Cape*, 170–171, 216, 182.

110. See pp. 225–26 for a fuller description of Bowen's visual-narrative conceptualization of background and foreground, landscape and characters.

111. EB to Daniel George, June 2,1948, HRC 10.4.

112. *HD*, 4.

113. EB to Daniel George, June 2, 1948, HRC 10.4.

114. EB to Frank Rouda, March 1, 1946. HL, Box 1.

115. Bowen, "Summer Night," in *CS*, 389.

116. Woolf, "Narrow Bridge of Art," 20.

117. EB to Frank Rouda, March 1, 1946, HL, Box 1.

118. Bowen, "Poetic Element," 18.

119. Neil Corcoran, Maud Ellmann, and Hermione Lee, among the first to register the "strangeness" of Bowen's style; more recently Susan Osborn and Anna Teekell, have taken on Bowen's "deviations" and odd syntax.

120. "Elizabeth Bowen and Jocelyn Brooke—An Interview," December 15, 1950, NSA.

121. A.E. Coppard to EB, September 5, 1935, HRC 10.6.

122. DeVries, "Touch and Go."

123. David, *Olivia Manning*, 11.

124. SS to EB, April 19, 1935, HRC 12.1.

125. Bowen, "Poetic Element," 4.

126. Bowen, "We Write Novels," 28.

127. Bowen, "Poetic Element," 13, 14.

128. EB to WP, June 27, 1936, DUR 19.

5

Love and Lovers

"Great Grey Pigeon": Alan Cameron

Paradoxically, Bowen longed for stability in a home, and, eventually, marriage; at the same time, she reached for independence with the freedom of loves "outside the home." Her friend, David Cecil confirmed this asserting that she was loyal to the institution of marriage but adventurous in seeking out other romantic relationships alongside it.[1] Her known loves were Humphry House, Goronwy Rees, Sean O'Faolain, May Sarton and Charles Ritchie. Alan Cameron's accommodation to her needs and "genius" were established early in their married relationship, and he stood loyally by while she sought a broader range of emotional, intellectual, and sexual experiences. Sean O'Faolain ironically noted that Bowen had married "sagely"; and Isaiah Berlin remarked, she "had affairs with other men, not often; her husband didn't mind, he thought he was married to a genius. She must be allowed to do what she wished."[2] Intelligent and nurturing, Cameron offered stability and kindness, yet was generally viewed as a bore. Bowen's friend John Bayley said that Bowen had a "happy marriage to a dull but kind man, unjealous."[3] Cameron would sometimes refer to Bowen's male admirers as Black Hats—a row of hats often greeted him as he entered their Clarence Terrace apartment. He confided to Audrey Fiennes, Bowen's cousin, "Don't you see—all these things minister to something in Elizabeth."[4] Her increasingly separate life paid homage to his belief in her gifts. Viewing it through a woman's lens a generation later, Penelope Lively saw it as "an unhappy marriage, stable without romance"; Lee added that Cameron "was not a man one leaves," accommodating presence that he was.[5] They both observed that Bowen valued Cameron's unwaving support, kindness, and loyalty, though other social, intellectual, and sexual needs were

© The Author(s), under exclusive license to Springer Nature Switzerland AG 2021
P. Laurence, *Elizabeth Bowen*, Literary Lives, https://doi.org/10.1007/978-3-030-71360-7_5

unmet. Some of her love relationships were raw and left emotional wreckage but reveal the untamed side of her personality, exploding the myth of her reserve. These loves not only feuled but lead us to read her novels in new ways.

Beginning, however, with her marriage to Alan Cameron, he was viewed by Bowen in a sheltering role as a "great grey pigeon."[6] Introduced by her aunt Gertrude, Cameron was thought to be a "suitable" match: a World War I veteran who had survived gassing, an Oxford graduate, and a candidate for the position of assistant for education in Oxfordshire. During their short courtship, Bowen addressed him as "angel face," drawn to his good looks. In a letter written to him before their marriage, she described her love as "very childish—I mean sexless and imaginative. You see I have loved you for a long time as a friend, and that goes deepest and doesn't seem to have changed very much."[7] She was 24 and he, 30 when they married on August 4, 1923, in the Blisworth, Northamptonshire rectory of her uncle, the Reverend Wingfield, after knowing each other for a year (Figs. 5.1 and 5.2). It was the year that she

Fig. 5.1 Elizabeth and Alan Cameron, wedding at Blisworth Rectory, Northamptonshire, England, April 4, 1923. Rights holder and Courtesy of Laetitia Lefroy

Fig. 5.2 Bowen's wedding group, married by her uncle, Reverend Wingfield (far left). Rights holder and Courtesy of Laetitia Lefroy

published her first short-story collection, *Encounters*, and encouraged by Cameron, continued to develop as a writer. Her first novel, *The Hotel*, was published in 1927; her second, *The Last September*, in 1929, during the time they lived in Oxford. Cameron shaped the socially awkward Bowen during the early years being older, better educated, and more worldly. She acknowledged her inexperience, "Do you realize—in the worst sense—how young I am? You are a real person who has come in contact with real things, and I've lived altogether inside myself, all my experiences have been subjective … You can make me grow up" (Figs. 5.1 and 5.2).

Bowen believed she was perceived as "a born to the bone provincial, like my ancestors, and in a twisted and haughty way rather proud of it."[8] John Bayley found touching her confession that "she couldn't buy a pair of shoes without him [Cameron]."[9] She paid attention to vanishing creams as well as clothes, having learned at the age of 14 that it was necessary not only to be nice but to look nice. She wrote that in those days, fashion took no account of the teenager, and she made her errors: the pink parasol that almost poked out someone's eye at a cricket match, the muslin dress with blue bows that she wore to a beach picnic, which she had to dispose of by slipping it off a rock into the sea.[10] In later years, she would refer to enjoyable shopping trips in her letters to Charles Ritchie, her friend and lover, once reporting that she had bought a dashing bright green-blue tweed suit, brighter than usual. She sought his approval of her dress, mentioning a smart new hat "to be black (as usual) with two feathers of curious blue-green curling against the cheek."[11] She liked elegance, and thanked Ritchie on one occasion for the gift of a flawless bag from Paris. "Every time I take that bag to a party, I shall feel in the tactile sense that you're coming too. I don't think anything, I mean any object, you could have given me could have made me more happy."[12] She confessed, "I can see what would happen to my clothes if I lived in Ireland: my eyes would get slightly out [adopting a] dowdy and bad style."[13] Yet she had her vulnerabilities, and her friend, Molly Keane, once remarked that Bowen didn't think she was good-looking even though she attracted the attention of men and women.[14] Writing to her lover, Charles Ritchie at the age of 51, she said "See me—I wish I were more beautiful—even if it hurts."[15]

Cameron was six years older than Bowen and a soldier during the years that she was going to bed to the sound of bombs near the Downe House School. He fought with distinction in the Eighth Devonshire Regiment, entering the French theater on April 25, 1914, as Germany attacked France. The Western Front was the most important field of action at that time, and he later fought in the Battle of the Somme, beginning as a Devon regimental captain and achieving the rank of sergeant. He received three medals: one of them, the Star Medal was automatically awarded to soldiers who left England for battle elsewhere, and records confirm that Captain A.C. Cameron applied for it 1914–15 and received it in 1920. And like all other officers, he automatically received the British Medal and the Victory Medal.[16] Bowen referred in letters to the eye poisoning that he suffered during the war, an injury that plagued him throughout his life; some friends said that he was traumatized by his war experience, and showed lifelong signs of depression and alcoholism. Bowen maintained silence on these matters. But his war record and suffering rebut the facile evaluations of some of Bowen's friends and critics today.

In Oxford in 1925, she was "located, married, the mistress of a house," and to her, "the sensation of living anywhere … was new." Marriage provided her with a social perch from which to launch her life. Cameron came from the academic upper-middle class and offered financial and social stability. She clung to her home with its security and the certainty of the writing table and was validated through early publication of *Encounters* and good reviews. Cameron believed in her and Sarton recalled that he would sometimes recite passages from Bowen's books while walking up and down the room. He supported women's causes and, at one time, a postwar female Labor candidate when Bowen did not. She never wrote much about her relationship, nor did she include husbands, in general, in her stories. But in an early novel, *Friends and Relations*, written in 1931, before any of her known affairs, she wrote of marital confusions and complications. She wrote of secret loves outside marriage and the irony of Edward rejecting his mother's affair with Considine Studdart, a family friend, while being secretly in love with his wife's sister, Janet. Despite intense feeling between Janet and Edward, they repress their emotions, hide their attraction, and steer clear of an affair: a Victorian resolution. Perhaps Bowen at that stage in her life, stood as her character, Janet, "powerless, looking at her life [...] her whole habit of mind. This like a house long inhabited without feeling and vacated easily."[17]

Elizabeth Bowen was of a generation of women writers—like Rosamond Lehmann—who believed in romantic love with all its joys and yet wrote with acerbic intelligence that romance carried "death between its lips": it destroys Max in *The House in Paris* and Emmeline and Markie in *To the North*. She was a sceptic and the passion of romance and the grace of married love is often missing as in her story, "Firelight in the Flat." Nevertheless, her honest, loving, distressed, and, sometimes, searing letters to her lovers reveal another Elizabeth Bowen. Beneath her reserved demeanor were tensions, dissonances and passions in her nature that fueled her writing rather than dislocating her as surmised by early critics and biographers.

But who was this complex woman? Often described as "striking," her copper hair pulled back tightly, her face "a classical mask, powerful, sibylline-unique."[18] Like her father, she was tall, large-boned, with prominent cheekbones: some said she was handsome or masculine looking, never pretty. Molly Keane, her writer friend, remarked that "she wasn't beautiful strictly speaking but she dressed as remarkably as any beauty dares to and with a careless distinction."[19] She cared about clothes, and when Bowen entered a room, "the atmosphere changed"; both men and women paid attention. She typically wore a dashing tweed suit, and sometimes a black hat with feathers, often white doeskin gloves, and heavy Renaissance style junk jewelry. Behind her impeccable style and reserve was a restless, adventurous, brilliant, and talented woman. She had the air, Keane said, of "an aristocratic Elizabethan adventurer" home from a sea voyage of discovery, particularly after finishing a novel. Many noted her youthful spirit and physical hardiness well into her later years, her capacity for the enjoyment of the everyday, and her derring-do.

She was attractive to men and women and her loves are presented here in the light of Michael Holroyd's 1967 expose of Bloomsbury sexual liaisons that represented a break in biography. These revelations, part of a sexual revolution, not only touched Bowen's life and biography but shaped the themes she and others wrote about in the modern novel. Ten years into her marriage, in 1933, Bowen became restless and unapologetically entered into a romantic affair with the literary critic, Humphrey House, the beginning of her separation from what Patricia Craig called a "companionate" marriage. Bored, she remarked to Ritchie in 1945 that her husband was like a character in a Chekhov play who "always repeats the same lines at his entrances and exits."[20] Her daily life, however, was enmeshed with his—their walks and talks—and she depended on his welcoming presence in their homes in Knights Lane, Northampton (1923–25); Old Headington, Oxford (1925–35); Regent's Park in London (1935–52); and, sometimes, Bowen's Court, Kildorrery (1952–54). As she developed various liaisons, she carefully balanced her roles as a woman, wife, intellectual, and writer. She expressed feelings of wifely duty in 1935 to Virginia Woolf after having to cancel a visit to Rodmell because of a conference she had to attend with Cameron. She ruefully noted that she was "so seldom a useful wife to Alan," and so stayed with him over the course of a week—"fearfully" wanting to visit Woolf, but feeling "it really would be rather mean of me to go away leaving him over-run with people that he had to be genial to."[21]

Many of her friends looked upon her marriage as a mystery. Peter Quennell, describing a visit to Cameron's quarters on the lower floor of Clarence Terrace, observed "a big dusky room, which contained pipe-racks, bags of golf clubs, a wooden shield bearing college arms and an old fashioned mahogany tantalus [a cabinet for spirits]." Around the room, he snidely noted, were numerous pictures of cats painted in the Victorian style. When Quennell admired them, Cameron led him from portrait to portrait, discussing their special qualities in a "deep and rasping purr." Quennell quoted Cameron: "A magnificent mouser he was! Now old Ginger over there, I've never known such pluck."[22] They had a drink from the tantalus; Eddy Sackville-West when asked about Cameron's drinking in later life, observed that "one hears the bottle and the glass soon after breakfast."[23] Then Cameron and Quennell went upstairs to Bowen's drawing room for literary conversation about Lehmann's or Woolf's or Murdoch's latest novels, a conversation, observed Quennell, in which Cameron felt somewhat uncomfortable. There were other friends of Bowen, however, who looked upon him as a proud and doting husband. Bowra described him as "an attentive host who had much interest in academic and intellectual matters, which he saw the more clearly because he was not attached to the University."[24]

Despite their separations and incompatibilities, Bowen was distraught and haunted by Cameron's death in 1952. She wrote to Isaiah Berlin that she could not stop weeping. She revealed how much her relationship mattered to her good friend, Leslie Hartley, "It seems so odd that this is the one experience I cannot talk over with him."[25] Theirs had been a marriage of 29 years, unconventional in the independence it afforded Bowen. Molly O'Brien, the housekeeper at Bowen's Court, clipped a romantic story, "Elizabeth and her Highland Scot," purportedly about Bowen and Cameron seen walking hand-in-hand across the private estate of Bowen's Court.[26] The story preserves a fictional Elizabeth, mistress of Bowen's Court, as an adoring newlywed with her Scots husband, seen through the admiring eyes of their Kildorrery neighbors and servants. But Bowen's life was nothing like this story. To Bowen, Cameron was not a romantic figure, rather the still point in her swirling personal and literary world. "Our emotions, even our senses, don't they seek something stable to cling to," wrote Bowen. "How can we not seek, in some form, an abiding city? We continue to cry out for the well known, the comfortable, the dear, for protecting walls round the soul."[27] Because of her itinerant life as a child, marriage and a home was a welcome respite from movement: she confided to Berlin that what she lost with Cameron's death was "the feeling of being located, fixed, and held by someone else not only in affection but in their sense of reality."[28] This is the emotional key, perhaps the rejoinder to queries as to why she never divorced Cameron. He was like her mother and father, she said, but brought closer to her by being a contemporary. Being an only child, no next of kin but 15 first cousins, Cameron was her attachment. She wrote to Sarton, "I feel him so constantly close to me in the house. The chief, sad thing is, not being able to talk. And without him, I feel so cold. I think no presence than his can have been warmer."[29] He also provided, a kind of assurance of "moral good" in the world, a sort of principle of "good sense." He was, she said, the one who read *The Times* every morning. Intriguingly, she described her *state* of grief, "almost like a state in the geographic sense, with a climate and landscape of its own."[30] Feeling is located in sensation. A year later, she wrote to Spender that it was a "lost-feeling year," and "the house of sensation is, as you'll know, so very capable of being haunted."[31] She confided a guilt, the unequal caring in the relationship that others observed; her own, caring "often so careless, so selfish."

Bowen would not brook any criticism of Cameron from friends. The maintenance of her marriage inspired a protective silence on her part, and she spoke of him only to a loyal few. She was open with Audrey Fiennes, her cousin who was a good friend to Cameron, and shared her thoughts with Sarton, Ritchie, Bayley, Plomer, and House. Sarton was one of her few friends who appreciated Cameron, but she incurred Bowen's ire when she fictionalized him and her as characters in her novel *A Shower of Summer Days* without seeking Bowen's permission. Charles is portrayed as a loving, supportive husband who takes pleasure in the management and care of the business of Dene's Court. He is tolerant of Violet's (Bowen's?) moods and focuses on the practical aspects of running the estate, while Violet represents "the tightly drawn web of forces and feelings" arising from the past.[32] Bowen's first known lover, Humphry House respected her marital relationship and wrote in 1933 that he did not want to "intrude" with Cameron, and surmised, there is "a whole area of your life in which he was what you wanted." But added, "in all of which I may have been hopelessly wrong."[33] Virginia Woolf, known for her barbed observations, softened criticism of Cameron, and wrote after a visit to Bowen's Court in 1934, "We spent a n[igh]t with the Bowens […] E was very nice, and her husband though stout and garrulous was better than rumour reported."[34] The whole trip was garrulous; "we never stopped talking. The Irish are the most gifted people in that line." Nevertheless, the negative view persisted and in 1936, Isaiah Berlin wrote to Marion Frankfurter that "Alan Cameron is daily becoming kinder and more intolerable."[35]

There is then speculation about why Bowen stayed with Cameron after she met the love of her life, Ritchie, the then-unmarried, talented, glamorous Canadian ambassador, in 1941. Did Ritchie propose marriage at this time? As her career thrived and her circle of literary friendships widened, she increasingly led her social and intellectual life apart from Cameron. An itinerant child, she had lived between two homes, two countries, and separated parents; as an adult, she lived between different kinds of love, hungry for romantic, erotic, and intellectual experience that sometimes intruded on other people's homes, yet clinging to a stable one of her own.

Few of Cameron's letters and remarks survive; he remains a silent partner with some pitying traces appearing in others' letters. Nevertheless, his accomplishments cannot be ignored: besides his distinguished military record, he made significant contributions to the new medium of educational film at the BBC in the senior position of secretary to the Central Council School of the School of Broadcasting, and, later, gramophone records at EMI, which became a legendary British label for major artists. At Cameron's retirement in 1952, Bowen praised these accomplishments as well as his earlier position as director of education in Oxford. Throughout Bowen's "vagaries," as she once termed them, he remained proud of her success as she spread her wings socially and professionally. Like Leonard Woolf, who recognized Virginia's genius, Cameron, in his fashion, enabled Bowen to experience life fully that contributed not only to her pleasures but to her development as an outstanding modern writer. Cameron was also her business manager, not only handling their day-to-day domestic business but managing both the Clarence Terrace apartment in Regent's Park and the maintenance of Bowen's Court (accounts, gardening, trees) from 1930 until his death. He also oversaw her book contracts, and correspondence in the Curtis Brown publishing files reveals that he specifically negotiated many of them.[36]

Mention of Cameron's infirmities began to surface in the early 1940s, when Bowen was passionately in love with Ritchie and writing her brilliant wartime novel, *The Heat of the Day*. She wrote Ritchie from Waldencote that she "must be seeing [Cameron] in, packing him up, cheering him up, etc." sounding very much the dutiful wife. In 1944, Bowen wrote to Sarton of Cameron's heart troubles, a concern that surfaced again in 1948. She reported that Cameron was going into the hospital "for treatment of his eye—the remains of war poisoning," a diminishing sight that forced his retirement from the BBC in 1947. In 1949, she wrote about Cameron returning from London, ill again, and in August 1951, he was treated for a case of "roaring diabetes." Cameron's ill health led to a heart attack in the spring of 1951. In 1952, under some financial stress, they decided to sell their apartment in London and move to Bowen's Court. In the last year of her husband's life, she wrote to Ritchie, "One can know somebody is dying, and yet frantically hold out against the truth, like holding a position in a war." She created a poignant sketch of Cameron: "He's in a very sweet and touching, in an uncontentious mood, wanders about the place in a sort of dream. Deprived of his cat, he is now falling in love with trees, the trees here. A most curious development."[37] She acknowledged that Cameron suffered in his life, not only from ill health but from the sacrifices he had made in his life with her. He "wrung my heart by saying suddenly, 'Do you realize these have been the happiest months of my life.'" In 1962 when Ritchie was appointed Canadian ambassador to the United Nations, she wrote, oddly, that this would have pleased Cameron. Even as she wrote of his death, she recalled his generosity of spirit, speculating that he would have been proud of her lover's accomplishments.

Remarks on Love

We find women in love in Bowen's stories but they are not in ecstatic states of body and spirit as in D.H. Lawrence, but engaged in a more nuanced intellectual and emotional intertwining. Sexuality flashes in her writing but it is largely left to the imagination of the reader. When Karen and Max in *The House in Paris* meet in Boulogne for a romantic rendezvous having long been attracted to one another, they discuss their "unwilling love" and the shadowy presence of Naomi, Max's fiancée and Karen's friend. Karen in exasperation arrests the conversation: "'Why must I listen to all this when you never say you love me?' Max's eyes fell from her eyes to her breast."[38] Max, a man of experience with women, confesses that he likes to see his way to his pleasures. They climb the stairs up to a parapet and their encounter is described with restraint and silences marked by an ellipsis:

The leaves behind their heads and the leaves under them kept shifting in the uncertain air that drew out the flags. An incoming tide of apartness began to creep between Max and Karen, till, moving like someone under the influence of a pursuing dream, he drew the cigarette from between her fingers and threw it over onto the boulevard. Moving up the parapet, he kissed her, and with his fingers began to explore her hand. Their movements, cautious because of the drop below, were underlined by long pauses. They were hypnotized by each other, the height, the leaves … Later they began hearing voices on the steps.

Each is conscious of his or her betrayal, but they abandon restraint. A week later, they met in Hythe and spent the day in a hotel. "Rain made the day dark for day, but till late the light did not change. Saturday stayed late, reflected on wet roofs […] At nine they went out."

In a letter about the explicit description of sex in the modern novel, John Bayley wrote Bowen that, "By stating sex, as now, they make it impossible for the reader to imagine it."[39] He asked, "Doesn't the novel work at getting behind things? It seems to be that form is absolutely tied, historically, to concealment of what can't be imagined." Bayley noted that Dickens is full of sex and so is Bowen, "but it is free, that is to say, imagined." He concluded that the modern novelist "who is always in bed fills me with gloom and is offensive." He did though have a particular view of sex revealed in an interview after the death of his wife, Iris Murdoch, acknowledging that he did not have much erotic feeling, and that passion played no part in his relationship with her. Bayley went on to compliment Bowen's contribution to the modern novel: inventing new "conventions for concealment" for sex and other issues. Sex is dangerous and restrained in expression in her novels unlike her life; in her letters, she openly displays its pleasures and disappointments. Her correspondence refracts what she termed "a woman's checked and puzzled life to which intelligence only gives further distorted pattern." A woman of intelligence and talent, she had difficulty finding a man who would offer what she needed. George Eliot perhaps best represents the dilemma in *Middlemarch*. Lydgate is torn between two women: the beautiful, materialistic Rosamond Vincy and the independent, intelligent, and plain-looking Dorothea Brooke. He chooses Rosamond for a wife, revealing how Dorothea is "checked" by an unconventional mind and interests that make her "unmarriageable." Bowen was unconventional, brilliant, and often "formidable" to others in her psychological acuity as well as her talent. Nevertheless, her experiences electrify the intelligent women in love in her novels.

Ten years into her marriage, Bowen sought an affair: it was rumored that her marriage was sexually unconsummated. She began her first known relationship in 1933 with Humphry House, drawn to his literary sensibility, character, and strong masculinity. House was at Wadham College, an Oxford fellow training to be a chaplain, and on the eve of his marriage to Madeline Church, Bowen still referred to the persistent strain of "the priest in him."[40] Bowen was involved with House for three years, from the spring of 1933 until the spring of 1936. When this affair ended, she turned to Goronwy Rees. An affair then followed with Sean O'Faolain, from the summer of 1937 to 1939 describing it to House, "It doesn't feel like a love affair, it feels like a marriage."[41] During this same period, she had an intermittent intimate relationship with May Sarton, a young American poet living in Boston, as well as unidentified relationships with other women at various times in her life. And in a troubled period after the death of her husband, and her waning relationship with Ritchie, around 1955–56, Bowen formed a close, nonsexual friendship with the aristocratic Eddie Sackville-West. But the passion of her life was the talented and cosmopolitan Ritchie, whom she met during the war when she was 42, a relationship that began in 1941 and continued until her death in 1973.

"Even when one is no longer attached to things, it's still something to have been attached to them," says Proust's Marcel, "because it was always for reasons which other people didn't grasp."[42] Bowen's friends did not always grasp the emotional, intellectual, and sensual reasons for Bowen's "attachments" or her marriage, but her correspondence reveals an attraction to men who offered not only heightened conversation but also a passion that, at times, borders on obsession, and that one might not detect from reading her novels. It also reveals, as Proust notes, that in life, if not in fiction, time and habit erode the intensity of those relationships. Poised, as always, Bowen fit her lovers into her life between writing hours and dinner parties. These relationships were the foundation for "pleasure," an oft-repeated word in her letters, and many of her stories open "like sort of a vitrine" the views of proud, intelligent women who discover that "love outside marriage is homeless."[43] She writes of both the pleasures and the disillusionments of romance. Similarly, Ritchie writes of the complexities of his relationships with women, of the link between his love for a woman—presumably his wife, Sylvia—and "a need to betray that love; a compulsion which I dread and desire" because of the "interminable dialogue" of marriage.[44]

Bowen was usually engaged with brilliant men. Her novelist friend Margaret Kennedy would deprecate her engagements with her male visitors in her Clarence Terrace apartment, terming it Bowen's "temple of the Muses," strewn with "frivolous followers."[45] But her visitors were anything but; rather, they were men "who cut ice," intellectually astute and a bit "savage." She viewed them with detachment and irony, as she did most of the romantic relationships in her life, except for her overwhelming relationship with Ritchie.

For Cameron, "the black hats" in their racks in the Clarence Terrace hallway signaled the presence not only of Bowen's admirers but also of her friends David Cecil, Plomer, and Berlin, as well as such luminaries as T. S. Eliot. Margaret Kennedy said the Camerons were not invited as a couple to social events, perhaps owing to the loudness of Alan's voice. He, then working for the BBC in London, was himself aware that his voice had unusual power and told Kennedy that though "standing two feet farther away than anyone else, he had already broken three microphones."[46] Though generally not invited, Cameron did sometimes join Isaiah Berlin and Cecil, remarking that he liked them as they were "not silly."

Loyal to Cameron in her fashion, Bowen paid lip service to a code of behavior informed by the propriety and manners of the Anglo-Irish. Yet she loved other men and their company, loves that Molly Keane observed were "necessary." Ritchie wrote in his journal that she acknowledged her personal doubleness when discussing *The Death of the Heart* with him in 1941. He surmised that she saw the two women in the novel, the adolescent Portia and Thomas' wife Anna, as two parts of herself: Portia is the hidden Bowen, the vulnerable adolescent who has the "naïveté of childhood or genius," and Anna, the more ruthless adult self that emerged in her affairs. Sixteen-year-old Portia innocently falls for Eddie, the carefree cad, and believes his expressions of love; Anna, the wife of her stepbrother, is also flirtatiously involved with him and designs a treacherous plot with him against Portia.

Bowen cannily tried to maintain a sense of propriety about her conduct, keeping her relationships in separate compartments. Borders, however, were porous. When her husband entered a room where she was writing to House, she scribbled, "Alan has come up to a conference party and is wandering round the room, so I can't write any more."[47] While writing to Ritchie and looking glowingly at a bouquet of yellow flowers he had sent, she summarily interrupted the letter to say she must take a walk with Cameron. She maintained daily life with him while riding the waves of other romances.

"Poor Incompetent Angel": Humphrey House

In Bowen's early affair with Humphry House, critic and scholar, she became his mentor as well as his lover. She had insight into human character and House—like Goronwy Rees, May Sarton, Sean O'Faolain, and Charles Ritchie who would follow as lovers—knew he was dealing with an unusual, brilliant, sensuous, and talented woman who would make her needs known. What emerged were other "I's" in her flickering self—the naïve Elizabeth new to affairs and the more ruthless Elizabeth who pursued what she wanted. The affair began in spring 1933, about ten years after a marriage that did not satisfy her sensually, leaving her open to experience, and about nine months before House's marriage to Madeline Church on December 21, 1933. It effectively ended when he left for India with his wife and child in June 1936. The letters between them offer a glimpse of her underside, she, ruefully admitting to House that to be "a so-called clever woman is to be acting blindly and drunkenly under a crust of myself all the time."[48] "I am," she continued, "partly a clever woman, but also very much more and very much less." The careful reader of Bowen discovers glimpses of the same beneath seemingly conventional women characters.

When Bowen and House met, he was 24, a budding scholar, moody and gauche. The first in his family to attend college, he had achieved a first at Oxford in *literae humaniores*, the classics, and a second in modern history in 1929.[49] It was a year after he had resigned as fellow and deacon of Wadham, lacking the theological conviction, he said, to take priestly orders. The integrity of this decision would cost him the security of employment his whole life. He had an unstable career, chasing after different academic jobs, according to his son, the late art historian John House, until at the end of his life he returned, in full dignity, as a senior research fellow to Wadham. But when they met, Bowen was ten years older, a confident and accomplished writer having published four novels and three collections of stories; he was at loose ends, uncertain of his future profession, and inexperienced in the ways of conducting an affair, particularly, as she noted, to the standards of one of the leading women writers in England. And though she spoke with more bravado than he, she too was learning about relationships outside marriage. Nevertheless, he was avid for sexual experience and his literary interests were firmly rooted: these passions drew them together. They would read passages from the *Aeneid* together, quote Spender's poetry, and talk about literature, particularly Jane Austen and Charles Dickens. House enhanced Bowen's literary background, as had Cecil and Connolly at Oxford. She acknowledged in one letter his assistance with an Austen essay, saying that she had "a very untrained mind."[50]

Bowen set the moral, aesthetic, and sensuous bar for the relationship with the repeated refrain, "if you cannot [...] then you and I have no future." This led to House's complaint that she was 'overbearing,' an accusation from other men—O'Faolain and Ritchie—who would follow. The conditions behind the threat were: the artist will have her way; intellectual conversation is important; her house and home with Cameron are to be respected; marriage is to be set apart and not mixed into their affair; wives and their demands do not figure; and she is not to be bullied. This high tone, however, vacillated between vulnerability and desire and was accompanied by the fear that House might drop her. She reminded him of the value of her intellectual companionship as well as their sexual compatibility, warning that the loss of her might leave him stranded and unfulfilled in his marriage: "If you did let me go and if your home life and your marriage ever ceased to satisfy the whole of your nature, then you would have nothing to fall back on but petty muddles and lusts."[51] Despite the conditions, Bowen conceded to House's "greatness," a compliment she awarded liberally to all her lovers. It augurs her early ambitions for this relationship and the way that she would shape an "artistic couple" of her imagining. But she also told House he had far to go, as he was often in "a state of worried and humiliated adolescence."[52] Their first meeting was romantic. He invited her to a luncheon in Appleton, near Abingdon, where he was living. He jotted first impressions in a journal that he sent to her noting she talked too much yet let her know of "his awful need" and his awareness of her as a woman.[53] Just as House felt the spark of her womanliness, she felt the force of his masculinity. She wrote a corollary letter a month later, remembering standing under the same palm tree and becoming aware of the "man" in him.[54] Their romance, however, was riven by an early crisis. House related in a cryptic letter, his dismay at her reticence and "gloom" at breakfast after their first intimate encounter. He observed her discomfort and alluded to his puzzlement about her remark about virginity.

Nevertheless, the discomfort was not explained, and she received his letter after their encounter, passionate and weeping, moved by her experience with him (and her loss of virginity?). She wrote to him that she wandered about the room with an unlit cigarette, looking for lost ashtrays, and confessed to "a curious thump of the heart, one of those conventions which we so seldom have," when reading his letter.[55] Elizabeth Bowen, in love. House, however, aware of his inexperience, alluded in one of his early letters to Stendhal's comment that a young man's first mistress is usually above him in personal power, almost eliminating his own self. The relationship between House and Bowen was based, as House says, on complementary qualities of mind, a relationship, according to Bowen, that "with care and an eye on the emotional clock" should continue. After this experience with Bowen, House wrote that a young man often turns to a woman who is shy and domestic.

He was preparing to marry Madeline Church, a shy and intelligent woman with whom he had been having an affair. It was also an intense period in his relationship with Bowen, and he was conflicted: he felt married to Madeline, held by his past relationship, but at the same time, "terribly bound up" with Bowen and Bowen's Court, at least in 1933. In a letter written to Bowen the day before his wedding, House insisted that their relationship would not change as they were complementary and belonged to "one another's truth."[56] She strove for "honesty," a word she used in defining all her relationships, but she also had the impulse to withhold information. She hated explanations and situations that were overanalyzed—scenes, crises, and melodrama— though she sometimes provoked House's outbursts and then unfairly criticized them as "adolescent." His letters, often written during crises in their relationship, were melodramatic or self-pitying, according to Bowen, and at other times quite cogent, perceptive, and up to her romantic mark of irony and detachment. Her 11 known letters to House written between 1934 and 1937 are frank and long, from four to ten pages, and enumerate his misinterpretations of her behavior or her analyses of his "adolescent" actions.[57] House's jejune qualities surfaced during a Bowen's Court visit from Berlin who arrived with Mary Fisher, daughter of H. A. L. Fisher, Warden of New College, and Marie Lynd, who lived with the Fishers. During their stay, House followed Lynd around, to Berlin's dismay, "like a huge, lovelorn dog," and claimed to have fallen "in love, deeply, irrevocably," somehow spellbound.[58]

On another of House's visits to Bowen's Court, in August 1934, after his marriage, Bowen angrily wrote to Plomer about House being called home to Madeline because of her state of health, pregnancy. Her barely repressed animosity toward Madeline led to her petulant assertion that she had rarely spent any time with him that year. Egotistical and high-handed toward the wives of her lovers, she later insisted to House that she had behaved with self-restraint upon that occasion. Bowen wrote scathingly to Plomer that she had sent off a telegram to him "in that queer little claustrophobic house of theirs. It's really rather touching, that little anxious bland woman and those little [plain?]

blond babies, and the little husky blond nurse—something between a doll's house and a rabbit hutch […] poor incompetent angel." The last phrase linked to House.[59] Upon House's marriage, Berlin wrote to Bowen that he would hear from House shortly "as he is to marry Madeline C. at Exeter on Thursday next. I had better not have anticipated his news, so please do not know till he tells you. We must just make the best of this. There is still a strain—to me at least—of the priest in him; one cannot combat the exaltation of someone doing what they think right."[60] Berlin countered Bowen's impressions when he met Madeline in the summer of 1934, a year after the marriage, writing that she was livelier and more secure, almost a mother; House, on the other hand, he observed was reduced and rather gloomy.

The sensuous imagination and the pleasures of the body and mind are exalted in these letters, privately countering the popular perception of Bowen as a woman of reserve. The same intemperance and passion that underlies the characters of Emmeline in *To the North*, Karen in *The House in Paris*, and Eva in *Eva Trout*. She often reminded House "what an immense power of pleasure, on all planes, in all ways, I have, and this pleasure is to a certain extent self-generated."[61] If Bowen had a gift to convey, this was it. Many of her friends remarked on her sense of enjoyment and how much she glowed with physical health and youthful energy.

Their relationship had weathered various difficulties by the time House decided to go to India. Though the letters start out romantically, differences in House's and Bowen's temperaments emerge. Being social was important to Bowen, and she wrote to Ritchie in 1948, "more and more do I think fully developed social instinct is one of the most attractive and even virtuous things in life."[62] House did not have this instinct, possessing a more somber, introspective, scholarly temperament—that she criticized as gloomy. He enjoyed being alone, telling Bowen that he was social only when invited out. Bowen, on the other hand, was a *salonière*, often inviting intellectuals and writers to Clarence Terrace and Bowen's Court, having been brought up to find great pleasure in conversation, dinners, and parties. She was good at being a hostess; House, at times, found her social "talk" and manner insincere. He recoiled from Bowen's "spontaneity" and her being "indiscriminately demonstrative." He criticized her "diplomatic manners, your enthusiasm and excitement in social situations [that] was alien to me; but I often felt it hard to see the difference between the tone and style of your social enthusiasm and your demonstrativeness with me. I knew well enough the feeling was different, but the style sometimes wasn't." House implied that she was false, a performer; Bowen admitted to "performance" and play-acting, and was expert at playing the role of "hostess." Offended by her style, he proposed that she had a social persona that corrupted their relationship. In a 1936 letter to him, she highlighted their differences, noting his lack of spontaneity and a social nature. But he was changing and becoming more self-confident vis-à-vis Bowen. He wrote defiantly later that month that he had rented a new house, northeast of Exeter, and asserted, yes, he was asocial and would lead a life that was authentically his own. His differences with Bowen were not only temperamental but also cultural and stylistic, given his unease with her tone and manner—what O'Faolain's wife would term her tendency to become "La Bowen."

Bowen articulated what she perceived as important in their relationship: "the life that we have in common is sensuous rather than intellectual life: intellect necessarily enters into our dealing with one another as we are both intellectual beings, but as friends go our purely intellectual interests and preoccupations are unusually far apart."[63] This was rather disingenuous given their shared interest in literature and writing. She continued, "if you cut away our sensuous feeling for one another there would be nothing left."

As time passed, House grew distant from Bowen, and his relationship with Madeline grew in companionable and scholarly closeness. Arthur Calder-Marshall, House's best friend and confidante, whom he met at Oxford, wrote to Bowen after a visit to Madeline when Humphry was in the hospital: "I think you are wrong about her. Away from Humphry, she is as much better than her married self as Humphry is away from her."[64] Following House's early death, Rupert Hart-Davis, House's publisher, praised Madeline's quiet virtues, which had suited House's temperament and literary work. After 22 years of marriage, House died from thrombosis at the age of 47, in Cambridge on February 14, 1955. Madeline was left with £200 a year and three children: Rachel, 21; Helen, 19; and John, 10. She had a difficult time but got a degree from Royal Holloway College in English, and proceeded to edit House's literary works. House had found affection and companionship in politics and literary scholarship, as well as relief from Bowen's restless demands in Madeline's calmer temperament.

He was a productive scholar who published the much-praised *Notebooks and Papers of G.M. Hopkins* in 1937 and *The Dickens World* in 1941, an important book on the historical and social background of Dickens' novels. He also began to collect and annotate Dickens' letters and novels. After his death, Madeline took over these projects, including the legendary critical annotations of Dickens' letters as well as the organization of House's papers. She removed some of Bowen's letters. Madeline saw through to publication the revised edition of *G.M. Hopkins*, completed by Graham Storey. She was also, impressively, one of the general editors, with Storey, of the Pilgrim edition of *The Letters of Charles Dickens* (in ten volumes, published from 1965 to 2002). John

House, their son, spoke sympathetically of his mother and the initial difficulties she must have had in "keeping up" with his father and his intellectual life and circle. She was an omnivorous reader, he said, and might often be seen coming down Culverly Road in Catford with a book propped up on the handlebars of her bicycle, reading while riding down the street. In addition to their literary companionship, which grew over the years, John said that Humphry and Madeline shared a strong socialist bond, certainly not shared with Bowen.[65]

In a recent obituary of John House, his father, Humphry, was described as talented but "austere." Some have said his presence was "forbidding." According to the writer George Steiner, "merriment … was not [Humphry's] strong suit." Steiner rather attested to his "sombre integrity" and "volcanic self-discipline," given his thorough and voluminous work on Hopkins and Dickens.[66] Bowra, once his colleague at Wadham, sketched another House, relating his enjoyment of his "sudden thirsts for blood" in argument and his genial way of telling his colleagues that they were no good.[67] These qualities of the scholar—integrity, hard work, and a disciplined nature—were combined with "moral" preoccupations about his relations with Bowen and Madeline. The words "exacting" and "pleasure" surface many times in their correspondence, forming the emotional poles of their relationship. Bowen was not shy in "exacting" certain kinds of behavior, in attacking his gloominess, suspiciousness, melodrama, lack of spontaneity, and reliance on other people, especially women, to bolster him. She was not jealous, and even taunted House, suggesting that he might find "another and better Elizabeth." Three years into their relationship, she encouraged him to see an unnamed woman, "B," and stated that his desire to see and enjoy her was "natural."

In May 1935 she wrote to House that she was revising *The House in Paris* in three weeks. Her discipline in writing never wavered as she juggled her married life with Cameron, moving from Oxford to London, and her affair with House. She announced to House, "it is hard for me (being a writer before I am a woman) to realize that anything—friendship or love especially—in which I participate imaginatively isn't a book too."[68] Accustomed to controlling the plot, she wrote *The House in Paris* as well as the life of an aesthetic couple at the same time. In the cracked mirror of her fiction, there are shards of her complex relationship with House. In the novel, Karen has a rendezvous with Max, her best friend's fiancé, in Boulogne. Both are in flight, as were Bowen and House, from a silent but present third who shadowed their experience, Madeline. The dreamlike passion of Max and Karen is poetically described, and Max's fiancée, Naomi, is silent in the background, "like furniture in the dark."[69] She is a comfortable and reassuring figure, like Madeline, who was already House's fiancée when Bowen and House's affair began. She, like the character, Naomi, is silent in the background and represents the calm and quiet that House would seek in marriage to her. Meanwhile, Max and Karen follow their desires and compelling passion. "Nobody speaks the truth when there's something they must have"—returns us to Bowen's bold expressions of desire in her letters to House.[70] In "Love Story," her character Frank asserts the same, "In love, there is no right or wrong, only the wish."[71] Bowen was grasping and made demeaning remarks about Madeline, asserting her own rights, ignoring House's upcoming marriage, and writing letters of passion. She related to House her dislike for the "woman" in herself, reflected in her quality of trying to grasp or hold onto a man. It is the same quality that Markie, the cold lover in *To the North*, detests in Emmeline. Bowen wrote, "What I said in *To the North* about that prehensile quality Markie detested in a woman, I put into him—as in other parts of the book—a good deal of dislike I feel for the woman in me."[72] Bowen put the "prehensile" quality into Emmeline that she exhibited in her relationship with House: both knew how to get their way yet Bowen, ambivalent, eschewed this "female" quality.

Though Bowen had always acknowledged that she had a good home with Cameron, she noted "my spirit stays homeless. So I am still alive." And "what seems sudden and most deprived about love outside marriage," she said, "is really its great strength, it has no home."[73] In letters, we hear of Bowen and House's meetings, sometimes at Bowen's Court, searching for "love without a home" as the lovers in her novel and the story "The Mysterious Kôr." Being homeless was independence. Throughout her life, the search for lovers and places to be with them, like the lovers adrift in her stories, signaled the liberating transiency of romantic relationships.

When House announced that he was going to India, Bowen was taken aback. She wrote to Plomer about having a row with House upon his departure and feeling sorry that he left under a cloud. House had some awful times in Calcutta, according to Bowen, given his bouts with flu and dysentery and a "persecuted time" when the Indian police opened his letters. He sided with the nationalists against the British colonialists, as his son, John House, reported—an unconventional position for an expatriate Englishman in India. House's anti-colonial position was of a piece with his commitment to socialism, his identification with Dickens' social reforms, and his support of the Labor Party, whose culture Bowen reviled, along with "LSE [London School of Economics] cuties."[74] Curiously, in the same letter, Bowen contradicted her usual politics and announced an odd temporary side effect of her relationship with House: "it has made a Communist of me." She began to question her conservative political views. After a discussion with House about Fascism and the authoritarianism of the dictator who makes the state his god, she began to distrust the values in her own life that Fascism defended: Fascism's "armed defense of the 'Mind'; a sense of the ego feeding on materially owned things, national or domestic; and "the terrific propaganda for the home and the family" that was touted. Bowen puzzled how hard it was to explain the realization that possessiveness corrupts people and relationships, and how this connected with House in her mind. And yet, she felt it did. She admitted to House about a year and a half into their relationship that she "had no idea that a political principle could have such deep psychological roots." Her questioning, however, did not last.

The Performing Self: Bowen the Artist

During her years with House, Bowen reminded him of her other persona, the writer: "Remember that you had Elizabeth Bowen to contend with—I mean, a confirmed writer. Someone accustomed to getting herself, or himself without outside opposition."[75] Bowen purposely used the pronoun, "himself," to underline traditionally "male," so-called aggressive qualities. She reminded him that she was domineering and had evolved into an independent woman who challenged traditional gender categories and clichés. Indeed, House, and later O'Faolain, mentioned her overbearing personality: its no-nonsense "mannishness" was sometimes attractive, but at other times, both men were taken aback by her high-handed attitude, as she pulled rank because of her age, personality, or stature as a writer. After all, she was a woman. "You must not mistake an artist's impatience to wish for everybody to live at the full height for an ordinary (and better) with a woman's caring love … I am not capable, and perhaps never may be, of a feeling like that. I am dishonest too, and play act more than you know—or I know myself."[76] She knew that she had strong opinions and presence, and did not play with "feminine" wiles or ways. Such notions of a new "feminine" inspired Bowen's character Marda Norton in *The Last September*, a strong-minded, independent-spirited woman whose manners annoy her host, Mrs. Naylor. Yet Marda inspires admiration in the young girl Lois, and reveals her toughness in concealing a wound after an encounter with an IRA "stranger" on a walk with Lois.

Bowen also revealed to House her struggles as a writer: "(The whole struggle, where work goes, for clear thought and absolute feeling is inside oneself—the writer.) One spends one's time objectifying one's inner life, and projecting one's thought and emotions into a form—a book." Once the inside difficulties are overcome, she announced, there "is the exercise of an unchecked power."[77] She asserted that being a writer was not as irrelevant as it might seem in their relationship, as she blurred distinctions between House and her fictional shaping of him. "If you cannot emerge imaginatively from your daily life enough to meet me imaginatively and to keep up this imaginative communication between us, then you and I have no future." The vocabulary is aesthetic, and the shaping of romance by taste and imagination, includes a warning that he must be free from ordinariness.

This led to the puzzles in Bowen's life. She encouraged House to keep his marriage separate from their relationship but when he chose not inform her of his marriage to Madeline that occurred while she was lecturing in New York, she was angry. The news was broken to her gently by Berlin in a letter. Later, when House failed to inform her of his wife's pregnancy, in October 1934, the shock brought into view Bowen's vulnerability and rarely expressed desire to have a child. When House's daughter, Rachel, was nine months old, Bowen charged that he had underrated how hard she was hit by the news of Madeline's pregnancy. She confessed, "you know the whole area is painful when I myself wanted a child so much," echoing Marda's sentiment as she approaches marriage in *The Last September*: "I should hate to be barren."[78] House aggressively responded to Bowen's angry letter when accused of lacking "simplicity" in not relating the information; he asserted that all contraceptive arrangements were up to Madeline, and railed, "should I have reported my bed life." He rejected her implication that he resented the child, and defended himself in admitting he had not told her because he knew she would be hurt. It was a raw moment of exposure of Bowen's pain about being childless, though according to the critic, Deirdre Toomey, this was a choice. Bowen, according to Toomey, told Iris Murdoch that she and her husband decided not to have children because of her dedication to writing, and Cameron's "horror of the modern world." It was a decision, Toomey reports, that according to Murdoch, they came to regret.[79] An additional factor is that Bowen, unlike most young, upper-class Anglo-Irish women of the time, had not been socialized into marriage and having children. She was taught that there were other the options for women in the early twentieth century by the headmistress of the Downe House School who encouraged women's self-reliance and achievement. Bowen recalled, "we were never addressed as future mothers." Ann Ridler, who wrote a history of the school, reports that when a survey of graduates was taken in 1922, about five years after Bowen's graduation, about 16 percent of the women had careers other than marriage, more than the graduates from other girls' boarding schools.[80]

When Bowen began her career as a writer early in her twenties, she rarely mentioned children, although her novelist friends Rosamond Lehmann and Margaret Kennedy would often describe their domestic juggling acts in letters as they tried to write and mother, particularly during the war. Books became Bowen's progeny and she gave birth to many imagined children—particularly lonely, sometimes mad or angry girls—and also explored the state of innocence as critic, Nicola Darwood, and readers have noted. She conjured children and adolescents from Portia in *The Death of the Heart* to Henrietta and Leopold in *The House in Paris* to Theodora in *Friends and Relations* and the schoolgirls in *The Little Girls* as well as the many children in her short stories.

These letters unmask a sexually passionate aspect of Bowen, the woman: though she asserted the conditions of the relationship, the letters, nevertheless, reveal that she was not always in control of the ground rules. Bowen was older, more socially experienced, and an established writer when she met House, but she was also sexually inexperienced and enthralled by the pleasures of a liaison with a younger man. House too enjoyed giving and taking pleasure, but aware of Bowen the author, he shyly thanked her early in their relationship for her "immense letters" that made him feel, at moments, "unequal." Later in the relationship, he criticized her demanding ways, mannered style, and a demonstrativeness that was temperamentally uncomfortable for him while forging a closer relationship with Madeline. After House left for India, Bowen's independent spirit roamed. Her roving eye turned toward Goronwy Rees.

Goronwy Rees, a Mercurial Welshman

Bowen met Rees in 1931. He was a writer, an editor at the *Spectator*, a Marxist, and briefly part of the network of Soviet agents in Britain that included Guy Burgess, Donald McLean, Anthony Blunt and others that he disengaged from after the Nazi-Soviet pact of 1939. Bowen was fascinated by him for a time, and he became one of her close friends. When invited to Bowen's Court in September 1936 with Isaiah Berlin, Stuart Hampshire, and the beautiful Rosamond Lehmann, among others, handsome Rees brought trouble. Bowen was attracted to him, a Welshman, a member of an electric and dubious "race" that always held a fascination for her. Not only did she share a streak of Welsh heritage but acknowledged that quite a few of the men in her books were "slightly Welsh." They possessed an edge, a wildness, a darkness like Markie in *To the North*.[81] Rees did also.

Desire trumped decorum on this infamous weekend at Bowen's Court in September 1936. After the weekend, Bowen was informed of an erotic encounter in an upstairs bedroom between beautiful Rosamond Lehmann and handsome Rees. Though Bowen's Court was sometimes a place where Bowen invited lovers, she would not brook others using it as a love nest, particularly when one of the lovers was her current flirtation. The house had an "aestheticized reality" for Bowen, a "rightness" about the manners of those living in it or visiting, a code of behavior dictated by the character of the house.[82] But it was destined to be invaded by modernity's manners and morals. It turned into a lot of "Bloomsbury nonsense," according to Isaiah Berlin, who afterwards was regarded as a disinterested observer and, therefore, the recipient of everyone's "ludicrous persecutions."[83] On the evening of the Rees and Lehmann encounter, Stuart Hampshire observed that Bowen was in a nervous state, smoking cigarette after cigarette. Goronwy Rees arrived, he said, like a toreador in *Carmen*. Lehmann sat in the drawing room, "her head carried with an adventurous tilt [...] and the eyes with their prevalent expression of attentive amazement."[84] Hampshire, gazing with admiration at Lehmann, observed Bowen watching Rees and surmised that she was in love with him, while Rees was gazing at Lehmann, "tall [and] statuesque, with almond shaped eyes, and a warm impulsive manner."[85] Rees flirted openly and attracted everyone's attention, and most of the guests, Hampshire said, left "the sinking ship."[86] Berlin looked back at the "enchanted atmosphere," borrowing Rees' description of them "sitting in timeless Toulouse-Lautrec postures," and noted "Alan's popping blue eyes and Elizabeth curiously on edge" with embarrassment.[87] Bowen's feelings of rage, no longer "withheld," arose when she later learned the details of the liaison from her niece, Noreen, who heard the encounter from her top-floor bedroom. Bowen initially denied being hurt: the amorous tryst has "nothing to do with me," she wrote to Berlin. It is an offense, she wrote, to the "dignity" of the house, as well an "insult" to her niece. In her letters to Berlin and some to Bowra, Bowen was hard on Lehmann—their relationship was interrupted for over a decade—but less so on Rees. Even after learning all that had happened, she confessed that she "had the solicitude and affection for him [Rees] that Maurice heard in my voice."[88] In addition, she wrote to Berlin on October 6 that she had received a series of affectionate letters from Rees. Bowen's initial ignorance of the situation revealed her habit of "not noticing" (a pose or sometimes claiming it was her nearsightedness for which she did not wear glasses), her notion of propriety in the Anglo-Irish house, her capacity to deny, her belief in discreet erotic arrangements, and, to some degree, her emotional innocence. The next day Lehmann left, but Noreen reported to Berlin: "I heard something I shouldn't have heard about Miss Lehmann and Mr Rees. Should I tell my aunt?" Berlin responded, "Certainly not, certainly not. Not a word, oh no."[89]

In a subsequent letter, Bowen surprisingly reported to Berlin that after Lehmann left, Rees "demonstrated towards me an affection which I believe in a curious way he really does feel; just as I feel a great affection for him."[90] Libidinous still? Things went on as usual for a week, but on the following Saturday, she and Rees had another midnight harangue that erupted into "the most awful nerve-storm, [he] wept, screamed, threw himself about the room said that I had an unholy power over him, that my point of view of things was killing him or sending him mad." Later, according to Glendinning, Bowen told Rees that her father had gone mad in Bowen's Court and maybe he would too if he stayed there with her. Rees conceded and Bowen acknowledged in the same letter that the house had become "a beautiful shell of horror." Then with characteristic understatement, she related to Berlin that after the stormy incident, "the day being Saturday, we all went out to tea."

Bowen carefully maintained her veneer and silences and introduced herself in professional circles as "Mrs. Cameron." The Roman ideal of virtue begins, she asserted, in the private space of the home—serenity, balance, wisdom, patience—and ripples outward to society. Her characters Julian and Celia get married in *To the North* to "maintain it," this integrity, but there were rifts in Bowen's own *virtu* and *domus*. Lehmann wrote in Bowen's obituary that there was embedded in her the social tradition and standards of an "Anglo-Irish gentlewoman" and warned, "woe betide" anyone who ignored this.[91] This feeling of betrayal in female friendship resurfaces in Bowen's writing in Naomi Fisher's wounded feelings when Karen, as romantically adventurous as Lehmann, runs off for a sexual escapade with her friend's fiancée, Max in *The House in Paris*. And in *Friends and Relations*, one man falls in love with two sisters, complicating their lives. Lehmann herself picked up the antagonism and jealousy between two sisters in love with the same man in *The Echoing Grove*, a novel reviewed by Bowen. In her later relationships with married men, Bowen would again try to contain her feelings of jealousy and anger; nevertheless, she once wrote to Ritchie that her lack of resignation "took such complex forms: I never know at what moment it isn't going to leap on me like a tiger."[92] This tiger arose after the infamous weekend.

She wrote to Berlin about her notion of privacy and resented the universal interest in others' affairs. "If any of my preoccupations with anyone had become as apparent I should be frenzied. But then I should always put up a defensive propaganda of running any object of my affection down, and eliminating by acid any threatening sympathy. Which to the subtle observer might make everything more obvious, but observers are not subtle, I always find."[93] When Francis King interviewed Bowen, she told him that any connection between her stories and her romantic experiences would be "damagingly public to explore."[94] Here Bowen revealed the elaborate damage control she would set in motion to protect herself from gossip or rumor by "running down the object of her affection" to throw people off the trail.

The Lehmann-Rees romance wounded Bowen, though earlier biographers, Glendinning and Craig, as well as Lehmann's biographer Selina Hastings, downplay the importance of this affair. Friends pointed out that Bowen had her revenge in fiction, imaginatively endowing the character of the cad, Eddie—who flirted with Daphne in *The Death of the Heart* published two years after the notorious weekend—with traces of Rees. Though hardly identifiable, Rees subsequently wrote to Berlin that he wanted to sue Bowen for libel, though all had been transformed into fiction.

She may have tried to displace the "insult" to herself onto Bowen's Court, but temperamentally, as Rees observed, she was churning with violent emotions. He wrote to Berlin after the weekend, "she frightens me as I've never been frightened by anyone before."[95] Ritchie also experienced her potent character, alluding to his case of "possession," she, "a witch who had put a spell" on him.[96] Rees said that she enjoyed none of the peace she had created at Bowen's Court, and the Lehmann incident unleashed a tumultuous aspect of her personality—a rage—that critics and biographers have failed to register. In a letter to Berlin, Rees foregrounded her "strange welter of desires and emotions" to which he was subject during that eventful week.[97] Her friend L.P. Hartley detected the same, mentioning Bowen's gift for conferring tranquility on others' minds, but wondering if she benefitted from it herself. This turbulence of spirit is unleashed in her fiction in Emmeline's murderous crash in *To the North*, Max's ghastly suicide by hanging in *The House in Paris*, and Eva, "the lunatic giant," driven by passion and intemperance. This rebellious and delinquent spirit is also aglow in the unhappy runaway, Portia, in *The Death of the Heart* and the tortured, motherless Leopold in *The House in Paris*.

Une Affaire du Tête: Sean O'Faolain

In her first passionate affair, with House, Bowen asserted that she was "a writer" before she was "a woman." No such pronouncements were necessary when she met O'Faolain, a gifted author of short stories, because he encountered her first as a writer. He belatedly read *The Last September* in 1937, and loved it. She was then on the verge of the publication of *The Death of the Heart*, while he still struggled in the more limited literary field of Ireland. Their enchantment with each other's written words, before they met, led Julia O'Faolain, Sean's daughter, to claim that theirs was *une affaire du tête*. But O'Faolain's reflections in his revised autobiography suggest otherwise: he found Bowen's attraction both as a woman and as a writer "irresistible."

Eager to meet Bowen, he asked Derek Verschoyle, writer and editor, to arrange an introduction. Within 48 hours of his arrival in London, Bowen and O'Faolain met at Verschoyle's London club. Years later, O'Faolain would reflect that he could not have foreseen that on that afternoon, he was beginning "a troubling and bizarre journey," an intense but intermittent two-and-a-half-year affair, from May 1937 until October 1939, and a continuing friendship. He wrote that upon first meeting Bowen he was attracted, and had invented a different role for her as "Woman" rather than "Writer" before the lunch was over. Though Verschoyle's wife had used the adjective "horsey" to describe Bowen, what he first saw was "a tall, sturdy, bejeweled, fashionably dressed, just perhaps a bit over-dressed, capable-looking woman smiling at me in an amiable if collected way, her fair hair parted centrally, gracefully waved, her hands rather mannish, her eyes unusually small, peering at the three of us like the helmsman of a yacht in a crowded harbor."[98] This first impression quickly faded into a different image: a naïve and defenseless woman, like a character who had perhaps strayed from *The Last September*, "one of its young Irish girls become fifteen years or so older," and then of "a far younger creature, girl rather than woman, vulnerable, more sensitive, private ... a quite different person."

Bowen was also attracted to O'Faolain before she met him. She had first encountered his writing when plowing through entries to select short stories for a Faber collection, *Best Short Stories of the Present Day*. The break in her tedium came when she read what she described as O'Faolain's "grand" "Midsummer Night Madness," about his Irish Civil War experiences, as well as his stories "The Small Lady" and "Bomb Stop." She wrote to Plomer in 1936:

> Yes, indeed I am doing those abominable short stories (the collection I mean). As far as I ever do read here, I read nothing else. 4/5ths of what I try out show a level of absolute mediocrity; arty they are, and mawkishly tenderhearted .... Really they are the hell ... I long more and more to make a collection of *Great Middlebrow Prose*. Would this be actionable?[99]

Plomer agreed that O'Faolain, Liam O'Flaherty, and Frank O'Connor were the best Irish writers in that collection. But on a more personal level, she asked Plomer about O'Faolain: "Have you met him? Is he nice? He might possibly be quite dim." Dim he was not; talented, he was, and heralded as one of the best of the young Irish writers to come out of a "backward" Ireland deemed indifferent to literature, art, and critical standards by the acute critic, David Garnett in 1932. O'Faolain was also editor of *The Bell*, a progressive cultural and literary magazine that sought writers who would focus on representing Irish life and culture, and who embraced European as well as Gaelic influences. Also, he was handsome. She discerned his talent and knew when she met him that he was "a stripper of veils" like herself, someone who sought honest and sincere romantic relations, at least with her. He also liked women, and as Bowen's taste in men tended toward the rakish, she picked up his libertine spirit as she had in Rees, and would later in Ritchie. She was always discreet but particularly private about this affair confiding in no one except House, then far away in India, and, later, to May Sarton. O'Faolain had been married for ten years and had a child, and wanted to protect that relationship, as she did hers with Cameron. Bowen wrote to House, "Nothing is easy […] So we are trying to pay for our happiness by being very good," noting that they both were by nature "extremely secretive."[100]

Their rendezvous were mainly at Bowen's Court or in Dublin, and occasionally, London. Their friendship continued into 1941, during her clandestine Ministry of Information (MOI) visits to Ireland, ostensibly to do research on her family history, *Bowen's Court*, but really on an "Irish errand" for the MOI to investigate Irish neutrality. During this period, she absorbed some of O'Faolain's strong feelings about Ireland and his interest in the cultivation and evolution of Irish literature, as Eibhear Walshe has argued in his critical book on Bowen's Irish writings.[101] But she had her own temperamental qualities, a responsiveness to mood and place that Eudora Welty identified, "an Irishness, a sense of your surroundings, very sensitive to what you can feel all the time." Welty admired Bowen's youthful spirit and physical hardiness well into her later years, as well as her capacity for enjoyment and derring-do. Bowen was not intimidated to learn of O'Faolain's radical past as a bomb-maker with the IRA, and then as a fighter in the Irish Civil War in 1922–23. She insisted, however, in her letter to House that "he is not at all like anybody's idea of an ex-gunman, he is a very gentle person with fair hair—or hair, at least about the colour of mine. We are the same age—and doing such very different things in the same years of our lives."[102] One of the different things she was doing while seeing him was having a brief but intimate flirtation with May Sarton, who lived in America but visited Bowen occasionally in London, Salzburg, or Bowen's Court. Sarton often sought out established literary figures, and the relationship began with a fan letter in April 1937, about a month before Bowen met O'Faolain.

Bowen's romance with one of Ireland's finest short-story writers was most intense just before she volunteered as an MOI agent. This reveals again the intricacies of her identity, or, as O'Faolain put it, "her cloven heart," riven by her loyalties to Ireland, England, and Europe.[103] He noted, "it took me a score of affectionate encounters to decide that her strength and her weaknesses were at least in part born of a division in her personality; for that I would ultimately decide, was what she was, a dreamer and a skeptic, a romantic and a realist, sometimes a yearner but as often a toughie."[104] Part of her was inevitably drawn closer to Ireland, its landscapes, and literature during the time of her affair with O'Faolain and they shared the cultural claustrophobia and restlessness of many Irish writers and intellectuals during the war.

After the affair, Bowen wrote a short story, "Summer Night," that takes place during the summer of 1940 when rumors of invasion threatened neutral

Ireland. The story illuminates Ireland's national indifference to and perceived betrayal of the war in Europe. It conveys the claustrophobia that O'Faolain felt, culturally cut off from Europe like Robinson, the intelligent Irishman, and Justin, his guest, who is "locked" into Ireland and unable to travel during the war. Justin visits Robinson with his deaf sister, Queenie—whose deafness may represent Ireland's decision to tune out the war—as Robinson waits for Emma, a married woman who streams through the Irish night for an assignation with him. Hints of impatience with Irish neutrality surface, and suggest Bowen and O'Faolain's anguish amidst "the war-broken towers of Europe [...where] In the heart of the neutral Irishman indirect suffering pulled like a crooked knife."[105] Though not engaged in the conflict, some Irish responded to the suffering of the war not only in their own wartime deprivations but the destruction of cities and lives suffered in Europe—when such news leaked through to Ireland. Being outside the conflict generated guilt, and this fleeting sentiment is also expressed by Mrs. Massey in "A Love Story" when she announces that she is ashamed of her country. Ireland is "an infected zone," and the national climate filters into the moral indifference of the lovers: Robinson who lives apart from his family and Emma who betrays hers with furtive, false phone calls. At the same time that there are traces of feeling against neutrality represented in some stories, Bowen displayed her understanding of the practical, military, and economic reasons for neutrality in her *Notes from Eire*. O'Faolain was a nationalist and also voiced his grievance about the political and cultural isolation created by Ireland's policy of neutrality during the Emergency, regretting not being part of the anti-Fascist campaign.

Bowen's relationship with O'Faolain, nevertheless, drew her closer to Ireland and awakened a homesickness, while O'Faolain in the flush of their affair in 1937 was grateful to be drawn away from Ireland into talk of her English and European literary circles. He was now her touchstone on Irish feeling, national politics, and contemporary Irish writing, and would continue to be so for a few more years as she visited Ireland for clandestine purposes of MOI at the beginning of the war. For O'Faolain, often isolated just before the declaration of Irish neutrality in the war, contact with London literary society and an established writer with liberal European views proved a turning point in his career. He craved wider experiences. He wanted to be a citizen of the world, not a figure in a postcolonial frame, a cultural leftover after British domination. Her activity on his behalf was evident as she offered an introduction to Virginia Woolf. Reciprocating, he introduced her to Yeats, who was drawn to her because she was part of the landed gentry, and a writer.

O'Faolain complained of the insularity of Ireland, stoked by the nationalism and the paternalism of the Catholic Church as represented by its 1929 Censorship of Publications Act that banned many promising Irish writers, including him. O'Faolain refused to honor the Church, observing its paralyzing effects on life, literature, and sex in Ireland. Like Bowen, his imagination embraced Europe, and he would write stories that showed the dreams of characters broken by the petty concerns of a provincial society that rejected literary representations of sexuality, infidelity, contraception, abortion, and prostitution.

In addition, he had "fallen utterly in love" with the author of *The Last September*, when he first read it, eight years after its publication. He wrote that on his way to London from County Wicklow he was in turmoil with the author

> who had Turgenev's triple trick of presenting reality to me as if it were a ball balanced on her five finger tips ... remaining both compassionate and ruthless about all those people in whom she presumably found, as every artist does, her subjective mirror.[106]

O'Faolain was smitten by her words, as well as her relationship to Ireland as expressed in the novel. He admired her control and "her sense of drama in small things," coveting the atmosphere she had created, claiming that he "could smell the hay, the wet, the mountain line." It challenged his perspective and demonstrated that one could be "a Turgenev when writing of holy, simple, pietistic, peasant, bogtrotting, jansenistic, lower-middle-class agricultural Ireland." He was bolstered by Bowen's representation of the ordinary life of the farmers and the roaming IRA in the neighborhood of an Anglo-Irish big house, and soon after his relationship with Bowen ended, he began to encourage a home-grown modern Irish culture and literature by establishing with Peadar O'Donnell a magazine, *The Bell*, which he would edit for the first five years. Ireland, neutral and geographically separated from the turmoil and destruction of Europe, could afford to focus on literature. Little information about the war traveled there. O'Faolain cultivated Irish talent, while some Irish and several authors of Anglo-Irish background looked for literature and culture outside its own shores: authors like Wilde, Shaw, Yeats, and Joyce. When the first issue of *The Bell* was published, in October 1940, it rang out with a new focus on social and political issues in Irish literature but received little attention in England; all that could be heard in the streets of London were sirens. O'Faolain turned away from "romantic" Ireland to a new "realism." He had no sympathy for the romantic and mythic tradition of Irish writing that Yeats represented. The stance of *The Bell* was culturally European-minded, yet removed from a Europe that was bursting into flames, as Clair Wills astutely notes. He continued to work in literary and intellectual circles to expand Ireland's vision of culture and literature, while Bowen turned to the war. *The Bell* struggled against Catholic influence and censorship of authors, and embraced taboo discussions in Ireland: the institutional abuse of women in the treatment of unmarried mothers, birth control, illegitimacy, homosexuality, divorce, mental illness, prostitution, jails, and crime. It trained its eye on Irish "realism" and everyday Irish life and rejected European modernism unlike Bowen who turned her narration inward using modernist techniques to capture consciousness.[107] O'Faolain said he would have rejected Eliot's "Wasteland" and Joyce's *Ulysses* for his publication, though he later changed his mind. His stated mission was simple, encouraging Irish authors to write "about our own people, our own generation, our own institutions" in a "decent, friendly, possibly hot-tempered, but always polite and constructive way."[108] He was editor of *The Bell* from 1940 to 1946, and solicited writing from Bowen for the publication (as well as Mary Lavin), adding a woman and an Anglo-Irish voice to a chorus of Catholic writers, drawing her into the Irish literary ranks. Taking on Bowen's critics in her day, he asserted that *The Last September* is "entirely Irish—if that matters a damn." He then alluded to the broader literary vision that he and Bowen shared: "(We're so sick of hearing our Nationalists ask for Irish literature—so thirsty for just literature.)"[109]

Different Irelands

Bowen viewed the Troubles mainly from the viewpoint of a big house in *The Last September*; O'Faolain's stunning story, "Midsummer Night Madness" adopted the view of the men who burned such houses down. *The Last September*, O'Faolain observed, was written "when Ireland was still, in some sort, her [Bowen's] home."[110] In a vivid and moving April 1937 letter, he said, "like a fool," he conceded that she had written "the history of a besieged city," but now "the siege is over."[111] Or are "the walls as high as ever? I fear to think it is." One heard in her novel historical noises in the background, and it was now time for the Irish novel to bring "the enemy," the Anglo-Irish, to the foreground, and join the divided worlds of Danielstown and Peter Connor's farm. He urged her to write another story "that was at least aware of the Ireland outside [the big house] that, perhaps, regretted the division enough to admit it was there."[112] The cultural division is desperate, and "no novelist could falsify or sentimentalise over it." He then asked, "Do you feel any of this?" She did. He reminded her that she was representing a besieged minority, the Anglo-Irish, whose cultural and political influence had waned, and urged each side to make up its losses. Bowen observed the cultural division in *The Last September*, and acknowledged it in *Bowen's Court*, but would not be the author to initiate the cultural dialogue that O'Faolain urged. It would be left to others like the Catholic poet, Seamus Heaney, to cross this boundary. Nor did Bowen ever directly address the partition of Ireland—Northern Ireland under the rule of the United Kingdom and the Southern Irish Free State established in 1922.

O'Faolain himself felt like a "spy" from another class and culture in the big house and wrote of this in "Midsummer Night's Madness." He represents a later historical phase of the big house than Bowen and exposes the immoral, corrupt, and mad owner of what had become a garrison house—a kind of fortification for the Black and Tans—and adds a cast of IRA characters whose morality also unravels. Bowen and O'Faolain came from different Irelands: she, the talented daughter of the Anglo-Irish Protestant elite, living most of her life in England, and now an accomplished writer; O'Faolain, the working-class son of an Irish constable and a pious Catholic mother, who emerged from a modest background, and became one of the best writers in Ireland. There were paradoxes in his family's alliances. His father was proudly part of the Royal Irish Constabulary, the armed police force of the United Kingdom in Ireland until 1922, a force that in certain climates was viewed as "disloyal" within Ireland. O'Faolain, nevertheless, violently opposed the British presence in Ireland and made bombs as an IRA activist to blow up British targets during the War of Independence.

These Irish-English tensions added a frisson to Bowen's affair, according to Julia O'Faolain, his daughter. She remembered that in the early 1970s, Bowen visited their London house and told them "with relish" that her name for Sean was "Johnny," a name historically connected to the English. Julia wondered if this was "a bit of closet imperialism?" She suspected that he called her "Eilis," a Gaelic variant on the name Elizabeth. But only Liz, Liza, and other affectionate nicknames appear in his letters.

Julia O'Faolain assessed her father's "chosen" lovers, in an afterword to his autobiography, *Vive Moi*, as having "wounded personalities" and, surprisingly to her, "a certain plainness," given her father's good looks: Bowen; Honor Tracy (a "castle Catholic," a term applied to Irish who were deemed too Anglophilic); and Kick Erlanger.[113] Julia berated "the stammering Elizabeth Bowen whose mad father and declining family fortunes drove her to snobbery and fiction." She asserted that her father's "heart" was not in the affair;

O'Faolain, however, disagreed, writing warmly years later about "my Eliza." Though O'Faolain perceived a vulnerability in Bowen upon meeting her, he came to see that there was little timidity in her character. He remarked upon her quality of determination, as did other friends, for choosing to live in London during the blitz, instead of retiring to Bowen's Court even after the bombing of her home in Clarence Terrace. In the end, though, he felt that her character was "too strong, deliberate and stubborn to the point of weakness," or to capture her in a Miltonic phrase, her "strength was her bane."[114] When meeting her for lunch in the early 1970s when she was dying of cancer, "all passion spent," he remarked that she had lost her "almost masculine sense of vigor" that had appealed so much to him.

There is some truth in Julia O'Faolain's view that O'Faolain's was "a willed encounter" with an "Irish Turgenev," who wrote of longing for a past world in *The Last September*. He was a budding writer still at 37, stuck, he thought, in a provincial society, "elementary" and culturally and intellectually isolated. "The Irish life—way before my time had been far too elementary to feed a Novel; one might as well hope to grow a whole garden in a flower pot."[115] He had been discovered and bolstered by David Garnett, the prescient English editor who supported his writing and the publication of the short-story collection *Midsummer Night Madness* in 1933, but he still struggled with Irish censorship and with making a living in his own country. The short-story form best suited his needs, as it could capture the fragmented life of Ireland of the first part of the twentieth century "after which our society began to fall to bits as a system like a tumbled jigsaw puzzle."

O'Faolain and Bowen were vivid souls, and maintained strict separations between their marriages and their affairs. Julia O'Faolain, however, did convince her father late in life to reveal and describe some of his affairs in her candid supplement to *Vive Moi*, written 20 years after Bowen's death. Here he said more, perceptively and eloquently, about "La Bowen" than any of her other lovers except Ritchie. Julia O'Faolain was only five at the time of O'Faolain's affair and so she recounts what her father told her with her own bias. A writer herself, Julia revealed her own strong views on women's historically limited roles inside and outside Ireland in such writing as *Not in God's Image: Women in History from the Greeks to the Victorians* (1973), *The Obedient Wife* (1982), and *The Irish Signorina* (1984). She recounted that throughout her childhood "la Bowen—as my mother called Elizabeth Bowen—was an offstage source of contention in that she invited you, but not Eileen, to house parties. 'They're probably professional gatherings!' you would argue with lofty perfidy, as you packed your bag."[116] La Bowen was not only a source of discord in O'Faolain's marriage, as she was in House and Ritchie's, but also a public figure to contend with.

O'Faolain confessed that "when our intimacy became as complete as, in our circumstances, it could ever be," he asked her a question about what he perceived as her split personality. Her response was "I see no reason why any writer should not be a man of the world as well as a writer": in other words, a woman writer engaged in acts of the imagination as well as one who is intellectually, culturally, and politically engaged in her times, a duality allowed to male writers without question. In later years, O'Faolain acknowledged that he had been foolish in his assessment. Appreciating the complexity of Bowen, a woman of talent who also wanted to be loved, he acknowledged: "A split personality. I now know it as an essential possession for all poets, politicians, philosophers, theologians, actors, authors, in short for everyone who is not a monomaniac."[117]

The End of the Affair

The affair ended, according to O'Faolain, on his last visit to Bowen's Clarence Terrace townhouse, on August 31, 1939. That day "as we lay-abed, passionsated, Alan rung from the office to tell her that the British fleet had been mobilized, 'Which means war.'"[118] Her relation to O'Faolain and Ireland changed with this report of war by her husband, as their loyalties were divided. He would later revise this account, as he did others relating to Bowen, stating that he was in County Mayo when war was announced. Nevertheless, they took sides. Bowen became engaged in wartime Britain, while O'Faolain tacked back to Ireland. After 1940, O'Faolain remarked that Bowen virtually disappeared for a few years, although they would occasionally cross paths when she visited on her wartime "Irish errand," though O'Faolain knew nothing of it at the time. Their conversations likely entered some of her *Reports from Eire to the Dominions office*. Certain shared opinions surface in both *The Bell* and Bowen's reports: Irish provincialism; the isolation of Irish intellectuals and writers from literary currents in Europe; and, for O'Faolain, the difficulty of getting a wartime visa to travel to Europe to connect with English and European writers.

The years 1936 and 1937, when she first met and engaged with O'Faolain, were turbulent ones for Bowen. She was professionally productive but personally adrift. She had wild success with her novel *The House in Paris*, published in 1935, and had begun to work on *The Death of the Heart*, but felt abandoned by House and rejected by Rees. Also, Cameron was gloomy because of professional squabbles at the BBC, a job that had motivated their move from Oxford to London in 1935. Bowen also was not in good health, and as early as November 1936, had a month of laryngitis, was spitting blood, and was warned by her doctors to stop smoking. In the spring of 1937, however, she perked up and began her affair with May Sarton concurrently with her romance with O'Faolain: two kinds of love. These multiple and sometimes overlapping relationships reveal Bowen's complicated truths and remarkable energy in sustaining relationships while writing her stories. They tell of her ability to expose, hide, and publicly juggle various aspects of herself: the woman, the lover, the writer, the intellectual, the hostess, the careerist, and the political agent.

The Smiles of Livia

Anyone interested in women, Bowen thought, must be interested in Livia. On a visit to Rome, she was struck by the *Smile of Livia*, a sculpture of the resourceful wife of Caesar Augustus who grappled with powerful men: first, the emperor, Nero; her second husband, Caesar; her son, Tiberius; and her grandson, Caligula, as well as politically complex situations. Bowen read into the secrets of this ruthless woman who survived many unsavory situations with poise and calm. She admired her ironic smile.

This same irony was woven into much of her writing, and her relationship with May Sarton who was one of the few women to break Bowen's taboo and document it.[119] In addition to her own relationship, Sarton related—according to critic Ann Waldron—that Bowen had other women lovers and a habit of intense friendships, "then dropping them ruthlessly."[120] Woolf described her as "a pale pretty Shelley imitation American girl."[121] Bowen's romantic episodes with Sarton followed a pattern with which she was comfortable: an older female mentor with a young admiring confidante. Bowen was a woman of 39; Sarton, 26. In speaking of women's friendships with Ritchie in 1942, she said that she did not define this kind of relationship as "lesbian." Considering Woolf's closeness with her niece Angelica, and Jane Austen with her niece Fanny Knight, Bowen said "that every young woman has such friendships and that the older woman puts into them all the lyrical, poetic side of her nature and that she lives her youth again."[122] She continued, "The girl finds so much pleasure in being seen through the eyes of love and admiration [by the older woman] that she may have a flirtation with a man simply for the pleasure of telling the other woman. This is all," she said to Ritchie, "quite apart from Lesbianism." Such a relationship appears in *The Last September*, in which Marda, the older, more cynical woman, becomes close to Lois, who is emerging into love. More menacingly in *The Hotel*, Mrs. Kerr, the older widow, subjects the young woman, Sydney Warren to her social demands. Ann Berthoff, who met Bowen when she was lecturing at Bryn Mawr, observed that Bowen was attracted to pretty young girls, was worshipped as a teacher, and sometimes became a confidante. Berthoff recounted that she was drawn to a young poet, Cynthia Lovelace Sears, "a good one, and very beautiful."[123] Sears in an interview related how mesmerized she was by Bowen's conversation. When Sears got back to London, she wrote to Bowen about how she had flirted with a young man, a pilot, on her trip back—the kind of confidential story from a younger woman to an older one that Bowen relished.

A similar confidante relationship developed with May Sarton. The correspondence between Bowen and Sarton, particularly from 1936 to 1938, reveals an intermittent intimacy. It elicited from Bowen a kind of amusement and tender language that one might use to address a child or a pet. Bowen's letters are ironic, playful, infrequent, and often guilty and apologetic in tone. "My sweet, you lacerate me when you are unhappy; you mustn't be that again. And don't ever shoot me: I wouldn't like that at all."[124] So wrote Bowen, saucily, to Sarton apologizing for not responding to her letters. Bowen was under pressure finishing *The Death of the Heart*, during which time Woolf warned her to dispatch "that goose May Sarton who sent me a gentian picked by Julian Huxley," thus dismissing Bowen's acolyte.[125] Bowen was preoccupied during the same month with O'Faolain, a relationship that she initially hid from Sarton, though she once confided that she was on her way to Boulogne to meet a man who would become her lover. Bowen enjoyed Sarton's flattery and gave her advice on writing and her career: Sarton, a talented poet, had just had four poems published by *Harper's Bazaar* in 1937, and was then working on her first novel, *The Single Hound*.

Ritchie noted in his diary that Bowen loved the adulation of young girls. In 1960, she gave a seminar at Vassar and he imagined "the frieze of young creatures drifting across the campus, the girls going to collect their letters like going to collect eggs on the farm, and a girl coming back reading hers as she walked and smiling to herself. The whole place threaded with stories. I wish ER [Elizabeth Ritchie, his niece] could know E at this stage, if E doesn't have too many girls in her life already. I think E an immensely potent witch."[126] Her presence, a combination of her appearance, intellect, and personality, was seductive, and "bewitching" was the word often applied by her friends. It was a force that attracted both men and women. Ritchie mentioned another young admirer, Marshall Berland, a student who was inspired by Bowen when she was teaching at the University of Wisconsin. Ritchie observed, "He loves and reveres her as I did once."[127]

Sarton often sought the approbation and support of older, established women writers. In addition to Bowen, she had crushes on and correspondence with H.D., Winifred Bryher, and Woolf. After reading a rather modest essay on manners that Bowen wrote for the *New Statesman* in 1935, she gushed, "I was simply and frankly bowled over by your personal brilliance, style, point of view."[128] According to Sarton, John Summerson, an architect writing a book about the Nash terraces (of which Bowen's apartment in Regent's Park was one), introduced her to Bowen and her husband. In May 1936, Sarton, Cecil, and Berlin attended a Bowen dinner and Sarton "was as dazzled as a moth by so much light … the brilliance of it all."[129] She shyly observed Bowen, who looked "like a drawing by Holbein. Hers was a handsome face, handsome rather than beautiful with its bold nose, high cheekbones and tall forehead; but the coloring was as delicate as the structure was strong—fine red-gold hair pulled straight back into a loose knot a her neck, faint eyebrows over pale-blue eyes." In August 1936, Sarton sent Bowen an admiring poem, "Portrait by Holbein": "Your face is drawn in pencil startling the senses."

After this meeting, Sarton began to obsess about Bowen, and though she lived in America, she made frequent trips to London. From America, she wrote adoring letters about Bowen's publications and her own sense of loneliness, uselessness, depressions, joys, relationships, and struggles with her poetry and novel writing. After reading *The Death of the Heart* in 1938, she wrote that she thought of Flaubert; "the smell, the taste of rooms, of the house, or people one can forget less than any real people. It did leave me with a feeling of distilled horror like the ash from a fire, a taste that I can't get out of my mouth."[130] The relationship continued, and on January 16, 1938, waiting for a new novel from Bowen, Sarton, always flattering, wrote, "There will soon be a revolution among your public."

As many friends complained, Bowen was not an attentive correspondent, and she and Sarton were separated for long periods of time. Bowen, probably relieved at the distance, appreciated the adulation, and half-humorously dealt with Sarton's jejune love pangs. But Sarton was talented, and to Bowen's delight, included sketches with her daily epistolary dramas. In one of her first letters, sent from the Hotel Russell on July 25, 1936, Sarton thanked Bowen for a copy of *The House in Paris* and included a sketch. Though Sarton states in her biography *A World of Light* that the affair began in May 1937, claiming there was only one intimate encounter, letters suggest more frequent meetings. Sarton adored Bowen but did not meet her again until the spring of 1937, when she rented Jeakes House with friends in Rye. Gravitating always toward women who could teach her, and something of a sycophant, she longed to be taken into Bowen's life. When she later invited Bowen to dinner at her new home, she discovered that they were alike in "their talent for instant intimacy." She wrote:

> There was a full moon on the night she spent at Jeakes House in late May. My study, high up, with a large studio window, looked out over the roofs and chimney pots to the wide lonely marshes, misty in the moonlight. We sat there talking, sometimes silent, for a long hour after dinner, and finally, Elizabeth so sensitized to atmosphere, to place, to the total content of a moment, responded to my passionate feelings for her. We slept together in my big bed after an exchange that had great tenderness in it.[131]

After this romantic encounter, Bowen would write frank notes to Sarton, with hints of the erotic. She acknowledged how infuriating her infrequent letters must be, explaining, "I can't communicate with anyone, however much I'd like to—in a way I don't want to. I think the Irish must be the most maddening race."[132] Surprisingly open, Bowen wrote intimately—or to use one of her own words, "claggily"—to Sarton with expressions that rarely appear in other letters, with the exception of those to Charles Ritchie, which were in a different key. On June 8, 1937, a week after meeting with Sarton in London, Bowen apostrophized from France, "you were so sweet last week-end: a perfect seraph. You are rather sweet when you're cro-ooss … Good bye for now, sweet one. I've got no name for you. XXE."[133] In the same letter, she described her view of a garden of roses from her window and asked Sarton, "What do your windows look at? Is it still very hot and are the lions and tigers turning up their flanks and panting." Other undated 1937 letters from Clarence Terrace anticipated meetings: "Tomorrow I'll see you darling? About six or something? And you're staying the night? Love love love." A few months later she wrote apologetically again, detailing all her work finishing *The Death of the Heart*, doing extra bits of journalism to pay for a trip to Salzburg where she would meet Sarton, and confessing that she "loves her letters with the flowers falling out."[134] She continued that she was not able to visit Sarton in Boston: "Forgive me darling child, for this long silence which must have seem unaffectionate and horrible but hasn't been so really. My love sweet one. E." A month later, at the end of August 1937, Bowen met Sarton; Tom Howard, an American friend; and Tony Butts, Plomer's intimate, in Salzburg. Bowen remembered the trip in a letter: "It was lovely like a dream."[135]

Bowen brought Sarton and Woolf together at a dinner at Clarence Terrace in April 1937, and, according to Woolf, Sarton "sat on the floor at my feet and, unfortunately, adores and worships and gave me primroses one day in the winter and her poems."[136] After that dinner Sarton pursued Woolf, as she had Bowen, and was humorously chided by Woolf after informing her that she was "frightened" of her: "But why should you have been frightened, considering that I am as tame and mild as a very old giraffe. I admit that the room looking onto the Lake [Regent's Park] dazzled me, but only as a giraffe might be afraid of the lights."[137] Woolf attempted to deflate Sarton's worship with wry humor. And later, when Sarton sent Woolf her novel *The Single Hound*, Woolf again rebuffed her adulation: "If you're in London later still want wild and random impressions verbally probably we could arrange it. And as for feeling suspense about my judgment—that seems to me absurd in the extreme." Sarton boldly noted in a letter to Bowen that Woolf's remark "made me laugh and if I were not twenty-six and a fortress of reserve I would write her a tremendous fan letter. But like Gogol's Madam, 'Silence, silence.'"[138] But what alienated Woolf, the adulation, the gushing, the sketches, the poems, the flowers falling from letters, attracted Bowen—for a time.

Sarton described her meeting with Woolf as "painful" and remarked, "she really has a phobia about having to say anything about people's work and so we made small talk until almost the end when she suddenly started talking very hard when I had to leave!"[139] Addressing Sarton's novel *The Single Hound* in the same conversation, Woolf told her that she had a tale, and liked the second part best; however, Woolf added that she "would be interested to see if I really had anything to say." Woolf also warned, "there is the danger of feeling too much and not thinking through hard enough." Sarton was impatient: "What a curious woman—I kept wanting to say for God's sake be simple—it was like looking down into one of those spiral shells." Sarton's conversations with Bowen were longer and more relaxed. A month earlier, in December 1938, Sarton had sketched an intimate scene in which she might come into a room and find Bowen "curled into the corner of the sofa, half smiling like the Primavera," Botticelli's fifteenth-century maiden.[140] Though generally reserved in letters, Bowen offered Sarton a frank and cynical assessment of her own personality:

> You mustn't spike yourself on things. It makes me reel when these sudden gulfs of unhappiness open up. I just feel you must think me the most awful old rook and cad—and oh, all sorts of things and worse. You must know how little feeling, *in general*, I have for women. I like to have in my house, on seemly occasions, anyone pretty and amiable. I'm a cynical and hard-bitten old hostess. Can't you—oh yes, you naturally can really—see the difference between that and anything else?[141]

This confirms her gravitation toward amiable young women, and reservations about women in traditional roles at that cultural point in time. Bowen, according to Ann Berthoff, invited Sears to Bowen's Court in the spring of 1953 at the same time as Sarton. Sears arrived, "glowing," and sparked Bowen's interest. Bowen's attention to Sarton was on the wane on this visit, and Sarton was jealous. In an interview, Sears described her exhilarating visit, being picked up at the airport in Shannon and driven to Bowen's Court, arriving in the light rain of evening.[142] The house, to Sears, was "richly dark, not gloomy, with lots of texture, something out of *The Secret Garden*," a magical children's book. She remembered the big table in the kitchen, the red flocked wallpaper, the library, and the tables piled with books, as well as the views from her bedroom window, both the evening moonlight and the daytime gorse and flowers, near the third-floor ballroom. Received graciously by Bowen in her usual tweed skirt, heavy sweater, and chunky jewelry, Sears exuded, "I adored her." But she was taken aback by Sarton's evident jealousy, and later when Sarton imitated Bowen's stutter when they were alone together, Sears could not believe she had been a dear friend of Bowen's for years. Sears also said that Bowen was a "good listener with complete focus" and "extremely attractive." Though Bowen never made any affectionate gesture toward her, Sears admitted that she would not be surprised if Bowen had affairs with women.

Bowen did not at first confide in Sarton about her relationship with O'Faolain, but it turned out that Sarton was more preoccupied with jealousy of Bowen's women friends. In July 1938, Sarton mentioned that her three meetings with Bowen were "blessed," implying intimacy. Bowen retained a friendship with Sarton and wrote to her in June 1944 about Cameron's heart trouble. Over the years, Sarton had become a friend of Cameron's on her visits to Bowen's Court and Clarence Terrace: she noted his "warmth," a quality that also accounts for Bowen's devotion. Since few of Bowen's friends liked Cameron, Bowen appreciated Sarton's responsiveness, and thanked her for sending him a gift of Silly Putty. In 1952, she wrote a letter to Sarton about Cameron's death, "so gently gone, poor man."[143]

Bowen visited Sarton shortly after Cameron's death grateful for her understanding and happy in the atmosphere of her home. She describes her state poignantly, "like a great incompetent flapping blind bird, not even an eagle, a hen-on the wing, or something flapping screeching in at one of your windows."[144] Fearing she exhausted her and her partner, Judy, she apologized. Yet she expressed impatience in her meeting with Sylvia Plath there. A year later, May 1953, the talented young poet, guest editor at *Mademoiselle*, interviewed Bowen for an article. Plath's vibrant smile in the interview photo captures the admiration of many young women that Bowen met, but belies Plath's depressed state as she began ECT treatments for manic-depression a few months later.

Bowen praised Sarton's novel *Shadow of a Man*; however, the publication of *A Shower of Summer Days* in 1952 caused a rift. Sarton created a character, Charles Gordon, based on Alan Cameron, and a big house, Bowen's Court. It was a turning point, and Sarton discovered from Howard Moss, a critic friend of Bowen's, that Bowen thought she was "cheeky" to have written about her without discussion. Sarton apologized, but disingenuously added in a 1965 letter, "I cannot believe that you and I have ceased to be friends." She added an invitation to her home in New Hampshire, reflecting, "I know so little of your life now, I hardly know to whom this is addressed […] a swanlike person with whom I fell in love thirty years ago."[145]

There are other hints of Bowen's intense friendships with women in her letters to Ritchie, but the editors of their correspondence, Victoria Glendinning and Judith Robertson, observe that she did not fully reveal these personal relationships to him. The editors, who had access to more correspondence than was published, surmise that "she had many 'girl-friends' of a certain age, mainly in Sussex and Kent, some of them emotionally linked, whom she met frequently. CR was not told much about this aspect of her social life."[146] Sarton had observed that Bowen had a pattern of intense friendships with women whom she then "ruthlessly" dropped: Sarton was one; Nancy Spain, another—entertaining but exhibitionist about her relationships; and a shadowy "B," Beatrice Horton who was a close friend. Carson McCullers also made advances to Bowen but was rejected. Nancy Spain was infatuated with Bowen and frequently visited her Clarence Terrace apartment to Alan's dismay, according to Rose Collis, but was "dropped" because of her flamboyance. Bowen never accepted the label, "lesbian," and was uncomfortable with the expression of sentimental or cloying feelings that she associated with such relationships. Temperamentally, she recoiled from the first signs of personal exposure or sensationalism or publicity.

Her friendship with Eudora Welty was also intense and for Welty, at times, ardent, judging from the heightened language in Welty's letters during 1951. This was the year before Cameron's death, when Welty visited Bowen's Court in the spring, and Bowen visited Welty in the autumn for Thanksgiving. Though Bowen's letters to Welty were not available and digitized through MDAH at the time of this inquiry, we do learn from Welty of her stay at Bowen's Court during the period when she was writing *The Bride of Innisfallen*, we do learn of Welty's stay at Bowen's Court during the period when she was writing "The Bride of the Innisfallen." Welty wrote of her longing to return, which she expressed in a series of tender letters after her visit. In a nine-page letter written from the Ile de France as Welty crossed to Europe in the spring of 1951, she wrote of missing Bowen intensely, wishing to hear her voice, even wondering what dress she was wearing. She alluded to the cable and yellow roses that Bowen had sent. It is a love letter, with Welty declaiming, "you were sweet—you are beyond any saying, all you thought and did and know and brought about—you did *so much*. But I let you, loved it and took my pleasure, I let you as I love you—and of course imagine how I would like doing so much for you [...] I'll never, never forget any of those days and nights."[147] Even on the ship, sensations from the visit reverberated: "once or twice I could feel the rhythm of trees passing overhead as we would drive down the avenue" during our wild car rides. In later letters she urged Bowen to visit the South, suggested meeting in New York City, and reminisced about going to Coney Island and walking along the East River in the fall. They did meet many times over the years: Welty gave lectures in Chicago in December 1951 at the same time that Bowen was lecturing there, and she visited two years after Cameron's death in September 1954 for two weeks. They also went on a six-day trip to the Mississippi coast, Thanksgiving 1951. In early 1961, they met at Bryn Mawr, where they taught together and then spent time in New York. It was a long, close friendship though not much correspondence survived, and their meetings trailed off in the mid-1960s.[148] Welty, increasingly aware that Bowen admirers sought her attention, described attempts to meet Bowen in 1968 on the occasion of Bill Koshland's, president of Knopf, party for her in NYC. Welty described "the mosaic of her visit," noting that she could only snatch a few precious minutes with her, remarking "I think too many people is an impoverishment."[149] Bowen's "uniqueness hardly went unnoticed," wrote her friend, Howard Moss, "and because she was never a bore. In her presence you felt warmed by her warmth, flattered by her distinction, stimulated by what she had to say and amused by the way she said it." And, he said, echoing another good friend, Isaiah Berlin, "she made you feel that you were absolutely at the top of your form." Welty, nevertheless continued to express her devotion to Bowen in letters to William Maxwell exclaiming how "lucky" she was to see Bowen when she was ill in 1970. And in the summer of 1973 after her death, Welty thanked Maxwell for his gift of a Bowen chapter corrected in her hand "which I treasure you know how deeply, and you know how gratefully." She sent him a picture that she took of Bowen on the back porch of a little hotel in Cahir, Tipperary, taken in 1956, on long ride in country, the same day they went to Cachel. Maxwell, also a great admirer and friend, responded, "I have one for myself and love having it in view," honoring Welty's affection with the comment that Bowen composed herself in the photo "for you, so that you would have all there was of her."[150] Whether Bowen's relations were sexual or not, she had a gift for intimacy given her unique and talented personality: she attracted women and formed close relationships, for a time.

Relationships between young girls emerge in her letters and fiction. In 1945, she wrote Ritchie from Bowen's Court: "Have you read—I've just read—Le Fanu's *Carmilla*, the first vampire story? It's most exquisite, delicate, beautiful an *amitie amoureuse*, between 2 young girls, one of whom turns out to be a vampire. It had the most erotic effect on me—more so than any book I have read for a long time. Do you think I have got a vampire complex?"[151] The vampire, Carmilla, is drawn to an innocent girl, Laura:

> In the rapture of my enormous humiliation I live in your warm life, and you shall die-die, sweetly die—into mine. I cannot help it; as I draw near to you, you, in your turn, will draw near to others, and learn the rapture of that cruelty, which yet is love; so, for a while, seek to know no more of me and mine, but trust me with all your loving spirit.[152]

Laura naively trusts Carmilla's honor but is rescued from her clutches by a doctor. This mixture of the gothic and the erotic that attracted Bowen appears in shadowy forms in the relationship between Eva and Elsinore in *Eva Trout*, though Bowen wrote the novel in what Ritchie curiously termed an "anti-lesbian" phase. In the novel, Eva, an adolescent, enters a school in a castle bought by her father for his lover. Here she meets the fairylike, suicidal, and dying Elsinore, and in time visualizes their room "levitating" to the top of a turret as a "marriage chamber."[153] Passionately responsive to Elsinore's suffering, Eva experiences a "solicitous sense of this other presence. Nothing forbad love. This deathly yet living stillness, together, of two beings, this unapartness, came to be the requital of all longing." Bowen represents lesbian love as Elsinore, at one point, pleads with Eva: "take me with you Trout, you never left me before […] no, reasoned Elsinore […] however could I? […] obstinate self determination […] both of them froze together." Eva's relationship more openly represents the Sapphic simmer between Sydney Warren and Miss Kerr and Miss Fitzgerald and Miss Pym in her first novel, *The Hotel*, 1927, sketched four decades earlier; a few years later represented in Theodora and her "fierce friend," Marisa, in *Friends and Relations*, 1931. In *Eva Trout*, Bowen sardonically mixes gothic elements and a homosexual theme, part of her pattern of taking a traditional style and transforming it to new uses, as she would later intertwine the gothic and the surreal.[154] Time and space are shattered in Eva's mind; they "lay about like various pieces of a fragmented picture. She remembered, that is to say, disjectedly [a diffusion of memory]. To reassemble the picture was impossible, too many of the pieces were lost, lacking."[155] Modernist, perhaps surrealist techniques, capture the pieces of Eva's life and mind in a narrative collage that mirrors her physical and emotional disfigurements, frequent changes of scene, and frustrated longing for a mother, a father, a lover, a child, indeed, a home.

Bowen's novel, *Eva Trout*, was published one year after the landmark Sexual Offenses Act of 1967 that partially decriminalized male homosexual acts in

England. This reform not only protected the private sex lives of citizens but also created a climate that liberated authors to write more freely about formerly taboo topics and relationships. Bowen's representation of several homosexual characters and relationships in *Eva Trout*—Willy Trout, Constantine Ormeau, Tony Clavering-Haight, Kenneth—might be seen as part of this literary liberation. Writing about such relationships in this repressive atmosphere was still considered scandalous and actionable. Yet the topic of homosexuality had surfaced in her letters beginning in the 1930s. Radclyffe Hall's novel of lesbianism and cross-dressing, *The Well of Loneliness* was published in 1928 to furor and censorship. It provoked spirited debate in literary circles about homosexuality, transsexuality, and freedom of speech. Virginia and Leonard Woolf went to court to defend Radclyffe Hall's right to free expression when her book was banned, although in their literary judgment it was "a meritorious dull book."[156] Bowen weighed in and agreed with them and T.S. Eliot: the book was tedious propaganda rather than an honest exploration of the theme. It is worth noting that in 1929, a year after the court case involving *The Well of Loneliness*, Bowen had considered the idea of writing about homosexuality, sending a proposal to A.C. Coppard of Golden Cockerel Press. He responded:

> If you write *Barren Love* I can't say what you will bring the GC [Golden Cockerel Press] in for—that depends on you. And I don't see why you call it Barren Love, except in the procreative sense which surely doesn't count in such a relation. It's a theme that might be beautifully done, but for myself I'd only use it if I saw some of its complication as fruitful material for art, not as propaganda a la Laurence or the Lonely Well Lady. Or otherwise you would have to treat it in a daintily pornographic style, for there is no point in just nibbling at the hook or book.[157]

Bowen's use of the biblical word "barren" to describe homosexual love is a clue to the influence of the sexual theories of Richard von Krafft-Ebing, popular at the time. He promoted the view that procreation was the origin of sexual desire, and that other expressions of sexuality were a perversion. Although *Barren Love* was never written, Bowen, like other writers, struggled to find a vocabulary to fit the sensations, experiences, and paradoxes of the varied relationships between men and women, and women and women. But like Proust, and unlike Woolf, she put aside gender as a necessary category to redefine her life and writing. She just lived it: she never accepted a label for herself—whether "lesbian, feminist, heterosexual, homosexual, or invert"—seeking in her life and writing what Woolf called "words not syllabled yet." In letters, she occasionally referred to herself as "a man" or ironically used the pronoun "he," eschewed traditional "feminine" roles, and was prescient about the shifting socially constructed notions of gender and sexuality that arose after World War I. She lived and wrote about postmodern sexual fluidity.

However, a year before the publication of Hall's novel, Rosamond Lehmann had also ventured into the field with *Dusty Answer*, 1927, a story of a woman who was attracted to both men and women. The book was a *succès de scandale*. Lesbian themes seemed to be more culturally acceptable and got more play in the public realm—though Radclyffe Hall was famously censored in 1928, the same year that Woolf circled around the same topic in her mock biography, *Orlando*, a love letter to Vita Sackville-West. Woolf's novel became a best-seller, under the radar of censorship because of the clever playfulness and understatement as Orlando transforms from a man to a woman:

> As all Orlando's loves had been women, now, through the culpable laggardry of the human frame to adapt itself to convention, though she herself was a woman, it was still a woman she loved; and if the consciousness of being of the same sex had any effect at all, it was to quicken and deepen those feelings which she had had as a man.[158]

About the time she wrote *Dusty Answer*, Lehmann remembered that there was a "great homosexual wave" at Cambridge and Oxford: everyone "either seemed homosexual or was pretending to be." She remarked that her first husband, Leslie Runciman, wrote to a Cambridge friend when they married, "You might think it degrading of me to settle for a woman, but she is different—she has the mind of a man."[159] This was the same "compliment" paid to Bowen.

The masking of homosexuality was not necessary in all social circles, as in the Oxford circle Bowen joined in the 1920s or in the frank society of Bloomsbury. In the 1920s, the fashion for "being Greek" was embraced at Oxford and Cambridge, and according to Lehmann, there was an openness at the beginning of the "great homosexual wave." She remembered it as a time when everyone was a homosexual or pretended to be. Others such as Woolf intuited that Bowen was attracted to women as well as men. Woolf wrote to Ethel Smyth in 1932 that "Miss Bowen" was visiting and "stammers and blushes."[160] Woolf also used the visit to incite jealousy in Vita Sackville-West with whom she had an erotic relationship, and she wrote to her in October 1932:

> My Elizabeth [Bowen] comes to see me alone, tomorrow. I rather think, as I told you, that her emotions sway in a certain way (that's an elegiac). I'm reading her novel to find out [*To the North*]. What's so interesting is when one uncovers an emotion that the person themselves, I should say herself, doesn't suspect. And it's a sort of duty don't you think—revealing peoples true selves to themselves? I don't like these sleeping princesses.[161]

Sly Virginia. But was Bowen "sleeping"?

A year before *Eva Trout* was published, Charles Ritchie noted in his journal, "I sympathise at the moment with E's anti-queer phase which was one of the precipitants of her new novel 'Eva Trout', now so nearly finished."[162] Though a puzzling remark given that the novel allows expression of homosexuality, it marks Bowen's concern with the topic. Was this a response to the 1967 Sexual Offenses Act? Or was it more personal? Bowen once related to Francis King that if any of her affairs became apparent to anyone else through rumor, she would defensively eliminate with "acid" any public suspicion. Was Bowen then working to squelch Ritchie's suspicion of her proclivities around the time she was writing *Eva Trout?* In the early 1950s, Bowen developed a friendship with flamboyant Nancy Spain, a journalist, broadcaster, and writer of detective stories who was also a media celebrity and lesbian icon at the time. Bowen wrote to Ritchie in January of that year that she went to a party with her "new girlfriend."[163] Bowen continued, she is "a great deal younger than me," 19 years, which followed Bowen's preferred pattern in relationships with women. She added: "I had a vacancy for a girl friend, and she just fills it … she's nice and gay and rattling." Bowen thought Spain was Anglo-Irish (she was not), and it prompted her to announce that she liked Anglo-Irish women "with make-up put on one-sidedly and generally a button off here or there or having forgotten one earring," better than intellectual or rich Englishwomen. Bowen's friend the novelist Jane Howard confirmed Bowen's relationship and said that in the summer of 1950–51, Spain had invited her to go to Bowen's Court with her, but she demurred, not really knowing Bowen at the time.[164] Bowen also entered the lesbian circle of "B," Beatrice Horton who was the sister of her literary agent, Curtis Brown, "B" worked as a freelance writer who wrote historical fiction that interested Bowen as well as children's stories; worked for the British Civil Service during the war and for the BBC Radio 3 from 1947 to 1956, during which time she interviewed Bowen. In 1960, when Bowen moved back to Old Headington, Oxford, she stayed with B. Horton in Lewes while her residence was being readied. Horton was part of a circle of her "girlfriends," as Ritchie termed them. These experiences flicker in her stories and novels. But the sustaining love of her life was Charles Ritchie.

"Interlocking Minds": Charles Ritchie

"It was my love for her that I was gradually putting together as one composes a book," reflects Proust's Marcel about his love for Gilberte; the same might be said of Bowen's 32-year passion for Charles Ritchie.[165] Ardent letters from an otherwise reserved Bowen reveal not only her strong attraction to Ritchie and the way in which she "made up" her life with him as a book (and in her books), but the neglected fact that romantic love was an important and absorbing emotion in her life and writing. For Ritchie, Bowen had the quality of a looking glass, as Virginia Woolf would quip, "possessing the magic and delicious power of reflecting the figure of man at twice its natural size." He commented on her ability to enhance his sense of himself, to remind him of his imaginative, poetic, and secret self hidden beneath his glittering social and diplomatic life. She sparked his sensibility, he said, and created inimitable conversation as no other woman could (and there were others). Bowen engaged in composing art and life side by side, not drawing conventional lines between the two. Her passion and feeling as expressed in letters, was seemingly greater than his: she returned all his letters to him at the end of her life, and he destroyed, according to Glendinning and Robertson, most of them, leaving us with her letters and his private diary. Her feeling was not "deadened," "disfigured," or "withheld," as critics often assert in life or literature in her passionate and frequent letters while waiting and longing for his "beloved blue envelopes." Bowen's meetings with Ritchie were furtive and infrequent, often for only a week at a time, at Bowen's Court in Ireland, Clarence Terrace in London, or at his diplomatic posts in Paris, Berlin, New York, Washington, and Canada. Yet her daily thoughts and writing were intertwined with him, particularly during their heightened affair in London during the blitz when "unmarriedness" was in the air for Bowen, and women like Louie in *The Heat of the Day*.[166] An intense sensual and emotional current flows through the relationships between men and women, and women and women, and the women in her writing do not fear or hold back feeling; in fact, an intimate narrative tension is created by their feeling too much and, sometimes, as in Bowen's relationship with Ritchie, more than the men or women with whom they are involved. The passion of Karen and Naomi for Max in *The House in Paris*; Portia for Eddie in *The Death of the Heart*; Antonia and Lilia for Guy in *A World of Love*; Stella for Kelway in *The Heat of the Day*; and Eva in *Eva Trout* overshoots their living (and sometimes dead) partners. Love leads to disappointment, frustration, rage, disillusionment, personal wreckage and, sometimes, death. Nevertheless, like a clever Jane Austen heroine, Bowen sought men in her life like Ritchie who were gifted, intellectual, articulate and, to some degree, literary and imaginative, craving as she did, mutual understanding and good conversation to strengthen the bond of "interlocking minds" and bodies.[167]

She and Charles Ritchie, the Canadian diplomat, first met on February 10, 1941, at the christening William (Billy) Buchan's daughter, Perdita, to whom Bowen was godmother. At that time, Bowen had been married for 18 years to Alan Cameron and had published six novels and four books of short stories. After meeting Bowen, Ritchie wrote in his journal that she was "well-dressed, intelligent, handsome face, watchful eyes."[168] He had expected "someone more

Irish, more silent and brooding and at the same time more irresponsible. I was slightly surprised by her being so much 'on the spot.'" Six months later, she seemed "all romance and girlish seriousness," but Ritchie soon recognized that she was "as acute as a razor blade and about as merciful."[169] He detected early a hardness in her that he and other lovers would suffer or relish in their relationship and conversation. Like Veronica in *The Hotel*, "There was something pleasantly hard about her; at every contact one was conscious of the blade in her deep down with a fine edge on it." If Ritchie noted her mind, he did not neglect her body, and eight months after they met, he again wrote in his journal, "The contrast between her face and body seems symbolic [...] It is a powerful, mature rather handsome face. But the body is that of a young woman. The most beautiful body I have seen. It is pure in line and contour, lovely long legs and small almost immature firm breasts. Naked she becomes poetic, ruthless and young."[170] Early on, his feelings wavered and he wished the affair over, but a year and a half later, he knew the relationship was not transient. Finding her in a room full of mirrors and flowers and books in her Clarence Terrace townhouse, he asked, "Of what is her magic made?" noting that she cast a spell and that her eye missed nothing. He captured her brilliance in his apt style: "Her uncanny intuitions, her flashes of insight like summer lightning at once fascinated and disturbed me. Now day by day I have been discovering more and more of her generous nature, her wit and funniness, the stammering flow of her enthralling talk, the idiosyncrasies, vagaries of her temperament."[171] He was 6 years her junior, a pattern in her love affairs: Humphrey House, 10 years younger; Goronwy Rees, 10; May Sarton, 15; Sean O'Faolain, a year.

In addition, Ritchie had to contend with her as a well-established writer who was in the center of some social and literary circles in London when they met. He queried in his journal whether he would ever have fallen for her if it were not for her books: "I very much doubt it. But now I can't separate her from her literary self. It's as if the woman I 'love' were always accompanied by a companion spirit infinitely more exciting and more poetic and more profound than E. herself."[172] Perhaps this doubleness enhances and is in the nature of relationships with artists, for the writer and the companion. When they met, he was a junior Canadian diplomat and she, a celebrated writer, having already published six novels and five collections of short stories. Her imagination fueled her novels, enhancing and sometimes burdening the relationship. Her writing, particularly the novel *The Heat of the Day*, transformed their wartime years in London into fiction, just as Ritchie's highly regarded memoir, *The Siren Years*, charts their days during the same years. He too was also always writing, not only official diplomatic documents but letters and his journal and Bowen treasured this aspect of his talents: "You see, along with the effective, operative side of yourself, you carry the burden of an imaginative nature—for it *is* a burden, as well as a gift, the equivalent of genius."[173] She nurtured his imaginative side, challenging his social, diplomatic self. Her belief in his talent and writing is confirmed in publication of three volumes of scintillating journals and writing about the war years and his life as a diplomat after her death.[174]

Bowen and Ritchie also shared the feeling of being outsiders in England and insiders in Ireland and Canada with a heritage of their own. They both saw England from an oblique angle. Ritchie was born into a well-established family in Halifax, Nova Scotia, boasted a lineage from England, and attended Pembroke College, Oxford; Bowen descended from a 300-year Anglo-Irish line of Bowens and Colleys in Ireland, living in England most of her life. They were "in" but not "of" England. They also shared a life of movement, both adapting to frequent travel in England, France, Germany, Italy, Canada, and America. Bowen said of their itinerant lives, "I think we are curiously self-made creatures, carrying our personal worlds around with us like snails their shell. I am strongly and idiosyncratically Irish in the same way that you are Canadian, cagey, recalcitrant, on the run, bristling with reservations and arrogances that one doesn't show."[175]

Bowen and Ritchie experienced their infrequent times together in an altered state, a romance heightened by the bombs that exploded around them during the war, days in London during the blitz that Bowen transformed into her brilliant wartime novel, *The Heat of the Day*, memoir, and essays; Ritchie, into his vibrant diary, *The Siren Years*. Their letters reveal that they rather self-consciously read each other's words. Ritchie falling in love with Bowen acknowledged his sensual passion but he also always praised her companion spirit as an artist: "I am in love with E imaginatively. She even has a strange beauty like a woman in a tapestry."[176] At other times, he felt "like a character in one of her stories—a romantic character obsessed with love and brought to liveliness by absurdities and vices."[177] In the same journal entry, written two years after their first meeting, he observed that he had taken a "mortal risk in becoming and remaining her lover." Bowen too took a risk and generally avoided noticing his marriage and other loves, particularly Ann Payne, whom he met in Paris in 1929 or 1930, and with whom he maintained a long relationship, along with other intermittent relationships over the years. She adored him and imaginatively embellished him, like a character in one of her books. When in Madrid in the 1950s, she writes to him about standing in a roomful of El Grecos where she realizes, "You are as I've always said very like something in an El Greco. The more El Grecos I see, the more I see that."[178] This quality exhilarated Ritchie, the "sudden outbreak of her odd, brilliant visual talk"[179] (Fig. 5.3).

Fig. 5.3 Charles Ritchie. Rights holder and Courtesy of the Estate of Judith Robertson

It was also a relationship, as Ritchie acknowledged, that "floated on alcohol." Bowen's cousin, Laetitia, observed of Bowen's drinking habits at Bowen's Court, "glasses started clinking early in the day, tea at 4, then gin on ice." She presents a memory of Bowen, cigarette and drink in hand, often coughing, and addressing her, Ritchie, and others she felt an affection for as "darling."

As Bowen continued to yearn, Ritchie's affections in 1945 vacillated among his fiancée Sylvia, Bowen, and other women. In April 1946, he wrote in his journal of his sexual excesses with another: "Symptoms 12 hrs after—rapid heart action, guilt, feverish erotic spasm, irritability and cruelty."[180] He was a man who liked his pleasures, acknowledging that there were different kinds of love. He may have been in flight from marriage, at times, fearful that Sylvia had become a "symbol of obligations, and this was stripping her of all charm [...] What can I do with my shifting irresolute nature which spoils other people's lives and my own."[181] Yet Ritchie was also aware of the heartbreak in his relationship with Bowen, tenaciously waiting in the background. He continued his lament, being frozen "in the same trance of indecision between love and doubt." He would compare himself in one letter to the characters in Somerset Maugham's book *The Narrow Corner*, where two men marooned in far-off Malaysia spar for the love of the same beautiful, tragic woman. Ritchie felt it was a perfect novel for his mood in 1947 as he usually was suspended between two (or more) women: Bowen accepted the triangle of his marriage, intuiting his other relationships.

November 1946 brought the first mention of Ritchie's intention to marry Sylvia Smellie, and Bowen took the high road: "Charles, I don't want you to think I am going to take your marriage *au grand tragique*. I can take it how you want me to, and I will."[182] Upon the eve of this marriage in 1948, Bowen wrote:

> You are extraordinary, I am extraordinary, we have been extraordinary together. I ought (I can see how you could feel it) to be able to take one more extraordinary thing (your marriage.) The incalculable thing is sadness—how it shoots one down. The moment one is sad one is ordinary.[183]

She was stricken by this relationship that drew Ritchie away from her to Sylvia and Canada, but willed herself not to be "sad," never one to engage in self-pity. She elevated Ritchie and herself as "extraordinary" people who would not let a conventional marriage interfere in their romance. What *is* extraordinary about Bowen is the strength of her resolve, her imagination, her belief in herself, and her bond with Ritchie, as well as her bravery in continuing their relationship. Bowen haunted Ritchie's marriage. Beginning in January 1947, Ritchie was in Paris for three years as counselor to the Canadian Embassy, and they would meet intermittently at 218 Boulevard St. Germaine, a place that Bowen loved. Ritchie wrote a charming letter that incidentally reveals his literary gifts to Lester Pearson, Canadian diplomat, claiming that this flat on the left bank was "too expensive for me, too large for me, too cold for me, but all the same very attractive."[184] It was here, about eight months before his marriage, that Bowen decided to give Ritchie a ring with the engraving of his family crest—"Virtute Aquiretur Honos," Let Honor Be Acquired by Virtue—longing "to have the ring to put on your finger, not just post."[185] Though it is not known if the ring was given, it is a poignant fantasy revealing again Bowen's longing to symbolically marry. During this same period, however, Ritchie's erotic interests were elsewhere and he related an affair with "M" from April through June 1947.[186] Her passion continued unabated. She wrote to him in the hospital of her frustration about not being able to communicate with him during the labor and postal strikes in Paris that year:

I suppose I'd have been more of a frenzy if I didn't feel so one with you … so indissolubly wrapped up in you: the feeling of closeness I've had to you here day and night, since you left has been extraordinary. You do completely colour and fill my life.

Nine months later, January 16, 1948, he married Sylvia. No letters survive from Bowen to Ritchie in the period that began eight months after his marriage, from September 1948 to March 1949. Though he was still in Paris, he was with Sylvia, which meant longer separations from Bowen who suffered his absence. Ever defended, stoic, and play-acting, she compared herself to a soldier's wife, noting how many wonderful women had to endure separations from husbands during the war. She asserted that she experienced no such separation and aggrandized her longing. Meanwhile, Ritchie, ever ambivalent, wrote in his journal in 1948 that leaving her like this was a kind of "death."

Sean O'Faolain implied that Cameron's lack of jealousy afforded Bowen this independent, guilt-free love life with Ritchie and others. In the heightened years of her relationship with him, about 1941–46, she balanced life with both men: she did not intend to leave her stable life with Cameron and Ritchie was not offering marriage. A year after Ritchie's marriage, however, Bowen's "extraordinariness" began to fade, as she could no longer cling to the belief that nothing would change. She described her inability to accept his marriage as a defect in herself, exhibiting a masochistic side in a letter to Ritchie: "I do know there is a fault in me, and I bless you for your forgivingness and understanding. I depend on you more than you perhaps even you know […] My inability—though this only breaks out from time to time—to take the fact of your being married to someone else is a sort of deformity in me, like my stammer. Help me with it. The thing—the un-resignation—takes such complex forms: I never know at what moment it isn't going to leap on me like a tiger."[187] Throughout their 32-year relationship, she struggled with imposed periods of self-denial and renunciation, especially since he was not only married but usually in another country and, sometimes, with another woman.

Ritchie had an evenness of temper and ability to balance loves of different kinds while, at the same time, leading a demanding diplomatic career. Discreet, unflappable, and distinguished, he had personal charms that Bowen prized: intellect, imagination, talent, social skills, wit in conversation, and sexiness. Sharing Bowen's distaste for what John Banville termed married "guilt," assessed as a conventional and unnecessary emotion, Ritchie led an independent love life. He confessed in his journal, "with me love for a woman is always linked with a need to betray that love; a compulsion which I dread and desire."[188] Nevertheless, his love for Bowen persisted as he believed she elicited his truer, creative, and more mature self. She loved his gay company, and when he was in his "bachelor phase" in 1955, she wrote from Rome: "My darling [...] Do you realize that going about by yourself you're a different man [...] That is your natural element—gaiety, élan, amusement."[189] But when they were separated, the agony of missing him and her "increasing unsatiable loneliness," particularly in the late 1950s, overcame her again and again.

Bowen's letters to Ritchie faltered around 1957–58, when Ritchie was in New York, acting distant. This was also a time when Eddie Sackville-West—music critic, novelist, and cousin of Vita Sackville-West—who was attracted to Bowen, moved to Ireland to be near her. A caring but platonic relationship evolved as he was homosexual and often sought the companionship of a strong woman. Bowen heard from Ritchie infrequently during this period, and welcomed Sackville-West's attention though the relationship was ultimately frustrated by his frequent illnesses, the sale of Bowen's Court, and her love for Ritchie.

What was extraordinary about Ritchie was not only his *bon vivant* personality, which attracted women, but also his talent as both a statesman and a writer. Bowen, a disciplined personality herself, admired not only these talents but his "fibre and self command."[190] Glendinning referred to him as "the least hysterical of men." Always insightful, Bowen, nevertheless, would attempt to domesticate him, and he acknowledged early in their relationship, "when she has finished with me, I may be grown up instead of a permanent adolescent."[191] Change of many kinds rocked their long relationship, but he acknowledged early on that Bowen was "the goal towards which part of my nature, the deepest laid and most personal part, has always been drawn."[192] He had other relationships but he found her a woman of unusual intellect, perspicacity, and talent, a kind of companionship unmatched anywhere else in his life. But his marriage, his wandering desire, his thriving diplomatic career, and Bowen's increasing success as a writer and a public intellectual created impediments to their union.

During her early years with Ritchie, Bowen knew that he was a sensuous man who had taken pleasure in a "bachelor life" before and after his marriage. He never said he planned to marry Bowen, and she did not press him, it seems, until Cameron's death in 1952. Ritchie, a man who delighted in the various textures of life and other women, registered, at times, "a little shock of distaste to have a competent and intellectually honest woman about. I like women extravagant, late for appointments, willful, fond of showy clothes and society, vague, drifting, dreamy."[193] In 1947, he partied in France with Greta Garbo, Lady Diana Cooper, and Nancy Mitford. A year later Bowen would warn him of his "dreary parties in Paris. If you keep grinning like a dog and running about the city," she said to Ritchie, he would lose his looks, his hair, and his fascination.[194] Involved at another time with a ballerina, he admitted that he sometimes sought qualities that were the opposite of Bowen: she was too competent, too forthright about her passion, and transparent in her affection. A year into his relationship with her in 1942, Richie announced that "indifference" went a long way with him in women.[195] Markie similarly says of Emmeline in *To the North* that her feeling and passion overshot his, making him uncomfortable.

In fiction she shaped what she could not control in life, particularly after her husband's death in 1952, when her emotional life tipped. Her experience contributed to the kinds of love she represented in her novels written during her long affair with Ritchie: love that is betrayed and disappointing, as with Stella in *The Heat of the Day*, or the competitive jealous love of Antonia and Lilia for the same man in *A World of Love*, or a frustrated love like Eva's love for Mr. Arable in *Eva Trout*. After 1952 there was an imbalance: she, a woman alone and lonely after Cameron's death; Ritchie, married, and a man about town. She was devastated when she finally abandoned hope of marrying Ritchie. When they squabbled in 1954, he reflected on the unreality of his happiness when he was with her, and she remarked on the unreality of her life when she was not with him. His defense always was to numb his feelings. Yet her frequent letters drew him closer, and he acknowledged attachment even after the "gashes" of her outbursts "poisoned" their relationship in incidents after Cameron's death. In a letter that provides no explanation, Ritchie reported an outburst in Bonn that almost ended their relationship: "we come back and back to the same subject [crossed out word, "marriage"] to have nothing to look forward to, that my feelings are getting number—yet not unhappy, her."[196] Such dialogue surfaced again and again but Ritchie was stunned when Bowen drove her desperate emotions underground—they "fuelled her writing"—and continued to write. When he read *The World of Love*, which she was writing during that 1954 Bonn visit, he realized it as "a triumph for her."[197] He found the "book racing through me, the happiness of this morning." He was astounded once more that, during this time of loneliness and despair, she could concentrate and write the final chapters "in the nightmare agitation of that visit to Bonn ... [when] she was distractedly unhappy." Her emotion was expressed in fiction though in life she held her feelings in check, sustained by temperament, habit, and social training. But an emotional abyss lay, at times, beneath her writing.

But Ritchie was "exhilarated" by her literary spirit; he loved Bowen the writer. He registered his contribution to her life, wryly adding that the book has "been bought at a price paid by her perhaps even more by me. It is our book as it contains our shared illusion of life, and could not, as they say in prefaces, have been written without me." Sometimes, though, Ritchie felt as if he were in a book, involved in a relationship of her composing. Just a year after they met, they strolled through Kew Gardens in a dreamlike state, a kind of "drifting" together that Ritchie mentioned often: "It was a day like a page from one of her books, the involved relationship between the two lovers who are wandering among the flower beds."[198] He mentioned the "giddy feeling of being carried along on the tide of her imagination, being transmuted into literature: sitting for my portrait or being swallowed alive." He was sometimes used and imaginatively shaped by Bowen. He concluded on that day in 1942 that the relationship had turned arid, saying that "desire is dead," a year after they met. But his feelings would wax and wane amid other relationships, reflecting what he described as his irresolute nature.

Writing, for Bowen, filled the gaps of Ritchie's absences; he living most of the time in Canada with his wife, and she, with Cameron in London. "What would I do (I mean under the circumstances) if I were not writing. I simply can't think. Writing […] is more than a compensation for not being with you: it's become an extension of us, a part of us."[199] And so her writing and his, particularly their letters, given that they were both of strong imagination, intellect, and talent, were an unusual part of the texture of their romantic life. This quality sometimes blurred the line between fiction and life. Bowen admitted no less, 15 years after they met: "I'm talking to you as though you were here. And you are here. Never has any one's house been so filled by any one person."[200] For Bowen, imagination did not admit absence.

Bowen and Ritchie's letters, memoir, and books extended and immortalized their relationship. When Bowen completed *The Heat of the Day* in 1948, dedicated to Ritchie, she wrote: "I love another letter you wrote me, about my novel. How extraordinary that it is your book and my book. Short of there having been a child there could be no other thing that was more you and me."[201] And when completing *Collected Impressions*, a book of her reviews, prefaces, and broadcasts, in 1950, she wrote that she once again had become "a mother." She ruminated in 1950, when she was 51, about having children when one is young, and wrote to Ritchie: "you are young still … you would have a very natural and egalitarian (inwardly) relationship with a child, a son, if you had one now … I feel it. And you know how I wish it … there is a genius in your nature that I feel is, somehow, bound to go on."[202]

Her life, however, was lived elsewhere, "round the edges of working on the novel [*The Heat of the Day*]. I am working at it about 8 hours a day (including the 2 or 3 hours I do after supper in the evenings)."[203] And yet she asserted that romance was necessary to her being, she could never "sublimate" and only "live for my work."[204] Her intertwined life and writing were sustained by Ritchie's intermittent visits, his words, his letters. When a letter did not arrive there was a rupture in her life, but when one did, in September 1945, she reflected:

> I don't know how I should live were it not for letters. How would one not (as you say), without the beloved evidence of a letter, come to torment oneself with the fear that love and the entire world of life that surrounds it was an illusion, subjective, brain-spun. As it is the unfolding of a letter from you, the whole cast and shape of the handwriting on the paper, even before I have begun to read what is written, gives me sort of a rush of nearness.[205]

She acknowledged a few years later that Ritchie had brought a new strength and growth to her writing, confirming that her books were also his: "You've given me not only greater comprehension but clearer vision than I had and made me more fearless. I feel this in my life: it would be strange if it didn't show at least to some extent in my writing."[206]

Bowen and Ritchie were sought-after guests, unlike Bowen and her husband. Ritchie knew many important people and celebrities, and loved parties, talk, and fun, as reflected in his memoir *Undiplomatic Diaries*, mentioning such personalities as Nancy Mitford, Marlene Dietrich, Anthony Powell, Angier Biddle Duke, and the Duchess of Westminster. Bowen, a hostess of repute, carried herself with élan and often entertained lavishly. She would tell the interviewer of a woman's magazine, *Housewife*, that she loved formal dress, candlelight, and flowers for her elegant dinner parties.

She dined with well-known writers and intellectuals: Berlin, Bowra, Connolly, and Cecil were favorites of Ritchie's. And there were excursions into Bloomsbury, though Ritchie found little originality there; he considered them a group of culturally agreeable people who thought alike. They also had a magical weekend with the eccentric writer, Stephen Tennant. Ritchie and Bowen enjoyed each other's company alone and with others. Even in the late fifties, the ebb of their relationship, Ritchie marveled at "the fascinating flow of E's talk, the pictures of places, people, the continual surprise and pleasure of her choice of a word, the funniness, poetry and brutality of her view of people and events."[207]

Both continued to write all their lives, through periods of personal and historical crisis. She always encouraged Ritchie's creative side, which she feared would be eclipsed by the rigors of his diplomatic career, and she continued to write through times of despair. In May 1956, during a period when Ritchie's ardor cooled and her relationship with Eddie Sackville-West developed, he, nevertheless visited her at Bowen's Court. He continued to delight in her zestful conversation, "her youthfulness, her childishness, her tearing energy," and yet feeling like an aging hypochondriac, he wondered what he could do.[208] Knowing his own feelings, he pulled back, recognizing the brave face Bowen put on her disappointment. It was four years after the death of her husband, and Bowen's fantasy of Ritchie leaving his wife and living with her at Bowen's Court was unfulfilled. He did not act. Ritchie wrote in his journal, "the weather outside these big windows in this bedroom has turned again from a hard light to a cloud. There is heartbreak in this house, in this person."[209] No absence blunted her sensuous imagination or tender feelings toward him though she was in despair in 1967 when she saw him for such short times. In 1969, a few years before her death, she again bought him a ring, a carnelian signet ring on Bond Street, something to remember her by, she said.[210] She associated her life with him so closely to Bowen's Court that she claimed that she would leave the house forever if her inner life with him died. When she finally moved to the small house in Hythe in her last years, there was always a room there for Ritchie's visits. Her longing to be with him persisted to the end of her life.

This dominant relationship, like her other romantic affairs, was expressed and judged by an intelligent, proud, and ironic self; at other times, when her emotions were unleashed, by an obsessed woman who became frustrated when she could not always have her way. In her fiction, she creatively embellished these relationships. Fueled by the complexity of a woman's needs, passions, pleasures, frustrations, and disappointments, her fiction portrays a world of values from the perspective of female characters. For example, she explores lesbian love in *The Hotel, Eva Trout* and other stories; the malaise of marriage in the character of Anna and the heartbreak of adolescent love in Portia in *The Death of the Heart*; the ruthlessness of furtive love expressed by Karen in her affair with her best friend's fiancée, Max, in *The House in Paris*; the haunted past love of Antonia for Guy, the dead soldier, in *A World of Love*; and the constriction of marriage in *Friends and Relations*. In her life and writing, Bowen depicted romance and sex through the lens of a perspicacious, adventurous, ironic or, sometimes, blinded modern woman. In *The House in Paris*, in Max's absence, Karen weeps and walks about the room repeating, "Max, Max, Max! This was a moment to meet; life stood at its height in this room and she wanted him to come in," echoing Bowen's own exclamation in letters, "Charles, Charles, Charles."[211] Bowen's lovers not only evade the marriage plot and gender categories but, sometimes, embrace death. Max and Karen will never marry and Max will commit suicide; Emmeline and Markie's sexual drive will lead them to death on a dark road. O'Faolain caught the perturbation and threat of love and death beneath Bowen's romance: "Eliza's tremulous to terrible theme is that although love is, indeed, the one experience worthy to be crowned, its mask carries death between its lips."[212]

Notes

1. David Cecil's comments, "Sunday Feature: Radio 3," April 2, 2000, BBC, NSA.
2. Berlin, interview by Michael Ignatieff, May 7, 1991, MI Tape 13, p. 16. Berlin was 81 years old.
3. Corcoran, "Sunday Feature: Radio 3," April 2, 2000, BBC, NSA.
4. Glendinning, *Elizabeth Bowen*, 106.
5. "Woman's Hour," Lee and Lively.
6. Glendinning, *Elizabeth Bowen*, 51.
7. *MT*, 194–195.
8. EB to CR, November 18, 1945, *LCW*, 45.
9. Corcoran, "Sunday Feature: Radio 3," April 2, 2000, BBC, NSA.
10. "Horrors of Childhood," 111—see Hepburn, Essays?*
11. EB to CR, November 23, 1946, *LCW*, 101–102.
12. Bowen, letter to Charles Ritchie, December 20, 1957, Glendinning LCW, 192.
13. *BC*, 75.
14. Molly Keane, "Life with the Lid Off," September 28, 1983, BBC, NSA.
15. EB to CR, January 5, 1950, *LCW*, 149.
16. National Archive sources and National Archive Medal Cards (WO372), BNL.
17. *FR*, 91.
18. Lehmann, "Elizabeth Bowen—Obituary."
19. Molly Keane, "Elizabeth of Bowen's Court," *The Irish Times* [ca 1973]*.
20. EB to CR, January 30, 1945, *LCW*, 42.
21. EB to VW, August 26, 1935, SU.
22. Quennell, *Customs and Characters*, 89.
23. Glendinning, *Elizabeth Bowen*, 210.
24. Bowra, *Memories*, 190.
25. EB to Leslie Hartley, October 21, 1952, JRUL, MS Letters.
26. "Elizabeth and Her Highland Scot," Hennessy, Miscellaneous Files.
27. Bowen, "The Culture of Nostalgia," in Hepburn, *Listening In*, 98. "An abiding city," Bowen's recurrent phrase from Hebrews 1 3:14.
28. EB to IB, October 8, 1952, BOD, MS. Berlin 145v.
29. EB to MS, October 6, 1952, NYPL, MS. Sarton.
30. EB to IB, October 8, 1952, BOD, MS. Berlin 145r.
31. EB to SS, August 4, 1953, BOD, MS. Spender 39.

32. Sarton, *Shower of Summer Days*, 49.
33. HH to EB, July 12, 1933. HHC. With permission from the Literary Estate of Humphry House.
34. Woolf, letter to Vanessa Bell, May 4, 1934, *Letters* 5, 299.
35. IB to Marion Frankfurter, June 3, 1936, Berlin, *Flourishing*, 171.
36. See Curtis Brown files, HRC 10.5, January 28, and 46 other instances.
37. EB to CR, April 14, 1949, *LCW*, 136.
38. *HP*, 153, 157, 164.
39. John Bayley to EB (ca. 1968), about *ET*, HRC, Bowen 10.6.
40. EB, December 18, 1933, BOD, MS. Berlin 292, folio 14r.
41. EB to HH, fragment, 1937, HHC.
42. Proust, *Sodom and Gomorrah*, 139.
43. EB to HH, November 8, 1934, HHC.
44. CR journal, August 18, 1952, *LCW*, 182.
45. Powell, *Constant Novelist*, 120–21, 8.
46. Ibid., 8.
47. EB to HH, July 13, 1937, HHC.
48. Ibid., July 12, 1933.
49. *Dictionary of National Biography*, s.v. "Humphry House."
50. Ibid., June 3, 1936.
51. EB to HH, March 16, 1955, HHC.
52. Ibid., January 20, 1936.
53. HH to EB, June 14, 1933, HHC. With permission from the Literary Estate of Humphry House.
54. EB to HH, July 12, 1933, HHC.
55. EB to HH, July 12, 1933, HHC.
56. HH to EB, December 20, 1933, HHC. With permission from the Literary Estate of Humphry House.
57. Bowen's letters to House missing after 1934: in Madeline's possession after House's death, 1955, probably repressed or destroyed.
58. IB to Maire Gaster née Lynd, January 11, 1982, Berlin, *Flourishing*, 52n1.
59. EB to WP, August 3, 1927, DUR 19.
60. IB to EB, December 1933, BOD Ms Berlin, 245, folio 14.
61. EB to HH, January 20, 1936, HHC.
62. EB to CR, September 7, 1948, *LCW*, 134.
63. EB to HH, January 20, 1936, HHC.
64. Arthur Calder-Marshall to EB (n.d.), HRC, 10.6.
65. John House, interview by PL, London, June 2011.
66. Masters, "John House—Obituary."
67. Maurice Bowra to EB, February 24, 1955, HRC 10.6.
68. EB to HH, November 8, 1934, HHC.
69. *HP*, 159, 55.
70. Ibid., 55.

71. *CS*, 510.
72. EB to HH, July 12, 1933, HHC.
73. Ibid. November 8, 1934.
74. Ibid.
75. Ibid.
76. Ibid., May 18, 1935.
77. Ibid., June 6, 1934.
78. *LS*, 128.
79. Dierdre Toomey: *Dictionary of National Biography*, s.v. "Humphrey House."
80. Ridler, *Olive Willis and Downe House*.
81. EB to CR, November 18, 1945, *LCW*, 74.
82. Kreilkamp, in Walshe, *Elizabeth Bowen: Visions and Revisions*, 11.
83. IB to Mary Fisher, October 23, 1936, Berlin, *Flourishing*, 210.
84. Plomer, sketch from *At Home*, 52.
85. Rees, *Looking for Mr. Nobody*, 83–84.
86. Ibid., 85.
87. IB to Rosamond Lehmann, early October 1936, Berlin, *Flourishing*, 203–204.
88. EB to IB, shortly after September 23, 1936, BOD, MS. Berlin 245, fols. 64–5.
89. Berlin, interview by Michael Ignatieff, May 7, 1991, MI, Tape 13, p. 17.
90. Ibid.
91. Lehmann, "Elizabeth Bowen—Obituary."
92. EB to CR, October 24, 1949, *LCW*, 142–143.
93. EB to IB, September [n.d.] 1936, BOD, MS. Berlin 245.
94. See David, *Olivia Manning*, 11.
95. GR to IB, September 26, 1936, BOD, MS. Berlin 274, folio 27.
96. CR journal, January 30, 1943, *LCW*, 36.
97. GR to IB, September 26, 1936, BOD, MS. Berlin 274, folio 27.
98. O'Faolain, *Vive Moi*, 301–303.
99. EB to WP, August 17, 1936, DUR 19.
100. EB to HH, May [n.d.], 1937, HHC.
101. *SIW*, preface.
102. EB to HH, May [n.d.], 1937, HHC.
103. SOF to EB, July 1939, HRC 11.7.
104. O'Faolain, *Vive Moi*, 304.
105. Bowen, "Summer Night," *CS*, 588.
106. Ibid., 300–301.
107. See Heather Ingman, 96ff.
108. O'Faolain, ed., *The Bell*, February 1941.
109. SOF to EB, April 22, 1937, HRC 11.6.
110. O'Faolain, *Vive Moi*, 311.
111. SOF to EB, April 22, 1937, HRC 11.6.

112. Ibid.
113. Julia O'Faolain, afterword to *Vive Moi*, xiii.
114. Ibid. 304–305.
115. Ibid., 301.
116. Ibid., xi.
117. Ibid., 304–307.
118. Ibid., 310.
119. EB to MS, 1936–1956, NYPL, MSS Sarton.
120. Ann Waldron. *Eudora Welty, A Writer's Life*, 209.
121. Woolf, April 9, 1937, *Letters* 6, 118n2.
122. EB to CR, January 11, 1942, in Ritchie, *Siren Years*, 131.
123. Berthoff interview.
124. EB to MS, May 31, 1937, NYPL, MSS Sarton.
125. Woolf, October 9, 1937, *Letters* 6, 181.
126. CR to EB, April 22, 1960, *LCW*, 396.
127. CR journal, June 28, 1959, *LCW*, 324–325.
128. MS to EB, November 20, 1935, NYPL, MSS Sarton.
129. Sarton, *World of Light*, 192–193.
130. MS to EB, December 11, 1938, NYPL, MSS Sarton.
131. Sarton, *World of Light*, 197.
132. EB to MS, n.d., 1937, NYPL, MSS Sarton.
133. Ibid., June 8, 1937.
134. Ibid., August 1, 1937.
135. Ibid., August 30, 1937.
136. VW to EB, April 9, 1937. See *Letters* 6, 119 n2.
137. VW to MS, June 16, 1937, *Letters* 6, 137.
138. MS to EB, May 26, 1939, HRC 12.2.
139. Ibid., January 16, 1938.
140. Ibid., December 11, 1938.
141. EB to MS, May 31, 1937, HRC 12.2.
142. Cynthia Lovelace Sears, interview by PL, New York, May 8, 2008.
143. EB to MS, October 6, 1952, NYPL, MSS Sarton.
144. EB to MS, June 9, 1952. HRC 12.2.
145. MS to EB, August 25, 1965, HRC 12.2.
146. *LCW*, Comment, 358.
147. EW to EB, n.d. (ca. spring 1951), HRC 12.3.
148. Marrs, *Eudora Welty*, 190–202.
149. Welty to Maxwell, *What There is to Say…* March 30, 1968, 248–249.
150. Ibid., September 4, 1983, 386.
151. EB to CR, October 22, 1945, *LCW*, 71.
152. LeFanu, *Carmilla*, 32.
153. *ET*, 54.
154. Lassner and Derdiger, "Domestic Gothic," 195–214.

155. *ET*, 40.
156. Woolf, *Diary*, 3, 193.
157. A.E. Coppard to EB, August 12, 1932, HRC 10.6.
158. Woolf, *Orlando*, 161.
159. Lehmann, "Rosamond Lehmann—Interview," *Paris Review*.
160. VW to Ethel Smyth, March 17, 1932, *Letters* 5, 35.
161. VW to Vita Sackville-West, October 18, 1932, *Letters* 5, 111.
162. *CR Journal*, November 20, 1967, *LCW*, 446.
163. EB to CR, January 7, 1950, *LCW*, 152–153.
164. Howard, *Slipstream*, 218.
165. Proust, *Swann's Way*, 571.
166. *HD*, 49. Also see Feigel, *The Love Charm of Bombs*, traces the love lives of five writers during the London blitz—including Bowen.
167. EB to CR, May 7, 1962, *LCW*, 385.
168. Ritchie, *Siren Years*, 88.
169. Ibid., 22.
170. CR journal, September 29, 1941, *LCW*, 24.
171. Ritchie, *Siren Years*, 143.
172. Feigel, *Love Charm of Bombs*, 176–177.
173. EB to CR, January 1958, *LCW*, 13.
174. *The Siren Years: A Canadian Diplomat Abroad*, 1937–1945; *An Appetite for Life: The Education of a Young Diplomat*, 1924–1927; *Diplomatic Passport: More Unpublished Diaries*, 1946–1962.
175. Glendinning, *Elizabeth Bowen*.
176. Ritchie, *Siren Years*, May 25, 1982, 177.
177. CR journal, January 30, 1943, *LCW*, 36.
178. Ibid., October 6, 1954, 193.
179. CR journal, October 29, 1967, *LCW*, 445.
180. Ibid., April 7, 1946, 89.
181. Ibid., December 25, 1945, 81.
182. EB to CR, November 18, 1946, *LCW*, 99–100.
183. Ibid., January 16, 1948, 121.
184. CR to Lester Pearson, February 24, 1947.
185. EB to CR, April 2, 1947, *LCW*, 11.
186. CR journal, April 1, 1947. *LCW*, 107.
187. EB to CR, October 24, 1949, *LCW*, 141.
188. CR journal, August 18, 1953, *LCW*, 182.
189. EB to CR, March 16, 1955, *LCW*, 207–208.
190. Ibid., January 1958, 13.
191. CR journal, June 13, 1942, *LCW*, 33.
192. Ibid., September19, 1948, 133.
193. Ibid., May 1, 1947, 108.
194. EB to CR, August 1, 1948, *LCW*, 128.

195. CR journal, April 21, 1942, *LCW*, 32.
196. Ibid., December 9, 1954, 198.
197. Ibid.
198. Ibid., May 24, 1942, 32.
199. EB to CR, June 6, 1964, *LCW*, 424.
200. Ibid., May 15, 1956, 233.
201. EB to CR, June 17, 1948, *LCW*, 124.
202. Ibid., April 11, 1950, 166.
203. Ibid., December 6, 1947, 112–113.
204. Ibid., August 1, 1950, 175.
205. Ibid., September 2, 1945, 58–60.
206. EB to CR, December 6, 1947, *LCW* 113.
207. CR journal, May 9, 1955, *LCW*, 212–213.
208. Ibid., May 12, 1956, 232.
209. Ibid.
210. EB to CR, April 14, 1969, *LCW*, 454.
211. *HP*, 137.
212. O'Faolain, *Vive Moi*, 309.

6

Snapshots of War (1939–1945)

The Wars of the Century

Bowen grew up with the instabilities of war. She was, as she often said, the same age as the century, and after feeling the vibrations of the Great War when she was a teenager, she went to Dublin in 1919 to serve as a volunteer nurse for Irish soldiers who had served and returned with post-traumatic stress syndrome. The Irish fought with the British promise to end partition in mind—as a reward for their participation—but this never came to be, embittering many Irish. She observed not only the psychological pain of those soldiers, but later the convulsions and divisions of the Irish War of Independence.[1]

Bowen was prepared, she said, at the age of 12 "to handle any book like a bomb." Her charged words, describing her reading of Rider Haggard's *She*, exploded like the Great War around her. This book that had a "violent impact on her," would always remain intertwined with the landscapes of war.[2] Less than a mile from the Downe House School in Orpington, Kent, where Bowen was devouring this book, British military flights were taking off at the Biggin Hill Aerodrome to defend against German zeppelins. It was May 1915, the first time in history that London—as well as the Home Counties—was bombed from the air. Ramsgate, a Kentish coastal town about 60 miles from Bowen's school, was also bombed that year.[3] World War I had begun: "Hearing a clock strike, one morning, with more meaning than usual I stopped halfway up a grandstand to realize that time held war. The hour was more than my hour."[4] Rumors of violence outside brought, she said, "moral stress" to the students. Though she had no brothers in the war, and she rarely read newspapers, these years sharpened her awareness that there was a world beyond her

© The Author(s), under exclusive license to Springer Nature Switzerland AG 2021   **181**
P. Laurence, *Elizabeth Bowen*, Literary Lives, https://doi.org/10.1007/978-3-030-71360-7_6

personal one and she was living in history. This heightened historical consciousness marked her actions and writing for life that spanned World War I, the Irish War of Independence, World War II, the Cold War and the Vietnam War, major historic events in which the issues of colonialism, postcolonialism, Fascism, Nazism, and violence exploded. Bowen as a part of the beleaguered Anglo-Irish minority reveals not only a class but individual responses to these forces, and reading her anticipates in ways our thinking across cultures today. When Bowen returned to Ireland, the tension between the IRA and the Black and Tans was heightening.[5] She felt the threat to Bowen's Court and recalled her feelings at the age of 19 when living in Ireland. Her early life there, she said, affected her work in giving her an "objective view" of England.[6]

Later, when traveling in Italy, she saw demonstrations of Fascism. She took the Republican side in the Spanish Civil War in the late 1930s, and noted in one of her later wartime reports that Catholic support of Franco was "Catholic Fascism" or "pharisseeism."[7] Reflecting on the violence and despair of her generation as a result of these experiences, the narrator in *The Heat of the Day* comments on the numbness of people who got "all sealed up."[8] Bowen was of the same generation as Gavin in "Ivy Gripped the Steps," which "had seen the face of somebody dead who was still there—'old' because of the presence, under an icy screen, of a whole stopped mechanism for feeling."[9]

During World War II, living in London, Bowen was again troubled with war in the air, the "buzz bomberries," as she called them, guided missiles being used by the Luftwaffe, interrupting her work on her novel. The war reorganized her values and she and Cameron lived with the constant fear that bombs would strike their Clarence Terrace home, and part of her home was destroyed toward the end of the war. She wrote astutely about the convulsive effects of wartime not only on cities but on people's temperaments and relationships. Readers and critics notice how violence tears through her writings as she retreats to her writing table.

She knew the consequences of war in the lives of children. At the beginning of the war, Margaret Kennedy, her writer friend, had recounted evacuating her children from London; Rosamond Lehmann also wrote that she was moving to the country with her children and Cecil Day-Lewis, her lover. "Nothing undoes the years away when children are evacuated and return after the war," she asserted in her essay, "Opening Up the House." "The children who were in nursery school are at school; the children who were at school have grown up." Their lives are disrupted and when they return, the past is lost to them: their homes are unfamiliar, and to those children born somewhere else during the war, "this is going to be an unknown house. They sniff about for its history."[10] Understanding this, Bowen described the evacuation of children and the elderly in the seacoast towns just across from Calais, and how they lived out the war in her essays, "Dover" and "Folkestone." She sketches history ripping through the life of a young child in her story "Tears, Idle Tears." She is attuned to the dislocations, geographical and psychological, of children during the war. In her threatening story, "Summer Night," "the blood of the world is poisoned … There are no more children, the children are born knowing."[11] The mother in this story who is flying away to a lover "and not saying why or where" leaves her children at home. In this story, a "burning child," Vivie, acts out the anarchy in her home and in the world. The night her mother is out, she takes out a box of chalks and tattoos her naked body with snakes and stars and streams into the night like an animal. Her aunt finding her sweeps an eiderdown around her naked body, "wrap up, wrap up." All over Europe, children were dying, "and to wrap the burning child did not put out the fire" of the black tide of war.

A World of Love is also haunted by war. Though Jane, a beautiful teenage girl, is born after the war, a dead soldier shadows her young life when she learns through letters of her mother and Antonia's past love for him. The packet of his letters to her mother or Antonia (or do we know to whom the letters were directed?) "belonged to history" and through them the "wreckage left by the past" is forced upon her consciousness.[12] She senses the "bad odour" of the war—it is a sensation—and feels disequilibrium and heaviness, as "she had grown up amid extreme situations and frantic statements," and knew no one "apart from her own contemporaries, who did not speak of it either with falsifying piety or with bitterness." Similarly, in *The Little Girls*, a postwar novel, three old friends meet to recover their childhoods in Southstone, based on Bowen's remembered stability in her childhood town, Folkestone, in southeast England, blitzed in the war.

Imaginative Writing and History

Margaret Kennedy, her friend, wrote that "despite the force of bombs," literature still mattered.[13] She wrote an appreciative note to Bowen upon the publication of *The Death of the Heart*, noting that it "offered some of the pleasures of civilized life, which we think we have abandoned forever early last week." In spite of falling bombs, she asserted, "Whatever happens next, and I take the blackest view of it, some things are going on that might have vanished." Bowen continued to write throughout the war, and stated in her preface to "Ivy Gripped the Steps" that they were "between-time stories—mostly reactions from, or intermissions between major events."[14]

During this decade, she also attended the World Conference of Writers in 1941, the Paris Peace Conference in 1946 as a freelance journalist, and as a correspondent and cultural ambassador for the British government after the war. In February 1941, she met Ritchie and they spent the most extended period of their romance in wartime London. *The Heat of the Day*, which emerged from that period, "could only have been lived during the long progress of the war."[15] While writing this novel that captures the undercurrent of violent personal and national intrigue, she was also writing her family history, *Bowen's Court*. The big house is represented in these works with both a positive and negative charge. *Bowen's Court* was a project that Clair Wills, among others, believes was a cover for her Ministry of Information work in Ireland, as it enabled her to obtain a visa for her investigation of attitudes towards Irish neutrality, the sought-after ports, and to explore the Irish moral equivalency of the British and the Germans. Yet at least a year before she joined the MOI, she wrote to Humphry House of her "obsession" with the writing of her family history, unable to work on a Dickens essay she had promised, "Sorry about my dilatoriness and silence and un-progressiveness over the Dickens Book [...] since I was in Ireland, in this other thing I am doing, the Bowen's Court book, something between a chore and a tour de force, has become really rather an obsession—more so than any novel."[16]

Bowen did not focus her family's colonial history until writing *Bowen's Court* during World War II, and her political role as an agent for the British Ministry of Information at this time perhaps brought it into awareness. It led her to compare the Anglo-Irish colonization of Ireland in the seventeenth century to contemporary Fascism, and her ancestors' will to power in Ireland to Hitler's conquests across Europe. Both, she said, revealed the "subjection to fantasy and infatuation with the idea of power"; both drives began, she said, "in the heated brain" of a Cromwell, a Hitler, or a Mussolini.[17] Yet in her fiction, the big house, Mount Morris, is also an idyll of peace far from besieged London in *The Heat of the Day*.

Bowen professed that any imaginative writing was also always about history. "Ivy Gripped the Steps" registers historical changes in a decaying house through a young man's "tour of annihilation" in the town of Southstone that he knew as a child. The opening image is of ivy that "gripped and sucked at the flight of steps down which with such a deceptive wildness it seemed to be flowing like a cascade": a metaphor for the war that sucked the life out of the people and town. Ivy gripped the sealed gothic house, almost a tomb.[18] Bowen darkens her previously sunny childhood images of Folkestone as history enters her imaginative postwar writing creating an eerie atmosphere through a ghostly figure emerging in a crumbling house and town in "desuetude and decay" in 1944. Soldiers and ATS, a women's voluntary service during the war, still occupy parts of the town, and one figure emerges as Gavin walks around another house, the Concannons. An ATS girl in a khaki shirt, her face "abrupt with youth," sits at a window waiting to draw a blackout curtain. Gavin calls out, saying he used to know people who lived there. "'People lived there?' she said. 'Just fancy. I know I'd sooner live in a tomb. And that goes for all these places.'" In her preface to these stories in 1945, Bowen initiated a feminist perspective about women's wartime writing and what happened at home in the spaces between battles. "These are all wartime, none of them war, stories," she said. "There are no accounts of war action even as I knew it—for instance, air raids. Only one character in 'Mysterious Kor' is a soldier, and he only appears as a homeless wanderer round a city."

Bowen's "we" is distinguished from that of Ritchie and some other wartime men and women writers. In *The Heat of the Day*, Stella resents counterspy Harrison's use of the "perpetual we" of war. Your "we," Stella asserts, expressing the wartime feeling of community, is her "they."[19] Stella distinguishes herself as a mother and a woman on the homefront from the feeling that "war made us one big family."[20] She reacts to the war and what "they," the Army and war machine of which Harrison is a part, had "done" to her son, Roderick, that rendered him another person, in her view, emotionally impoverished. When he returns on furlough, visiting her in an "unfamiliar" flat, he is not the Roderick she remembered. "The Army," she thought, "was out to obliterate [him] in the course of a process, she could do nothing to stop it." Roderick projects a wariness, she thinks, a fear of the "expenditure of feeling" that the war has bred, and she perceives the "dissolution" of his words. Stella senses the impoverishment or diminution of his language with traces of the army, and, in the same vein, resents being "bludgeoned" by Harrison, the counterspy's language, his words resonant with police or military brutality. Bowen's liminal style blurs the line between outer and inner (like a moebius strip, a surface with only one side) in her depiction of how the war has personally diminished people, places and language. The room where Stella and her son meet is a "void" where time and the sense of hearing is cut off. Rooms had no names and nothing spoke—"silence was the blackout, registered by the hearing"—reminding us of the cerebral rooms of Beckett. It is "without environment" and Stella has the sensation of being on "furlough" from her own life. Though Bowen felt the war had to be fought, she registers the cost in human feeling, rooms, relationships, and language in her novel in which much of the story of the war is unsaid.

Stella is also betrayed by love, discovering that her embittered lover, Robert Kelway, is a Nazi spy. He is a survivor of Dunkirk, disaffected by his middle-class background. She rails against him: "if only you loved me, I could do no worse than not love you back; but there has been something worse—somehow you've distorted love" by intertwining her in his political betrayal. She too is turned into a spy on him as she dares not ask if he is a spy: "You may not feel what it feels like to be a spy; I do—ever since you came to me with that story. You've banked on my not having the courage to ask one question, and you've been right, so far." The distinction between personal and political collapses, and she is further estranged by the counterspy, Harrison, who makes repulsive attempts to blackmail her into sleeping with him to save her lover from punishment for treason. Bowen exposes Stella, as a mother and a woman and a spy, experiencing the explosive effects of war in her personal relations. She makes us sense and "feel" war in a woman.

Louie, the saucy, working-class young woman in the novel, enters into the bonding "we" of wartime feeling as she reads the daily newspaper accounts of war. Though she may feel a different "we" than Stella as she waits for her soldier husband to return, she also articulates a cultural bond, "women are all in one boat." It is this "we" that Bowen and other women writers explore in their war writing. Yet Ritchie and others came to a realization of another "we," writing in his memoir, *Siren Years* about everyday shock cases of wartime London. Though he once feared that his diaries were "too personal to see the light of day," 30 years later, in 1974, the "personal," he said, seemed "to merge into the 'we' of wartime London days." The diary, he says, brings "a breath of immediacy" to the war, but life is not transmuted into art in his diary. That, he said, is to be found only in a "work of genius," Bowen's *The Heat of the Day*. Bowen did not keep a diary; her wartime fiction represents her war experiences.

"The war changed everything," said John Bayley.[21] Ritchie's *The Siren Years* recounts the compelling day-to-day changes and catastrophes as well as flashes of his early romantic days with Bowen in the "stepped-up atmosphere of war with its cracking crises, its snatched pleasures and its doldrums."[22] He describes the daily air raids that Londoners experienced. The silent empty streets wait, he said, for the shock. A day later, September 16, 1940, he wrote, "The attacks on London have only been going on for ten days. So far people are steady, there has been no panic. But they are depressed. Everyone is suffering from lack of sleep and nervous tension. There is some feeling that the poor are taking it the hardest and many complaints about lack of shelters." As the bombs increase, he writes, "It has come to a state where none of us can be sure that we shall meet each other the next day and we begin to look for a gap in the party. Bombs have been raining around here, Berkeley Square, Park Lane and Regent Street. So far none in St James's Street or Pall Mall, but this must be pure luck, and there is more than a chance that we shall get it in the next week. Life is 'nasty, brutish and short.'" Yet the war makes Ritchie realize his existence as a member of a community in a way that he had not experienced before. Fancying himself a "cosmopolitan" and laughing at "blimpish patriotism," he nevertheless finds himself taken with "cracker mottoes" that are now taken for "eternal truths." Ritchie also reveals his temperamental affinity with Bowen and others who refused to let the war blot out beauty. One diary entry juxtaposes his observations of the city's destruction with a note on a lunchtime ballet, and how wonderful it was to see *Les Sylphides*: "The permanent importance of an art compared with the noisy, accidental crashing of tons of high explosives. Aesthetic standards are the only ones that stand up in these times." He again cites *The Heat of the Day* as "the brilliant transformation" into fiction of what he and Bowen lived through. Bowen's wartime writing questions the ability of language to describe experiences of the war. All the old-fashioned words—"valor," "honor," "patriotism"—had been swallowed up in its violent convulsions.

Bowen invented a way of saying what was unsaid, registering loss, absence, violence, and silence. Words or the lack of them became her theme. Virginia Woolf believed that there was a different kind of music in people's conversation after World War I; Bowen also discovered "the music of the familiar" disappeared during World War II and after, there was an "imprisoned humming" and one could no longer "set that humming noise to words." Stella describes the "imprisoned humming" inside her head in the autumn of 1940.[23] The harmony of the music stopped. Through this pattern of words, interruptions, and silences, Bowen transformed the way fiction represented war. She wrote outside the historic, impersonal, "male" tradition of reportage and alighted upon themes of espionage, treason, and betrayal of love in wartime from the "inside." She marked this turn when she wrote to Humphrey House in India in 1939 that she was interested, as a writer, in the general forces of history, no longer in just the individual personality. Her concept of character evolved as she shifted to a stance of the unknowability of people. In another letter to House, she asserted that too much value had been placed on what we think of as "personality" in life and writing.[24] This regard, she thought, was misplaced and emotionally and intellectually messy: a "gothic hangover" of too much expressed emotion. "New art," she noted, "seems to be tending to overshoot personality, and I feel sure that's a good thing. I mean, it tends to see people as at once more flat and more fluid," and adds that "passions [and] interests involving loyalties interests me more and more [...] romantic individualism seems to me played out."[25] *The Heat of the Day* demonstrates her new focus: loyalties and betrayals are worked out in the national and private passions of Stella, Harrison, Kelway, and Louie in a stream of the "general" current of the times, an atmosphere. Kelway betrays England, and also Stella's love, both with his Nazi espionage and his use of her politically and personally; Harrison morally betrays Stella in an attempt to blackmail her sexually and emotionally; Louie betrays her soldier husband in acting on her "unmarriedness." In Bowen's "new" art, characters are fluid, and sometimes flat, and turn away (as modernists do) from the expression of emotion—to the dismay of critics with different expectations. Critics then and now object to the lack of human dimension, character delineation, and clear motivation in *The Heat of the Day*. Stella like most of Bowen's women is the most clearly developed character: an intelligent, middle-class divorcée, a mother, a spy with connections to the Anglo-Irish landed gentry. Other characters are sketched only in outline as types: Harrison, a gauche counterspy; Kelway, a middle-class spy for the Nazis; Louie, a working-class married woman.

Despite what she said, Elizabeth Taylor, Bowen's novelist friend would find her characters "all real, and physically real," in *The Heat of the Day*. "When they lift a hand, or laugh, it is a real thing that is done." In fact, she thinks "Robert the best of them all" though there are those critics, in opposition, who assess Robert Kelway, Stella's lover, as "unreal," murky in outline along with his unexplained Nazi identification.[26] The word "real" takes on certain overtones among novelists after the war, and Taylor is hinting that the modernists before the war or high modernists do not write about the "real." Yet as Virginia Woolf queries, "what is real and to whom." It is a contested word particularly in the 1930s given the infusion of documentary and factual writing into so-called literary writing: the word, "real," subject to the reshaping by intermodernist critics. Taylor, unwittingly, is also reshaping analytical tools for reading late modernist writing between and after the devastation of wars that changed writers' views about the working and middle class, about espousing political causes, about the definition and value of what is popular and what is literary, and also what is considered masculine and feminine.

Bowen highlights issues of loyalty and treason, intertwining always the personal and the national. The figure of the traitor first entered British living rooms when the Nazi propagandist, William Joyce, an American-born Irishman known as Lord Haw-Haw, began broadcasting false news from Germany in 1940: the BBC countered with its own propaganda, "Postscripts," commentary on the night's news, to keep listeners from flipping the switch. Rebecca West's vivid account of Joyce's personality during his trial in 1945 in *The Meaning of Treason* filters into Bowen's spy, Robert Kelway in *The Heat of the Day*. Similarly, Storm Jameson explored the life of a Communist spy in her polemical novel, *A Cup of Tea for Mr. Thorgill*. Bowen and Jameson (along with West, in other writings) defy Diana Trilling's 1948 charge that the work of the most talented and conscientious women writers of the day focused only on the internal and subjective, ignoring external reality.[27] Bowen and Jameson believed "the essential concern of the novel is with men and women *in their times*" and not only the expression of "feeling" or subjectivity traditionally associated with women writers.[28]

This atmosphere of war, treason, and secrets enveloped Bowen. It was a climate in which much was unsaid—"loose lips sink ships"—and her literary voice and style embody concealment. From the 1930s on, clandestine political conversations swirled around her and eased her voluntary movement into the MOI and other propaganda activities. In "A Love Story," two men with double identities are hidden away as spies in the same Irish hotel during the Emergency but they say little to one another. And *The Heat of the Day* is a novel about silence: listening (muffled sounds, hums) and watching (despite black outs), alert to what's said or unsaid. As Roderick, Stella's returning son relates when questioned about taking notes on a conversation, "'really, Mother,' he exclaimed 'conversations are the leading thing in this war! [...] Everything you and I have to do is the result of something that's been said. How far do you think we'd get without conversations?'" Stella, a spy herself, knows this living at "the edge of a clique of war knowing who should know what commanding a sort of language in which nothing need ever be said." Also living at "the edge of a clique of war," Bowen would transform what she experienced in World War II into *The Heat of the Day*, and her wartime stories, *Ivy Gripped the Steps*, fiction that will surface more fully in "Art and Intelligence." In her intelligence *Reports from Eire*, 1940–1942, her multiple, sometimes shifting ethical and patriotic loyalties are revealed illustrating a tilt toward England or Ireland or both or neither. At various times, including today, critics and reader perceive her allegiance to one or the other. Such coexisting complexities of identity have often been denied, simplified or neglected by critics.

Notes

1. Twenty-six counties of Ireland became independent from Britain, Eire; six counties in the north remained loyal to Britain.
2. BBC Interview, February 28, 1947, Rider Haggard's *She*, BBC, NSA.
3. Biggin Hill Aerodrome, opened by Royal Flying Corps, World War I to defend against German zeppelin attacks. http://rdcamsgatehistory.com/zoomify/zeppelins_1915_viewer.htm, *Daily Mail*, May 18, 1915.
4. *SW*, 26.
5. The Black and Tans, British forces recruited to fight in the Irish War of Independence.
6. Bowen, "Frankly Speaking."
7. Noted by Fisk in "Turning One's Back on the Fire of Life."
8. EB to VW, February 1941, SU.

9. *IGS*, 182.
10. *PPT*, 134.
11. "Summer Night," *CS*, 599.
12. *WL*, 34, 43.
13. Margaret Kennedy to EB, n.d. 1938, HRC 11.6.
14. *IGS*, xii.
15. *HD*, Knopf Records, NYPL, box 102, folder 18.
16. EB to HH, July 9, 1939, HHC.
17. *BC*, 455.
18. *IGS*, 138, 182.
19. *HD*, 40, 152–3, 50, 156.
20. Ibid., 152–3.
21. John Bayley to EB, n.d. (ca. 1965), HRC 10.6.
22. Ritchie, *Siren Years*, 8, 66, 67, 74, 67, 100.
23. *HD*, 100.
24. EB to HH, June 29, 1936, HHC.
25. Ibid., January 20, 1936.
26. Elizabeth Taylor to EB, February 24 and March 14, 1949, HRC 12.1.
27. Trilling, "Fiction in Review," 254.
28. Jameson, *Novel in Contemporary Life*, 2.

7

Art and Intelligence (1940–1950)

Art and Politics

H.G. Wells famously declared, "I'll be damned if I lend myself to any government propaganda."[1] Bowen did. Despite her skepticism about the state's merging of art and politics in World War II, she allied herself with the British, taking a moral stance against Fascism. She lent herself as a writer to what she was enlisted to do, to spy on neutral Ireland at a time of great difficulty and importance and to write reports for the British Ministry of Information. She was also a wartime writer; later, a journalist covering peace conferences and a lecturer for the British Council. She was a cultural ambassador, a propagandist contributing to a morale-boosting film script and postwar situation reports; a public personality participating in panels on BBC's Third Programme; and a member of the British Royal Commission on Capital Punishment.[2] At the same time, she was one of the most popular writers in Britain and America in the1940s and 1950s. In an interview in 1960, she defended the importance of her writing as well as her propaganda activities: "Just as in an air raid, if you were a warden, which I was, you stump up and down the streets making a clatter with the boots you are wearing [...] You know," she said, that "you can't prevent a bomb falling, but thinking, 'At any rate I'm taking part in this. I may be doing some good.'"[3] She challenged Wells' assertion that any writer of repute who collaborated with the state failed "to grasp his real significance in the world."[4] She did not lose her independence or get into "low company" or fall short of "the essential aristocracy of … her profession" as a writer, as Wells had warned. Cyril Connolly had similarly cautioned artists about propaganda and the seductions of the state in an issue of *Horizon*:

© The Author(s), under exclusive license to Springer Nature Switzerland AG 2021
P. Laurence, *Elizabeth Bowen*, Literary Lives, https://doi.org/10.1007/978-3-030-71360-7_7

War artists are not art [...] the BBC is not art, all the Penguins [John Lehmann's literary series], all the CEMA shows [Council for the Encouragement of Music and Art], all the ABCA [Army Bureau of Current Affairs] lectures, all the discussion groups and MOI films and pamphlets will avail nothing if we deny independence, leisure and privacy to the artist himself.[5]

Bowen continued to be an independent thinker and writer—distinguished not only by her art but also her brilliant intelligence—living fully in her times as an intellectual, sometime activist, and writer of fiction. She seriously considered her responsibility as an artist in society.

Her boots actually were on the ground and a tin hat atop her head during the blitz when she and her husband served as volunteer air raid wardens. Trolling the streets of London, she lived "both as a civilian and a writer, with every pore open, living so many lives, and living among the packed repercussions of so many thousands of other lives, all under stress."[6] She wrote to Ritchie about going to an air-raid precaution lecture where she was instructed how to issue gas masks, direct people to prefab or tube station air-raid shelters, aid in recovery work after bombings, and maintain the blackout during the particularly intense Nazi aerial bombardment of London, September 7–May 11, 1941. This filtered into her fiction. "When I reread a story," she wrote, "I relive the moment from which it sprang. A scene burned itself into me, a building magnetized me, a mood or season of Nature's penetrated me, history suddenly appeared to me in some tiny act or a face had begun to haunt me before I glanced at it."[7] She infused her stories and modern novels with this sense of the historical moment and intrigue. When asked about the role of an artist in society on a BBC panel with Graham Greene and V.S. Pritchett in 1948, she responded: "My books are my relation to society. Why should people come and ask me what this relation is? It is the other people, the readers who should know."

Taking Sides

Bowen strongly believed in the artist's responsibility to speak out, act, and write during convulsive times. In 1939, Britain realized that independent Ireland had become "Hibernia incognita," as Eunan O'Halpin, an authority on British intelligence and Ireland, observed.[8] And after the fall of France, the British fear was focused on the unprotected ports in Ireland that they had ceded in 1938—Cobh, Berehaven, Lough Swilly—and the roaming German North Atlantic convoys. Ireland, in short, was vulnerable to a German invasion, a steppingstone to Britain. Ireland was neutral in the war, and at the beginning it was not known whether the Irish hated the English occupiers more than the German Nazis.

As Germany's panzer divisions advanced across Holland, Belgium, and France in the spring and summer of 1940, they set off international alarms and mobilized the British people. In addition, Ireland was perceived to have an "enemy within,"[9] pro-German sympathy was on the rise in May 1940,[10] and, according to the historian Paul McMahon, British military intelligence was alarmed by a burst of German propaganda there.[11] The British were threatened by defenseless Ireland as Hitler escalated the sea and air war and created a blockade against all shipping to England. Bowen feared this too. Her Irish and British loyalties were aroused as she witnessed the daily destruction of London from Germany's airborne invasion, the growing threat of Nazism and possible occupation.

Was neutral Ireland ready for a stealth invader? Britain decided to find out with a surveillance operation, establishing the Ministry of Information, a system of "lower-level liaison on intelligence matters." Counter-propaganda was needed in southern Ireland, but MOI strategized mainly with John Betjeman, a Press Attaché in Eire. They advised that personal communication among elite individuals and certain cultural groups would be the most effective propaganda.[12] Enter Elizabeth Bowen and four other agents sent to Ireland in the summer of 1940 to test and pump up anti-German feeling as propagandists, writers, and radio personalities: Ian Morrow about whom little is known; Arnold Lunn, a writer for the Catholic journal, *The Tablet*; and Miss Maxwell, an Anglo-Irish MOI employee with a home in Dublin. When Elizabeth Bowen volunteered, she became part of a system of intelligence and a network with writers like John Betjeman who were "deputized," as Heather Jordan notes, "to gather salient details about the life of the nation for its own use" and security.[13] They were the shadowy corps that gathered intelligence pertinent to the security of England but the MOI was advised to use *soft power*. It was lodged in the Senate House at London University and organized into four divisions: the first, in which Bowen participated, was propaganda at home and in foreign countries; others were censorship, news, and press relations; the production of publicity material; and administration. There is no doubt that Bowen felt the pull of duty to England, and in a letter to Virginia Woolf in July 1940, she asserted that her MOI work "was wanted."[14] Her role first to spread the British point of view to the intellectuals, parliamentarians, clergy and people she met; second, to "listen in" and report Irish opinion to the Dominions office to help determine effective propaganda strategies. She would produce reports on any errant elements that might support the Germans over the English.

Her letter to Woolf also provides the first clue to her political network as she was planning to meet Harold Nicolson, the diplomat, politician, and writer, and the husband of Vita Sackville-West. He was then the parliamentary secretary, the official MOI censor in the wartime cabinet, and became himself an effective propagandist on his visit to Ireland during the war. She downplayed her role to Woolf, describing her work innocuously as listening to and shaping Irish "talk" in official reports on opinion. In a later report, she wrote that more people like her should be sent to Ireland to oppose rumors, "(I mean talk in ordinary conversation) in this country cuts more ice than anything else."[15]

Bowen would not sport a dart pen or lapel knife, but would disappear from time to time, gathering information in Dublin and Cork investigating public opinion on neutrality, the British, the Germans, and the possible leasing of the treaty ports in the south and west of Ireland to England. She moved easily in intellectual and political circles under cover of being an established writer working on her family history. The MOI welcomed her as she fit the agency's new profile. In July 1941, it decided to recruit from outside government personnel because of criticism of the non-specialists with social connections who had been hired at the time of its founding. MOI now wanted agents who had experience in journalism, writing, propaganda, or publicity.[16] She was an established author in plain sight with knowledge of the intellectual and political circles and culture of Ireland. Her skills of observation—her temperamental ability to wait, watch and listen that also made her into a writer—were needed. Her many MOI reports were subsequently praised by the agency for being observant, sane, well written and interesting. Historically, she joined a cadre of women on the edges or between cultures who were both spies and writers.[17]

Journalist and writer Bruce Arnold observed that Bowen's formative years in England and her Anglo-Irish background naturally led her into reporting for the British: "it got her dubbed a spy. She wasn't a spy; she was actually reflecting a majority view of the Irish people that was pro-Britain. But, unfortunately, the government was not pro-Britain. It was sort of neutral with quite a decided preference for Germany because it was a government of old men who had fought through the War of Independence and so on."[18] Though Victoria Glendinning states that Bowen was a volunteer, MOI records reveal that Bowen was still a paid agent and in 1944–45, earning £115 and 10 shillings for her work at that time.[19]

Paul McMahon reports that the British knew of Sinn Fein and IRA activities in 1940, then at their most intense, and had a pre-emptive plan for invasion of Southern Ireland.[20] In 1940, when Bowen was informing, the British government was in conversation with deValera about admitting British forces or ceding ports in the event of such an invasion. They knew of the influence of Frank Aiken, his Minister of Defense, and Joe Walsh, Secretary of the Department of External Affairs, both of whom were vigorously anti-British and pro-German, as well as in touch with the extremists in the IRA in the early part of the war. Part of the British strategy under Betjeman was to initiate a strong counterpropaganda campaign in Ireland including business schemes and economic sanctions to sway ordinary people, particularly farmers, to feel the impact of economic loss and take Britain's side, and even rise up against deValera to adopt a favorable pro-British, pro-Ally position. Betjeman's scheme was to pressure Eire's business community to realize its economic connection and debt to the United Kingdom, the Empire and the United States, and spread the word to others in Ireland.[21] In a July 7, 1941, memo, he proposed that propaganda pamphlets supported by the business community (and based loosely on a similar South African campaign) might convince workers that their economic well-being was dependent on the United Kingdom. According to Lord Davidson, £ 300,000, 000 of British capital was invested in Ireland's business.[22] A scheme was devised to establish an organization in Eire using commercial channels to influence people and businesses like Arthur Guinness Son & Company. Betjeman made the proposal to John Rodgers, MOI, and given the delicate situation of the British in Ireland, he was warned of its riskiness if knowledge of it fell into the hands of "enemies" in Eire. Nevertheless, numerous messages concerning the use of economic channels for propaganda traveled between Betjeman and John Maffey, one of the most important UK representatives resident in Dublin who brought to Ireland the lessons he learned about nationalism and the indirect rule of the UK in the north west Indian frontier and the Sudan. Maffey is reported to have kept a successful balance between deValera's nationalism and the imperialist Churchill during his decade in Ireland, 1939–49.

Betjeman was eccentric and popular in Ireland and also worked on radio broadcasts with John Maffey, posing as a press attaché with the assistance of Nicholas Mansergh who had been head of the Empire Division for MOI and who strongly defended Irish neutrality. John Betjeman—who changed his name to "Sean" for his assignment—engaged in activities to reduce tensions between the United Kingdom and Ireland to counter the stepped-up propaganda activities of the German Press Agency in Eire through his radio program—Irish Free Radio. He sponsored talks and journalism, and like Stephen Spender, masked the extent of his wartime work for the MOI by claiming it was no secret. Eager to counter the Irish press, German broadcasts, and Lord Haw Haw, he enlisted popular literary figures like Frank O'Connor, a friend, and Sean O'Faolain, a popular writer of short stories—and even Patrick Kavanagh, the poet, at the urging of John Maffey—to broadcast talks, stories, and poetry.

Betjeman also knew Bowen, admired *The Death of the Heart*, and had written in October 1938, the book "is a winner—an absolute winner, a stunner, a topper."[23] He mentioned his odd, favorite phrase in her writing, "eyes like urgent poached eggs," and compared her to Thackeray, pointing out that they shared the same "richness" of atmosphere and observation of class distinctions. "Dear God," he exclaimed, "how I loved it [...] your book goes to prove my contention that the Anglo-Irish are the greatest race in Western Civilization": it was observed that Betjeman had developed influential friendships with many Anglo-Irish figures during his time in Ireland, even converting from Catholicism to Anglicanism.

Louis MacNeice, poet and dramatist, was also drawn into BBC propaganda work in London during the war. A memorandum in the BBC archives, January 9, 1941, indicates that he wrote asking if he could do propaganda work to America.[24] He was hired by the Features Department, the BBC semi-governmental propaganda unit, and worked there for 20 years fearing (like many writers of the time) that his radio propaganda work would eclipse his lyrical, poetic voice. Actually, as Emily Bloom has illuminated, radio work brought him out of his insularity and energized him: his distinction between the poetic "I" and the communal "we" collapsed as the war progressed and his dramatic work at the BBC evolved. The documentary elements became part of the texture of his new voice, now intertwined with war and history as with other intermodernist writers. He would find his voice, like many women writers, at home rather than in field of battle. Radio broadcasting would change the sounds of poetry as it became more aural and enlisted new sound effects to communicate with listening audiences. And history entered poetry in new ways. MacNeice, for example, disagreed with Ireland's position of neutrality and this filtered into bitter lines. "Off your own shores, the mackerel are fat on the flesh of your kin."[25] He indicted the Irish for being uncaring about the Irish seamen on its coast being blown up by German mines while patrolling the North Atlantic sea for merchant and enemy ships: the seamen would have been defended by Allies and saved had Ireland abandoned neutrality and been part of the war against Fascism. MacNeice was unable to position himself in a nation or religion—born into an Anglo-Irish family and spending most of his life in America and England. Nor could he draw a line between the space of propaganda and poetry. Instead, he stood like the budgerigar of his poem "who was not born for nothing" and stood "at his post on the burning perch/I twitter Am—and peeps like a television Actor/Admiring himself in the monitor."[26] Aware of the tragedy of the war, watching the human race recede and dwindle, he, nevertheless, sang a song of self in poetry. In addition, he developed the aesthetics of the Features Department of the BBC, writing several morale-building scripts for the series, "The Stones Cry Out," documenting the history and stories surrounding London buildings damaged or destroyed by bombs in the blitz, among other successful dramatic projects.

The war and literature were linked in MacNeice's work as they were in Bowen. Her feelings of patriotism extended to British culture and literature, and she became one of the founding members of the Jane Austen Society in the same month that she volunteered to be an MOI agent. She was loyal to England, British literature, and the preservation of English heritage. Though to some, the project to buy and preserve Jane Austen's home at Chawton was folly during wartime, Bowen did not agree. R.W. Chambers of the Austen Society argued that the war was being fought for the preservation of national heritage. At the Austen Society's annual meeting in 1951, Bowen "gave a brilliant address on Jane Austen's art" according to a prominent society member.[27] In 1949, Chawton was finally purchased by Mr. Thomas Edward Carpenter who created a trust in memory of his son who was killed during the war in 1944. A few years earlier in 1942, Bowen also upheld the importance of the literary tradition by writing a short survey, *English Novelists*, about those who, she said, were honored in name only. "Now when the English spirit stands at its full height," it would be a double loss as "England's past in art, as well as in history, has helped to build up her heroic To-day. It is natural to want our writers beside us as we face this new phase of human experience." Her book was part of a beautifully illustrated Collins series on British culture and history—nationalist propaganda published during and after the war. Art and intelligence joined forces. But it must not be forgotten that her loyalties and tastes also extended to Irish, French, and American literature.

Wartime Stories

Bowen's allegiance to Britain would shape not only her government reports, journalism, film scripts, and BBC broadcasts, but also her fiction for at least a decade. Britain, Ireland and Europe became the historical and cultural terrain of her writing. In her complex and brilliant story, "Summer Night," impatience with Irish neutrality during the war is expressed in the thoughts of Justin, a man "locked" into Ireland visiting his deaf sister, unable to travel to Europe because of the ban. "The war-broken towers of Europe" haunt him, and he lives with impotent feelings and perhaps guilty thoughts about Ireland's choice of neutrality, "In the heart of the neutral Irishman indirect suffering pulled like a crooked knife."[28] He lives in an "infected zone" with others in Ireland because "each moment is everywhere, it holds the war in its crystal, there is no elsewhere … the enemy is within it, creeping about."[29] The atmosphere of the war travels to neutral Ireland, though supposedly outside of it, and brings a "stop to the senses" and a moral indifference to national and personal relations. Emma and Robinson in the story feel "unmarried" and have an affair ignoring the reverberations in home and family. In the background, Queenie, Justin's deaf sister, smiles and pours tea, and may represent a benign aspect of Ireland's necessary deafness to the war in Europe. This Irish indifference is also expressed in Bowen's story, "Sunday Afternoon." Henry living through the London blitz returns home to Ireland briefly to find that his friends are "secluded behind glass" and do not want him to say much of London's wartime destruction.

Bowen lived in this atmosphere of telling "a little but not much," knowing the power of holding or withholding information. This intrigue enters not only into her stories but *The Heat of the Day*, her wartime novel about secrets and betrayal—personal and national—as well as the porousness between the two. It is a compelling story of love and espionage in which Stella Rodney learns that her lover is a Nazi spy through a British agent who propositions her to obtain her lover's freedom. Bowen is suspended between her various identities in the early years of the war: writer, spy, and lover, and this mix enters her novel.

The Difficulty of Saying "I"

Bowen's fictional characters, like her, learn that much is unknowable about other people's motives in love and war. She felt that she was "fully intelligent" only when writing, and in a 1951 essay, "Disloyalties," on Graham Greene's letters, she distinguishes between two kinds of writers: the intellectual novelist building upon "a framework of ideas" and "the aesthetic-intuitive, working mainly on memories and impressions." In the former, the "seat of integrity is the brain, in the other, feeling."[30] She incorporates both strains in her oeuvre engaging in current events and political crises, writing official reports and documents as well as non-fiction essays; at other times, she transforms history and politics into fiction. Language becomes "dead currency" to Stella in *The Heat of the Day*: meaning empties out when she discovers her lover's betrayal of her and of Britain as a Nazi spy, as well as the counterspy Harrison's betrayal through blackmail.[31] She hears Harrison and "listens [...] as silence mounted the stairs," her mind "opaquely clouded water." But in the same essay, she absolves writers, including herself from charges of "disloyalty" as they are "fifth columnists" and do not owe allegiance to country or nation but a larger and less-known imaginative and geopolitical terrain.[32] Bowen further explores this topic quoting Greene's assertion that "disloyalty" is the writer's virtue. The essay proceeds as a kind of shadow justification for her *Reports from Eire* as she too was branded as disloyal by a portion of the Irish. She quotes Greene:

> Loyalty confines us to accepted opinions; loyalty forbids us to comprehend sympathetically our dissident fellows; but disloyalty encourages us to roam experimentally through any human mind, it gives to the novel the extra dimension of sympathy.[33]

Bowen adheres to Greene's claim that the writer of imagination has to be a brave guardian of human values—and to have multiple "I's"—always mobile and shifting, and rejecting any restrictions on his explorations in life or art.

The charge of disloyalty that floats across the critical screen of Bowen's work contains a popular notion of a "self" that is single and solitary, but she encourages sympathy with other points of view and selves encouraging writers "to roam experimentally through any human mind." Loyalty is not the simple morality we find in Aristotle and Plato or a fixed, patriotic relationship to religion or state, but interwoven and multiple. Alliances during periods of turmoil are shifting as reflected in the personal and public lives of those who fought in the Irish Civil War and became a part of the Troubles. In *The Last September*, Lois, a young woman muses about the complexity of her future in Ireland—outside the big house: "she was fitted for this being twice as complex as their generation [Mrs. Montmorency and Lady Naylor] for she must be double as many people having gone into the making of her."[34] The same might be said of Elizabeth Bowen.

She defends the intellectual writer's "choice" to defend certain values—in this case, anti-Fascism—as he turns away "from resting places, from lighted doorways, to pursue his alternatives and troubling regrets."[35] Through her review, Bowen subtly asserts her choices. She had probably signed the Official Secrets Act, and so only occasionally admitted her activities as in signing her essay on Dover, British Ministry of Information in *Collected Impressions*. Bowen let that happen as she transformed her experiences into her fiction, her novel of love and spying in *The Heat of the Day*, writing, as Christa Wolf, a leading German writer, advocated, "from the inside out."

Wolf and Bowen, both lived in partitioned countries with complicated loyalties during their period of informing. When Christa Wolf's "Perpetrator's File" was released by the STASI in 1993 (the Berlin wall had come down in 1989), she—having spied on fellow writers before this time was taken aback, remembering, she said, "one of the many I's who have taken shifts in me, replacing one another in sequence, slowly or quickly."[36] Bowen never publicly confronted identities taking shifts within her during or after her period of informing. Christa Wolf also evaded admitting her spying on fellow authors and spoke, instead, of feeling "soiled" by the STASI reports she read about herself, particularly the language of the secret police who described her: "the brutal way they took your lives and made them trite, over hundreds and hundreds of pages." Would Bowen have felt the same when the Aubane Historical Society exposed her MOI reports on Eire in their 2007 pamphlet. Christa Wolf astutely noted that if there was anything to learn from the reports on her activities, "it's what language can do to the truth. Those files were in the language of the secret police, completely incapable of capturing a real life informer."[37] Nevertheless, Wolf was shocked into getting to know herself down to the bottom—yet rather indirectly with a lapse of about 48 years—through telling the story in her fragmented writing, her novel, *The Quest for Christa T*, and *The City of Angels*, in which she attempts to explain her earlier informing. There she writes of "The Overcoat of Dr. Freud," "You know, the coat that keeps you warm but also hidden, that you have to turn inside out. To make the invisible visible."[38] Stella, the translator-spy in Bowen's novel, also feels "soiled" when she comes in contact with the blackmailing British spy, Harrison—his sexual manipulation, his surveillance of her private life with Robert, and his coarse language. She resents his use of the "perpetual we." Your "we," she asserts—the wartime feeling of community—is my "they." Stella separates herself as an individual, a mother, a woman from the feeling that "war made us one big family."[39]

She reacts to the war and what "they"—the war machine and system—had "done" to her son that molded him into another person, alienated, dissolute. She sees what the war did to her lover, and Harrison, the British spy. As a woman, she experienced the dissolute effects of the war in her personal relationships. On the other hand, Louie, the working-class girl enters into the "we" of wartime feeling as engendered in the daily propaganda and newspapers she reads. Bowen, as Christa Wolf had urged, gives us glimpse of the overcoat turned inside out, the invisible made visible, in her fiction. The war comes through a new lens with a divided self.

Bowen could not foresee what self-divisions the war would exact. Sean O'Faolain, her lover at the time, described the drama in his last meeting with her before the war on August 31, 1939 when she received a call from her husband that the British fleet was mobilized. This announcement sent O'Faolain back to Ireland and his wife, separating him from Bowen, politically and geographically, virtually for the duration of the war.[40] He saw her once two or three years later in Dublin, where he took her to lunch at Jammets and with "false gaiety" said, "Well, Elizabeth? So it is taking a world war to divorce us?" She was unemotional, but O'Faolain reported that she said, "I have never before felt so completely a leader." What she hinted at, not fully revealed until about 20 years later, was her engagement as an agent for the MOI in Ireland. Though separated, their friendship continued, given the appearance of her essays, reviews, and stories in *The Bell*, of which he was then editor. He sought to incorporate her perspectives. In March 1941, she wrote a piece on James Joyce; in August 1942, he ran a review of *Bowen's Court*; in September 1942, a piece appeared, "Meet Elizabeth Bowen"; and in 1940–41, three of her stories appeared. She reviewed his *Come Back to Erin* in December

1940, and he reviewed *The Demon Lover* in April 1946. She shared his views on Irish parochialism, often expressed in *The Bell*, and some of these views filtered into her MOI reports. They agreed on the isolating effect of neutrality on Irish culture and thinking, the nation's growing claustrophobia, the constricting values of the Catholic Church, and the negative effects of literary and political censorship, as well as the denial of visas to Irish writers during the war. In O'Faolain's 1993 revised version of his autobiography, *Vive Moi*, he reminisced more candidly about his life 40 years earlier with Bowen. He mentioned the Dublin gossip in the 1950s that Bowen had been writing reports for the War and Dominions Office in 1940–42, just after their affair ended. But O'Faolain, unlike others, forgave Bowen's actions and affirmed that despite some claims among the Irish to the contrary, Bowen had a heartfelt relationship to Ireland:

> All this is now over forty years ago but I can still wince a little at us all—at Elizabeth, at myself, at some patriotic woman who wrote to the press about visiting spies disguised as harmless visitors, at Harold Nicolson, at the BMI; or else I see the whole trivial incident as a tiny symbol of the sort of thing that war does to people. It puts an end to that civilized balance of values that normally encourage us to see everybody's dilemma from another angle beside our own … If the British had found it necessary to seize our harbours and ports, men, guns and planes they could have done it, and would have had to do it if the Germans had forestalled them. The very thought of Ireland at war would have torn Elizabeth's heart apart.[41]

"What war does to people" was O'Faolain's defense of Bowen's intelligence activity in Ireland.

Bowen was drawn to O'Faolain's charm, personality and good looks but also—as he was to her—by his dazzling, lyrical writing. In a letter to Peter Davidson, his editor at the *Atlantic Monthly*, and his wife, Peggy—after reading a piece by William Abraham on Bowen—he assessed her literary position: "I put her with Waugh, Joyce, Forster as the 4 best British novelists of the ¾ of this century. She'd pretend to be cross and say 'I am Irish'—the beloved Crook!": an epithet that still sticks in some quarters of Ireland.[42]

The war, O'Faolain asserted, changed people. Bowen felt strongly about the Nazi threat to Britain, but she also feared a German invasion of Ireland. Both moved her to act. If "character is isolated by a deed," as Yeats claims, then Bowen's silhouette was clear in July 1940."[43] While still O'Faolain's friend and writing pieces for his magazine, she was gathering information for MOI in Cork and Dublin, speaking with Irish contacts and reporting back to the Dominions Office. Did Bowen lose her "civilized balance," as O'Faolain termed it, in being spy, friend, and lover, Irish and English, anti-Fascist and nationalist? Acknowledging the tough choices of wartime, Bowen wryly observed the powerlessness of artists and thinkers like herself against the wave of Fascism: "And to what did our fine feeling, our regard for the arts, our intimacies, our inspiring conversations, our will to be fair to everyone bring us? To 1939?"[44] War was declared on September 1, 1939.

Pen Portrait of a Nation: *Reports from Eire, 1940–42*

Bowen's reports to the British MOI are historical documents sketching the attitudes and consequences of Irish neutrality in daily life. Though only nine survive, they are "a pen portrait" of Eire balanced by her novel, *The Heat of the Day*, her transformation of "belligerent" England under the blitz beginning in autumn 1940. The Aubane Historical Society published 13 of the reports; Eibhear Walshe in his collection of Bowen's Irish writing, eight (overlapping with Aubane).[45] Bowen spoke with politicians, members of the Irish parliament, intellectuals, writers, clergy, and people on the streets of Cork and Dublin. She occupied a small flat in St. Stephen's Green during her intermittent mission over two years, and "was able, under these circumstances, to see again, over tea or sherry, people [she] had met elsewhere and to continue conversations that had promised to be interesting."

About 15 percent of her rumored 200 reports have been recovered.[46] According to Robert Fisk, many documents in London were "destroyed under statute"; none of Bowen's reports was uncovered in Ireland as "in 1945 Irish authorities shredded 70 tons of documents considered too sensitive for scrutiny," and in Northern Ireland, records were weeded.[47] The full extent of Bowen's reports to the Dominions Office in Dublin or War Office in London where they were sent will remain "history's missing dimension," as the historian Andrew Christopher terms it.[48] In addition, the British Public Record Office, now TNA, made a decision in 1967 to open government documents after 30 rather than 50 years, as had been the case, and departments, according to Simon Fowler, a researcher at TNA, this meant they had to work very hard to get wartime material to the PRO in time for their release in 1972. In addition to written reports, there are the unrecorded talks with various officials that Bowen alluded to in a 1942 letter to Woolf, in which she states that she had visited the Dominions Office because "there were things I wanted to say that I couldn't write."[49] She talked to Lord Cranborne: "I say talked, because he listened with very sympathetic and charming [David] Cecil politeness. I know he had seen the reports I'd been sending in." Bowen then described a cloak-and-dagger scene, embellishing, as she loved to do in her letters to Woolf: the challenge of finding and gaining admission into the Dominions Office given that Bowen and the taxi driver did not know exactly where to go. Finally, getting to an entranceway, she raised suspicion: "We were challenged by bayonets, and I said each time in a more quavering but more aggressive voice that I had an appointment."[50] Once inside, the building was as she had imagined it: "there were forms to fill in, then the long passages that though very hot still managed to smell of stone. There were outer courts of rooms of gentlemen's secretaries and files, then his room, which was nice and long, with boarded-up windows, a stretch of Turkey carpet, a roaring fire." Her reports were generally sent to the Dominions Office because the Irish Free State was still, to some degree, under the sovereignty of the British, others were kicked upstairs to the War Office in London. In another letter to Woolf, she noted that the last time she was in London, she went to the War Office, "also on an Irish errand." There at 11 o'clock, she was amused to find them all drinking glasses of milk.

Bowen's method of reporting, from the sample of communiqués, alternated views of the Irish from the "outside" and from the "inside." From the outside, the reports detailed the British government's frustration with Irish neutrality fearing German invasion of Southern Ireland, and, subsequently, England; and from "inside" Ireland, Bowen gleaned that the majority of the Irish people were in favor of de Valera's practical stance in the war given the country's economic and military vulnerability.[51] She described wartime Cork and Dublin: the fragile economy; the lack of military resources and trained militia; shortages of tea, radio batteries, paper, and gas; censorship of newspapers and movies; fear of bombing and isolation. Bowen's last available report, one she considered important, July 25–31, 1942, described these deprivations and attacked the British press campaign that alluded to their daily "comforts." She also urged, along with John Betjeman, more tactful and fewer anti-Irish British radio broadcasts to Ireland.

Sensitive to the politics of language, she found Irish "talk" more interesting and animated than English, as the Irish isolated by rigid censorship of newspapers and movies, were eager to ask questions and gather fresh news of the war. British conversation was more predictable and formulaic, studded with slogans created by the media to build people's morale during the blitz.[52] She noted that the Irish used religious rhetoric, critically viewing the English as "ungodly" for their materialism. She focused—myopically perhaps—only on Irish sacrifice never bringing in other nations in her available reports. Norway, for example, was also the country that had also declared neutrality, but was occupied by the Germans in 1940. The Marchioness of Londonderry expressed her disbelief in Ireland's "antiquated notions of neutrality [that] would not be considered for a moment by the modern Hun" in a letter to an Ulster newspaper.[53]The fact that Norway had been invaded gave the British pause about the vulnerability of Ireland. But it was not until 1942 that Bowen herself would observe the commonalities in contributing to a film script on Norway. Though fragmentary, her reports do give, as one journalist said, "the pen portrait of a nation."

Her reports downplayed Irish sympathy toward Germany, although Robert Fisk and other historians confirm the pro-German, anti-Semitic attitudes present in the culture, particularly early in the war. One MOI document asserts that 75 percent of the Irish population were "fanatically" anti-British, particularly in the Midlands, counties Kerry, Mayo, and Donegal. In Bowen's more benign and perhaps uninformed view, the Irish were heavily pro-Ally: British charges of Irish disloyalty in the press or on the radio were not only unearned, she believed, but inflamed Irish feeling, and insulted "the inherent temperamental 'anti-Nazism' of the country."[54] She repeated this opinion in a 1941 review of Jim Phelan's book *Ireland-Atlantic Gateway*.[55] The review was written about the same time as her secret MOI reports, and she asserted that the Nazi propagandist was not on firm ground in Ireland, as he committed himself on different occasions to promises (support for the Rising and Home Rule) on which he was unable to deliver. Hubert Butler, more sanguine, speculated that the citizens of Ireland, "finding indulgence" in the Germans, and "having been led to expect violence," might "easily have been tricked into easygoing collaboration" through manipulations of piety and patriotism.[56] Robert Fisk observed that in the early part of the war, anti-Semitic, pro-German pamphlets were distributed in Dublin by Sinn Fein, the party historically associated with the IRA.[57] According to Fisk, the IRA became passive as time went on, given that de Valera had imprisoned many of its members beginning in 1939. One of Bowen's reports does, however, acknowledge that Irish anti-Semitism was on the rise, attributable, partly, to jealousy of Jews in business in Dublin, as well as the result of European anti-Semitic propaganda.[58]

Bowen advised against British counterpropaganda and Irish entrance into the war. Her preference—"I [...] wish that the English kept history in mind more, that the Irish kept it in mind less"—reflects her opinion that the British tended to ignore their brutal colonization of Ireland, while the Irish kept their grievances against English oppression in focus.[59] She expressed irritation with the British, defending the Irish against charges of "disloyalty," reminding the British of "the plain facts of history." Bowen also signaled the British press about its "tactlessness" toward the Irish stance, and the damage of its "whispering campaign," the spreading of rumor by agents in Ireland. The British realized through Bowen's and other reports that they had underestimated Anglophobic opinion in Ireland.

As a strategy for persuasion, Bowen and other British agents recommended the soft power of personal contact and the unofficial diplomacy of talk, of the kind in which she was engaged. While on her Irish errand, Bowen tellingly became friends with James Dillon, almost the only member of the Irish Parliament in Leinster House who was against Ireland's stance of neutrality.[60] Early on, she viewed Dillon as a British ally and reported, "all sensible people in this country follow the line taken by Mr. James Dillon."[61] She viewed him as someone who might lead the Irish away from what the British and Americans then considered a "belligerent" stance about withholding the treaty ports. She falsely claimed, "Mr. Churchill no more than deprecated the loss of the ports as bases, making no demands nor threats." She described Dillon as one of the ablest members of Parliament, someone who could take on de Valera's policy: courageous, able, and dynamic.[62] But she misread him and the climate: his position was unpopular, and after a rousing speech as deputy leader in 1942 when he petitioned the government to abandon neutrality, side with the Allies and go to war, he was forced to resign. In the 1970s, when Robert Fisk, historian, revealed to Dillon that Bowen had been reporting his opinions to the Dominion Office in Ireland and the War Office in London, Dillon was taken aback. According to Fisk, when Dillon read the secret memorandum, he showed no bitterness, stating "only that she had abused his hospitality in 1940 by breaking the confidentiality of the meeting."[63] And in response to her description of his "religious fanaticism," in the report he snapped back about her "unhappy agnosticism." Bowen's loyalty to Britain and the anti-Fascist cause led her to break Irish trust as perceived in some quarters of the country.

Bowen was an intelligent and keen observer, and a persuasive writer. Her gifts as a novelist contributed to the accessibility of her reports, as she generally knew how to read people and sketch character. Lord Cranborne commended her work: "Her previous reports have struck us as very sensible and well balanced. The present report also strikes one as a shrewd appreciation of the position"[64] (Fig. 7.1). Her knowledge of Irish culture, her intelligence, and her reputation as a writer gave her a perch from which to assess the state of official opinion. In an essay that distilled her reports, "Eire," written for the *New Statesman and Nation* in 1941, Bowen drew from her MOI reports, summed up the political complexity, and defended Irish neutrality. She listed British charges against Ireland's "pigheadedness, ostracism, childishness, and apathy as to the fate of civilization and even a dishonorable timidity," but nevertheless asserted that Eire's stance was one of integrity. "Eire feels as strongly, one might say as religiously, about her neutrality as Britain feels

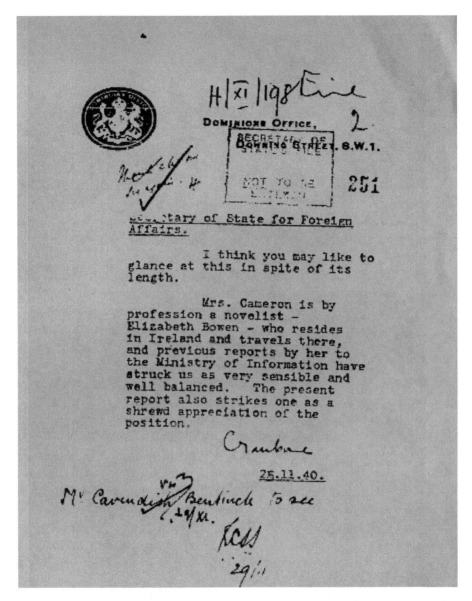

Fig. 7.1 Lord Cranborne, Praise of Bowen's work in MOI, November 25, 1940. Rights holder and Courtesy of TNA (The National Archives, Kew, England)

about her part in the war."[65] Echoing British views, she asserted that the Irish are naive in politics and "not yet adult in citizenship." She was most concerned about the "dwarfing" effect of wartime isolation on Ireland's cultural future. Irish censorship blacked out news of the war. Nevertheless, 70,000 soldiers from Eire and 50,000 from Northern Ireland fought in the war and those killed were not listed in the Irish newspapers, British newspapers were absent from the newsstands, and war scenes from newsreels were banned. The "dwarfing," Bowen stated, was enhanced by the Catholic Church's opposition to progress, as "enlightened Catholics" like O'Faolain had complained. He noted the strange Irish mentality about religion, "the contradictions, the deep piety, the absence of any real morality, the clash between desire and religion—the odd types, the Anglicanism, who finds faith, the theorist who reasons towards belief, the Franciscan filled with love & suffering." Bowen was also critical of the Anglo-Irish who continued to separate themselves from the Irish and adopt an attitude of "defeatism" toward the war.

What is most intriguing throughout the reports is Bowen's flickering "I," the continuing difficulty of saying "I." Aspects of her English, Irish, and European identifications as well as views of the Allies, Anglo-Irish, and Irish are reflected by turns. She tilts in the end toward an Ireland of reconciliation among religions, cultures, and political rivalries. She alludes in her report to St. Columba's, her father's school, as a model of integration, given that it was a Protestant institution then accepting Roman Catholic students. She urged the reconciliation of the Irish and Anglo-Irish in an essay on "The Big House" in *The Bell*: it "seems to me a pity" that the gulf between "the two Irelands" was still experienced by young people in 1940.[66] A 1942 MOI report notes that the Irish were beginning to favor the formation of "a third party" to erase the divisions left by the Civil War."[67] What she most feared, and O'Faolain and MacNeice agreed, was that Eire's isolation from European ideas and culture might breed a "national childishness" bred by censorship of newspapers, authors, and intellectuals, and the parochial influence of the Catholic Church.[68]

Bowen's sensibility matured during the war and she captured the mental, moral, and emotional climate of London in autumn 1940 in *The Heat of the Day*: "the tideless, hypnotic, featureless day-to-day way of life." The emotional tension is heightened by the war but the death and the destruction are not explicitly expressed. Stella, a divorced woman over 40 "on happy sensuous terms with life" articulates Bowen's view that "conversations are the leading thing in this war" and "talk" was to be avoided.[69] Stella, like Bowen, had some notion of what she might most "usefully do" when the war began, and worked as a spy in a secret organization, Y.X.D., to support the Allied position. Stella noted that in the years between the wars, she had traveled, and had "known whom to ask to support her application" when the time came for espionage. Bowen did also. Her subtle portrait of Stella and the other women—working-class Louie and Connie—and Robert's middle-class mother and sister—outshine the disaffected and flat men in the shadows of the novel as do most of the women in her novels. The theme of silence and hiddenness continues in the story "Careless Talk," as Eric who works at the War Office, arrives for lunch, and Joanna, his friend, naively asks, "how do you think the war is going." "Oh we mustn't ask him things," says Mary quickly. "He's doing frightfully secret work."[70] This national stance, particularly targeting women, encouraged a habit of guardedness shared not only by Mary and her friends in the story, but by Bowen and other writers.

Cultural Fallout

In 1993, Frank Clifford and Jack Lane of the Aubane Historical Society of County Cork were the first to target Bowen's secret wartime activities after Robert Fisk's 1979 revelations. The same exigency that drives Derrida to write things under erasure (sous rature)—to write a word and then cross it out but then print the word and the deletion—motivated Clifford and Lane in their treatment of Bowen in *The North Cork Anthology*. Though they included a few passages from *The Last September* in the anthology, a black line is drawn through her name in the table of contents to mark her exclusion (Fig. 7.2). At the same time that she and her writing are present, she is denied status as a North Cork resident (though born in Cork) or even an Irish author, asserting that her themes and characters were drawn from English culture. The absent "trace" of Bowen's past as an informant in Ireland is present in their reading though their gesture is now discredited. How do we incorporate local complexity into the transnational and rethink and breathe new life into this debate? The Dublin media responded with outrage to Lane and Clifford's charges, and Fisk revealed that demonstrations surfaced in the 1999 centenary celebration of her birth at University College, Cork, where Clifford and Lane distributed some of her espionage reports in a pamphlet, *Notes on Eire: Reports to Winston Churchill, 1940–1942*; more reports followed in 2009. The contretemps persisted, and in 2007 a debate about Bowen's wartime activities surfaced again in the *Irish Examiner* as English and Irish writers and politicians took sides. Declan Kiberd in a radio broadcast charged Lane and Clifford with being "awful Neanderthals," for which he later apologized; Roy Foster, a distinguished professor of Irish literature living in England parodied the pair in a novel, *Paddy and Punch*. Clifford and Lane struck back in a pamphlet, "Aubane vs. Oxford," in which they pitted academics against "the little men" of Ireland like themselves. The Aubane group's nationalism went far: "The part of the world that made her buzz was Kent."[71] On the other side, Nicholson claimed her as "Irish," mitigating her MOI activity by labeling her an "unofficial correspondent" in work

A North Cork
Anthology

250 Years of Writings
from the region of
Millstreet, Duhallow,
Slieve Luachra and thereabouts

By
Jack Lane
And
Brendan Clifford

AUBANE HISTORICAL SOCIETY,
Aubane,
Millstreet,
Co. Cork.

Contents

Fig. 7.2 *North Cork Anthology*, erasure of Bowen's name, Table of Contents, Rights holder and Courtesy of Jack Lane of Aubane Historical Society, Ireland

that "was helpful to both countries [...] in a sense, she was an agent of both." In fact, she was a paid as an "official" agent of the British. Yet according to one prescient historian, "had Britain re-invaded the South, a substantial amount of Bowen's information would have been of use." Others stated that she "was just reporting the public mood": nevertheless, the reports were marked "secret" and not available for researchers until after her death, a signal that they contained classified information that was thought significant. The debate illustrates both the doubleness and insufficiency of language to pin down a stable meaning of the concept of nation and who belongs. For Bowen, as a woman and a writer she eludes borders—as Virginia Woolf asserts, "she has no country."

While Bowen's kaleidoscopic self and actions would escape nationalists such as Clifford and Lane who demanded fixed selves and stable positions from Irish authors, Bowen was "unstuck," as she said, from a particular country or place. She was drawn to many places—England, Ireland, America, Italy, and France, and concluded, in 1962, "After all, what a non-attached divided life I've led, since childhood, haven't I? Nothing ever particularly is the norm, which I suppose is why I attach myself to any surroundings of the moment and live in the moment so very nearly completely."[72]

Propaganda

Though nothing was the norm, Bowen demonstrated her loyalty to Britain and the Allied cause in various ways, including through the medium of film. Shortly after her stint as an informant for the MOI, she signed a contract to write a script for the Strand Film Company that produced wartime documentary propaganda films.[73] Bowen, acquainted with her husband's work in educational film at the BBC, knew of the propaganda, and while taking sides against Fascism also sought the income that script writing would produce. Dylan Thomas had also been enlisted to write scripts for Strand. Her collaboration on a film, *All for Norway*, 1943, was part of the British propaganda effort to build the morale of the Norwegian government in exile in London after the Nazi occupation in April 1940. Her scripts became part of the released film, "Fighting Norway," (Fig. 7.3) that focused on the resistance of the Norwegian trade unions and schools to the occupation of the country (small and neutral like Ireland). Bowen worked on the script with others over a period of three months and received a letter from Donald Taylor of Strand in 1942, agreeing to pay her £50, indicating that "the said film will contain a substantial part of the Writer's work."[74]

Bowen continued to be employed by the MOI throughout and after the war, writing situation reports toward the end of the war on the condition of the seaside towns Dover, Hythe, and Folkstone. Some of them became essays

Fig. 7.3 "Fighting Norway," 1943 propaganda film, partly scripted by Bowen. Public Domain and Courtesy of National Film Board of Canada

published in journals signed as MOI contributions, and, later, in *Collected Impressions*. Alan Hepburn reports that tax records reveal that the MOI paid Bowen from 1944 to 1947.[75] It was during this time that she traveled to her childhood towns that were also the port cities heavily shelled by the Germans in the war. Dover was only 21 miles from Calais, France, and she described its mood: "For four years, since France fell to the Nazis, Dover has watched, waited." In 1944, the town still listened to the hammering of Allied guns across the Channel having evacuated its children and elderly. She recounted the damage to High Street, passing by "the gay, cracked, shaken buildings," walking through tunnels, down ramps and across bridges. She saw invasion barges floating below her in the harbor "like painted ships … painted canvas, waiting to carry history." Dover was a town "full of secrets": hidden explosives in the harbor, guns still poised on the Channel, and patrols on the docks. "London is kept as ignorant of what goes on in Dover as might be Berlin." It waits for D-Day.[76]

Her essay, "Folkestone," July 1945, appeared in *Collected Impressions*, and Alan Hepburn's careful study reveals that the published version of this essay ends with a sentence that evokes the hazards of war for children: "For the child of 1945 Folkestone bristles with barbed wire." The earlier draft of this essay in the Ransom archives is more benign ending with a variation on this idea: "For the child—even of several decades back—Folkestone, as seaside, bristles with frustrations."[77] Hepburn notes that the earlier draft of the essay suggests the future possibilities of Folkestone, but the later publication published after the war describes the ravaged condition of the town.

Postwar Writing and De-Nazification

After the war, the British surveillance networks moved to the center of British culture, and the Ministry of Information became the Central Office of Information. Bowen's political focus then shifted from anti-Fascism to the culture wars and, eventually, the Cold War. She participated in influencing public opinion and policies abroad to bolster democratic values before the emergence of the Cold War. She was enlisted to write a "London Letter," published abroad for the British Office of Information in 1945–1946. She also attended the Paris Peace Conference in July–August 1946, as did Charles Ritchie, having acquired credentials as a freelance journalist to attend talks and report her impressions to the *Cork Examiner*. Serendipitously, she dined with Charles Ritchie every day. She was there to picture history in the making, and produced articles that had a good deal of what she called "photography": portraits of particular conference participants, the atmosphere of the courts, and the debates.[78] Her contrasting portraits of the Russians, M. Vishinsky and M. Molotov colorfully parodies them.

Bowen also became a part of the de-Nazification program in Germany in April 1946 when she was asked to recommend British books for translation and publication in Germany and Austria. After World War II, according to Sandra Schwabe, "the British controlled the selection of world and local news for German newspapers in their zone, aiming to develop a healthy political life and outlook in the country, that is to be swayed toward democratic values," as well as to broaden the mental horizons of intelligent Germans.[79] Guidelines were drawn up for "books for the multitude" on music, architecture, art, history, sociology, and representations of the British way of life. The British believed that literature had more impact on the reading public than books with more didactic intent. This cultural work was considered crucial in transmitting the socially inclusive values of Britain and America to a country that had been mired in bigotry against Jews, gypsies, homosexuals, and the disabled since Hitler's rise to power in March 1933. Many American and British writers and artists were invited to Germany after the war to witness, record, help create this book culture, and spread American ideals.

Bowen recommended works for translation, including several of her friends' books, signaling what she considered culturally important in contemporary British and Irish writing. Her suggestions represent a range of values: for example, the story of the Blitz in Henry Green's 1943 novel *Caught*, and the Irish rebellion against British occupiers in O'Faolain's 1922 novel *A Nest of Simple Folk*. The committee instead chose nonpolitical works: Ivy Compton-Burnett's 1944 *Elders and Betters*, a witty novel about Edwardian families; and Maurice Bowra's study of symbols in art, *The Heritage of Symbolism*. Later the committee added two of Bowen's works to its list: her wartime stories in *Demon Lover and Other Stories* and *The House in Paris*, which captures the prewar atmosphere in Paris.[80]

Goronwy Rees was also on the committee, surprising, given that he was implicated as a Communist informer for a short period in the late 1930s. Spender, another friend of Bowen's with previous Communist affiliation, was also cleared to do work for the Control Commission in Germany.[81] She was part of a network. This is confirmed by Noel Barber—a novelist and foreign correspondent known for his propaganda work for Britain in Malay and Morocco—who wrote to Bowen in February 1946, soliciting articles for the *Continental Daily Mail* in Paris.[82] He mentioned in passing that he appreciated the pieces she had written for the MOI, and enclosed two of them.[83]

In 1949 Bowen turned her intellectual gaze back to England. She was invited to join the Royal Commission on Capital Punishment, to decide whether to modify or end capital punishment. She visited cities in England, Scotland, and America as part of the study: she learned not to take a "squeamish" or "emotional" view of the agonizing materials the committee handled; she visited prisons and saw demonstrations of execution implements but declined an invitation to witness an execution. She reported "being in the middle of a nightmare" on her visit to a Maidstone jail, "each of the prisoners in some indefinable way [...] a bit off [...] the stench of squalour and slyness about them all."[84] The Commission recommended the abolishment of capital punishment in 1952, but the death penalty for murder continued until 1965, and for treason, until 1998. Bowen contributed psychologically subtle recommendations to the commission on a few points of law. First, under the existing law, "only physical provocation counted as a provocation which can turn murder into manslaughter or make it just another homicide." Bowen recommended "the inclusion of *verbal* provocation" as a factor that could reduce murder to manslaughter, noting that it "may have been either as a writer and an imaginative person, or as a woman, that to her continuous mental torture is equally provocative." Her suggestion was accepted. She also contested the point of law that "clemency is extended to a man who finds that his wife has been unfaithful" and not to a man who discovers that his mistress has insulted him with betrayal; Bowen argued that a man who murders a deceitful mistress is more likely to have the law against him, yet the law should recognize that uncontrollable "passion and jealousy is likely to arise more fully in a sexual relationship" with a mistress than in a marital relationship.[85]

In this same period, Bowen agreed to be a cultural ambassador, lecturer, and propagandist for the British Council in Eastern and Central Europe in 1948–1949, visiting Czechoslovakia and Hungary, both on the verge of Communist coups; and later, she would visit Austria, grappling with the aftermath of the Nazi occupation.[86] Bowen was a successful cultural ambassador, offering public lectures, reports to the council, and essays on her East European tour. As in her reports on Eire, she gave general impressions of a country: vivid descriptions of places, the psychology and morale of the people, sketches of character, surveys of public opinion, commentary on different factions and groups, historical background, and astute political observations, with advice sprinkled throughout. Czechoslovakia inspired her most effusive writing, but also self-censorship (perhaps at the direction of the British Council) as the country was in political crisis—a coup was brewing when she was there[87] The British were watching developments in Eastern Europe closely. Her trip to Czechoslovakia in February 1948 just preceded the coup, and Bowen took sides against the Communists, working and lecturing intensely in her two-week visit. A few weeks later, the Czech Communist Party, with Soviet backing, established a dictatorship that would last four decades. Her essay, "Prague and the Crisis," begins, "'Best of all,' everyone said to me, 'you should have come to Prague at the blossom time'"—code for the coup.[88] It is curious that Dylan Thomas also flew to Prague in this same year as a guest of the

Czechoslovak Writer's Union: he, a known propagandist and spy for the British.[89] These literary visits were a cover for British propaganda, the use of personal communication among elite individuals being a style of persuasion developed earlier by the MOI during the war years. Ostensibly, the cultural side effect, was secondary.

Her lectures, "The Technique of the Novel," presented to the Czech Syndicate of Writers, and "The English Novel in the Twentieth Century," for members of the British Institute and Charles University, drew large crowds. In a BBC broadcast in March 1948, she noted that she had "never spoken to an audience whose interest in literature could be felt to be more vital or sincere" than in those lectures. She toured the city, admiring the modern housing, industrial buildings, public libraries, and the magnificent opera house. As always, the landscape imprinted itself on her memory: "the great open sweeps of tillage, the mysterious forests, the noble ranges of mountain, the sky-reflecting rivers, the churches perched on hilltops, the villages in the valleys." The British Council report also detailed her visit to the pioneering film studios of Jiri Trnka, an original and innovative Czech puppet maker, internationally recognized. Trnka had an extensive career as an illustrator of children's books and his animation of folktales, literary works, and the political impact of Hitler earned him the reputation as the Walt Disney of Eastern Europe—though his films are more beautiful and refined. Bowen spent an enchanted afternoon watching his film *A Year in Bohemia*, a homage to the endurance of Czech peasants represented as dolls. Bowen proclaimed it to be "great art," revealing her abiding interest in dolls, puppets, and the potential of the cinema.

She also gave literary lectures in Austria for more than two weeks, and the Vienna office viewed the substance as excellent and "greatly appreciated her clear and (intentionally) slower delivery," confirming that her stammering was present but not an issue. She drew an audience of 400 in Vienna, 120 in Salzburg, and 160 in Innsbruck. British Council reports indicate that she showed "untiring interest in everything she saw and everyone she met and undoubtedly enjoyed the programs arranged for her without for a moment forgetting, or asking to be spared her duties as a literary ambassador."[90] The Austrian newspaper heralded her presence as more than a literary event: "the windows of Europe are open wide."

The British Council commented that Bowen was introduced as "a most famous English authoress" according to the Hungarian *Village Citizen's Democratic Daily*.[91] None of her novels had yet been translated into Hungarian, and she was hardly known; she was, however, a novelty, a British literary lady, described as "tall, interesting looking, fair … like a figure stepping out of some English novel" and a representative of Western values. She experienced Hungary as a most depressing "occupied country" in the sphere of Soviet influence, "in which any genuine life was being lived surreptitiously."[92] Non-Communist parties in Hungary were repressed in 1947, and in 1948 the pretense of democracy was dropped as opposition leaders were sent into exile or imprisoned and the red star was added to the Hungarian flag. Given the dire conditions, Bowen was much more political and open about Communist oppression there than she was about Czechoslovakia, and her essay "Hungary" reads, at times, like propaganda. She absorbed its clandestine atmosphere and nervousness of people to whom she spoke, knowing that they were being watched. In conversation with students, she noted their caution but curiosity about American and British students. They were a generation, she said, whose ambitions were grimly national rather than personal. This anxious feeling extended to other communications with, for example, the dean of arts at Budapest University who, she said, "had the sense of a gagged person speaking with the eyes." In a large café, she had the sense of being in "a hall of whispers" where people breathed secrets under the din of the orchestra. She witnessed the "warping and distorting" power of the Soviet regime, but nevertheless felt an "unformulated resistance" to the regime in the Hungarian temperament and people, and a receptivity to Britain and the West. She cannily observed that British Council lecturers had freer contacts with individuals than the members of the legation, expressing surprise at "how far a British person could travel on the cultural ticket" that she was riding. Although she was not well known, her British Council affiliation gave her access to some members of the cultural elite, from whom she could perhaps gather information. She asserted that the distribution of modern English literature could influence the population's ideas of the West. After her trip to what she termed a backward and beautiful country, she advised against Britain loosening ties with Hungary, which would "not only be a blunder but a betrayal."

The British Council's literary and cultural challenge to Hungary included Bowen's lecture on James Joyce. He was a lively topic as the first Hungarian edition of *Ulysses*, translated by Endre Gaspar, had just been published in 1947, and was almost immediately banned. It was a brave effort as the eminent Hungarian Marxist historian, Georg Lukács, played a major role for decades in rejecting Joyce's modernist style.[93] Championing Soviet "realism," he denounced Joyce's focus on individual consciousness, isolation, and stream-of-consciousness. Both Gaspar's translation and Bowen's lecture were early challenges to this view of Joyce, who did not gain acceptance in Eastern Europe until the 1980s.[94]

Reparative Reading

Was Bowen an intelligence agent, a consultant for the British government, a spy, a propagandist? The meanings of these words are manifold and interwoven, their charge depending on the context of a national or community discourse, a particular historical moment, a particular country or point of view. Bowen, for example, was accused of being "disloyal" by some in Ireland—in informing on the Irish for the British MOI during the early part of the war (1940–1942)—yet reminds readers in her essay, "Disloyalty" that one can have a geopolitical allegiance that is larger than loyalty to nation or country. Justin Stover has incisively written about this elusive concept of "loyalty" that "is formed in an individual through a combination of social factors, including the influence of longstanding cultural elements, contemporary community standards, and interpersonal relationships."[95] "Loyalty" to a cause might sometimes be linked to violent acts; "treason" might be defined by Irish participation in the British army or an Irish girl's dating a British man; a "propagandist" might be viewed positively or negatively depending on community opinion of the cause. Consequently, the meaning of these words in an ethical or patriotic sense is not static but shifts with the changing values of the individual, community and the politics of the day. They surface here because Bowen bears traces of many of these words in the critical literature surrounding her activities and writing during World War II and after. The words are open to interpretation and re-interpretation as their meanings and the reception of Bowen and her writing shift according to the political and ethical allegiances of the reader, and the critic and the country in which she is read.

Clair Wills attests that "espionage is too strong as well as too narrow a term for Bowen's activities," because Bowen went beyond the usual definition of espionage in transforming her reports into journalism, fiction, and nonfiction that continues to be read. Yet Eunan O'Halpin writes that the charge of "spy" stuck to Bowen once it was confirmed that her reports on Irish opinion were sent up from the Dominions Office, a quasi-intelligence facility in Dublin, to Winston Churchill in the War Office in London that influenced Britain's military operations. Paul McMahon, another historian, also has no qualms classifying Bowen as a spy given his broad definition: one engaged in "the collection and processing of all information, whether open or secret, pertaining to the security of the state."[96] Bowen herself used the word "reporting," perhaps coyly, to describe and mitigate her activities in a 1959 interview. She said she was "doing a good deal of reporting work for the Ministry of Information during the war, of different kinds," adding, "I don't know whether that would rank as journalism or not."[97]

A "reparative reading," an approach suggested by Eve Kosofsky Sedgwick in another context, prompts us to reinvent and reread Bowen.[98] Critics ignore the intelligence and propaganda activities of authors at their peril. Once Bowen's role as an informant was confirmed, she became a cultural flash point, revealing much about the culture and politics of her time as well as the country in which she is perceived. How does this information, now established, inform our reading of Bowen's wartime writing and affect, more broadly, her literary reputation and how she is read? Although the archive of letters and documents presented here direct us to the past and Bowen's activities in the 1940s and 1950s, it expands into the future as new interpretations are placed upon Bowen's work for MOI, and its transformation into official reports, journalism, non-fiction, and fiction.[99] These responses too become a part of Bowen's "archive" as presented here as she, like all authors, is subject to changing views of the Irish, English, and, indeed, the world. From the Irish perspective, Bowen's pro-British, anti-Fascist and MOI activities in Ireland are viewed by some as a "betrayal" in working undercover for the English; from the British and Allied point of view, Bowen was admirably and correctly anti-Nazi in gathering information on Ireland's stance of neutrality, her role justified by the fear of German invasion of England through Ireland as well as the possible German occupation of Ireland.

Britain appreciated her service to the anti-Fascist cause. Four weeks after she was accepted as an agent, M.E. Antrobus, British representative to Eire, wrote to John Stephenson, July 27, 1940, praising her reports as "sane and interesting," in addition to revealing silly confusion with another novelist, Marjorie Bowen, suggesting how little she was known outside British literary circles.[100] Another letter followed from Lord Cranborne in November 1940.

The MOI, Dominions Office in Ireland, and the War Department in London valued Bowen's insights, poised perspectives, and ability to write persuasively without the jargon typical of government reports. These reports on Ireland, as well as her propaganda and situation reports after the war, were clear and focused, with none of the elusiveness of her fiction.

Notes

1. Butler, "Writer as Independent Spirit," 527.
2. See Hepburn, ed. *Listening In.*
3. Bowen, "Frankly Speaking."
4. Butler, "Writer as Independent Spirit," 527.
5. Connolly, "Comment," 9.

6. *IGS*, viii.
7. *MT*, 129.
8. O'Halpin, *Spying on Ireland*, 2.
9. A wartime rumor that Irish ports were being mined in cooperation with the English is discredited by historian, Thomas Hachey, who asserts there is no evidence for the charge (e-mail to PL, December 6, 2014).
10. Wills, *That Neutral Island*, 148.
11. McMahon, *British Spies and Irish Rebels*, 378. Examined British and Irish intelligence archives, 2011.
12. Edward Corse.
13. Jordan, *How Will the Heart Endure*, 98.
14. EB to VW, July 1940, SU.
15. *Notes on Eire*, July 13, 1940.
16. McLaine, *Ministry of Morale*, 39.
17. See Phyllis Lassner, "Women Writers," in *Espionage and Exile*.
18. Arnold interview.
19. Jordan, *How Will the Heart Endure?* 210.
20. McMahon, *British Spies and Irish Rebels*, 375.
21. Betjeman to Rodgers, (MOI), TNA PRO INF August 10, 1941.
22. TNA, INF1/539. Lord Davidson to John Rodgers, July 2, 1941.
23. Betjeman, *Letters*, 216.
24. Mahon, "MacNeice, the War and the BBC."
25. MacNeice, "Neutrality."
26. "Budgie."
27. Jenkins, introduction to *Collected Reports*, ix.
28. "Summer Night," *CS*, 588.
29. "Summer Night," *CS*, 599.
30. Bowen, "Disloyalties," 61.
31. *HD*, 22, 29.
32. "Disloyalties," Lee, *The Mulberry Tree*, 61.
33. "Disloyalties," Lee, *The Mulberry Tree*, 60.
34. *LS*, 36.
35. "Disloyalties," *The Mulberry Tree*, 61.
36. *City of Angels*, 161.
37. *City of Angels*, 137.
38. *The City of Angels*, 197.
39. *The City of Angels*, 40, 48–49, 152–153.
40. See also lively account of this event in Feigel, *Love Charm of Bombs*.
41. Ibid., 311.
42. SOF to Peter Davidson, *Atlantic Monthly's* editor, May 7, 1974, UCC, BL/L/PD, 1963–1974, 272.
43. Yeats, "The Circus Animal's Desertion," *Complete Poems*, 336.
44. *BC*, 92.

45. Clifford and Lane, *Notes on Eire*, 3rd edition includes thirteen reports (including those in Aubane's earlier editions). Walshe in *Elizabeth Bowen, Selected Irish Writings*, includes eight reports, omitting Bowen's early 1940 reports. Walshe's eight reports overlap with Clifford and Lane, but the editing differs.

46. *SIW*, 52–99.

47. Fisk, *In Time of War*, ix.

48. Christopher, *Defense of the Realm*, 1.

49. EB to VW, n.d. (ca. December) 1941, SU.

50. Ibid.

51. There were varied views of Irish "neutrality." Thomas Hachey views it as deValera's pragmatic, strategic, and at times, rhetorical policy. Churchill's criticisms of deValera's obstinacy earned a reply from de Valera when he asserted that the independence of a still-wounded Ireland, and "ensured that neutrality [during the war] would henceforth be worn as a badge of honor by Irish nationalists of every hue" ("Rhetoric and Reality," 37).

52. See Porcelli, "Between British Commitment and Irish Neutrality."

53. TNA PREM 453/2.

54. *SIW*, 77.

55. Bowen, review, *Spectator*, September 5, 1941, *WWF*, 118.

56. Butler, "Invader Wore Slippers," 375–76, 383–384.

57. Fisk, *In Time of War*, 431.

58. *SIW*, 60, 59, 81, 67.

59. Ibid.

60. McMahon notes that Frank McDermott and Seanad Eireann were the only other members of Parliament who favored Irish entry into the war.

61. *SIW*, 52–53.

62. Ibid., 60.

63. Fisk, *In Time of War*, 423.

64. Bowen, *Notes on Eire*, 11.

65. Bowen, "Eire."

66. *SIW*, 59.

67. Ibid., 81.

68. Ibid., 67.

69. *HD*, 63, 23.

70. Bowen, "Careless Talk," *IGS*, 108. Porcelli's research reveals that the slogan "Careless Talk" appeared on 2.5 million posters from 1940 on, along with other slogans: "Don't forget, the wall has ears," and "Keep it under your hat."

71. Lane and Clifford, "Elizabeth Bowen: A 'Debate' in *The Irish Examiner*." Letters including those of Martin Mansergh and Jack Lane: http://aubane-historicalsociety.org/irishexaminerbowendebate.pdf. Accessed May 2015.

72. *LCW*, 389.

73. Allan Hepburn also referenced Bowen's participation in "War in the Archives."

74. Strand Film Co. to EB, December 21, 1942, HRC.

75. *PPT*, 13. Hepburn's research reveals that MOI paid Bowen £115 in 1944–1945; £117.12.0 in 1946; and £21.3.0 in 1946–1947. HRC 12.5–6.

76. *CI*, 221–225.

77. Bluemel, 136.

78. Bowen, "Paris Peace Conference," 66.

79. Schwabe, "Literary Criticism." Gratitude to Jonathan Laurence for translation of parts of this dissertation on the British book-printing program in postwar Germany.

80. Bowen's books are listed in Alan Bance, ed., *The Cultural Legacy of the British Occupation in Germany*, 120.

81. Smith, *British Writers and MI5 Surveillance*, 57.

82. Noel Barber wrote *The War of the Running Dogs* about the Malay Emergency, violent conflicts between the Commonwealth and the Communist party in Malaysia: he was engaged in a British propaganda mission in the country.

83. Noel Barber to EB, February 4, 1946, HL.

84. EB to CR, January 22, 1950, *LCW*, 157–158.

85. Bowen, "Frankly Speaking."

86. Watanabe, "Cold War."

87. The Cold War materializing when Bowen visited; the February 1948 coup d'état followed her visit.

88. Bowen, "Impressions of Czechoslovakia," in Hepburn, *Listening In*, 82, 87, 88.

89. See Stefania Porcelli.

90. British Council Reports, NGC FW TNA1400990811: Austria BW13; Czechoslovakia BW 27; Hungary BW 36, BNA.

91. *Village Citizen's Democratic Daily* (ca. 1946), miscellaneous clipping file of Brenda Hennessy.

92. Bowen, "Hungary," *PPT*, 87, 90, 87, 90.

93. See Goldman, "Belated Reception."

94. See Gula, "Lost a Bob but Found a Tanner," Hungarian translations of Joyce's *Ulysses*.

95. Justin Stover: http://ak-militaergeschichte.de/stover_allegiances (accessed September 2020).

96. McMahon, *British Spies and Irish Rebels*, 2.

97. Bowen, "Frankly Speaking."

98. Kosofsky-Sedgwick, "Paranoid Reading and Reparative Reading," 4. Important points are made about "paranoid" readings and "performative effects" of such positions, applied to Bowen.

99. Derrida, *Archive Fever*.

100. M. E. Antrobus, UK representative in Eire, to John Stephenson, BNA, DO_35/1011/3/001, 178/40.

8

The Roving Eye

Transience

Bowen was drawn not only drawn to clandestine watching and spying, but to the ephemeral, the transience of what the eye perceived. When asked about the part that light played in her work, she said, "I was unconscious of it," but added that she saw things "at first glance as a dazzling blur or shadow." Her shortsightedness had something to do with it. She added, "in Ireland, light is a factor, an immense factor, always changing, and it conditions everything, almost magical, celestial to the starkly grimly gruffly ugly [...] and determines one's mood."[1] And so her eye wandered to other arts and new media that radiated not only with light but also with waves of sound: the new media of photography, cinema, and the surrealist art movement as well as the radio and telephone that took her beyond the human eye and ear into different instruments of consciousness.

A writer, she believed, always keeps a "roving eye," "some faculty free to veer and wander," to find a story to tell and a way to tell it.[2] Sometimes in her writing, she deepens a scene like a painter who creates a setting in which to immerse her figures or her eyes reel past a landscape like a film, or takes a still photograph. She becomes an instrument, a kind of screen upon which images are projected. This exploration propelled her to a new narrative space occupied by other modernist and intermodernist authors.

When she was 18, in September 1917, she fulfilled her wish to become an artist and enrolled in the London Council School of Arts and Crafts. This was the same year that Mainie Jellett, an Irish painter, went to the Westminster

© The Author(s), under exclusive license to Springer Nature Switzerland AG 2021
P. Laurence, *Elizabeth Bowen*, Literary Lives, https://doi.org/10.1007/978-3-030-71360-7_8

School in London to work with Walter Sickert, part of the avant-garde Camden Town Group; then on to Paris with Evie Hone, a stained-glass artist, to study with Andre Lhote. Hone, along with Jellett and Mary Swanzy, made modernism current in Ireland. According to Bowen, Jellett "brought back to her native city [Dublin] a dynamism that, at first, as she had expected, was found unfriendly, destructive, even repellent." Bowen, appreciative of their modern impulses, said Ireland was not ready for the "ice of abstract terms" that Jellett introduced.[3] But Bowen was not part of this avant-garde movement.

Nor was Bowen ready for The London Council School, a fledgling institution seeking to establish itself in the field of design in the way that Slade and the Royal Academy had for fine arts. Bowen told a Hungarian interviewer in 1948 that she had wanted to become a book illustrator, and on the face of it her qualifications seemed inadequate for a school that was established to provide specialist art training for those in trades or crafts. She attended for two terms, entering about a decade after the new department of book illustration and poster production was created. The founder recognized that unless the craft was taught, the incipient private-press movement would be doomed. It is likely that Bowen took courses in book illustration, poster design, drawing, and etching, and would also have attended the required lectures on Hogarth, Reynolds, Gainsborough, Blake, the countryside in art, and the nature study of Turner and Constable. Bowen's drawing skills did not develop: "I discovered myself to be bored, and an art school dunce. So I gave up."[4]

Like Karen in *The House in Paris*, she was working "with a dead brush," no longer animated by talent or interest.[5] Yet her initial movement toward the visual arts at this cutting-edge art school and her interest in book illustration are clues to how she looked at the world and treasured, as she later said, what was "riveting to the eye."[6] She regretted that "lost gift," and said, "often when I write I am trying to make words do the work of line and color. I have the painter's sensitivity to light. Much (and perhaps the best) of my writing is verbal painting."[7] Yet she realized the difficulties of translating painting into writing; the simultaneity of experience in a visual image could not easily be captured in the sequential syntax of a written sentence. She drew attention to her narrative attempt to write "a visual sentence" in *A World of Love* in an interview with Walter Allen. Jane, the young girl, enters a drawing room and notes, "pyramidal the flowers were on the piano." Bowen defended the odd placement of the word "pyramidal" because it was the shape of the pyramid that the girl *first* perceived as she entered the room; then she sees the flowers on the piano.[8] Bowen explained that many of her syntactic inversions come from that kind of visual perception.

She became a painter's writer. In a 1955 letter, Rose Macaulay praised Bowen for showing differentiated characters seen from the outside comparing them favorably to the disembodied, polite, and in her view, flawed characters of another serious novelist of the day, Ivy Compton-Burnett. She complained that Compton-Burnett's background in her novel, *A House and its Head*, was unspecified and indeterminate in comparison to Bowen who "like a painter's sketching of his figures set in a drawn landscape all shimmering to some life that ambiances turn like water and [realize?] their individuality."[9] This shimmering with alternations of sunshine and candlelight is captured in a cemetery scene when the young Sydney Warren escapes from Mrs. Kerr with her friend Claudia in *The Hotel*.

> The cemetery seemed quite deserted. Gashes of over-charged daylight pressed in through the cypresses on to the graves [...] candles for the peculiar glory of the lately dead had been stuck in the unhealed earth: here and there a flame in a glass shade, opaque in the sunshine. Above all this uneasy rustle of remembrance, white angels poised forward to admonish. The superlatives crowding each epitaph hissed out their "issims" and "issime" from under the millinery of death. Everywhere, in ribbons, marbles, porcelains was a suggestion of the salon, and nowhere could the significance of death have been brought forward more startlingly.[10]

This cemetery scene, graced with poetry and brilliant word choice absorbs the lively social atmosphere of the salon and elegance of the nearby hotel; nevertheless, it is a cemetery and the "rustle" of death lurks beneath the glitter of life. Bowen artfully captures the haunting doubleness of life and death as the angels lean forward to admonish, and the frippery of the decorations on tombstones point to mortality.

To explain her narrative patterning of characters and places in her writing, she once employed a painterly description of a Dutch interior. The texture of *The Heat of the Day*, she said, develops through the narrative interrelationship of setting, place, and character. The figures in the painting, for example, "Dutch Interior" by Pieter Elinga (1660), like the characters in her novels, are a part of a pattern of the whole and not a narrative focal point:

> The book is, in fact, not at all like one of those Italian fourteenth century pictures in which a foreground group is seen against a far distant landscape, but rather is it like one of the Dutch interiors where, although there are central figures the character of the whole picture comes as much from the background as from the figures themselves.[11]

Though the details in the painting might suggest "realism"—as some critics have described Bowen's style—a longer look suggests that the patterning points toward "abstraction." The interior of the room, the designs, shapes, patterns and objects and the figures are a part of the whole. The idea might be applied to a new understanding of Bowen's style (the relationship among the characters, setting, plot, action) as well as a way of reading: external landscapes and interiors rooms in which she places her characters are an integral part of who they are and the texture of the whole picture. Objects, patternings and figures "speak" in her writing.

Later, as a mature writer, Bowen was praised for her "word pictures." She was grateful when Derek Hill, the painter, highlighted this quality in her writing: "Thank you for what you say about Co. Cork, and also about my word-picture of it. All the same, I would rather paint. Only colour and light can render colour and light: the written word's always thick and cold."[12] In her story "Requiescat," she sketches an Italian lakeside scene. Here a widow meets her husband's old friend, "Now it was the time of the Angelus, and bells answered one another from the campaniles of the clustered villages across the lake. A steamer, still gold in the sun, cleft a long bright furrow in the shadowy water." Bowen observed, "The scene had all the passionless clarity of a Victorian water-colour."[13] When traveling in Austria, she noted "the metallic looking trees and the immense velvety mountains," and remarked that she could see why the Austrians did not paint landscapes, but were drawn to engraving instead.[14] In an engraving, the image of the silver trees would appear to be incised on the surface of the flat, "velvety" mountains, creating a sense of depth not easily achieved in a painting.

Bowen's gift also engages readers in her act of seeing as a painterly writer. In *The Little Girls*, Clare, Dicey, and Sheikie meet for a reunion in childhood Seale (a mythical Hythe), and come upon an old High Street window that offers the unusual sensation "of looking at pictures of where one was."[15] The back of the window displayed masterpieces like "Hope" with a harp; the front of the window showed etchings, drawings, and paintings of High Street where they stood. The girls were fascinated by the perception that what was "in" the pictures was actually "outside" the pictures where they stood. In addition, they see a double reflection of themselves in the street in the shop window and in the glass frames of the paintings themselves. "The reflection looked like a large painting." Here we have a succession of images, moving from inside to outside the painting that enhances what we see. But then, surprisingly, the metaphors of High Street become actual, visible, and audible, and the street speaks: "'All right, then, I am picturesque!' the street must have said." Things speak. The street has voice. Bowen's presentation of these flickering visual and aural perceptions suggests a threshold of the "real" that the painter or the writer steps over: an actual physical place is transformed into art. We hover in this liminal space with Bowen, both watching and joining the little girls in their discovery of multiple levels of imagery and "reality." This space reveals Bowen's finely nuanced play with multiple reflections, like the kaleidoscope that transforms the way we see patterns and colors.[16] This pattern of seeing and then seeing again persists in her writing. For Bowen, language is the "glass" wall, the barrier that separates and distances her from experience. Language is often *manqué*; words can capture only the glancing sensations, colors, and experiences of life. She reflected that this novel, *The Little Girls* is what Americans would call "a recall of sensory experience book," aligned with her own "echo-track of sensation" from childhood that surfaces in her subtle writing.[17]

In daily life, Bowen often visualized absent people. In 1948, she wrote Ritchie from Bowen's Court, "I wish I were an Impressionist painter and could paint pictures of you as you were here—halfway up or down on the stairs, coming in through doors, standing leaning against the mantelpiece. The things I think of you and the ways I see you would sound foolish said or written even to you. I wish I could show you the pictures I would paint."[18] When standing in a room of El Grecos in Mexico in 1950, she compares Ritchie's figure to those she sees in the paintings.

Light and Speed

Light plays variously in her work: it could be sunlight, moonlight, twilight, candlelight, electric light, or cinematic light; shadow in a painting; or doubleness or specters in photography or rayographs. She acknowledged at one time, "I do write, I think, from the eyes. I always see things."[19] To use Bowen's own vocabulary, she moves as a writer from "seeing" toward a "situation" or an "action" that implies some kind of "mood," from which her characters and story emerge: she dismisses "analysis" as a conscious element in her work. Light extends from a physical sensation to something that is not visible to the eye. It hits a scene, for example, the driveway up to a big house in *The Last September*. Or it is absent, exposing a dark line like the obelisk in *A World of Love* that reappears in silhouette throughout the novel, a monument, a symbol. Antonia and Lilia lived and loved in the shadow of this obelisk near the ruins of a big house, and, young Jane of the next generation reads love letters of a deceased soldier in its shade. All that matters in this novel, as Rose Macaulay observed, is the texture of writing and the assemblage of people. Bowen's line, the obelisk may reflect the line drawn down the center of Lily Briscoe's painting in *To the Lighthouse* that divides two worlds: the common, everyday life and the spectral or haunted domain of the past.

Light illuminates, mirrors, reflects, deflects, or blinds. In *A World of Love*, golden-haired Jane visits wealthy Lady Latterly and spends time with her in her luxurious light-shot bedroom before a party:

> The bedroom gained still more unreality by now seeming trapped between day and night—this marvel of marbling and mirror-topping, mirror-building-in and prismatic whatnots being at the moment a battleground of clashing dazzling reflections and refractions. Crystal the chandelier dripped into the sunset; tense little lit lamps under peach shades were easily floated in upon by the gold of evening.[20]

Outside the bedroom, a ray of light blinds Lady Latterly and enchants Jane.

In addition to light, Bowen was drawn to the sensation of speed that she believed also alerted vision. Speed became the locus of the modern to Bowen and other writers, and attests to her fascination with the movement and sensations of bicycles, cars, and planes, and their effect on visual perception. Speed was, she said, "exciting to have grown up with. It alerts vision, making vision retentive with regard to what only may have been seen for a split second."[21] This would apply to the click of the camera, as well as travel as Bowen was often in motion. First, she was reckless on a bicycle when she was 13. Her Aunt Laura gave her a bike, saying, "Now this is yours." and she recounted, "first riding the Raleigh, I dismounted, often, simply to stand and look at it. This, my first machine, had an intrinsic beauty." She recounts the dares of riding blindfolded on a bike, some of the little girls in her novel experiencing the "birdlike" freedom. She was also attracted to the speed of cars, and in August 1936, told Plomer that she was learning to drive. She was a joyrider, noting that she drove "far from brilliantly, but not, I hope, to the public danger."[22] She found that she drove faster by herself: "the 30 mile average always bores me." Eudora Welty, when visiting Bowen's Court in 1953, observed that Bowen drove quite recklessly around country roads, and had great fun doing so. Her cousin, Laetitia, recalled her terror when driving with Bowen to get a driver's license, and how much Bowen depended on the horn to get cars out of the way; another cousin said there were rumors that her neighbors in Hythe removed their gate posts in frustration after she had crashed into them on several occasions. Even market researchers in the Nuffield Organization were interested in Bowen's opinion of her 1929 Morris Oxford Tourer. She noted in their market research questionnaire that she loved driving fast and found driving or being driven "stimulating to the invention of stories."[23]

Speed, planes, and cars come into view in *To the North*. Emmeline and Markie's wild car ride and their later flight to Paris reflect intense desire and madness. Bowen imagines speed and its delights and dangers and represents it cinematically in her final scene of the novel, a tour de force. As they drive a "glow slipped from the sky and the North laid its first chilly fingers upon their temples, creeping down into his collar and stirring her hair at the roots." As they passed petrol pumps, "red and yellow, veins of all speed and dangerous, leapt giant to their lights." They head uphill to a "funnel point in the darkness—for though lamps dotted the kerb the road ran and deepened ahead into shade of pitch like a river—this icy rim to the known world began to possess his fancy, till he half expected its pale reflection ahead."[24] In the dark, Markie begins to see the end of the road of life with fascination. Speed mounts in Emmeline's nerves: she cannot stop. The speed of the car offers the sensation of flight, their earlier flight to Paris, and unmoors her body. The ending appears as if on a screen. Driving up the Great North Road with her, we close our eyes as if in a movie theater when a white glare blinds us as the car crashes and ends the film. We discover the menace and murderous wishes beneath the seeming gentleness of a women caught in the urgency of love and pain. Bowen's narrative eye rivets the cinematic scene. She states that she wants to obliterate words and "to give the full possibility of sensation and visual power in *words* so that the sensation I have in mind when I write should go straight to the readers."[25]

Images of flight along with the speed of the car suggest Markie and Emmeline's mounting attraction and sexual tension: a nuance of sexuality for which, John Bayley, the critic, complimented Bowen. In the novel, Markie, at one point, recalls their trip to Paris: "'I wish we were still flying.'... 'So do I,' she said with an irrepressible smile. 'I wish it were still that day.'"[26] Surrealist images emerge in their flight to Paris: "earth had slipped from their wheels that, spinning, rushed up the air. They were off. Dipping, balancing, with a complete lack of impetus." There was "no noise, no glass, no upholstery that boxed her up from the extraordinary: as they smoothly mounted and throbbed through the shining element she watched trees and fields in the blue June haze take on that immaterial loveliness, that foreign and clear intensity one expects of the sky." The surreal flight of the body in this clear yet ominous sky lights their erotic path to Paris. Bowen learned to drive, and flew in a plane for the first time four years after this novel was published in 1936. She imagined and described speeding cars and the sensation of flight, interestingly, before she experienced it.

The Photographic Eye

This altered sense of sight, sound, speed, and time experienced in modern transit extended to the instrument of the camera: the instant click of the photograph and the whirr of the movie camera. Photography opened up another way of seeing with its ability to record multiple images, moments, and changing moods that could adapt to a mobile narrative technique that would relieve her from presenting a fixed image of a character or society. The camera, according to Bowen, made "vision retentive with regard to what only may have been seen for a split second."[27] The camera eye, unlike the human eye, could make time stop. "Any artist," she said, "is a walking camera—sometimes consciously, sometimes not, he is forever making exposure, then developing, in his internals, the results."[28] She compares memory to a photographic plate being developed in a darkroom: as light hits the plate, it reveals images; patches of remembered experience appear. She thought of her own wartime short stories not as flashy reportage but as "disjected snapshots [dispersed impressions]—snapshots taken from close up, too close up, in the middle of the mêlée of a battle."[29] Bowen, like other wartime women writers, downplays events to spotlight a character, a feeling, a mood, and, importantly, a narrative sense of slow time. In "Ivy Gripped the Steps," Gavin's memories are close-ups.

An early short story, "Recent Photograph," narrates the importance of an actual photograph to a journalist hungry for details at a crime scene; her reports include snapshots of people. These brief character sketches lend concentrated photographic vividness to Bowen's writing. She describes seeing February afternoon light falling upon the "winter-worn phantasmagoric city" of Prague on her British Council trip in 1947. It had "the ghostly hyper-reality of a photograph: a grey-brown print cunningly tinted in."[30]

And yet there are, at times, that she announces the limitations of the photographic eye when compared to the imagination. *The House in Paris* spotlights the prejudiced perceptions of Mrs. Michaelis by noting that a camera eye can blind one "to those accidents that make a face that face, a scene that scene, and float the object, alive, in your desire and ignorance."[31] Mrs.

Michaelis misses the accidents of Max's personality and flattens him "like a flower in a book." Karen observes that her mother's "well-lit explanations of people were like photographs taken when the camera could not lie," but stunned the imagination.[32] Bowen opposes this photographic eye to the superior "imaginative eye" of Karen, who accords Max a mystery and personality "like a road running into a dark tunnel." Bowen releases Max from Mrs. Michaelis' fixed, anti-Semitic photographic gaze, and allows him possibilities as a complex character through the imagination.

The idea of photography continued to evolve in Bowen's art. She informed documentary photographer Dorothea Lange that she was writing a novel with a photographer as its main character. Lange told Berenice Abbott that Bowen wanted to know "what kind of people we [photographers] are and what it feels like to be one." Lange "was struck by how close what she [Bowen] describes comes to what we do," referring to a piece that Bowen wrote for the *Times*, "The Roving Eye."[33] Bowen then did briefly sketch a free-spirited, successful female artist photographer, Antonia, in *A World of Love*.

Royal Photos

A little-known aspect of Bowen's interest in photography was also her attraction to photographic postcards of Victorian royalty. Postcards and photos of British and European kings and queens are mentioned in her correspondence with William Plomer, satirically engaged as they were, at times, with the personalities, breeding, and conventions surrounding royalty. In a 1936 letter to Bowen, Plomer alluded to a caricature of Queen Elizabeth I that she might use in her long projected album similar to his own albums of photos of royals.[34] His friends mention these scurrilous albums in which he mocked the pomp and posturing of stuffy or silly kings, queens, princes, and princesses of England and Europe, sometimes with sexual overtones (Fig. 8.1). Plomer and Bowen were ambivalent: he, a passionate royalist at times; Bowen, sentimental. She wrote to House that when the news of George V's death was announced, she felt "a surprisingly genuine stab of national grief."[35] Plomer reminded her that they had both attended George's funeral, and she recalled having arisen at four in the morning to watch the procession, meeting Plomer and T.S. Eliot afterward. She wrote to Plomer, "You crystallize things I didn't know I had felt or thought," grateful for his reminder that she was drawn to the ceremonial pomp of the occasion.[36] Bowen's ambivalence toward royalty separated her from most Catholic Irish who, at the time, would not bow to the queen.

THE THREE KINGS AND FIVE QUEENS

Fig. 8.1 Plomer's Royal Photo, "The Three Kings and Five Queens." Rights holder and Courtesy of Durham Library, England

The coronation of Queen Elizabeth II provided a spectacle—the scepter, the crown, the robes, the queen's carriage for writers, photographers, radio broadcasters and, particularly, television crews who filmed the first coronation in Westminster Abbey. Bowen, in awe of the occasion, wrote an impressionistic piece for *Vogue*. Standing among the millions lining the streets of London, she observed "an enormous channel of expectation."[37] Her first impression of Elizabeth on her way to the Abbey was "pure fairy tale"; a trail of "radiance … left by the young beauty seated beside her husband, who seems to accompany her on a joyous journey." Bowen's focus, however, is on the isolation of her queenly role: "What has to be the extent of her dedication? How dare we compute the weight of the Crown?" In her radio broadcast of May 1953, Bowen specified this "weight," the royal family decision to remain and endure the blitz in London to bolster the spirit of the people. She wonders "will the queen be aged by the crown, or stripped of herself by the mystical ceremonial." Bowen ends her article with a triumphant homage: "We behold ELIZABETH, our undoubted Queen."

Bowen identified with the young queen. In a heartbreaking letter to Ritchie in 1959, distraught after the sale of Bowen's Court, she wrote,

In a way, I am like Elizabeth II—run as she was, by a succession of different people. She was a marvelous actress, giving the full to the role given to her to play. But somebody else jolly well had to write the play. In a smaller, alas very much smaller way, I am like that. People make a mistake when they identify the performance I give with my real being.[38]

Her friend, William Plomer was also engaged with Elizabeth II having been commissioned to write the libretto for Benjamin Britten's celebratory, *Gloriana* composed for the occasion of her coronation. Plomer irreverently based it upon Lytton Strachey's colorful work on Elizabeth I's troubled relationship with Robert Devereux, *Elizabeth and Essex*. Rose Macaulay took a more traditional stance in her 1953 BBC broadcast, "The Virtue of Queenship," trumpeting "how popular monarchy is" and how people have always liked kings and queens. She relished the extravagant spectacle and the "royal fever" that might convert even "our late colonist, Americans" to resurrect the monarchy they discarded one hundred seventy years ago."[39] Veronica Wedgwood also joined the chorus in *Vogue* noting that the people's faith in Elizabeth was deep-rooted in historical memory. She noted in a 1993 BBC broadcast that her family's well-known Wedgwood china firm would mark the coronation with the production of a blue jasperware teapot with white laurel leaf and berry wreaths around the profiles of Queen Elizabeth. This traditional commemorative still graced British tea tables to ward off the ambivalent views of royalty projected by the outsiders, Bowen and Plomer.

Film

In addition to photography, Bowen was captivated by film and the wireless, novelties of the post-war era. Her roving eye is drawn to film and camerawork, and she writes that they are a worthwhile study for a novelist in "Notes on Writing a Novel." She asks, "where is the camera eye to be located?" in her essay, and asks the same of her narrative.[40] She enlarges what can be "seen" in literature by incorporating not only the eye of the photograph—the "snapshot"—into her narration, but also the succession of images projected by a movie camera. In 1924, just after the publication of her first book, *Encounters*, she was urged to go to the cinema by John Strachey, the editor of the *Spectator*, who had solicited her first short story, "Ann Lee." Silent films were shifting to talkies, film "was just then emerging from disrepute," and there was much to be learned from it.[41] Film's flickering realities are reflected in her narrative eye in her 1920s story, "Dead Mabelle," in which William, a naïve filmgoer, confuses actuality and his screen dream of a beautiful actress, a line that the medium seeks to erase. Bowen uses the technique in *Friends and Relations* to train an impersonal camera eye upon a scene and makes an empty room "look" as we, the viewer, might look upon such a room in a film. After a quarrel between Edward and his sister-in-law, Janet, who share a secret but unconsummated love, Edward leaves the room. His mother, Lady Elfrida looked down with surprise from her bedroom landing at his [Edward] descending head. She, of course, reproached herself. The long low little room, left alone with Janet, was mortally disconcerted; the lamps staring. A room does not easily re-compose itself, laugh, remark some inconsequence, remember a tune. Lady Elfrida would have recovered herself almost at once. "Gone?" she said, coming in.[42]

Here Bowen pauses her text, a still shot in a movie, and animates a room where something has happened. She creates a sense of interiority in stopping the forward movement of the plot to suspend us in this silent room. The "disconcerted" room in which Janet remains after her contretemps with Edward has "staring lamps" and holds the sense of the argument that has just taken place. In swift little turns, Bowen shifts from a human gaze to an impersonal eye revealing through objects the feeling of a place where something has happened. The atmosphere of a room does not recover as quickly as people do, Bowen seems to say. Atmospheres hang over rooms, and reveal character. The narrator of *The Heat of the Day* also reels past a description of Robert Kelway's boyhood room in Holme Dene: "a varsity chair … a swirl lamp … A turkey carpet … and sixty or seventy photographs" on the wall, all featuring Robert. These are snapshots of the smug middle-class home where Kelway developed his disaffection with the class "without a middle." Does it smack of Bowen's prejudice against middle-class breeding and preoccupations as Elizabeth Hardwick suggests? This culture turned him, Kelway said, against his own country and into a spy, a stance unconvincing to readers. The optics of film, as revealed in Kelway's room, however, engaged Bowen: it offered new resources for narrating character through telling objects. Modernist gestures emerged as possibilities to develop in narration: "Oblique narration, cutting (as in the cinema), the unlikely placing of emphasis, or symbolism (the telling use of an object for its own sake and as an image)."[43]

In *The Heat of the Day*, she creates a succession of images, as in a film, to express the mutability of a character, Harrison, a mysterious figure who appears and disappears in a series of shadowy, flickering appearances befitting a spy throughout the novel. Stella does not experience his character as continuous, "By the rules of fiction, which life to be credible must comply, he was a character 'impossible'—each time they met, he showed not shred or trace of having been continuous since they last met … coming out of the vacuum."[44] When Stella looks at Harrison "close-up" during their discussion of Robert's treason, she could not see "what was queer, wrong, off, out of the straight in the cast of Harrison's eyes." She sees only the "expression of urgency, the pupils' microcosm, black little condensations of a world too internal to know what expression was." The human eye is evasive in this world of doubleness, and the camera eye useful in capturing intrigue, spies, and double agents. Even Robert, her treasonous lover, Stella remembers, found the human eye "embarrassingly repugnant," avoiding direct gazes. Cinema offers "half-light" as Harrison's face is in "photographic half-light [and] looked indoor and weathered at the same time."

Bowen ends *The Heat of the Day* with a cinematic rooftop scene as Kelway, having been discovered as a Nazi spy, escapes from Stella's apartment to the roof, knowing that his time has run out. He remarks, "There's one great thing about a roof; there's one way off it." Bowen visualizes his climbing up the ladder through the trapdoor in the skylight. "That day whose start in darkness covered Robert's fall or leap from the roof had not yet fully broken." Another scene in the novel is a still: Robert "stayed with his thumb in his lighter. So in the cinema some break-down of protection leaves one short of action immobilized, frozen onto the screen."[45]

In her travel book *A Time in Rome*, the city "reels past like a silent film."[46] Early silent films are on her mind, and she follows the activity in the city, she said, "with the greater, closer, more spellbound and fascinating attention for the absence of explanatory wordy sound tracks." She prefers seeing the city silently. Her review of H.G. Wells' 1936 film *Things to Come* critiqued its dialogue: "Colloquially didactic, almost all sentimental, much of the talk is cackle and I wish he had cut it." More responsive to the poetic shots than the words, she remarks that visual images "woo the imagination instead of bludgeoning it." Sally Phipps, Molly Keane's daughter, remembers her husband talking with Bowen about American silent movies in 1920s–30s, "she absolutely adored them and was knowledgeable."

On a visit to Venice in 1953, she reported a lively philosophical dinner conversation in which the guests debated "whether one thinks in images or words," a topic, she said, that "splits intellectual Italy to the core." In the debate, Bowen took the firm position that "one thinks in images and the language found for them is nothing more than a translation." She was hotly supported in her position by a professor who was a "Croce-ite." The philosopher Benedetto Croce believed, like Bowen, that the "intuited image" preceded the first stroke of the brush.[47] Because she was drawn to the image in writing, she responded to Proust. In her essay on "Bergotte," she describes Proust as "a visual writer. Imagery rendered his cadenced prose, above all, sensuous and concrete. The art in his novels acted upon the reader as does a spectacle on an onlooker."[48] Moved by the power of the visual, even seeking at times to "obliterate" words, Bowen sought to incorporate these sensuous and concrete qualities in her own writing.

She moved in circles with people who were engaged with the new medium of film. Paralleling her new interest, her husband wrote a little-known progressive report, "The Film in National Life," in 1932 about films that the state supported, celebrating empire and the centrality of London to the colonies.

Also, John Houston visited and stayed at Bowen's Court.[49] Houston's films would have appealed to Bowen given their artistry as he had been an accomplished painter before becoming a film director. Bowen was also a reader of and drama critic for her friend Graham Greene's *Night and Day*, a high-brow literary magazine that reviewed films. Greene reviewed "cinema" as opposed to "movies" until the magazine's early demise after six months, because of a scandal over Greene's review of a Shirley Temple film.[50]

During the war, Bowen wrote part of a propaganda script for a film that became "All for Norway" in 1942 and her interest resurfaced when she wrote the script for a sentimental CBS documentary on Ireland, *A Tear and the Smile*, narrated by Walter Cronkite and Brendan Behan, produced in January 1961. In 1962, she wrote to Ritchie that she was on her way to Seville to write about the filming of David Lean's *Laurence of Arabia* with Peter O'Toole, an assignment commissioned by *Show* magazine. She was paid $1,000, and was pleased because she wanted to have money in New York in March when she would visit him.[51] She believed *The House in Paris* was the most screen-worthy of her novels, and praised the BBC television production by Julian Aymes, transmitted September 1, 1959.[52] She wished, she said, that they could make a film with the same cast, as it "kept the tension and atmosphere of the story," unlike an earlier dramatic production. In 1999 Scott O'Mordha also directed a production of *The Death of the Heat* for RTE.

Disembodied Voices

Bowen, however, was not only drawn to the screen—"the oblong opening into a world of fantasy"—but to the world of sound, the wireless and the BBC. Always susceptible to the unseen, the unknown, and past hauntings, she is responsive to both the gothic tradition, the modern movement of surrealism, and contemporary sounds. She wrote to William Plomer of "psychic waves" of before-the-war feeling in 1946. She was ripe then for radio with its disembodied voices communicated over electronic waves—an aural counterpoint to the spectral surrealism that also drew her in: both carrying traces of absence or the ghostly. World War II was the first war broadcast by the radio; the Vietnam War, by television. Voices entered people's living room: "Hitler yells on the wireless," wrote the poet, Louis MacNeice in "Autumn Journal" and people sometimes tried to shut the radio off and the war out as in Bowen's "Love Story." After the war, radio moved away from reporting and expanded into culture: the BBC opened a new wavelength, the Third Programme, for serious listeners in response to what was perceived as the "mediocrity" of most programming. It was to begin on September 29, 1946, and BBC producers feeling overburdened by the classics solicited Bowen, a leading modern writer, the summer before to contribute to this popular new media. As a contributor and a listener like other civilians—"radio was god" in Ireland and England during the war—she became more attuned to sound. The BBC producer, Stephen Potter, encouraged her to write a script, "Return Journey: Elizabeth Bowen in Rye," reminding her that she should suggest sound effects, and invited to contribute to a "Living Writers" series. Bowen's short stories, considered easily adaptable, were also aired frequently, particularly those from her wartime collection, *Ivy Gripped the Steps*, and her novel, *The Little Girls*. A.E. Coppard, friend and editor, noted the stories, "The Man of the Family" and "The Cat Jumps" as superb for the radio or the stage. Her agent, Curtis Brown, reported the requests for radio adaptations in his letters, and this surely added to her income. Despite her struggle with a stammer, she, herself, would sometimes read from her stories or participate in literary panels on the BBC. Surprisingly, Eudora Welty reported that after meeting the poet and editor Howard Moss in New York with Bowen, they discussed "what would happen if Elizabeth Bowen could take over a radio station" given her conversational skills with no mention of her stammer.[53] Other modern writers like Ezra Pound and Gertrude Stein also considered the medium: Pound wrote radio operas for the BBC in 1930s and Gertrude Stein spoke of a new kind of radio audience that critics say, affected her writing.

In her essay, "After November, 1918," she announces, "the novelist in England, like the individual, found himself face to face with the great void of peace. The effect, like that of facing a blank page, was intimidating."[54] Yet Bowen scripts the sounds of World War I into her radio play, "A Year I Remember-1918": the guns, the cannons, the Senior Male Voice that intones "Your firing line is in the works or the offices in which you do your bit; the shop or the kitchen in which you spend or save; the bank or the post office in which you buy your War Bonds."[55] A Young Girl in the play lives hospital days to music as the volunteers "tore about, stacked plates, served dinners, washed up. Whistling, singing, gramophones in the bus." The Second Young Girl wonders if she will be a widow without being a wife, "There may not be anyone left for us at this rate." And throughout the play, the songs of the war are woven, the whistling of "Tipperary"; girls' voices singing "Do it for Me," "Going Up," and "Over There." In some stories, the radio itself, its voice is a presence without a hearer. "Sunday Afternoon" opens, "From a cabinet came a voice announcing the six o-clock news. In the middle of this, three berries fell from a bowl of holly and patterned noisily into a brass tray." The radio provides the background war in homes removed from battle. The telephone was another instrument that piqued Bowen's interest in the disembodied voice. Sounds and human voices emerge from an earpiece or a radio cabinet— a hidden place—and enter the home interrupting conversation with news of the world, sometimes signaling alarm. In "Summer Night," a story about a couple's illicit meeting in neutral Ireland, the telephone's ring startles Emma's family when she calls them from a roadside booth. She presses her mouth to the telephone like a "conspirator," a word that rebounds from the national lexicon, secrets and collusion, a salient national issue during the war. The national mood invades the personal telephone. Later when Emma calls her lover to signal her imminent arrival, "talk" among his guests is "torn" by the ring: Interruption, pauses, and jars become a new rhythm in Bowen's syntax, inspired by her response to the telephone and the secret interludes in conversation in the war.

From Gothic to Surrealism

Disembodied voices, shadows, spectres, dreams, and hauntings are part of the experience of reading Bowen. Breton, the founder of surrealism, was the first to articulate the thread that Bowen had long intuited from the eighteenth-century gothic and Celtic iconography to the twentieth-century surrealist imagination as Keri Walshe perceptively noted in her important early work on Bowen and surrealism. When the first International Surrealist Exhibition came to London in the 1930s she was already there to receive a new force and vocabulary that set out to liberate the power of unconscious as well as the latencies of objects into an art. It fit her sensibility. She channeled past traditions into this exciting, new stream of art: her "hauntings" attributed to her uneasy position as an Irish author[56]; to the spectres of the Gothic tradition; to Freud's psychological "uncanny"; to notions of the "return" in trauma[57]; to Celtic mythology in which objects contain spirits that become animate; and to Irish fairy and folk tales in which the dead arise from the "other side." For Bowen, earlier hauntings, phantoms, and dreams surfaced in a surrealist "spectrality." The new form of the rayograph—a photographic process that obtained silhouettes, shadows, and doubling of people and objects—is the objective correlative of her sensibility: her notions of life, character, time, and memory, in short, the presence of the past in the present. This bringing together of two times or states of mind or dream and reality into a "surreality" was already part of Bowen's elusive and sometimes puzzling composite aesthetic. Unsupervised hauntings from the dead or dreams permeated her work from her first published stories in 1923 as she picked up the thread of the gothic imagination, a supernatural tradition in Ireland that extended from Sheridan Le Fanu to Bram Stoker and Yeats. Bowen had grown up with Celtic mythology and Irish fairy tales, and her writing vibrates with the Celtic belief that "the souls of those whom we have lost are held captive [in a plant, stone, some inanimate object], and thus effectively lost to us until the day (which to many never come) when we happen to pass by the tree or to obtain possession of the object which forms their prison."[58] Such souls call out, according to Proust, with whom Bowen shared this belief, and when recognized, are "delivered by us, they have overcome death and return to share in our life." Her work also vibrates to the notion of the "revenant," the shadow of a thing, an object, or a person that returns, part of Bowen's aesthetic, and visualized in the rayograph.

Surrealism was an international system of ideas that came late to England. It drew her in, based as it is upon a belief in the omnipotence of dreams, the power of the unconscious and the irrational in art and life. She attended the First International Surrealist Exhibit in the summer of 1936 at the New Burlington Galleries in London, and wrote to her friend, William Plomer, "I missed you at that Surrealist opening. What chaos."[59] Max Ernst, Juan Miro, Salvador Dali, Rene Magritte, Hans Bellmer, Giorgio de Chirico, Giacometti and Marcel Duchamps were featured, with paintings, sculptures, found objects, photographs, printed words, postcards, and books, all demonstrating the centrality of poetry and the play of the unconscious. She was ready for one of the iconic images of surrealism: a dreamlike encounter between a sewing machine and an umbrella on a dissecting table.[60]

Bowen's works express worlds of queasy sensation, the felt presence of the dead and the return of the past. She finds latencies in objects, as the pillow that is "all eyes" in *The House in Paris*; the lamps that "stare" or the "prim attentive chairs that are like a world waiting" in *Friends and Relations*; the windows that "listen" to the talk of Cecilia and Julian; and the rooms that sit up "visibly" when a character enters in *To the North*.[61] She was also drawn to the scientific ideas of Arthur Eddington, who theorized that latent energy is present in all objects. Strange objects appeared in surrealist exhibits, and Bowen was drawn to them. One might find, for example, a walking stick; a found object; masks or shields; objects from Africa, America, or New Guinea; or a familiar object, such as a colander, liberated from its usual association with food. To startle viewers into a new awareness, such objects were defamiliarized by the artists. Bowen was open to this new art, writing with disappointment about traditional paintings at the Royal Academy show a few years later, pejoratively referring to the academy's *rentier* point of view. It was, she said, a conservative institution that depended for support from people with money but not necessarily taste, an academy with an old-fashioned aim "to inspire, to elevate, to console, and to titivate leisured fancy."[62] The academy had none of the verve or currency of the avant-garde movement to which she was drawn.

Earlier, Bowen had encountered smaller exhibits of Surrealist painters at Zwemmer's, a progressive bookstore and art gallery in London. In 1934, when she was writing *The Death of the Heart*, she mentioned the first exhibition of Salvador Dali in Britain at Zwemmer's in a letter to House.[63] Daliesque traces surface in her description of Regent's Park in an essay: the light of the sunset affects and "takes on the queerness of Dali rocks."[64] House was curious about the exhibit at Zwemmers:

> What is all this about Zwemmer's? They sound very exciting. I know hardly anything about Surrealism at all; remember an exhibition I saw in London several years ago when Fornari (I think) [an Italian Futurist] and one or two others made some impression on me; but do not know their literature at all: have indeed been always, in ignorance, more amused than expectant.[65]

House voiced his suspicions of automatic writing mentioned as part of the exhibit: words dictated unconsciously to the reader who mysteriously becomes a medium. Bowen shared his doubts, and they enter into her story "Tommy Crans," in which she parodies such writing. The metaphor of witchcraft, nevertheless, enters her writings, and writing is sometimes described as a hand that moves by itself. The chauffeur in the story "The Disinherited," after writing a letter to his dead girlfriend, guiltily dropped the pen "as though it were burning. He watched it, frightfully animate, roll to the edge of the table."[66] And in some of the last notes of her life, written toward an autobiography, she outlined a section she called "Witchcraft: A query." Here she asks, "Is anything uncanny involved in the process of writing?"[67] She muses whether a resurgence of images while writing, unconscious flashes from past experiences, is allied with witchcraft, a metaphor she preferred to automatic writing. She was magnetized by the hidden arts, and expressed a fascination with a necromancer, Mr. Wade of Snowshill, whom she visited with Susan Tweedsmuir Buchan and Woolf in the 1930s.

Machine automation also filters into Bowen's writing expressing a rhythm of coldness and inhumanity. Objects in the modern office become metaphors of mind. Bowen felt like an automaton when learning to type in May 1936. She wrote to House about "this funny machine [which] is like a clattery steel hedge between myself and half my faculties." A month later she was happy "to be delivered" from her handwriting and noted the automatic nature of things as "a sentence becomes not me the moment it is on paper, and the unsympathetic clatter of the keys has something astringent about it." But she is also skeptical whether she could write fiction or criticism of any importance "without my almost erotic fondling of the pen," and notes that she is beginning her new novel, *The Death of the Heart*, slowly by hand with her Biro pen.[68] A year later, writing to Plomer, she apologizes for typing a letter, remembering that he had once complimented her on her stylish handwriting. She adds that though she makes errors, typing still gives her "a most exhilarating sense of power, in fact it feels unlike me to be doing it at all. I stop to contemplate the most banal sentence with absolute rapture. I suppose you, like everyone else, have been doing it for years."[69] She related to Jocelyn Brooke in 1950 that typing took over from her favorite Biro pen, altering her writing practices. She said that she worked straight onto a typewriter, her typing slow and bad—"about thought speed"—and liked the "impersonality" of seeing a sentence or paragraph in typescript.[70] Surrealist techniques, using typed calligrams—words playfully arranged to form a visual image—interested her also, given her new typing skill.

Beginning in the early 1930s, Bowen engaged with landscapes of cold light surfaced with a surrealist glint. Traces appear in *To the North*, *The Death of the Heart*, and in her later collections of short stories, *Ivy Gripped the Steps* and *The Cat Jumps*. In *To the North*, "north" is a place in the mind or heart. Here she liberates her characters from fixed social positions and ordinary space and time. It is a novel lit by the white light of the moon, a surrealist moon that also shines in her postwar story, "The Mysterious Kor." The cold, white, abstract light creates the psychological chill of the novel that emanates from Markie's fixed "basilisk eye," a venomous eye from legend that can kill with one look. Markie's impact on Emmeline is out of proportion and her gentle eyes turn mad, "icy" and "glassy," pointing to the "northern" regions of the mind and heart. After a meeting with Markie one afternoon, Emmeline returns to her job, unable to keep up the "pretense of industry: in vain the clock: place and time, shivered to radiant atoms, were in disorder." Thinking of their planned trip to Paris, she is threatened with a sense of "levitation." Emmeline grips the edge of her rolltop desk. "There was no afternoon," Bowen wrote, "the sun, forgetting decline, irresponsibly spun like a coin at the height of noonday."[71] We might be in a blazing Dali landscape, a place and time disordered and "shivered to radiant atoms." This impossible love skids into a surreal London newly ringed by sprawling suburbs and factories. As Emmeline drives, turning "north" toward Uxbridge, they see that "small new shops stood distracted among the buttercups; in the distance aerial glassy factories were beginning to go up among forlorn trees, branch lines and rusty gardens. Dream and actuality are interwoven. She gently smiles at this London "where her friends still slept under the haze of shining smoke" as she skirted "the ribs of the White City." She presses her silver slipper against the gas pedal, the speedometer mounting as Markie panics beside her. As Emmeline drives, Bowen captures her unconscious flight, north. Her eyes that had "a wandering icy gentleness like insanity's, gentleness with no object."[72] But the "north is never where you stop," remarks Mary Ann Caws, "the idea of North, it is where you know what wanting is."[73] We are left at the end of this novel with Emmeline's murderous longing.

Violet Hunt, a friend of Bowen's known for her literary salons, wrote, "this is modern love," upon reading *To the North*. She reminded Bowen how new this kind of passionate and unrequited love was a subject for a novel, and how it reflected the lives of women like Bowen who exercised sexual freedom before or after marriage. Hunt wrote, "It is all of Love—like the old ones, but modern Love. Dreadful, devastating, because there is no longer room for it as an absorbing emotion. In these easy days all experience what they call Love, and it attacks & hampers the free as well as the woman that a remnant of convention protects."[74] Modern love may "absorb" women, but not necessarily men, and women have only a shred of convention to protect their reputations and feelings. Though this novel was written in 1932, before Bowen met Charles Ritchie, it is prescient. It reveals her early insight into unfulfilled love, a devastating state she intuited in her character, Emmeline.

Surrealist images also surface on the road in *A World of Love*. Antonia and her young protégé, Jane, return from a party and speed ahead in a strange landscape. "Jane's ecstatic *willingness* to be silent … preyed on Antonia as the night jolted past them. The swerving course of the Ford made honeysuckle, a boot caught on the hedge, the cadaverous chimney-end of a vanished cottage, a hallucinated wandering white horse, lurch out, from one side then the other, into glaring view: their way seemed to be posted along with warnings," in spite of which Antonia spoke and said:

"This road I knew before you were born."
"Oh was there always that white horse?"
"Why?"
"Only I think we drove right through it."[75]

Surrealist Skies in Wartime

During and after the war, Bowen looked up at skies that were lit with aerial fire or an empty dust. These skies described in her wartime stories signal a changed vision. Though she entered into the play of surrealism before the war; the violence and aggression of the wartime years signalled that the time for such playfulness was over and surrealist light would enter differently into her writing. She writes of "walking in the darkness of the nights of six years (darkness which transformed a capital city into a network of inscrutable canyons) one developed new bare alert senses."[76] The landscape changed daily, and, her skies, so carefully painted in her earlier novels, reveal now a white light from the moon, an eruption into flames or airborne dust from the destruction of buildings. One of her most successful stories of the war, "Mysterious Kor," is created from the blitzed ruins of London. Bowen said of this story, "I saw Kor before I saw London; I was a provincial child … I was inclined to see London as Kor with the roofs on. The idea that life in any capital city must be ephemeral, and with a doom ahead, remained with me, a curious obsession for an Edwardian child."[77] Cities do not have solidity; they do not last. The certainty of "places" became no-places during the war, and the surrealist light of wartime London was cast into mythical Kor:

Bright fell the moonlight on pillar and court and shattered wall, hiding all their rents and imperfections in its silver garment, and clothing their hoar majesty with the peculiar glory of the night. It was a wonderful sight to see the full moon looking down on the ruined fane of Kor. It was a wonderful thing to think for how many thousands of years the dead orb above and the dead city below had gazed thus upon each other and in the utter solitude of space poured forth each to each the tale of their lost life and long-departed glory. The white light fell.[78]

The white light cloaks the ruins of the city with the cold silence of a de Chirico painting. Another sky in "Summer Night" though in Ireland holds the crystal of the war in Europe. Emma reflects, "you cannot look at the sky without seeing the shadow, the men destroying each other. What is the matter tonight—is there a battle?"[79] A strange melting sky of glass and fire opens the story, Emma, like so many others during the war, lives in "a rising tide of hallucination" and sees everyday skies as if in a nightmare or a trance:

As the sun set its light slowly melted the landscape, till everything was made of fire and glass. Released from the glare of noon, the haycocks now seem to float on the after grass […] it would be a pleasure of heaven to stand up there, where no foot ever seems to have trodden, on the spaces of wood soft as powder dusted over with gold.[80]

Bowen witnessed the solidity of objects and buildings turning to dust or bursting into flame during the blitz, ending her illusions about the solidity of objects. Landscapes were "always convulsed by some new change" as "the power of irrationality," she said, "was unloosed in the world in Hitler's fanatical march to power across Europe.[81] She was always yearning "to find an abiding city," a place of the mind like a Biblical city or ancient Rome which she considered a bulwark of civilization. Drawn into the vortex of the war while living in London, she became modern, if to be modern is "to experience personal and social life as a maelstrom, to find one's world and oneself in perpetual disintegration and renewal, trouble and anguish, ambiguity and contradiction."[82] This state departs from her prewar feelings when "the destruction of buildings and furniture [was] more palpably dreadful to the spirit than the destruction of human life."[83] The objects and buildings were civilization. In *The Death of the Heart*, 1938, Matchett, the maid, asserts her relationship to the furniture in the Quayles' house. "Furniture's knowing all right. Not much gets past the things in a room, I daresay." Furniture has a force.[84] Despite the comfort of its solidity, Bowen presents Matchett in a "phosphorescent apron" in startling silhouette against a patch of surrealist sky:

> [She] sat sideways on to the bed, her knees towards Portia's pillow, her dark skirts flowing into the dark round, only her apron showing. Her top part loomed against the tawny square of sky in uncertain silhouette; her face, eroded by darkness like a car fanned light on it. Up to now she had sat erect, partly judicial, partly as though her body were a vaseful of memory that must not be spilled.

This uncertain image of Matchett recalls surrealist "rayographs," named after painter and photographer Man Ray, who obtained silhouettes by exposing ordinary objects to light on photosensitive paper. Matchett's figure looms in the dark, her face fanned with light: she is both the reliable servant who cares for the furniture in the house, and a subversive figure, a "vaseful of memory" who speaks the truth. Usually depicted as silent and still, she is almost an object herself. But under her watchful eye and care, the potential of material objects is unleashed in time; they contain a connection with past owners.

Bowen was always fascinated by objects and admitted to being a magpie, a scavenger, and loved browsing through Victorian jumble—the curios and antiques in flea markets near Islington—and buying furniture, curtains, and pillows for her house. In *The Little Girls*, the children go to rag-and-bone and curio shops on High Street, searching for a coffer in which to bury some objects, "the more battered the better."[85] Squinting at the windows, they see "knives and forks, half dozens of napkin rings, pepper and salt sets … fancy tea spoons, tied up with rotting ribbons, lay among tangled corals, dishonoured medals and lacquer and other visiting card cases; and in between verticals such as statuary, domed or naked clocks, decanters with dust in their cut glass, grand jettisoned oil lamps, cruets for ogres." There was always something marvelous for Bowen; always something marvelous about this world of possessions and the links between various objects and realities that she happened upon in flea markets and surrealist exhibitions.

Surrealist Collage

In addition to her attraction to spectrality and ghostliness—and fascination with disparate objects that represented different domains and displacements— Bowen was drawn to a form of surrealist play, the collage. This involved a piecing or pasting together of fragments or bits of things into a pattern, a practice that would influence her narrative form, particularly during and after World War II. In a little-known photo, Bowen is pictured in her study sitting at her typewriter—books and papers scattered across her desk—next to a screen, a collage, that divides the room. The caption states: "Morning and afternoon, Elizabeth Bowen works in a study adjoining her bedroom on the first floor. She uses one of her 'surrealist' screens to divide the two rooms." Bowen explained to the interviewer, "I paste *New Yorker* cuttings and Christmas cards on to a canvas base and varnish the complete patchwork."[86] Collage was then a form of play and, eventually, a writing technique. When asked by a Hungarian interviewer in 1948 about her hobbies, she responded that one was cutting out colored papers and pasting them on oatmeal containers, making collage boxes.

During the war, Bowen observed that in order to go on, people had to "save bits of themselves" from the ruins of war. They assembled who they were from bits of remembered stories and poems, or from what they remembered of one another like a collage. In *Ivy Gripped the Steps*, Bowen commented on her story writing technique: "I cannot paint or photograph [instead] I have isolated; I have made for the particular, spot-lighting faces or cutting out of gestures."[87] The stories were "flying particles of something enormous and inchoate that had been going on. They were sparks from experience."[88] Similarly, she described the disruptions in narration in her wartime novel, *The Heat of the Day*, as "patchwork." She believed that if things could be "blown out" during the war, they could also, through self-assemblage, and a new kind of writing, be blown back in. "Outwardly, we accepted that at this time individual destiny had to count for nothing: inwardly, individual destiny became an obsession in every heart."[89]

Contrasts and dislocations and patches of place, memory, and feeling then became the philosophical underpinning of her narrative practice. She wrote in her late memoir:

Imagination of my kind is most caught, most fired, most worked upon by the unfamiliar. I have thriven, accordingly, on the changes and chances, the dislocations … the contrasts that have made up so much of my life. That may be why "my" world (my world as a writer) is something of a mosaic.[90]

The "mosaic" of her life prepared her as a writer to assemble experiences in unfamiliar ways: her sentences yoke the commonplace and the strange. She alludes to a collage or "scrap screen" again in a letter to Ritchie upon the publication of *Collected Impressions,*

> a collection of which I think I vaguely talked to you, of reviews, prefaces, broadcasts, occasional pieces, etc. … any style it has, I think, is in the arrangement: it was interesting arranging the stuff, like making a sort of scrap screen out of my own work.[91]

Narrative collage appealed to Bowen's sensibility. The notion also enters into her perception of India as described by Humphry House in a 1936 letter.

> You make me see Calcutta very plainly—how correctly, of course, I shall never know. But you have it vivid: I almost experience it. How odd, this business of constructing a picture inside oneself, according to some one else's directions—which is what a description amounts to—is. I mean, what a scrap-drawer of images one draws on—images come by in the queerest ways. In this case—water-colours in drawing rooms, lantern slides at missionary lectures, illustrations to missionary magazines, uncharacteristically concrete phrases in Anglo-Indian's talk, rather crude descriptions in Anglo-Indian novels, travel circulars, snapshot-albums of traveled majors' wives. It is like ransacking everything from rare editions to shop catalogues to make a surrealist collage.[92]

Bowen here reveals not only House's experience in India but her surrealist "reading" of his letter and her composing process. Her visual imagination was piqued by book illustrations as a child; by the formal study of painting and illustration as a young woman afoot in London; by the contrasts of landscape as she moved from Ireland to England; and, later, by photography, film, and surrealism, the technologies and arts developing in her day. Two planes of reality, the actual and the image, are always at play in her work as she negotiates the space between seeing and writing. For Bowen, the visual imagination of the painter remained with her and the question always was, how to transform sensations—what she saw and heard—into words and pictures.

Notes

1. "Elizabeth Bowen and Jocelyn Brooke."
2. Bowen, "Roving Eye," *MT*, 63.
3. Arnold, *Mainie Jellett*, 118.

4. Bowen, "Autobiographical Note," *WWF*, 267.
5. *HP*, 86.
6. Bowen, "Poetic Element," 9.
7. Bowen, "Autobiographical Note," *WWF*, 267.
8. Bowen, "We Write Novels," 28.
9. Rose Macaulay to EB, n.d. (ca. 1955), HRC 11.6.
10. Bowen, *Hotel*, 86.
11. Bowen, *HD Blurb*, Knopf Records, NYPL, box 102, folder 18.
12. EB to DH, December 16, n.d., PRONI D4400/C/2/27.
13. Bowen, "Requiescat," *CS*, 45.
14. EB to IB, August 19, 1937, BOD, MS. Berlin 245.
15. *TLG*, 121, 120–122.
16. Barthes, *Pleasure of the Text*: there is no "one" reading of a text but multiple readers, cultures, places, and times of reception.
17. EB to WP, June 1, 1963, DUR 19.
18. EB to CR, September 4, 1948, *LCW*, 132.
19. Bowen, "We Write Novels," 24.
20. *WL*, 71–72.
21. *PC*, 44, 4.
22. From a Nuffield Organization questionnaire that Bowen responded to, April 12, 1945, HL, HM 52840.
23. At same time that Bowen bought her car, Clair Wills reports, 209 people were killed on the roads and 10,852 injured through dangerous driving. Motor offenses rivaled bicycle crimes in 1937. Wills, *Neutral Ireland*, 34.
24. *TN*, 296–297.
25. Bowen, "We Write Novels," 28.
26. *TN*, 306, 296, 298, 168.
27. *PC*, 44.
28. Bowen, review, April 28, 1948, *WWF*, 221.
29. *IGS*, xiv.
30. Bowen, "Prague and the Crisis," *PPT*, 81.
31. *HP*, 126.
32. *HD*, 125.
33. Owe this reference to Julia Van Haaften, author of *Berenice Abbott, Photographer: A Modern Vision* (1989), and a member of the WWWL.
34. WP to EB, September 2, n.d. (ca. 1936), HRC 11.8.
35. EB to HH, June 12, 1936, HHC.
36. EB to WP, May 6, 1958, DUR 19.
37. "An Enormous Channel of Expectation," in *PPT*, 366, 368, 369.
38. EB to CR, December 8, 1959, *LCW*, 351.
39. BBC Broadcast, May 31, 1952.
40. Bowen, "Notes on Writing a Novel," 184.
41. *ES*, xiv.

42. *FR*, 49–50.
43. *FBMS*, 7–8.
44. *HD*, 155, 254, 9.
45. MS of *HD*, HRC, MS V, 7–12; HD 106.
46. *TR*, 165.
47. EB to CR, March 27, 1953, *LCW*, 187.
48. Bowen, "The Art of Bergotte," *PC*, 95–96.
49. Hone interview.
50. Graham Greene to EB, April 13, 1938, HRC.
51. EB to CR, January 28, 1962, *LCW*, 382.
52. Ibid., September 2, 1959, 337.
53. Maars, *Eudora Welty*, 284.
54. Herpburn, LI, 135.
55. Hepburn, *Listening In*, 66.
56. Roy Forster, *Modern Ireland*, 168.
57. See Gildersleeve.
58. Proust, *Swann's Way*, 59.
59. EB to WP, June 27, 1937, DUR 19.
60. Image emerged in Comte de Lautreamont, *Les Chantes de Maldoror, 1869*, a misanthropic figure of evil that inspired many surrealist artists.
61. *HP*, 39; *FR*, 134; *TN*, 208, 239.
62. Bowen, "The 1938 Academy: An Unprofessional View." In Hepburn, PPT, 29.
63. Halliday, "Gallery and Surrealism." Dali Exhibit, 1934.
64. Bowen, "Regent's Park," 150.
65. HH to EB, February 5, 1934. HHC. With permission from the Literary Estate of Humphry House.
66. Bowen, "The Disinherited," *CS* 398.
67. *PC*, 63.
68. EB to HH, May 28 and June 1, 1936, HHC.
69. EB to WP, June 27, 1937, DUR 19.
70. "Elizabeth Bowen and Jocelyn Brooke.
71. *TN*, 146, 79.
72. Ibid., 284. Emmeline has the same glassy eyes that repulsed Bowen in dolls, separating her from this surrealist fascination, represented by Hans Bellmer.
73. Caws, "Thinking North."
74. Violet Hueffer Hunt to EB, n.d. (ca. 1932), HRC 11.5.
75. *WL*, 93.
76. *IGS*, xiii.
77. Bowen, "Rider Haggard," *MT*, 247.
78. Bowen, "Mysterious Kor," *MT*, 292.
79. "Summer Night," *CS*, 599.
80. Bowen, "Summer Night," *CS*, 583.
81. *PC*, xiv.

82. Berman, *All That Is Solid Melts into Air*, 345–346.
83. *DH*, 207, 128, 81, 93.
84. See Bennett and Royle, 77 ff.
85. *LG*, 124, 93.
86. Bennett, "House."
87. *IGS*, xiv, viii, xi.
88. Ibid., viii.
89. Ibid., xi.
90. *PC*, 37.
91. EB to CR, May 6, 1950, *LCW*, 169.
92. EB to HH, 1936, HHC.

9

Reading Backwards

Literary Traces

Bowen's fiction is an original amalgam, hewing to no specific aesthetic or place in conventional literary history. Derrida suggests that the laws of reading should be determined by the specific text being read, and if we respect this stance, we abandon previous expectations of literary schools, groups, and circles, and allow the traces of Bowen's reading and influences to filter into ours. As we read her, we observe her updating the "homelessness" of the dispossessed Anglo-Irish to the dislocations of refugees of her generation after the war or the Irish people in relation to English colonialism; the "burning" of big houses to themes of conflagration in World War II; the gothic hauntings in the Irish tradition to the "uncanny" of Freud and the shadowy dreams of the modernist art movement of surrealism. She also reinvests the word "home" for women from its stable place in the Victorian marriage plot to the modern psychic "homelessness" of loves outside marriage.

She enjoyed and admired English, Irish, and European writers from the eighteenth to the twentieth centuries, and had close friendships with Virginia Woolf, Rosamond Lehmann, and Eudora Welty—as well as Elizabeth Taylor. She read widely, reviewed perhaps too generously, and aspired to be a writer but projected no sense that she had a professional strategy for her literary career. As a young woman of 20, a literary aspirant, Bowen arrived in London in awe of writers and compared literature to a landscape: in the foreground were contemporaries too close in some ways to be judged. At the Poetry Bookshop in London, she listened to Ezra Pound reading "what was hypnotically unintelligible to me by the light of one dark candle"[1] and

P. Laurence, *Elizabeth Bowen*, Literary Lives, https://doi.org/10.1007/978-3-030-71360-7_9

devoured the pile of orange-covered *London Mercury* literary issues. In the background were the "elect" writers from the past showing "those mountain ranges that are the classics—but even these seem to change, seem more or less distant, higher or lower, in the varying, changing lights of our own day." She admired the Irish writers, Jonathan Swift, Sheridan Le Fanu, Richard Sheridan, Maria Edgeworth, Somerville and Ross, and Bram Stoker; English authors, Jane Austen and Charles Dickens; the modernists, Marcel Proust, Henry James, James Joyce, and Virginia Woolf.[2] Bowen's first biographer, Victoria Glendinning, views her as an exceptional writer because she merges these figures, cultures, and traditions of English, Irish, and Anglo-Irish writers with European modernism into an original style.

Bowen was drawn into particular friendship and dialogue with three women writers, Virginia Woolf, Rosamond Lehmann and Eudora Welty as revealed in letters. She sat at Woolf's modernist table and enjoyed Bloomsbury entertainments, but remained on the margins of such literary circles, by choice. She wrote to her friend, William Plomer about "What an agreeable life we all had, seeing each other without being a group. Perhaps ours was, is, the only non-grouping generation."[3] It is misleading, she asserted, "with regard to English, as apart from Continental writing—to speak of 'groups' or 'schools.'"[4] She shied away from the literary glare and the cult of personality that animates writers today. Writing to Virginia Woolf in July 1937, she noted that she attended a literary dinner that went on "too long [...] I felt bored and rather degraded, so I went home. The whole thing was—frightening, new—literature."[5]

She started writing stories at the Downe House School, and, afterwards, attended art school for a year discovering that she had no talent. She then turned to literature and yearned to know writers. Her literary career took off when Olive Willis, former headmistress of the Downe House school, introduced her to Rose Macaulay who brought her into the same rooms as Edith Sitwell, Walter de la Mare, and Aldous Huxley. Macaulay supported the typing of the manuscript of her first collection of stories, *Encounters* (1923), and sympathized when Frank Sidgwick of Sidgwick and Johnson rejected her first novel, *The Hotel* (1927), eventually published by Constable. Bowen in return often reviewed Macaulay's novels in later years, but increasingly cooled and shared William Plomer's irreverence toward her: "Rose Macaulay, breathing purposefully in my eye, wished to know what I thought of her book about Foster. As I hadn't read it, the occasion called for as much tact as you displayed in reviewing the books."[6]

"Like no other": Virginia Woolf

Virginia Woolf, of an earlier generation, born in 1882, and a more established author, was admired by both Bowen and Lehmann. Both looked to her as an innovator, and Bloomsbury as the most important and influential literary circle in England. Early on, Bowen's stories were noticed by Woolf and Lehmann, and the three became friends in the early 1930s, all of them living not far from Oxford: Lehmann in Ipsden and Woolf, Sussex. When they met, Bowen had published *Encounters* (1923), *The Hotel* (1927), and *The Last September* (1929); Woolf, *Orlando* (1928) and *A Room of One's Own* (1929); and Lehmann, *Dusty Answer* (1927).

Ottoline Morrell introduced Bowen to Virginia Woolf at Garsington Manor, and she became one of Bowen's most treasured friends. Woolf observed upon their meeting in February 1932, "Miss Bowen, shy, stammering, to tea."[7] Four years later, still sensitive to her style and manner, Woolf met Bowen at her Clarence Terrace townhouse "in her glass shining contemporary room. Like a French picture—2 ladies looking at a lake."[8] Years later, Woolf acknowledged Bowen's sharp intellect: "E Bowen to tea; cut out of coloured cardboard but sterling and sharp edged." She came to appreciate Bowen's acute intelligence and frankness, if not aspects of her writing. Through Woolf, Bowen met leading intellectuals and writers, including T.S. Eliot, Stephen Spender, Maynard Keynes, Susan and John Buchan (Tweedsmuirs), Rosamond and John Lehmann, and Dorothy Strachey. One evening in 1934, she entered a Bloomsbury conversation about continuity, tradition, and religion. Virginia asked the young Julian Bell, her sister's son, who lived a wild, romantic life abroad in China, how he would live, "you who have no moral strictness?"[9] Julian responded that he would "miss your morality which has landed us in psycho-analysis, but I prefer my life in many ways." On this occasion, Woolf observed Bowen's stuttering and speculated that she "had also been brought up to repress by moral ancestors." Bowen enjoyed Bloomsbury talk, but confided to Charles Ritchie her unease about the "in-growingness" of this world, "their appalling habit of writing endless letters to each other, of analyzing, betraying, mocking, envying each other, of the kind of amusement they had, and the kind of pains of jealousy and treachery which they inflicted on each other."[10] From the outside, Bloomsbury was a talented, racy, bohemian set with an exhibitionism that did not attract Bowen. Yet she was as independent and exploratory as any in Bloomsbury—romantically, sexually, intellectually, politically, and as a writer—but not as flamboyant. She had a different style and politics. Near the end of her life, she capped her view of the circle in a letter to Lehmann: "Noble tho' they all were, they were smug. And their godlessness gives me—a feeling of depression, and what else—claustrophobia."[11]

Bloomsbury was not the only group Bowen circled. Ottoline Morrell, expansive and gossipy, also drew her into her salon where she received introductions to outstanding literary figures in the Thursday evening salons when living in Oxford and, later, at Gower Street, London: Spender, D.H. Lawrence, Hope Mirlees, and Eliot, among others.[12] Though Bloomsbury and others mocked the appearance and eccentricities of Ottoline Morrell (or Lady Immoraline, as Edith Sitwell dubbed her), Bowen admired Morrell as a literary socialite, reader, and hostess. Bowen told Morrell that her time and place was in the Renaissance. Always drawn to people at home in their settings, Bowen wrote, "I love seeing you and I love seeing your house. How happy you make us all."[13] William Plomer, with his gift for reading character, delighted in Morrell's eccentric style, warmth, enterprise, and interest in creative individuals, many of whom enjoyed not only her hospitality but benefitted professionally from her introductions. Once when Woolf was sitting next to Morrell on a sofa, Plomer noticed "two profiles on some Renaissance medal— two strange, queenly figures evolved in the leisured and ceremonious days of the nineteenth century. Each, by being herself, won an allegiance to herself in the twentieth." They both had "presence," what Plomer defined as "a kind of stateliness, a kind of simple, unfussy dignity."[14]

Bowen who had a sense of childish fun—remarked upon by Charles Ritchie and Howard Moss—was initially drawn by Woolf's laughter and like-minded mischief—as well as being an admired writer. She loved her comic exuberance, and their friendship she wrote, was "chiefly laughter and pleasure, and on entering, in her company, into the rapture caused her by the unexpected, the spectacular, the inordinate, the improbable, and the preposterous."[15] Bowen believed the "spring and principle of her art was joy."[16] In 1958, she wrote to William Plomer who was on the fringes of Bloomsbury, confiding that only he seemed "able to bring back Virginia's laughter—I get so *bored* and irked by that tragic fiction which has been manufactured about her since 1941."[17]

There were occasional gaps in their relationship. Woolf, at times, spitefully described Bowen in her diaries; and Bowen had her reservations about the smugness and claustrophobia of Bloomsbury. Ritchie and Bowen discussed Woolf in 1956, and he ruefully noted in his journal that Woolf's unpublished diaries revealed that she "had no fondness for her friends including E." When he related this to Bowen, she did not take offense, coolly noting, "perhaps her affection was intermittent (as mine is for so many people)."[18] Nevertheless, Woolf and Bowen relished each other's company—most of the time— beginning in the early 1930s.

We can only imagine what they said to one another—about life and writing—and their letters convey the charm of sharp observation, mischief, intelligence, and wit that they shared in each other's company. Woolf is the more playful in letters, and Bowen seemed to make more of an effort to be entertaining in hers, writing in a lively spirit with descriptions of odd and funny things from her travels, not always present in letters to others. She was sometimes a lax correspondent even with Woolf, not sharing Bloomsbury's letter writing habits, not giving time to letters as she had in the 1930s given her immersion in writing. She spoke of Woolf with Isaiah Berlin, whose salient impression when he met her at a dinner party at the Fishers Oxford in 1933 was that she was both a genius and "the most beautiful person I've ever seen. I can also imagine what she looks like when she goes mad, as I believe, she occasionally does."[19] Bowen reflected how remarkable it was to be a woman so beautiful that she had no need to look into a mirror. She related to Ritchie "how [Woolf] looked, tall and graceful and wearing some flowing dress of mauve or grey and her incomparable conversation."[20] Consequently, Bowen regretted that Berlin had not been seated next to Woolf at an Oxford dinner, describing her as "a tête-à-tête-ist: she doesn't like parties at all. She puts a spell on one. She talks best in the dark. When a lamp has to be lit she puts the lamp on the floor. One's brain begins racing."[21] It did not escape her sharp observation, however, that Woolf sheltered in Bloomsbury had "a sort of 'fairy cruelty' and could be sadistic." "She had always lived in a sort of Chinese world of intelligent complicated people who made a cult of her," related Bowen. The political and social sameness of Bloomsbury, as she perceived it, as well as the irreligion alienated her. Woolf's letters to Bowen titillate, inviting her to visit and hear the story of the Woolfs' troubles—for example, the tale of moth powder in Leonard's pajamas. "Don't sprinkle Alan's. I'll tell you why if you come."[22] And they exchanged gifts. "What a dangerous friend you are!" announces Woolf in a 1933 letter to Bowen, early in their relationship. "One says casually, I like shortbread—and behold shortbread arrives. Now had I said I like young elephants, would the same thing have happened?" Woolf wickedly decides, "The only way to neutralize the poison is to cancel it with something you don't want. Here's a book therefore. But be warned—I often make tea caddies in magenta plush-that will be your fate on the next occasion. I embroider them with forget-me-nots in gold." Woolf said that she gulped down the shortbread, having a bare cupboard, and reported that being ill should have been her fate, but "not at all—I dressed up as Queen Victoria on her wedding night [...] fell into the arms of the Prince Consort. The effect upon the Royal line has yet to be discovered. But it will be laid to your door."[23] At times, early in their relationship, Bowen expressed feelings of "tremendous inferiority" to Woolf as a woman. After an excellent dinner that she and Alan enjoyed at the Woolfs' in 1933, Bowen had occasion to say "if Virginia can provide food like that, why can't I," lamenting that Woolf organized her practical life better than she did.

Virginia and Leonard visited Bowen's Court in 1934 and enthusiastically thanked Bowen for her "island seduction"; at the same time, Woolf caustically wrote to others that Bowen's Court was "a stone cold Georgian box." Bowen, on the other hand, was unequivocally charmed by her visit to Monk's House, Rodmell, in July 1940 and again in February 1941, about a month before Woolf's suicide. She wrote that she "never imagined a place and people in which and with whom one felt so perfectly happy that one felt suspended the whole time, and at the same wanting to smile, and smiling, continuously like a dog."[24]

Woolf, aware of Bowen's worldliness and physical hardiness, remarked admiringly how she "moves about the world" in a letter to her niece Angelica Bell; in another, how well she "coped" with London. Woolf whose life was bounded by bouts of manic-depressive illness confides in her letters to Bowen, more than to others, the frequency of her headaches that sometimes confined her to bed for weeks. Bowen, having experienced her father's mental illness, understood more than most. She, always a woman of robust health until her final years with cancer, combined—unlike Woolf—daily engagements with society—that bred popular writing, official reports, journalism, movie scripts, and documents—alongside her aesthetic and fictional pursuits. She took clear public and moral stances against Fascism (as did Woolf) but led a more public life during and after World War II. Her daily life was intertwined with society and politics in ways that Woolf's—because of temperament and ill health—was not. However, though this engagement positions Bowen—in some critics' minds—within the formation of intermodernism, and the exclusion of Woolf from this formation is suspect. Intermodernism—a new literary formation with an emphasis on the values, politics, and subjects of authors who wrote during and between the wars, theorizes commonalities among these writers: those who share an interest in working-class culture, and sometimes, language; are politically radical; work for a cause; and are politically engaged in the war.[25] Woolf is often excluded from the ideology, and classed as a removed modernist along with T.S. Eliot who declared that the poet is not primarily responsible to "the people" but to language. Woolf and Bowen never assumed Eliot's position, and could be seen along a modernism-intermodernism spectrum. After Bowen's visit to Rodmell in July 1940, Woolf gave her a copy of her essay, "The Leaning Tower," that plots the relationship of politics to art in 1930s. The essay illuminates how "it was impossible—if you were young, sensitive, imaginative—not to be interested in politics, not to find public causes of much more pressing interest than philosophy." Woolf details the social confusions that the war brought to England in the sphere of education, gender, and class that is then reflected in the literature of young men like Spender and Isherwood. Bowen after reading the essay noted that she never thought herself "into the position" of the young, upper-class educated men writing in "the tower," now threatened and leaning because of "chasm" in the road, the war. She concurred with Woolf that the upper-class position of these men led to an odd angle of vision, "an element of fuss" and a kind of barrenness.[26] Curiously, Bowen does not comment in her letter on the valued position of women as "outsiders" that Woolf puts forth—or even her own "outsider" Anglo-Irish point of view." Both seemed to agree that not being inscribed with 11 years of expensive education—as the young, privileged men—women are in a different cultural position and are able to cast fresh outlook on society.

During World War I, Woolf was, nevertheless, detached from society "to the point of complete alienation, only to be explained by the fact that she had to spend the first year and a half of that war suffering from intermittent, but very serious mental illness."[27] Nevertheless, traces of the apocalypse of war and death appear in *To the Lighthouse*, and the radical thinking of *A Room of One's Own* and *Three Guineas* has had lasting impact on the women's thinking, the women's movement and position in society. In the 1930s as with many writers, Virginia Woolf's "I" became a "we" as people banded together before and during the war. The death of her young nephew, Julian Bell, in the Spanish Civil War as well as the photos of thousands of Basque children, orphans of war, being evacuated from Bilbao, Spain, splashed across the newspapers, moved her to write about the Spanish Civil War and approaching World War II. She wrote openly about the dangers of Fascism in *Three Guineas*, and recorded as well her preoccupations and fears in the writing notebooks for this work. The whole argument in *Three Guineas*, published in 1937, should be allowed to breathe in intermodernist thinking. In this polemic, she yokes feminism and anti-militarism and asserts that the same political and social system that makes war also makes women's education and resistance possible. She indicts the quackery of the fascists and the Nazis that threatens to engulf Europe as well as the British politicians and intellectuals who collude with them. In 1940, a year before her death "like a chasm in a smooth road the war came," and Woolf registered the attendant confusions in "The Leaning Tower."[28]

Similarly, there is a neglected modernist strain in Bowen's writing, evident in the structuring, themes, language, and atmosphere of *To the North*, *The House in Paris*, *The Heat of the Day*, and the post-modernist, *Eva Trout*. Speed and the new technology of machines (typewriters, adding machines, phones, planes, cars) infuses the language and themes of *To the North*; the play with time in the tripartite structure of Present, Past, Present infuses *The House in Paris*; the jar and fissures of war as well as a hallucinatory atmosphere permeates the style of *The Heat of the Day*; and refraction and distortions of perception and consciousness inform *Eva Trout*. A blurring of the line then between modernism and intermodernism might rescue both Bowen and Woolf from a Procrustean bed. Admittedly, Bowen helped to diminish the borders of high, middle, and low culture along with other interwar authors like George Orwell, Storm Jameson, Winifred Holtby, Sylvia Townsend Warner, Rose Macaulay, and Stella Gibbons, as Kristin Bluemel has noted in her work. Yet she is also separated from them by her Irish Ascendancy class, her anti-feminist rhetoric, her lack of sympathy for the Labor Party and the working class, her personal manner, her elusive language, her conservative political values, and being an inheritor and proud hostess of an Irish estate founded on British colonialism.

The whistle of bombs and sirens of war interrupted Woolf and Bowen's friendship, domestic lives, and conversations. The Woolf's home in Mecklenburgh Square was destroyed on September 16–17, 1940; a month later, their house in Tavistock Square, where they had their press and lived since 1924, also. Woolf would write of cycling to Newhaven on October 29, 1940: "25 bombs dropped, a little girl killed; the sirens sounding one evening just as she closed her curtains in Rodmell.[29] "Who'll be killed tonight?" she asks. "Not us, I suppose."[30] Three years after Woolf's death, Bowen's Clarence Terrace apartment on Regent's Square was bombed during a two-week period, July 10–24, 1944. Bowen, mannerly even in wartime, wrote of an evening when she apologized to guests for the noise of bombs and sirens during a dinner party. Woolf and Bowen saved remnants of the experience for their writing—Woolf in *Between the Acts* and essays and Bowen in *The Heat of the Day* and her wartime stories—and evaded the loudspeaker voice that threatened to drown them out. Both authors were fearful of the loss of the individual and personal voice in the cacophony of war rhetoric heightened on the radio and in the newspapers.

Bowen comforted Woolf after hearing of the destruction of her home, confessing that for months afterwards she felt "completely dumb: there seemed to be nothing to add to anything, even in what I said to you … I think about you so much, especially shredding those red currants in the evening up in that top room. And were all those streets that were burnt the streets we walked about? I have never seen them since." Bowen unlike Woolf, focused on lost objects, the "things" that comforted her. She asked, "When your flat went did that mean all the things in it too? All my life I have said, 'Whatever happens there will always be tables and chairs'—and what a mistake."[31] Bowen's places became no-place during the war. Woolf, in contrast, noted her liberation from possessions after the bombing:

> Now we seem quit of London [...] Exhilaration at losing possessions—save at times I want my books & chairs & carpets & beds—How I worked to buy them—One by one. And the pictures. But to be free of Meck [Mecklenburgh] Wd now be a relief. Almost certainly it will be destroyed—& our queer tenancy of the sunny flat over [...] But it's odd—the relief at losing possessions. I shd like to start life, in peace, almost bare—free to go anywhere.[32]

Bowen and Woolf experienced the devastation and emptiness of "ruined houses" and the war that they would transform in their writing. In this, they confirm Stella's observation in *The Heat of the Day* that "Art, is the only thing that can go on mattering once it has stopped hurting."[33] Differences, however, in their sensibility, values, and treatment of war also surface. They both contain wartime emptiness and loss of feeling in a domestic space—but with a difference: Bowen centers on a room in a flat in London in *The Heat of the Day*; Woolf, a house by the seaside in *To the Lighthouse*; Bowen sees from a human perspective; Woolf from a perspective outside the self; Bowen represents the alienation of people, objects, and things in a room; Woolf through things that once had a human shape and family feeling—objects— like shells on a beach—once inhabited, and clothes once worn and left.

What magnetized Woolf and Bowen's relationship was their writing. Bowen admired Woolf's literary style—"like no one else's," she said, and she was particularly struck by her experimentation, never using "the same form or combination twice."[34] She was "of most value as a novelist because she can't be pinned down inside the frame of a novel."[35] Bowen also varied her approach with each novel, but stopped short of Woolf's bolder narrative experiments; nevertheless, she sent her novels to Woolf for comment; Virginia did not do likewise. In July 1932, Bowen sent her *To the North* and Woolf found it "a real book after all this rubbish."[36] Woolf commented most extensively on Bowen's *The House in Paris*: "I liked it very much. In fact I think I like it best of all your books." She wrote in September 1935 that the novel "goes deeper with less effort and the cleverness pulls its weight instead of lying to dazzle on the top."[37] She made pointed observations on the structure, noting that this novel, Bowen's third, had more of an architecture because she had something to write about. She liked the book's coming around in a circle and found the play with time (the three sections of the Present, the Past, the Present) was very "satisfactory." Yet, a reservation, that it also had "the air of something too exact too definite for the context." She continued, we are afraid "of the human heart (& with reason); & until we can write with all our faculties in action (even the big toe) but under the water, submerged, then we must be clever like the rest of the modern Hicklebacks."[38] Woolf apologizes for lecturing Bowen on "the heart—not a thing I know much about," in the same letter. She also gently goaded Bowen to write particular works—her family history, *Bowen's Court*, and to develop the "idea of a diary of books not events—I mean not tea parties but Milton and so on."

Bowen reviewed several of Woolf's novels, beginning in 1927. Seeing Woolf from afar, she, at first, assessed *Orlando* as a personal, "insider" book addressed to Woolf's coterie, but recanted in 1960, acknowledging that she was "young and stupid" and missed the playful experiment and rebellion against gender categories in the mock biography. Bowen considered *To the Lighthouse* the most perfect of Woolf's novels, and in reviewing *Between the Acts* in 1941 judged that Woolf had successfully created characters integral to the plot, not just "vision" as in earlier novels.

Bowen visited Woolf at Monk's House about seven weeks before her death recalling,

> The last day I saw her I was staying at Rodmell and I remember her kneeling back on the floor—we were tacking away, mending a torn Spanish curtain in the house—and she sat back on her heels and put her head back in a patch of sun, early spring sun. Then she laughed in this consuming, choking, delightful, hooting way. And *that* is what has remained with me.[39]

Women's Movements

At the same time that Woolf wrote about the exclusion of women from fiction, education, and careers in *A Room of One's Own*, Bowen and Lehmann, privileged and independent, were either indifferent to or in denial of the importance of the women's movement outside their door—at least, rhetorically. Bowen asserted that women had already achieved their social and political goals through suffrage, education, and access to jobs; nevertheless, both she and Lehmann challenged conventional domestic female roles in their lives and writing. Bowen observed the women's movement swirling around her, yet argued that women had no right to a grievance; nevertheless, she worked among rural women in Oxford. Her obdurate stance and limited understanding of women's positions in other classes in urban situations is revelatory when brought into relief with Woolf's receptive and open-minded consideration of the label "feminist." It is a mark of distinction between the two writers. Not only did/do women writers and intellectuals sometimes reject the label as part of their refusal to be judged in a separate gender category (viewed as second-class in some contexts) but, like Woolf, they avoid essentialist definitions of what being a woman means. In *A Room of One's Own*, Woolf shirks "the duty of coming to a conclusion upon … the true nature of woman … what is a woman, I assure you I do not know, I do not believe that you know; I do not believe anybody can know until she has expressed herself in all the arts and professions known to human skill."[40]

Bowen, unlike Woolf, did not write self-consciously of gender as a separate category in thinking of herself as a woman or a writer until late in her life. Hostile to the word "feminism" and the movement, she picked up on the aggrieved note in women's voices and criticized Virginia Woolf: "From whence, then, came this obsession of hers that women were being martyred humanly, inhibited creatively, by the stupidities of a man-made world?"[41] Ironically, it was Cameron who appeared to be the feminist in the household. Not only did he wholeheartedly support Bowen's writing career but he also supported women's fuller participation in English society. Bowen suggests this in a June 1945 letter to Ritchie: "Alan says he's going to vote Labor because the Labor candidate is a woman (his 1912 feminism). I ask him whether he wants this country run by Jews and Welshmen."[42] Women, Jews, and Welshman, outsiders all.

Nevertheless, Bowen did have a commitment to women as a group in her little-known work for the Women's Institute in Old Headington. Her work for this organization—founded during World War I to revitalize communities of women to help in food production—demonstrates her belief in women's historical connection to the home, and its practical extensions into the world. She identified less with vocal urban feminists than with the countrywomen's cause, feeling a kind of community and nationalism in rural England. Typical Women's Institute talks when Bowen was a member were on railways, roads, produce, gardens, and charitable programs such as "Freedom from Hunger." In 1941, during the war, she wrote to Woolf about how much she missed her connection to the institute: "As a matter of fact […] since I came to live in London I don't live in England at all." When she moved back to Old Headington in 1960, she again became involved, and was elected president of the local branch. She wrote to Ritchie that the institute was fun, explaining her predilection for practical work with women: "I get on so much better with women if I have works to do with them—I mean work along with them (e.g. Vassar). It's only in vacuo that women rather paralyse me, unless," she added wryly, "they're my favorite ones."[43] The next year she attended the annual meeting of the National Federation of Women's Institutes in Albert Hall and found it "inspirational," with 6000 women from all over England, Wales, the Channel Islands, and the Isle of Man.[44] When she was president, the programs bore her signature: a lecture on drama by Margaret Kennedy; "Civil War in Oxfordshire" by her historian friend, Veronica Wedgwood; and a program on ghost stories, a genre to which she was partial.

While Bowen and Lehmann fidgeted with the labels and rhetoric of the feminist movement in 1920–30s, writers like Rebecca West focused on getting women the vote. Nevertheless, Bowen and Lehmann foregrounded women's lived experience in their writing, reevaluating the relations between the sexes, homosexuality, and the popular dichotomy between femininity and feminism. Bowen never denied women's intellectual abilities: "Intellect is outside the mould of sex."[45] Yet in 1936, she myopically asserted, "the woman's movement has accomplished itself," and women are now "free to do what they ought, what they can, what they have it in them to do: they have no excuse for not doing it." Speaking from her middle-class, privileged perspective, Bowen observed "innate passivity" in women, an essentialist position denying the educational, economic, and social forces that shape women.[46]

The year 1934, however, marks a rare public "sisterly" moment in Bowen's career with the submission of *To the North* for the "Prix Femina," a French literary award decided by an "all-female jury" for a work of imagination to an English author whose work was "insufficiently known or appreciated." E.M. Forster won for *A Passage to India* in 1925 and Woolf, *To the Lighthouse* in 1928. Bowen's circle agreed that she had the best claim with *To the North*, despite the entry of Lehmann, who had more recognition and popularity than Bowen at the time. Woolf stated that she felt Bowen or Lehmann deserved the prize, and, in the end, like others, was taken aback when they gave the £40 prize to Stella Gibbons for *Cold Comfort Farm*: "still now you and Rosamond can join in blaming her. Who is she? What is this book?" Gibbon's was a comic novel, a parody of rural Sussex life and people and those authors who wrote about them. It appealed more to the prewar temper and readers than Bowen's romantic tragic tale. Then moving to another pertinent topic related to the prize—money—Woolf adds, "and so you can't buy your carpet."[47] Lehmann was indignant that Bowen was not awarded the prize, as was Violet Hunt, the activist founder of the Women's Writers Suffrage League; Welty also weighed in in favor of Bowen. The event drew her into a community and discussion of women writers, not a group she publicly sought.

After the war, Bowen was placed on two committees because she was told they needed a woman member: the de-Nazification literary committee for Germany and the British Royal Commission on Capital Punishment. She acknowledged then that feminine qualities might bring a fresh point of view to public issues. Yet Bowen often portrayed feminists as women who built their achievements on the perceived failures of men. Her remarks contradict her own active life in journalism, espionage, royal commissions, and BBC and British Council activities, as well as her observations on the historical evolution of women: "The home was her sphere, and now the world is her home," she announced.[48] In addition, "her gift for understanding and testing the constraints of social and political codes merged with her imagination to devise plots which overturned convention to highlight a 'new woman's' energy."[49] This recognition of her insistent writing about intelligent, independent, and sometimes disappointed and betrayed women has led to several studies of Bowen's writing from a woman's perspective, beginning with the critic, Phyllis Lassner. Displaying a greater awareness later in life, she began a BBC broadcast in 1964 citing Elizabeth Coxhead's provocative assertion that Ireland "more than most is a men's country … Women are not welcome" in Irish public life. In reviewing *The Daughters of Erin*, she offered Coxhead's counterexamples of the lives of two revolutionary women and three artists: Maude Gonne, the English-born Irish beauty and revolutionary who so captivated Yeats; Constance Markievicz, a gun-carrying fighter born of the ascendancy class; Sarah Perser, hostess and founder of a renowned stained-glass workshop; and Sara and Mara Allgood, accomplished actresses. Bowen did not usually assert the primacy of gender, yet she agreed to promote the book, and commented at the end of the broadcast that the featured women "did what they did not in spite of being women but because of it," a seeming shift in perspective.[50]

Lehmann also stood back from the women's movement with a touch of class hauteur. In a 1985 interview, she charged the movement with being "too aggressive," labeling it a kind of "cult." Selecting an extreme stance to illustrate her point, she said in an interview, "I am told some advocate lesbianism as a matter of principle," and this is "a total breach. How can the majority of women go along with that?" Not attuned to change through collective social action, Lehmann advocated that a women's crusade had to be personal and individual.[51] Nevertheless, Rebecca West—the most stalwart of feminists—did not count Lehmann out. She considered her a serious writer and said upon the publication of *The Swan in Evening: Fragments of a Life*, "I have always admired your books because they are truly feminine, they do a woman's job of revealing the world women see."

West was dazzled by the famously beautiful Lehmann, as were others by the ethereally beautiful Woolf. Women's physical appearance—even among women writers—is a fraught topic, and it cannot be denied that Bowen was usually described as "handsome," rather than "beautiful." She writes of suffering from her image in the mirror as an adolescent, and expressed a longing to be more beautiful for her lover, Ritchie. Sally Phipps, the daughter of Molly Keane, nevertheless wrote that Bowen had a unique look and supported herself with style, taking great care in grooming and dress, often making a dramatic impression on men and women in a room.

Rosamond Lehmann: Romance

Bowen, Lehmann, and Woolf resisted what critics label the conventional marriage plot in their lives and fiction. They sought independent love lives separate from their marriages, and, to some degree, economic independence from their husbands, earning their own money through writing. Bowen and Lehmann wrote of love as a spellbinding emotion and the risks of romance—sometimes extreme and not always susceptible to reason—that operated in their lives, if not in their writing. Lehmann explored "femininity" rather than "feminism," and aspired like Woolf to "one day [when] men and women will be able to speak the truth with each other."[52] Many of her novels, often unfairly dismissed by progressive women readers, chart not only disappointed romance but needed changes in gender relations, parent–child relations and society, in general.

In a later stage in their relationship, Bowen and Lehmann developed a sympathetic relationship as writers—what Lehmann would term "sisterliness." The difficulties that surface in Lehmann's letters about the life of a writer with two children are striking. She confessed to Bowen, who had already published four novels and four collections of short stories, that she felt "a limited character—and now perhaps too fixed in my domestic life to stretch anymore," having two children.[53] Lehmann appreciated Bowen's attention to her novels and wrote gushing letters about hers. After receiving Bowen's praise upon publication of *The Weather in the Streets*, she exclaimed, "But oh how warming your letter is"; the novel had been criticized as "upsetting" because of the topic of abortion. Lehmann complained about the "children's various peregrinations and redistributions" as she left them with her in-laws so she could write."[54] Bowen sympathetically responded that if Lehmann wanted to combine being in London with working, she could visit her Regent's Park apartment that offered "several writing tables during the day and a reasonable silence." And after the tragic death of Lehmann's daughter, Sally, at the age of 24, Bowen was also sympathetic to Lehmann's paranormal communications with her daughter through a ouija board. The poet Kathleen Raine sensitively wrote to Lehmann that *The Sea Grape*, her book about these experiences, was the most important book for the 1970s not because Lehmann was "trying to tell of the other world ... but because you have re-told the secret of woman's love of true feeling, of the vulnerable, delicate reality of earthly love."[55] Lehmann was courageous in standing by her experience as a woman, a mother, and a spiritualist pouring this honestly into her novel: a perspective not always read sympathetically by critics.

In these relationships in the 1940s, Bowen appears to have come to terms with her own childlessness. After their reconciliation after the Rees affair,

Bowen sent Lehmann a copy of *The Heat of the Day*. Lehmann responding in her usual effusive manner, said she had just finished reading the novel again "and again in a state of almost unbearable emotion—exaltation and scorching tears … My sense of identification with Stella is intense! Not only because of the living in war in London in wartime—but also because of the relationship with Roderick. This is uncanny. You don't know Hugo [Lehmann's son], but it *is* Hugo. Cecil [Day-Lewis, her husband at the time] felt exactly the same."[56] Lehmann's motherhood also led her to respond to Bowen's representation of children. Though she thought *The House in Paris* a triumph, she noted the Salinger-like quality in Leopold, who was not like a "real" child. She wrote, "The only thing I'm not sure about is Leopold in the last part. I can't absolutely be convinced a child of mine would react in the way he did to that letter he read from his awful guardians. Would he, could he know so clearly from such a letter that he must abandon them?—that he disliked them so intensely? I'm not sure what it is that bothers me—his age, or such a letter to produce such a result, a kind of Henry James child touch about the whole situation. Perhaps I'm wrong."[57]

Lehmann's work also contained reverberations of the war, though critics often viewed her writing as more narrowly focused on romance and family life. Bowen wrote a review of *The Echoing Grove* in 1953, teaching readers how to read Lehmann in the midst of cultural change. She reminded readers that Lehmann infuses the climate of the day into a war between two sisters, and is not averse to disrupting family myths. Modern love, noted Bowen, is not as it was before the war, and Lehmann courageously focused upon its complications. It is Lehmann's most successful novel, presenting the rivalry of two sisters, Madeline and Dinah, for the love of the same man, Madeline's husband, a theme that also surfaces in Bowen's novels. Bowen termed this claustrophobic triangle, in which voices multiply and echo, "the tragic contemporary predicament, Modern Love."[58] The theme of both attraction and enmity between sisters (and female friends) and the complications of modern love was not just a fictional plot: it was a triangle that entangled Lehmann, Bowen, and Goronwy Rees on the infamous weekend at Bowen's Court in September, 1936. After this weekend when Lehmann and Rees (then Bowen's current flirtation) were invited with a group of friends to Bowen's Court, Bowen was informed of Lehmann and Rees' erotic encounter in an upstairs bedroom. Bowen was jealous, enraged, and betrayed and would not brook having others use Bowen's Court as a love nest, not only insulting, she said, the "dignity" of the house but interfering in her relationship. Lehmann's amorous relationship with Goronwy Rees beginning then and continuing for several years—a rivalry echoing Lehman's plot—cost, for a while, her relationship with Bowen. It was a very public rift and Bowen abhorred public interest in private affairs, fearing not only the "creeping squalour of misused thought and feeling" but rumors that Rees was maligning her character to Berlin.[59] In her writing, she staunchly refers to these extramarital romances as "love[s] without a home,"—and she and her lovers sometimes furtively sought a place for romance. Nevertheless, she also implies the liberation in such romantic encounters—though in other contexts, she paradoxically longed for a "home." Such romantic experiences would electrify Bowen's independent and unconventional women characters who impatiently struggled with society against the confines of traditional roles, beginning with eccentric Lady Elfrida, who has an affair with Considine to her son's disapproval in *Friends and Relations*; followed by Karen, who has an affair with her best friend's fiancée in *The House in Paris*; then Emmeline whose unbound love of Markie leads to murder and suicide in *To the North*; then Stella bound in love and loyalty to a spy in *The Heat of the Day*; and Eva Trout who betrays her teacher, Mrs. Arable, by recklessly seducing her husband, destroying all their relationships. Bowen had a lifelong habit of distancing her feelings, and the shield of *politesse* hardly defends her or her characters from the charge of hypocrisy. She asserts a standard, and yet signals in her stories and novels beginning in the 1930s that such standards were crumbling. Nevertheless, there was a ten-year rift in her relationship with Rosamond Lehmann.

Bowen, also romantically adventurous, shared with Lehmann this attraction to unavailable men, some like Rees with poor character. And she guiltlessly became involved in marital triangles. They both wrote about adventurous women usually in the context of the British upper classes. Bowen acknowledged that she was often attracted to a socially untamed quality in men that flashes out not only in the handsome Rees but in the cad Eddie in *The Death of the Heart*, Max in *The House in Paris*, and Markie in *To the North*. Girls, "loving art better than life," want men to be actors, asserts the knowing narrator in *The House in Paris*. "Only an actor moves them, with his telling smile, undomestic, out of touch with the everyday that they dread. They love to enjoy love as a system of doubts and shocks." The narrator observes of the girls that "not seeking husbands yet, they have no need to be social." This same male excess unwittingly draws Portia, the naïve adolescent, to Eddie, who is in a flirtatious relationship not only with Portia's brother's wife, Anna, but also with Daphne, a seaside girl, in *The Death of the Heart*. Bowen's young, impulsive female characters experience early disillusionments in love with cads who are socially difficult, leading O'Faolain to label Bowen's common plot "the kid and the cad."[60] Lehmann's life, more bounded by her several marriages, the tragic death of her 24-year-old daughter, and other domestic blows, never expanded as did Bowen's into the life of a public intellectual or activist in the national sphere. Alert to politics through her husband at the time, Wogan Phillips, she was a patriot and anti-Fascist, yet naïve about her intermittent friendship with Communist traitors like Guy Burgess and Anthony Blunt. Nevertheless, like Bowen she was passionately interested in women's lives, particularly romance, and how adults interpreted children. Her writing drew attention to the emotions simmering beneath domestic and married relationships.

Place in Fiction: Eudora Welty

If Bowen's personality is illuminated in her friendship and writing about war in relation to Woolf, and elevated in her treatment of romance in relationship to Lehman, then the importance of place in her writing surfaces in her friendship and conversation with the southern American writer, Eudora Welty. Though images, landscapes, and actual places are central to her writing, Bowen remarked that critics and readers were seldom curious about these settings of her novels. "Were I to meet a writer, living or dead, whose work has so percolated into my own experience as to become part of it, his places would be what I should first want to discuss."[61] She resurrects actual places in her writing, locales in England and Ireland—places like London, Hythe and Folkestone and Kildorrery—and they are as traceable in her novels as the precise Dublin sites James Joyce reawakened in *Ulysses*. Such places emerge from childhood memories: Proust's descriptions of a childhood in Combray in *Swann's Way* emerge from visits to his aunt and uncle in Illiers, France; Joyce's Dublin, from his acute memory map of the city of his youth; Welty's Southern towns, shaped by her days in Jackson; and Faulkner, his mythical town of Yoknapatawpha inspired by Lafayette County, Mississippi. Bowen acknowledged in an interview, "internally, yes. Since I started writing, I have been welding together an inner landscape, assembled anything but at random … a recognizable world, geographically consistent … and [yet] having … a super reality." She concedes that in addition to an actual place, the imagination is always working to recast and recreate. What emerges in her writing may be a mosaic of natural sites, historical remnants, fragments from books, foreign travel, myth or remembered or imagined feelings. What piques our interest is this welding of the planes of "place": its actual "geography" and its transcendent reality composed of memory, feeling, and history.

Bowen and Eudora Welty first met in the fall of 1949 when Welty con-
tacted Bowen on a whim on her way back from Italy and France on a
Guggenheim fellowship. She was invited to Bowen's Court, and it was the
start of a close, late-life friendship. It led not only to an appreciation of each
other's landscapes but also conversations about place (about which they both
used the term, "geographical sensations in the senses" in letters), their life
choices (perhaps about the often absent men that they loved), and writing.
Welty intuited how the opening landscapes in Bowen novels took on the disposition of a premonition, pointing to a world of feeling within soon-to-
appear characters. In *A World of Love*, the beautiful, ruined southern Ireland
big house setting prepares us for the figure of Guy, the dead soldier who
haunts the story. The house is no longer welcoming with "an air of having
gone down," yet the light in the landscape is expectant, foreshadowing Lilia's
daughter, Jane, "a shower of gold," who finds Guy's old letters in a trunk and
reawakens the unfulfilled romance in the lives of these women.[62] It was also a
landscape that captivated Welty on her visit to Bowen's Court in 1951. She
wrote in a letter to her friend John Robinson:

> It was so lovely coming. First night for coming anywhere you love—the boat
> enters Cork by a 3 hour journey up the river … in early morning—passing by
> little towns of pink and buff and gray houses in lines up the green hills up &
> over the hills here … you do feel it as a geographical sensation in the senses.
> Cold as it may get here it is the South in every way.[63]

This crisscrossing of the two writers, each rooted in her home, illuminates
the "Southerness" of temperament that they both felt. Welty visited Bowen's
Court several times in the early 1950s and was fascinated by and took photos
of the house, and Bowen later traveled to Welty's home in Jackson,
Mississippi. Fascinated by the landscape, she asked Welty to send her a
haunting Currier and Ives print, "Through the Bayou by Torchlight" when
she arrived home. Welty called Bowen a "Southerner" in manner and
hospitality; Bowen often wrote about the passing of social graces and reticence
from the world, and preserved them in her own manners and hospitality.
Welty shared her reserve and gentility. "Wherever she went, in the whole
world almost, the Southerners were always different from the northerners.
She always felt the congeniality."[64]

One might initially wonder about the affinity. Bowen was an independent,
upper-middle-class woman of cosmopolitan tastes and manners, and sexually
adventurous. She lived the lifestyle of a salonnière, often elegantly entertaining
English and Irish intellectuals and writers. She had been a pampered only
child in her first seven years, yet her childhood was one of displacements.

Welty, on the other hand, was the eldest of three children in a close-knit family, and lived most of her life in the same childhood home in provincial Jackson. Her father was an insurance broker; her mother, a homemaker. Her life was one of continuity and stability, yet the culture of the south was such that once when Welty tried to find a place to write in nearby Learned, the landlord refused her offer to buy as he was reluctant to sell to a single woman. Bowen once told a visitor with hauteur that Welty was "a perfectly remarkable woman to have come out of that circumstance." A pause. "Mississippi," she added.[65] In 1949, she emerged and traveled to Italy and France and stopped in Ireland to meet Bowen when she received a Guggenheim fellowship at the age of 40.

Though she never married, Welty had a close relationship with John Robinson, whose writing she selflessly supported, and to whom she wrote often though he spent most of his life with his partner in Europe. Beginning in 1970, she also had a romantic but not sexual relationship with Kenneth Millar to whom she also wrote intense letters: writing and love of Robinson and Millar were inseparably connected. Millar was married, and she wrote to him and sometimes his wife, Emmy, twice a month over 20 years, but they spent only about six weeks in each other's company.[66] This pattern of intimate letters and infrequent meetings was one Bowen would understand; her relationship with Charles Ritchie was sustained by correspondence— given his absence and her writing life.

Welty said of Bowen: "she was a marvelous lady, a responsive person, you know, to mood and place, and she was so happy, so delighted by things in life. And very apprehensive too. It was an Irishness, a sense of your surroundings, very sensitive to what you can feel all the time."[67] Before a visit to Bowen's Court in 1951, Welty wrote an effusive letter from Dublin. "It's always enough to make me happy," she reminisced, "just to think of Bowen's Court and you there—then to come and see you, and even to do a piece of work in the middle of happiness—well a story I would most wish were good (whatever it is, it broke out of a shell that had troubled me, so its work meant ever so much to me). I'll bring it and you'll see but it's not good enough."[68] Welty brought her story, "The Bride of the Innisfallen," in which she presents a variety of characters, American, Welsh, Irish, including, briefly, a bride, and they all travel together from London to Cork in a train compartment, and, later, a boat named "Innisfallen." She drew on her actual journey from London to Cork and related what she saw and overheard in conversations on the train in a letter to Robinson.

The train journey was grand—you're in Ireland the minute you get on the car in Paddington Station (I was in a compartment with 6 Irish and 1 Welshman who got on in Cardiff) … the other called her "the bride."[69]

The mythic and impressionistic quality of the lit train compartment—the dark outside, the mood, and the conversation among the strangers—may suggest the shaping influence of Bowen that some Welty readers view as a fault. Nevertheless, she piqued Welty to think and write about being removed from realistic, regional characters who found their identities firmly planted in the American South. After consulting with Bowen and before sending in the second draft of the story to the *New Yorker*, she made it "a little clearer and better," and inscribed and sent a copy to Bowen that remains in the Ransom Center.[70] It was the first story of Welty's that the *New Yorker* accepted in 1951, urged by William Maxwell and Gus Lebrano who had earlier rejected three Welty stories in 1940–1941 as being too "arty."

About ten years later, Bowen took a car journey to the American South with her friend Catherine Collins, wife of the president of Curtis Brown, her agent. She was on assignment for *Holiday* magazine, writing an article, "A Ride to the South."[71] The car trip started on the New Jersey Turnpike near the Collins home in Hopewell, and the magnetism of history emerges in Bowen's description. She careened down US 1, observing the school buses that "deposited white children," and she felt despair in Vicksburg, Mississippi, "the spring grass with blood in its confederate ancestry." She found a Bowen to have been among the Confederate dead. She stopped in Jackson to visit Welty. As she proceeded from Jackson to New Orleans, she observed small antebellum cotton towns; listened to folklore about French and Indian robbers; and viewed the Louisiana plantation homes, "feminine houses, some named after ladies." It was all at once, Bowen said, "a continuous living through the eye," like a scene in a musical. But a supplement to living through the eye was "the enforced return," the reoccurrence of memory of past writers and books. She travelled back to women writers who had who created the "big house" tradition.

The Big House Tradition

Among the books that Bowen returned to were those of Jane Austen, Maria Edgeworth, and Somerville and Ross. Austen and Edgeworth are engraved in the tradition of big house fiction but from very different cultural and political positions: at the turn of the nineteenth century, Austen wrote from a culturally stable British perspective in *Pride and Prejudice*—a book Bowen admired—satirizing middle-class women aspiring to marriage with men of fortune of the

British gentry; Maria Edgeworth writing in the same period wrote with the consciousness of a culturally-divided Ireland. Though living most of her life in England, she was surrounded by the political crisis of land reform in Ireland and exposed a big house in ruin in her novel, *Castle Rackrent*, in which Thadys Quirk, a loyal family servant astutely and comically details the irresponsibility and corruption of the Anglo-Irish landlord class. Ireland did not have the political and social coherence of England—preoccupied by the ruptures and violence of land reform and divisions of culture and religion in the nineteenth century—to approach the social issues of the English novel with the same equanimity and balance.

Somerville and Ross at the turn of the twentieth century continued to write from a vantage of cultural division between Ascendancy landlords and farmer-tenants in *The Real Charlotte*. In a talk Bowen gave on Somerville and Ross she did not simply view them as writers who recorded the descent of the Anglo-Irish ascendancy but praised their depiction of the Irish and Anglo-Irish character and the terror of landowners.[72] In the novel, Charlotte Mullen, a plain Anglo-Irish woman with an inheritance, is socially and psychologically pitted against Francie Fitzpatrick—her pretty, naïve, poor Irish cousin coming from the County of Lismoyle in the west of Ireland. Charlotte, jealous of her cousin's attractiveness and popularity, nevertheless, plots to have her marry a wealthy man to enhance her own social position. Early in the novel, Charlotte's Anglo-Irish image has traces of a champing horse pinioning Charlotte's ugliness and nature: "Her face reddened, and she opened her wide mouth for a retort, but before she had time for more than the champings as of a horse with a heavy bit, which preceded her more incisive repartees ... [and Charlotte] showed all her teeth in a forced smile."[73] She tries in a land grab, a typical Anglo-Irish gesture, to wrench a farm away from a poor tenant, Julia Duffy. Julia, however, "felt all the Protestant and aristocratic association" of her father's name and reminded Charlotte and Mr. Benjamin, the estate owner, that a promise was made to her that her land holdings would not be disturbed. She is, nevertheless, rebuffed. Subtle anti-English humor threads the novel and Charlotte announces her loathing for "fine" English ladies, "lazy hunks," sitting about waiting to be waited upon unlike her energetic and self-sufficient Anglo-Irish self. Irony and satire thread the novel as Charlotte's "refined" humor is wasted on Lady Dysart, an Englishwoman, who "was constitutionally unable to discern perfectly the subtle grades of Irish vulgarity." Lady Dysart also enjoys talking to Charlotte about a range of lively topics ignoring the inequalities of class and Charlotte's accent that to her English ears was "merely the expression of a vigorous individuality." Charlotte, despite this overt prejudice against her, sizes up Christopher Dysart, Lady Dysart's son, as a potential suitor for Francie, her cousin, as well as for being "a real gentleman" and having "not a drop of dirty Saxon blood in him." Charlotte's plots fail and signal the corruption and decline of the Anglo-Irish ascendancy. Bowen admired the satire and grasp of everyday Irish life in this novel and longed, she said in her talk, for such a novel in the tradition of realism to emerge in Ireland in the 1970s.

Bowen would join this tradition in her 1928 novel, *The Last September*, to capture the atmosphere of a big house in the midst of the crisis of the Civil War in Ireland, 1920–1922. She, however, wrote the novel six years after the Civil War while living in England, and adopted a position of cultural ambivalence toward the Ascendancy family and local farmers. It was a novel that Sean O'Faolain later observed, was written "when Ireland was still, in some sort, her home." His own stunning story, *Midsummer Night's Madness*, was written from the viewpoint of men who burned such houses down: it was an ironic story that Bowen selected for her collection, *Great Middlebrow Prose*. In a vivid and moving letter in April 1937, admitting that he was writing "like a fool," he conceded that she had written "the history of a besieged city," but now "the siege is over." Or are "the walls as high as ever? I fear to think it is." As a novelist, he felt "like a spy" inside the big house, and he challenged Bowen, daughter of this cultural house, to write the story about a Danielstown that was aware of the people—the Ireland outside it—or "regretted the division enough to admit it was there." One heard in her novel, he said, historical noises off and O'Faolain thought it was now time for the Irish novel to bring "the enemy," the Anglo-Irish, to the foreground as, in fact, he did in his own story. The cultural division, he asserted, is desperate, and "no novelist could falsify or sentimentalise over it." He then asked, "Do you feel any of this?" An open question. Bowen's response is not recorded, but she never did write of the several planes of class and religion in Irish society, except to acknowledge in her family history of Bowen's Court that the divisions O'Faolain highlighted still existed and troubled her. It is a border she did not cross in her 1929 novel or approach in any other afterward, drawn as she was into the war which became her subject in the 1940s.

O'Faolain, though greatly admiring her style in *The Last September*, wrote about its cultural narrowness. He is perhaps the most prescient critic of Bowen's equivocal cultural position in the novel that balances the value of the Anglo-Irish traditions in the big house while also preserving its sympathy for resistant Irish neighbors. In O'Faolain's letter to her, he asserts that "he kept wanting 'the enemy' to come into the foreground a bit." Reminding her that she was representing a besieged culture, he asked if she felt that each side now "has to make up its losses." In the same letter, he related a poignant incident in which he stayed with some nice people, the Griffins in a big house, Alta

Villa (which he asserted should have been Ait a'Shille, the old Irish form) and observed an old man "sidling with his hat in hand"—who might have been his father as he emerged from the hills where O'Faolain's folks came from. As the old man approached the big house, a butler emerged to ward him off from the lady in the house. Observing the cultural complexity, he noted that the butler might have been the man's second cousin, and the whole scene made O'Faolain sick to see "the two men talk to one another in that way, and to have to keep silent, and not say, 'Hello, Tom, or Jerry,' or whatever his name was." To O'Faolain "the wall between the big house and the Irish farmer was as high as ever in 1937 and it made him feel 'like a spy' inside the big house." The cultural division, he asserted is desperate, and "no novelist could falsify or sentimentalise over it." He challenges Bowen to write a story about a Danielstown that was aware of the people—the Ireland outside it—or "regretted the division enough to admit it was there." She never did.

In his own story, *Midsummer Night Madness*, Blake House "bursts into flames" just as Bowen's door to Danielstown opened "like a furnace in *The Last September*." It was an image that haunted her. Writing of a later period, O'Faolain sketches the Renn House in a state of decay, physically and morally, while Bowen's big house still carries on earlier Anglo-Irish traditions of parties, dances, and tennis—magic still emanating into their days as in the big house representations of William Trevor and Jennifer Johnston. Henn's point of view is represented, and the IRA agent sees "for the first time how deep the hate on his side could be, as deep as the hate in ours, as deep and as terrible."

What O'Faolain does not see is that Bowen's story is as much about a young girl's dilemmas as it is about the Troubles, the national reverberating in the personal. Despite their different Irelands, O'Faolain admired Bowen's "control" and "her sense of drama in small things": he particularly coveted the atmosphere in her novel, claiming that he "could smell the hay, the wet, the mountain line." Taking on past and contemporary critics of Bowen, he asserted that the novel is "entirely Irish—if that matters a damn." He then added, in an aside, the broader literary vision that he and Bowen shared: "(We're so sick of hearing our Nationalists ask for Irish literature—so thirsty for just literature)."[74]

O'Faolain, the less established writer, realized his "impertinence" in suggesting themes to Bowen, yet he ventured because he believed an "Irish novel about Ireland would get down to the reality of things-happening better if it chose a Big House that had no, or few, escapes." He wanted a novel from her that would reveal the life of the Ascendancy now, not in the 1920s as in *The Last September*. She could write a book about the difficulties and yet the loveliness and independence in the big houses—its flowers, its traditions—so that those outside the walls would realize it was "a real, full life. An admirable, a kindly, a comic, a tender, life." Instead, he said, Irish stories have been "in water tight compartments"—culturally separate.

Abandonment: Charles Dickens and Henry James

Charles Dickens in the same century was also an author whose perspectives reverberated in Bowen's life and writing as did Henry James: both wrote of abandoned children. Much has been written about her affinity to James, but she was closer in feeling to Dickens, and, to technique in James. After visiting Charles Dickens' house, Broadstairs, on Fort Hill on the Kent coast in 1965 where she grew up, Bowen related a "terrifying illumination" about abandonment. In Broadstairs, she told Charles Ritchie, Dickens wrote many books that "really are the roots of so many things I have felt, or perhaps my way of feeling things and seeing them."[75] Bowen's favorite was *David Copperfield* and she considered the first chapter, the best she knew, "I was born with a caul," according to Sally Phipps. The misery of Sissy Jupe, abandoned by her father in *Hard Times*, and the disfigurement of Esther in *Bleak House* prefigure the unhappiness of children in Bowen's own stories: Theodora, Portia, Eva, Leopold, and Henrietta. The social and cultural background of these children captivated Bowen, and like Dickens, she exposed their wounds.

Henry James, another of her favorite authors, was similarly preoccupied with abandonment. But he portrays an adolescent in the midst of her parent's contentious divorce in *What Maisie Knew* with a different technique for revealing Maisie. Character, in Bowen's view, "should on the whole, be under rather than over articulated. What they intend to say should be more evident [...] than what they arrive at saying."[76] Bowen's Portia in *The Death of the Heart* says little as she enters the unwelcoming household of her half-brother and his wife after the death of her parents. She "writes" what she thinks and feels in her diary that we glimpse only in fragments when Anna, her step-mother, reads it aloud to a friend. We are left to imagine Portia's feelings in between the accusations and observations in her written diary. James, on the other hand, over articulates and narrates what the beleaguered, precocious Maisie knows and "thinks" as she navigates the difficult emotional territory of her parents' divorce and their desperate and destructive attempts to win her over. Both girls, however, will learn to negotiate the social expectations and hypocrisy of the adult world. Bowen, however, will illuminate how writing in letters and diaries saves and guides Portia through adolescence, as it did for Bowen.

Henry James, nevertheless, mesmerized Bowen. She noted in an interview that he, an American, saw England better than the English, just as she, being Irish and living in England, had a superior angle on the English. In conversation with Isaiah Berlin, she sought his views of James and Austen and he found Austen's "preoccupation with marriage [...] terrifying and only too psychoanalysable."[77] He was not responsive, as Bowen was, to Austen's comedy of behavior or the satire on the darker economic and social motives beneath marital preoccupations. James offered more to the novelist, Bowen, than to Berlin, the intellectual historian. She was drawn to his cerebral style, even his asexuality, but when asked about him in a 1968 interview, she responded,

> I think his stories are wonderful. If I had known him, though, I would have sent him a blue pencil. Oh those endless scenes in drawing rooms of sympathetic young ladies listening to neurotic young men. But his style is powerful. I would never read him when I was writing. He's infectious, like a rash.[78]

Modernists

Bowen's limitations as a modernist reader were revealed in her review of Joyce's *Ulysses* for *The Bell*, commissioned by Sean O'Faolain. She began with the rueful remark that the death of Joyce was felt by few in his own land as a personal tragedy given his exile from Dublin in 1904, and the unavailability of copies of *Ulysses* in Ireland (though not censored). She combined appreciation and rebuke recoiling first from its "stomach turning physical ugliness" which was hostile to the reader. Buoyed by her own style that valued restraint, indirection, stillness, and the unsaid, she was not sympathetic to Joyce's belief that no dimension of human experience should be excluded from literature. In appreciation, she highlights Joyce's lyrical side, expressing the wish that the Irish public would read certain passages at the beginning of "Proteus," "The Dead," and *Portrait of the Artist as a Young Man*. In that same month, she reviewed Herbert Gorman's biography of Joyce for the *Spectator*. She began by identifying Joyce as a European writer, yet asserting what he owed to Ireland.[79] "Never," she wrote, "was there a less pitiable man." She describes Joyce as having "that kind of hauteur, independent of circumstance, that Stendhal called *espagnolisme*," a kind of Spanish way of feeling and behaving, and yet "he had the Irish qualities shaped and steeled." She followed Joyce and when *Finnegan's Wake* was published in 1939, she marked her reading in a letter to Ritchie, assessing that the language was "pounded like jelly." What drew Bowen to

Joyce was that, "Sensation was, above all, his subject," as it was hers.[80] She was astute in noting that "the sensations that were his fever and pain are common—what remains extraordinary is the length he travelled in his efforts to put sensation into words." Yet, for her, "his youth in Dublin remains … inside the crystal of his art." In the end, she asserts that it is places and physical surroundings that link people, noting her familiarity with Joyce's streetscapes and landscapes. She ends with an image of him forever "walking the Dublin streets or looking with us along the wet sands of the Bay."

Finally, Bowen's writing life is bracketed by her reading of Proust whose sensibilities and visual imagination she shared. She wrote of first reading *A La Recherche du Temps Perdu* in French in the early 1920s and acknowledged his influence on her first novel, *The Hotel*, published in 1927. Bowen wrote to Charles Ritchie that the hotel scene came from Balbec in *A L'ombre de Jeune Fille en Fleur*, which she read during a boring winter with her mother's relatives, the Colleys, in a hotel on the Italian Riviera. She noted that after this depressing time in Italy, she later realized what Proust meant "about boredom being (subsequently) fruitful."[81] A decade later, in a letter to Ritchie from the elegant Dorchester Hotel, Bowen would jokingly write, "How I wish Proust were here." In her novel, Bowen, like Proust, swings open "on a hinge like the front of a doll's house…life within." Both reveal the society and traces of homosexuality in the relationships in the hotel, but Bowen is interested in women's lives, and Proust, in men's. Miss Kerr says in Bowen's novel, "I'm not a feminist but I do like being a woman," and the same might be said for Bowen and her characters in this novel and others as she finds women's lives "sensational." She illuminates, for example, "some types of women," in Miss Kerr and her "violent friendship" with Sydney and the "rifts" between Miss Pym and Miss Emily Fitzgerald.

Bowen's novels, like Proust's, recall social photography: snapshots of time, place, and class. Anachronistic, like Bowen, Proust embraces the myths of the *ancient regime* in its waning days, as Bowen did the dying rituals and traditions of the Anglo-Irish gentry. He shows the shift in social patterns after the Dreyfus affair and World War I in France; similarly, the social landscape in *The Last September* changes as the Anglo-Irish are displaced, their homes burned by the IRA, and Ireland struggles to become a republic. His reflections on the "intermittences of the heart," the changing faces of love, time present and time past, and memory also preoccupy Bowen.[82] Her blue-bound copies of Proust in the 1949 Scott Moncrieff English translation with Philippe Julian's illustrations stood on shelves in Carbery, her home in Hythe.[83] Bowen was also intrigued by Proust's life, comparing it to her own when reading George Painter's biography of him in 1959. The biography, she said, gave her a sort of terror about the infectiousness of "the neurotic set-up" in romance. Thankfully, she asserts that she and Ritchie are not neurotics, "why I don't know," conceding only that they are "highly nervous and highly organized."[84] They were both high voltage. At the end of her life, she returned to Proust, commissioned by Peter Quennel to write an essay. She wrote to Derek Hill that she was settling down in November 1967 "to a long Proust jag," to write "the long portentous essay," "The Art of Bergotte," now in *Pictures and Conversations.* The transcript of her 24 pages of handwritten quotes attests to her commitment. She selected the writer, Bergotte—one of the three artists, along with Elstir, the painter, and Vinteuil, the musician, in the work—that confirm for Proust, as for Bowen, that "the only truth in life is art." Bergotte was an unattractive person but a gifted artist. Her affinity is illuminated in her selected notes in which she focuses on the adolescent disillusionment of Marcel with the writer's "meaty physical personality," the kind of disappointment that many of the adolescents in her stories experience with idealized adults. In addition, Proust alights "on the paradox of romantic love—that what we possess, one can no longer desire"—a state she explored in her novels, if not in her relationship with Ritchie. Bowen often intertwined notions of art with romance. Bergotte, like Bowen, is a sensuous and visual writer and what was most effective in his writing, according to Marcel, "was the magic of the climate in which they floated," not the actual scene but the scene filtered through the writer's sensibility, an experience familiar to readers of Bowen.[85]

Notes

1. Bowen, "Coming to London," 88.
2. Bowen, "Review of Cyril Connolly's *The Condemned Playground*," MT, 170.
3. EB to WP, May 6, 1958, DUR 19.
4. *WWF*, 351.
5. EB to VW, July 31 (1937 or 1938), NYPL 64B5060.
6. WP to EB, May 31 [1936?] DUR 11.8.
7. Woolf, March 24, 1932, *Diary* 4, 86.
8. Woolf, March 16, 1936, *Diary* 5, 18, 133.
9. Woolf, April 19, 1934, *Diary* 4, 208.
10. CR journal, October 29, 1967, *LCW*, 455.
11. EB to RL, October 16, 1972, KC, 2.
12. See Morrell, *Lady Ottoline's Album.*
13. EB to OM, August 15, n.d., HRC 3.2.
14. Plomer, *At Home*, 45–46.
15. Bowen, "Preface to Orlando," *SW*, 135.

16. Bowen, "Achievement of Virginia Woolf."
17. EB to WP, May 6, 1958, DUR 19.
18. CR journal, May 13, 1956, *LCW*, 232.
19. IB to Mary Fisher, November 30, 1933, Berlin, *Flourishing*, 69.
20. CR journal, April 20, 1942, *LCW*, 30.
21. EB to IB, December 18, 1933, BOD, MS. Berlin 245, fol. 11.
22. VW to EB, January 29, 1939, HRC 12.4.
23. Ibid., January 3, 1933.
24. EB to VW, July 1, 1940, SU.
25. See Bluemel, Introduction, 1–14.
26. Elizabeth Bowen, letter to Woolf, July 1, 1940, HH.
27. Sybil Oldfield, *Women Against the Iron Fist, 103.*
28. Woolf, "The Leaning Tower," 136.
29. Two hundred German bombs targeting railway lines and air force bases fell on London but it was 10 Downing St., the War Office, the Treasury, Piccadilly Square, and St. James Square that were actually hit, and 300 people killed.
30. Woolf, October 17, 1940, *Diary* 5, 330.
31. EB to VW, January 5, 1940, SU.
32. Woolf, October 20, 1940, *Diary* 5, 331.
33. *HD*, 337.
34. *CI*, 74.
35. Bowen, "We Write Novels," 27.
36. VW to EB, July 20, 1933, in Woolf, *Letters* 5, 205.
37. VW to EB, September 26, 1935, HHC.
38. Ibid.
39. Woolf, *Letters* 6, 473n3.
40. *ROO*, 131.
41. *CI*, 81.
42. EB to CR, June 26, 1945, *LCW*, 52.
43. Ibid., November 21 and 28, 1961, 373–374.
44. Ibid., May 30, 1962, 388.
45. Bowen, "Frankly Speaking."
46. Bowen, "Ray Strachey's *Our Freedom.*"
47. VW to EB, Woolf, May 16, 1934, *Letters* 5, 303.
48. Bowen, "Women's Place," 379.
49. Lassner, *Elizabeth Bowen*, 1–2.
50. Bowen, "Daughters of Erin."
51. Lehmann, "Rosamond Lehmann—Interview."
52. Ibid.
53. RL to EB, July 8, 1935, HRC 11.6.
54. Ibid., August 25 (ca.1935).
55. Kathleen Raine to RL, November 7, 1976, KC 2.498.
56. RL to EB, March 3, 1949, KC 2.64.

57. Ibid., October 12, 1935.
58. Bowen, "Echoing Grove—Review."
59. EB to IB, shortly after September 1936, BOD, MS. Berlin 245.
60. O'Faolain, "Reading and Remembrance of Elizabeth Bowen," 59.
61. *PC*, 34–35, 36.
62. *WL*, 11.
63. EW to John Robinson, April 2, 1951, LSU, MS.4919.
64. Devlin, *Welty*, 5.
65. Devlin, *Welty*, 210 n. 9.
66. Marrs, *Eudora Welty*, 369ff.
67. Prenshaw, 4.
68. EW to EB, April 1951, HRC 12.1.
69. EW to John Robinson, April 2, 1951, LSU, MS.4919.
70. EW to EB, aboard *Ile de France*, August 1951, HRC 12.3; typescript of this story in HRC.
71. Bowen, "A Ride South," 165–188.
72. Irish Literary Weekend, sponsored by Lady Birley, June 25–July 4, 1971, Sussex.
73. *The Real Charlotte*, 15.
74. O'Faolain, Sean to EB, April 22, 1937. HRC Bowen Collection 11.6.
75. EB to CR, April 11, 1965, *LCW*, 439.
76. Bowen, "Notes on Writing a Novel," 182.
77. IB to EB, January 2, 1934, Berlin, *Flourishing*, 80.
78. Monaghan, "Portrait of a Woman Reading."
79. Bowen, review of James Joyce, March 14, 1941, *SIW*, 62–63.
80. Ibid., 246, 239–240.
81. EB to CR, September 2, 1949, *LCW*, 138–140.
82. Proust, *Sodom and Gomorrah*, Part II.
83. Auctioned after her death, now in library of Bruce Arnold.
84. EB to CR, October 21, 1959, *LCW*, 342.
85. Bowen, "The Art of Bergotte," *PC*, 102, 95.

10

Late Life Collage (1950–1959)

Drifting

"Look at my life since Alan died," wrote Bowen to Charles Ritchie: "when I'm not with you I simply go on drifting from one orbit of influence to another."[1] The years, 1952–1959, were bracketed by her husband's death and the sale and destruction of her beloved Bowen's Court. She moved from place to place during the 1950s, seeking direction, propelled by her need to earn money and find balance in her relationship with Ritchie: he, married; she, *femme seule*. Ritchie, at a high point in his career, 1958, was appointed Canadian ambassador to the UN and took up residence with his wife in New York City; at the same time, Bowen was an itinerant college lecturer. She wrote to Sarton that the decade of traveling to American colleges was, at times, "as high pressure as I had ever known." The pace revealed her remarkable energy and stoic temperament, though she was often distraught about her finances and what she considered an unnatural separation from Ritchie. Though resilient, she had dramatic outbursts with him despite her outwardly poised demeanor. In addition to lecturing extensively from 1952 into the early 1960s, she traveled to the American Academy in Rome to finish *A Time in Rome* and completed *The World of Love* in 1955. In addition, she wrote popular articles for *Vogue*, *Holiday*, *Saturday Evening Post*, *Ladies Home Journal*, *House & Garden*, *Harper's Bazaar, and McCall's*. In between, she traveled all over England and Scotland for the British Royal Commission on Capital Punishment.

She remained hopelessly, sometimes obsessively, in love. In a poignant note to Ritchie from Rome, where she retreated during the sale of Bowen's Court for six months from October through March 1959, she wrote:

© The Author(s), under exclusive license to Springer Nature Switzerland AG 2021
P. Laurence, *Elizabeth Bowen*, Literary Lives, https://doi.org/10.1007/978-3-030-71360-7_10

My darling, when you opened this letter a piece of satin probably fell out of it—do make a dive and retrieve it, even if the scene is in the middle of the UN General Assembly, at a tense moment. This is the stuff of the beautiful Roman evening dress you have given me, which I have finally found … less than the sum—the £200 that you—you dear and generous beloved—gave me to spend.[2]

Fine clothes and moving in high social circles in Roman society offered a distraction. Her passionate letters continued. She wrote that she lived in "that state of loneliness, almost like a climate or a sad terrain, which again and again settles down on me when we have been for any length of time apart."[3]

The postwar decade began with Bowen and Cameron leaving London in 1952, an economically motivated move. They had waited for the British postwar policy that allowed them to take money out of the country, financially dependent upon Cameron's pension from the BBC and Bowen's lecture and royalty fees. Cameron's health was poor and they hoped a more peaceful lifestyle at Bowen's Court might restore him. The move also marked Bowen's increasing alienation from the city of London as it emerged from postwar austerity. It was gray and depressing in her view as working class teddy boys roamed the streets, tasteless suburbs expanded, poverty increased, and crime statistics grew.

Bowen was further alienated by the Labor Party's 1945 victory. She and Ritchie admired Churchill's oratory and brash diatribes against the Nazis during the war: "One of the secrets of the hold of his oratory over the English People," said Ritchie, is that he makes them feel that they are living their history, that they are taking part in a great pageant. He gives them his own feeling of the continuity of English history."[4] But Bowen had warned that when Churchill went, she would go. The Conservatives did go in 1945 when the Labor Party formed a majority government under Clement Atlee. Though sharing some of the leftist views of her earlier Oxford circle friends and Auden and Isherwood early in the war, she turned and announced her opposition to the "Labour wets" of postwar Britain to Plomer.[5] She wrote to Ritchie that "like all provincials, I expect London, or any capital city, to be something terrific: hence my deep irritation and neurosis which you must have felt in my letters all those months after the official finish of the war when London in any way breaks down, when the illusion fails."[6] After all her anti-Fascist ardor, she experienced it as a flop; her "feeling was exhausted. And there was a majority guilt-feeling (wrong I think) about the atomic bomb." Only the searchlights made into a cathedral shape were the "music" of the event for her. She generally sided with the values of property, tradition, and authority, and was rarely sympathetic with the people, en masse. She was a hawk in her response to America's Pearl Harbor attack, unsympathetic to student protests against the

Vietnam War, and in favor of pro-white Rhodesia. And though she conceded that at least 20 percent of the Labor people had principles, she asserted that "the few good ones have the entourage of the sissy, the half-baked, the *manquées*, the people with the chips on their shoulder, the people who've never made any grade and are convinced that it must be the grade's fault." She grew closer to Ireland for its practical comforts and calming spirit, living there intermittently after Cameron's death. In 1956, she argued that her "ancestors didn't care a damn about English politics and how right they were. This country, come back to, seems very amiable, good and sweet (in the sense one speaks of air being sweet). Quite illicitly—I mean, in view of their having been neutrals—everybody is enjoying peace madly [...] In fact, the Irish are the only people I have met so far who really are getting 100% kick out of world peace …[they] always knew this war would end up in Bolshevism and they are gladder than ever they kept out of it."[7]

Cameron's Death and the Sale of Bowen's Court

Lodged in Bowen's Court beginning in January 1952, Bowen wrote to friends that Cameron was doing much better, despite his recent heart attack, periods of "roaring diabetes," and persistent problems with his eyes. She recounted to Derek Hill that Cameron enjoyed life at Bowen's Court, and both of them were happy.[8] Then he died suddenly in his sleep in August. Though Bowen had led a literary and social life seemingly independent of him for most of their married life, he was the anchor in her fast-paced world, and she was distraught and dislocated upon his death. She wrote to friends who had been sympathetic—House, Sarton, and Plomer—to say so. "He's not gone," she wrote to Sarton.

> Bless you for your letter, your understanding, the dear vivid things you say about Alan. In the end, it was all so very quiet, so very sudden; he simply did not awake from a night's sleep. His health in the months after we came to live here (we left London "for good" last Jan.) took such a blessedly better turn. We had a long mid-winter in this house, then a dazzling spring then a long bright summer—not like Irish weather at all. We were **so** *happy*.[9]

Then, a turn in events: he just went to sleep one quiet night near the end of August. She wrote to House, "if this had to happen, this was the place: London would have been terrible with its unreality. There is a dignity and fitness about things here. Everybody inside and outside this place has been so good; most realising that here it's natural to weep. Nobody is ignorant as to say 'Forget it.'"[10] After his death, Bowen resumed an itinerant life, familiar since she was a child in Kent. Movement was her norm. Nevertheless, she hoped to keep Bowen's Court. "This place," she wrote to Derek Hill, "now means more to me than ever, I hope to go on living here if I can afford it."[11]

"For seven years," she wrote to Ritchie, "I tried to do what was impossible." Bowen's Court was a "barrack of anxiety" and the constant traveling to earn money slowed down her writing.[12] She related to Plomer that she experienced "terrifyingly empty days" that contributed to her growing insecurity.[13] Friends like Plomer and Butts were a consolation, and she maintained her style of hospitality, entertaining lavishly. She confessed that the maintenance of Bowen's Court was not only sustained by money but the goodwill of the servants. In her posthumously published essay "The Most Unforgettable Character I Ever Met," she relates how she explained her financial affairs to one of her favorite servants, Sarah Barry. "Since my grandfather's death finances had not improved: I could only afford to keep Bowen's Court if I earned money. So [Sarah] saw that what I did, along with the much that she did, followed the same ideal—to keep things going."[14] And the servants did sacrifice and sustain it. Bowen commented, "You may say she gave her genius to a forlorn hope—to a house at the back of beyond, to a dying-out family. But I think no gift goes for nothing."[15] Bowen finally sold it at the end of 1959: the house had been in the family for two centuries, and she was the only female inheritor of the estate. But she was not the only Anglo-Irish owner who struggled out of pride to keep things going. She observed other families that "to their credit […] with grass almost up to their doors and hardly a sixpence to turn over […] continued to be resented by the rest of Ireland as being the heartless rich." Now, she said, "this myth is broken down. I think everyone knows that life is not all jam in the big house": nowadays, she said, people comment on "the futility of the sacrifice."[16] When it was sold, however, her fantasy about sharing her life with Ritchie—"we MUST have a house"—was shattered.

Eddie Sackville-West

Bowen exiled herself to Italy during the sale of the estate. When she returned, Eddie Sackville-West, her close friend, noted the extraordinary change in her appearance: "she looked like someone who had attended her own execution."[17] Distraught because Ritchie refused to offer her the security she longed for, she threw herself into a whirl of professional engagements that hid her fragile state. An emotional chasm opened in Bowen's life, and she wrote letters about her devastating loneliness to friends. She had always found it difficult to accept Ritchie's marriage, but particularly so after Cameron's death, and became less and less tolerant of Ritchie's wife Sylvia, openly expressing her hostility. The despair and volatility of these scenes sometimes drove Ritchie away.

Yet she kept writing. In 1954 during a very dramatic and unhappy visit to Ritchie in Bonn, he marveled that she finished the final chapters to *A World of Love* on the table in his verandah in a small German hotel. At that time, she also developed a strong friendship with Eddie Sackville-West—wealthy, aristocratic, witty, elegant, eccentric, and a homosexual—who had followed her to Ireland. He was the cousin of Vita Sackville-West, who famously resented his inheritance of Knole and the prevailing rule of primogeniture. In April 1955, Hartley wrote that Sackville-West was on his way to London "to receive the fortune almost literally on a salver."[18] They had known each other since the late 1940s and had exchanged visits, and she had been his guest at Long Crichel, Dorset, a kind of male intellectual salon, where he lived with his companions, Raymond Mortimer and Desmond Shaw Taylor. He remarked at the time that Bowen was reaping unaccustomed royalties after publication of *The Heat of the Day*, making welcome improvements in basins and bathrooms at Bowen's Court. He also observed "poor old Alan very subdued and tottery," not in good health, just a few years before Cameron and Bowen moved from London to Bowen's Court.[19]

Sackville-West brought her into stimulating social circles, and some speculated that if things had turned out differently, he might have helped her with her financial plight with Bowen's Court. In 1956, Bowen, clear-eyed, wrote to Ritchie that Sackville-West was not in love with her in the usual sense; it was "a kind of love which contents itself with the happiness they have with a person … in love with my companionship … the fact that he knows I am not 'disponible' [available].'"[20] When he first relocated to Ireland, he had stayed with Bowen in Bowen's Court, but moved into his own house in Cooleville in May 1956. She was relieved. Though she liked his style and found him engaging, she could not stand his depressing fuss when in ill health. Visitors streamed to his home, and in September 1956, she wrote Ritchie about her "restless summer […] as you know, we all here take in one another's washing."[21] She remarked that Raymond Mortimer and his friend Paul, who had a house in Canonbury, Islington, had visited and were "like witches on broomsticks." She learned that they had cast her in the role "of an elderly Irish rake," fearing that Eddie would "Take to the Bottle," as everyone in Ireland drinks so much. It was a charge she deeply resented.

Ritchie visited her again in spring 1956, and after his departure, the images in her letters were of being "torn apart," "maimed," "wounded [...] as though shot through one wing."[22] Her entanglement with Ritchie was well known; nevertheless, people gossiped about her and Sackville-West as they became closer. She described their companionable relationship, an elegant dinner with him and then listening to *Tosca* in June of the same year. Around the same time, Ritchie wrote in his journal that Bowen was indirectly warning him that if she did not see him more often, Sackville-West would come to occupy her life increasingly because of what she described as "his adhesiveness, his impermeable quality, which she said is like Sylvia's."[23] "Adhesiveness" was not Bowen's idea of love. In the story "Look at All Those Roses," Lou, determined to be a necessity to her married lover, Edward, "stuck to him out of contentiousness [...] she seldom let him out of her sight—her idea of love was adhesiveness."[24] If Bowen shuddered over this quality, a month later, Sackville-West winced at the feelings of jealousy entering their relationship. He wrote in his diary that he had come to dislike the expression of emotion and to be the object of jealousy between R[itchie] and Elizabeth Bowen.[25] Ritchie, then visiting Bowen's Court, was possessively and curiously—given that he had never expressed a strong wish to marry Bowen—worried about the possibility of Bowen marrying Sackville-West. "I should know what she knew when I married [...] it would be justice all right [...] I don't think he intends to [...] the ground cracks under me."[26] But Bowen, he said, had reassured him, "she could not give him up, and, could not marry Eddy." Were they play-acting?

In 1958, his affections wavering, Ritchie wrote in his journal that when he visited with Bowen in New York there was still much talk of Sackville-West: "E begins to fear that I resent this and was at pains to prove that he was 'only a friend.'"[27] Sackville-West's declining health is frequently mentioned in this period, as well as Bowen's preoccupation with her dwindling finances. Overwrought, she shared little information with family or friends about the demise and sale of Bowen's Court, including Sackville-West, to his dismay. Before her decision to sell, something happened between them, according to a friend, Norah Preece: one or the other of them had proposed marriage, and this had embarrassed them both, realizing its folly even though he had earlier proposed the same to the Countess De La Watt and Betty Fletcher Mossop.[28] On the positive side, however, Bowen and Sackville-West could have pooled financial resources to save Bowen's Court; on the negative, Bowen was still obsessed with Ritchie, and Sackville-West's frail health would have cast Bowen into the unfamiliar and unwanted role of a caretaker. Having decided on the sale of Bowen's Court, she went off to Rome, distracted and in nervous collapse, and did not even contact Sackville-West for 20 months. When he observed Bowen's Court "locked and barred"—she had sold it without telling him—he naturally "took umbrage," according to Ritchie. Sackville-West wrote to Mortimer: "I can't tell what her state of mind may be. It seems agreed that she looks much older; otherwise, there is no agreement about anything connected with her."[29] Their friendship did resume in the 1960s, and despite his asthma and other illnesses, he continued to enjoy his social life. But in July 1965, Bowen was taken aback when informed of his death by his sister Diana. Bowen had planned to stay with him a few days later. "The poor dear innocent creature," she remarked; "he wanted to live, so much."[30]

Ritchie, during this period, was away with his wife in New York, and also engaged in an affair with M, an unidentified woman—according to Victoria Glendinning and Judith Robertson—whom he had known in Paris and met again in New York around 1957–58. He wrote in a fragmentary journal entry of his feelings of distance from Bowen, and questioned whether his affair was "disloyalty" to her, not mentioning his wife, leading us to wonder about Ritchie's editing of his journals after Bowen's death.[31]

American Colleges

After her husband's death in 1952, Bowen was drawn to America where "any sensation of being at all myself, is suspended." With all the stimulation, she felt as though she were continuously at a movie and away from reminders of Alan's death and her lonely state. She stayed with a succession of people—the Collins', the Knopfs, the Blacks who offered her the quiet she needed to finish her novel, *The Little Girls*. She was welcomed and also lectured widely, having achieved celebrity with the Literary Guild selection of *The Heat of the Day*, building a readership larger than the one in England or Ireland. Despite her faltering relationship with Ritchie, their rendezvous continued during the decade. Knopf, her American publisher, kept her books in print. She used an agency, noting that lecturing novelists in America were "6 a penny." Bowen welcomed their haggling for her honoraria and creating her itinerary, but noted that they did charge 30 percent for the service.[32] Bowen, nevertheless, welcomed meeting Eudora Welty who flew up to Chicago in December 1951, and they had a fine time at the Drake Hotel and exploring different restaurants.

Her literary reputation was soaring. She was working hard and she wrote to Plomer that she was personally "enjoying the epoch—it is really the first one it seems to me, in which I feel 'grown-up'—as much as I expected to do when I was a child. The only sad thing is that owing to the necessity to work so hard, I have ceased to be able to write letters."[33] Indeed, her fullest letter-writing period was the 1930s; the 1940s were consumed with the war, and the 1950s with lecturing, success, and popularity. In 1948, she received the British award of excellence, the CBE, for her contributions to the arts; in 1949, she was awarded honorary doctorates in literature from Trinity College, Dublin, and in 1952, the University of Oxford. She worked tirelessly, exhibiting her enormous energy and received the coveted Lucy Martin Donnelly Fellowship at Bryn Mawr, and accepted it in 1956. It entailed few formal academic duties.

Bowen also formed a lasting relationship with the University of Wisconsin through repeated visits. She was introduced to the teeming university and pretty town in 1952, and though working harder than usual at teaching, she managed to have time to continue writing *The Little Girls*. She earned the devotion of the good-humored and clever students at the university and returned again to teach in 1958, re-experiencing the Midwest's "immense remoteness in space" and "blend of extreme friendliness and total incuriousity."[34] It suited her.

Two years later, in spring 1960, Bowen was again to take up residence at a college, Vassar, but having just emerged from the depressed period of the sale of Bowen's Court, she was not looking forward to it. She wrote to Ritchie, "heaven, between ourselves, I am terrified of Vassar," and looked to the residency with "alarm and despondency."[35] Nevertheless, she taught freshman English, "The Art of Reading and Writing," and a successful course in the short story, one that Ritchie later gave himself, reading O'Henry and Poe and Chekov. In this course she spoke of "the drama of sound" intrinsic to the human voice and the way in which dialogue in fiction distinguishes one character from another. Yet she also informed her students that not all dialogue is verbal, asserting that "there is a touch of the sphinx in many human beings, and this 'sphinx' quality is one which—quite often—the [short story] legitimately exploits." There is dialogue, she said, but it may be unspoken—a sentiment shared by many modernists.[36] From afar, Ritchie painted a portrait of Bowen as "a potent witch" at Vassar in winning the adulation of the girls, wishing that his niece, Elizabeth Ritchie, could connect with her. He imagined a "frieze of young creatures drifting across the campus, the girls going to collect their letters like going to collect eggs on the farm … the whole place threaded with stories."[37] In early 1960, Bowen was still writing to Ritchie, but the letters were hurried and uninformative, about people and events in her life, not full of affection and ideas as in the past. Despite geographical distance and her agony, their intermittent meetings continued.

In addition to writing *A Time in Rome* and popular articles such as "How to Be Yourself But Not Eccentric" and "The Case for Summer Romance," she completed *A World of Love* in 1955, and began *The Little Girls*. The writing of *The World of Love* spanned Cameron's illness and death, and reawakened her desire to marry Ritchie now that she was alone. In the novel Lilia talks openly to her husband, Fred, of her past love for another man who has been a shadowy "third" in their relationship. Overcast, "the chestnut, darkening to summer canopied them over; over their heads were its expired candles of blossom, brown—desiccated stamens were in the dust."[38] The passage exudes the sense of an ending, a dying, and canopies over Bowen's faltering relationship with Ritchie, another "third."

There were friends and relatives who thought that Bowen was having a breakdown on her feet during this period of frenzied travel. Laetitia Lefroy, her cousin, said that family and friends did not hear from her for many months and feared she was ill. Overwrought, she ran off to New York in 1958 for eight months, leaving Bowen's Court in the trust of a caretaker. Uncharacteristically, she left bills unpaid, for which her niece Audrey and Sackville-West assumed responsibility, to her later distress. She thought of selling the land surrounding Bowen's Court, reducing the size of the house and living in it, or calling upon her heir, Charles Bowen in Nyasaland, to take over the estate, but nothing came of it. Ritchie, feeling guilty about Bowen's Court, wrote in his journal, "How I wish she could bring off some fortunate coup, if they would make a hugely successful plan and movie out one of her books, if she could come into money in a big way. But Billy Buchan, typically is the first to put it to me in words, 'she isn't a very fashionable writer just now.' I can see why she isn't in the taste of the times, the more so because she was so very much in the taste of twenty years ago."[39] Ritchie joined her at Bowen's Court for a week before he assumed the presidency of the Security Council of the UN in May 1957; she was convinced he would make history. Two months later, back in Cork, she was in a frantic state, selling silver and pieces of jewelry to ease her financial crises. The rental of the grazing land and cottages for five pounds per year could hardly cover her expenses.

In June 1958, when she visited Ritchie in New York, there were tense scenes and he sought to avoid her. Five months later, Ritchie did, however, slip away to meet her, but noted her decline. She looked "feverish" and "her cheerfulness doesn't seem solid."[40] A year later he wrote in his journal that he looked back with horror upon the spring months in 1959, in which "he saw her from the outside for the first time in 20 years" and doubted their relationship.[41] What did he see? Bowen, then 60, run down, homeless, still hopelessly in love with him and crazed by his diminished feeling for her. In this depressed state, she nevertheless wrote admiringly: "you have so much more fibre and self-command than I have—indeed than most people have. You see, along with the effective, operative side of yourself, you carry the burden of an imaginative nature—for it is a burden, as well as a gift, the equivalent of genius."[42] Ritchie had an "angelic calm" throughout these turbulent periods, according to Bowen.

At the same time, Ritchie wrote in his journal in 1958 that Bowen herself was behaving in a more distant manner. But she tried to insinuate herself further into Ritchie's life visiting Canada and meeting with his mother, his younger brother and his wife, and their daughter. Ritchie was always close to his niece, Elizabeth, and Bowen, fond of her also, thought her beautiful. At other times, Bowen would socialize with the distinguished Lester (Mike) Pearson, Ritchie's colleague in Canadian diplomacy, who later became prime minister of Canada. If she could not see Ritchie, she would find comfort in seeing his relatives, and she pointedly reminded him how well she got along with them. In 1959, she confessed, "I sometimes wonder whether even you, knowing me as well as you do, really realize my horror of my state as a *femme seule* [legal definition] … I am slightly independent in my mind, that is my intellectual part—but quite outstandingly the reverse in disposition."[43] But Ritchie did not share her strong feelings and desires.

She had expressed her insatiable longing years earlier, terrified that "loneliness becoming a sort of dementia, equivalent to a breakdown, sending me battering round and round the rooms of this house, knocking myself against the furniture—like some unfortunate bird that has gone indoors … and proceeded to entirely lose its head."[44] But visiting Ritchie in New York in November 1961, reanimated her feeling, and she wrote of an evening with him on the town dancing at El Morocco. But Ritchie, at the time, was wavering again in his feelings and wrote dismissively about her in his journal, as well as his life with Sylvia: "what do I care that the new sitting room rug is the wrong color." He was then involved with another girlfriend, "D" who, he said, would rescue him. And there was another girlfriend, Ann Maher. He mused, "I wonder if E knew [about his affairs with other women] whether she would help me to someone else—find me a girl." Referring to Jean-Paul Sartre and Simone de Beauvoir's "arrangements," he remarked, "Do you know I believe if she knew, she would. Provided it was the girl of her choice."[45] Ritchie liked and charmed women and shared Bowen's social and sensuous nature. Bowen never read the diary entries revealing Ritchie's paramours in *The Siren Years: A Canadian Diplomat Abroad, 1937–1945*, published after her death. It is likely, however, that she knew.

In March 1962, Ritchie began to feel that Bowen herself was getting bored with their relationship and was reconciled to his departures. Yet "she moves me … such tangled feeling. Mostly when I think of her I feel an immense sadness."[46] Bowen though was still faithful in feeling. Living in White Lodge, Oxford, she wrote two months later that his life "is the only thing that interests me, rivets me, obsesses me."[47] It was her "relentless will," as Ritchie termed it, that prevailed, and he felt uncomfortable with her increasing loneliness and the pressure it put upon him.

Hardening

During Bowen's difficult years of recovering, writing, and traveling, her friends observed that her personality hardened. She mentioned to Ritchie that she was becoming more "recalcitrant" as she got older. For years, she said, she had accommodated herself to people as "sort of a Jew," but had now become more uncooperative, like her father.[48] In the late 1960s, Bruce Arnold observed her "very strong determined deep voice, and very outspoken views." Though admirable, he said, she was also somewhat "formidable."[49]

After Cameron's death, staying with friends allayed her loneliness. Three months after Alan's death, she spent time with Helen Arbuthnot, a friend of Beatrice Curtis—the sister of her literary agent—in London. After the first winter of lecturing in America, she stayed with Catherine and Allen Collins at Hunts House, Hopewell, New Jersey, and Alfred and Blanche Knopf in Purchase, NY, in the spring. Still she traveled around Italy and Spain, and plagued by feelings of vacancy and melancholy, she confided to Leslie Hartley in April that she wept on a bridge in Valencia. She lectured for the British Council and kept up her high pace, lecturing at Morley College in November 1954 and at a grammar school for boys in December. She continued to travel to Oxford to visit Berlin and Bowra, though in 1954, they had little time for her because of their demanding careers, unlike their early days together in the 1930s. She felt the difference.

Bowen lived like a snail, she said, and carried her literary and romantic worlds with her. There are critics who cast a dark eye on her "dislocations," yet she and her writing seemed to thrive on movement. Her early life was peripatetic, and as an adult, she traveled to Oxford, London, Rome, Paris, New York; small college towns in America; Hungary, Czechoslovakia, and Austria in 1950s and 1960s; as well as the big houses of friends. Her pleasure in country house visiting—often remarked upon in her letters—located her in both the Anglo-Irish tradition and the movement of modernity. Her writing table was mobile and she relished writing under other people's roofs: she wrote to Derek Hill that she enjoyed writing *The Little Girls* in his house in Donegal in 1962, "in a place one's happy in under a friend's roof"[50]; and proofs of that novel while staying with David Cecil in Dorset in 1963; and part of *A World of Love* under the Collinses' roof—Alan Collins, then president of Curtis Brown—Hunt's House in Hopewell, N.J. She preferred staying with aristocratic or wealthy families with lovely homes and estates in later years. In October 1954 she visited Jean and Barry Black, who had bought Creagh Castle in County Cork, where her friend Dorothy Bucknall had also lived, whose house may have also been the model for Mount Morris in *The Heat of the Day*. Jean Black was one of her closest friends in later years, and Bowen yearned to be rich enough to purchase such a place herself. She traveled with the Blacks to Madrid in October 1954 and described it "like going around Spain with the Marx brothers."[51] She noted the city's "Franco-Fascist atmosphere," which assaulted the senses. She also particularly enjoyed the hospitality of the Vernons in County Limerick, particularly Lady Ursula, a close friend who looked like Garbo and whose husband was bisexual. After Ursula's death, she often visited Stephen Vernon, who was paralyzed by polio, and always a generous host who entertained lavishly. After the war, these couples had fled the deprivations of postwar London and Atlee's high taxes to seek big houses in Ireland purchased for a song. They not only offered Bowen hospitality but also came to her rescue, as wealthier Anglo-Irish families often did, to help with expenses of Bowen's Court in the late 1950s before she sold it.

Derek Hill: Landscapes

Derek Hill, the landscape and portrait painter, was another late life friend, and Bowen initially met him in Cyril Connolly's *Horizon* circles. She felt an immediate affinity with his art, his Anthony Powell social set, and his beautiful house. Always responsive to other people's houses, she particularly enjoyed visiting "Circe-like" St. Colomb's in Donegal, Ireland: "It's got such a feeling about it—I'll never forget the beautiful glitter of the lake from between the trees coming into the rooms. But also you've interpreted it, and added to it, quite magically."[52] Hill was then a painter coming into his own, and Bowen had sent him to Bowen's Court to capture it in a portrait after its sale in 1959. In August 1960, she wrote to Hill: "I can't tell you how I long for that painting of Bowen's Court by you. Nothing could more prolong for me the life of the house. Dear Derek, you must not let the painting be a complete present."[53]

She encouraged Hill to stay with Sackville-West at Coleville while painting, and before he began she framed the view of the house and landscape for Hill in a sketch, revealing again her astonishing visual memory. She advised him that Bowen's Court always looked loveliest in September or October and "from up the field, one gets the best idea of the setting of the house (the hills behind, etc.)."[54] When he arrived, the roof was off Bowen's Court, but he would paint it on to spare her the pain of seeing her house in ruins. Bowen herself prolonged the life of the house not only in her family history, *Bowen's Court*, but also in three of her novels, acknowledging "it is part of the character of Bowen's Court to be, in sometimes its silent way, very much alive."[55] In gratitude to Hill, Bowen dedicated her 1962 collection of essays, *Afterthoughts,* to him. Bruce Arnold views Hill's painting of Bowen's Court as a visual lament having "a ghostly duality in which the hill, exaggerated in height and dark with threat, overshadows more than the empty house: a way of life, a departed family, a whole class."[56]

But Hill also brought her feelings and thoughts about the Anglo-Irish into relief. She started visiting him in Donegal more frequently after Cameron's death, sometimes with Sackville-West or Jean Black, when she was somewhat bereft. She was a devoted friend, and she wrote appreciatively to Hill in later years about the pleasure of being in his house and writing.

Bowen looked at his paintings with an artist's eye, particularly admiring the light in his Donegal and, later, his Tory Island landscapes, where he temporarily lived an isolated life in a small hut, off the southwest coast. Bowen described him as a "magnificent" painter, and in 1950, attended one of his few shows in London, as well as viewing his paintings in his Donegal home. She bought two of his earliest, *Boreen at Glenveigh* and *of Donegal Glen*, and after his show at the Leicester Galleries, one of Rome, a city that both she and Hill loved and where he lived for several years before moving to Ireland. She also owned his painting of *Bowen's Court*. Bowen's estimation of Hill was confirmed when his home in Donegal became a museum for his own paintings as well as his collection of paintings.[illus.]. He was a "vociferous conversationalist, fluent, elegant and perceptive," and enjoyed Bowen's visits and conversation.[57] But friendships were not enough to allay the increasing vacancy that Bowen felt.

Notes

1. EB to CR, December 2, 1959, *LCW*, 350.
2. Ibid., December 8, 1959, 351.
3. Ibid., November 11, 1959, 347.
4. *Siren Years*, June 12, 1942, 108.
5. EB to WP, September 24, 1945, DUR 19.

6. EB to CR, August 24, 1945, *LCW*, 56–57.

7. Ibid.

8. EB to DH, October 10, 1952, PRONI D4400/C/2/27.

9. EB to MS, October 6, 1952, NYPL, MSS Sarton.

10. EB to HH, September 16, 1952, HHC.

11. EB to DH, October 10, 1952, PRONI D4400/C/2/27.

12. CR journal, July 3, 1958, *LCW*, 312.

13. EB to WP, September 9, 1952, DUR 19.

14. *PC*, 262–265, 28, 24.

15. Ibid., 262–265.

16. Ibid., 28.

17. Glendinning, *Elizabeth Bowen*, 24.

18. Leslie Hartley to EB, April 3, 1955, HRC 11.5.

19. De-la-Noy, 282.

20. EB to CR, March 28, 1956, *LCW*, 228.

21. Ibid., February 29, 1956, 221.

22. Ibid., May 25, 1956, 236.

23. Ibid., May 11, 1956, 231.

24. Bowen, "Look at All Those Roses," *CS*, 515.

25. Eddy Sackville-West, diary, June 1956, in De-la-Noy, 281.

26. CR journal, September 17, 1957, *LCW*, 284.

27. Ibid., May 6, 1956, 229.

28. Glendinning, *Elizabeth Bowen*, 233.

29. De-la-Noy, 299.

30. EB to CR, July 18, 1965, *LCW*, 442.

31. CR journal, October 21, 1957, *LCW*, 286–287, and editorial comments.

32. EB to C.V. Wedgwood, April 10, 1932, BOD MS. C6289–41.

33. EB to WP, May 6, 1958, DUR 19.

34. EB to CR, University of Wisconsin, March 3, 10, and 18, 1958, *LCW*, 298–304.

35. EB to CR, June 12, 1956, *LCW*, 237–238.

36. Bowen, "Notes on the Short Story."

37. CR journal, April 22, 1960, *LCW*, 336.

38. *WL*, 125.

39. Ibid., February 4, 1960, 355.

40. Ibid., November 14, 1958, 318.

41. Ibid., June 11, 1960, 367.

42. EB to CR, January 29, 1958, *LCW*, 296.

43. Ibid., December 2, 1959, 350.

44. Ibid., December 30, 1957, 293–294.

45. CR journal, November 28, 1961, *LCW*, 374.

46. Ibid., March 27, 1962, 383.

47. EB to CR, May 7, 1962, *LCW*, 387.

48. EB to CR, May 8, 1956, *LCW*, 230.
49. Arnold interview.
50. EB to DH, September 1, 1962, PRONI D4400/C/2/27.
51. EB to CR, October 6, 1954, *LCW*, 194.
52. EB to DH, September 22, 1955, PRONI D4400/C/2/27.
53. Ibid., August 20, 1960, PRONI D4400/C/2/27.
54. Ibid.
55. *BC*, 459.
56. Arnold interview.
57. Arnold, *Derek Hill*, 250.

11

A Frightened Heart (1960–1973)

Emptiness

Standing on the Palatine, one of the Seven Hills of Rome that looks down upon the Forum and the Circus Maximus, Bowen wrote that it taught what "emptiness" can be. "Life has run out completely: it is alone there. Those existences, artificial as fireworks, died out on the forgetful dark."[1] The historical city reflected her emotional state: Rome was in ruins, and her dream of Bowen's Court with its promise to someday shelter her and Ritchie was ended. When Bowen's Court was demolished in 1960, Bowen suffered, hearing people say, "So, we hear you have had to sell your Irish castle." Though Bowen said it was "a clean end," as it was "better gone than having it degraded," the emotional reverberations of the sale haunted her until her death in 1973.[2]

Her travel book, *A Time in Rome*, unearths her love and continuing interest in the city, its myths, monuments, ruins, and sites. She wrote to Ritchie in 1958:

> I worked intensively at my Rome book. I'm reading a tremendous amount of Roman history, which does fascinate me: one book after another I can't put down […] why I ever read anything but Ancient history, I can't think. I think its slightly abstract quality (due to distance of time) plus the almost utter absence of personality–interest which I like so much.[3]

But the city also emotionally threatened with its solidity and permanence. "My object," she said of her trips in the late 1950s, "was to walk[…] [the city] into my head and (this time) keep it there."[4] Her sensuous temperament took in the massive ruins, the hard-edged shapes, as well as the touch, smell, and

© The Author(s), under exclusive license to Springer Nature Switzerland AG 2021
P. Laurence, *Elizabeth Bowen*, Literary Lives, https://doi.org/10.1007/978-3-030-71360-7_11

even "the tastes of different dusts." Yet during her stay, after the sale of Bowen's Court, her vulnerable emotional state erupted. Her sense of loss confirms Proust's insight that there are places "whose personality is so strong that some people die from them."[5] In October 1947, Bowen reflected this sense writing to Ritchie that she felt that every time she had to shut up the house and leave for London, something died in her. And cleaving to a word that reoccurs in her vocabulary, she noted that "she became a degree less *virtuous*."[6] When in Rome, Bowen experienced a breakdown. Zigzagging in wrong directions on Roman streets was a symptom, she reflected, of "inner trouble." Juxtaposed throughout her book on the city are the substantiality of Rome and her own feelings of dispossession: "when it comes to knowing, the senses are more honest than the intelligence. Nothing is more real than the first wall you lean up against sobbing with exhaustion."

In debt to the Romans for the concept of "home," Bowen praised their "domus-enshrined tradition [that] subordinated egotism and bred virtues which extended their value outside its walls" in her travel book. "It was the private source of the public character, educated, temperate, disciplined." The city echoes her own dispossession from Bowen's Court, and she recalls Cicero when in exile, pleading for the restoration of his home: "Leave it that to be dispossessed is horrible. To the banished races this was already known."[7] She leaves Rome, but "only from the train as it moved out of Rome" did she look, "backs of houses I have not ever seen before wavered into mists, stinging my eyes." Then the stunning cry that recalls her relationship with Ritchie: "My darling, my dealing, my darling. Here we have no abiding city." Her cry reverberates in the story, "Mysterious Kor," in which lovers displaced by the ruins of war, embattled, are unable to find a place to harbor their love. Though *A Time in Rome* begins with intriguing descriptions of the city, it ends with the mortal uncertainties of St. Paul that she soon faced.

The opening of the decade brought auguries of illness. When she returned to London from Italy, homeless, she found a temporary apartment in Stratford-on-Avon, and finished some commissioned jobs to make money so that she could get back to writing. Friends who visited described her as "frail but enchanting." She returned to stay with London friends, first Helen Arbuthnot's garden apartment, then, Rachel Ryan's home. About six months later, she was ill with a *coup de foudre*, as she said: another attack of pneumonia. This was part of a pattern of respiratory illness in her life that smoking abetted, and that doctors had warned her about since the 1930s.

Back to Oxford

In October 1960, she decided to set up house in Oxford, where she had friends, and planned for the decoration of a flat that she rented from Berlin in Old Headington. She moved in March 1961, and though the new house was small, it had the atmosphere of Bowen's Court: she decorated in a certain style and moved in furniture that reminded her of the past, said Jessica Rathdonnell. She liked the place, and in 1961 invited L.P. Hartley, a critic and friend, noting that it was really a portion of a large house with countless small staircases, a house in which one would not suffer from "claustrophobia or aggravated hostess-consciousness as one is liable to do staying with anybody in a flat."[8] She described the surroundings, large trees and lawn-like gardens, and it was, coincidentally, across from Waldencote, where she and Cameron had lived early in their marriage. Her friendship with Hartley began in 1929 during her years in Oxford and continued intermittently throughout her life. They shared an interest in reviewing, respect for each other's writing, and a love of Italy, where their paths crossed in the late twenties and early thirties in Venice. Politically, Hartley belonged to the conservative Asquith set often in conflict with the reform-minded liberal prime minister, Lloyd George. Consequently, he was snubbed by the politically liberal Bloomsbury group that Bowen enjoyed, at times, because of her friendship with Woolf, her connection with Harold Nicolson, and her reviews for the liberal *New Statesman*, for which Leonard Woolf also wrote.

Hartley became a frequent reviewer in the 1920s, and praised Bowen's first novel, *The Hotel*, in *The Spectator*. In 1955, he lauded her poetic novel *A World of Love*, writing, "whenever you write you add something to the field of fiction and a new perception of beauty. No one else does."[9] She also wrote several reviews praising Hartley's books, particularly *The Go-Between*, which gained him public recognition and was made into a successful film by Harold Pinter in 1971. Her reviews of his work were sharp and sincerely meant, unlike many others that she wrote that were encouraging but uncritical.[10] Her letters to him include more literary commentary than those to others. He was particularly appreciative of her critical observations of the macabre character of Hilda in his novel *Eustace and Hilda* before its publication in 1947. He wrote that not only was he pleased with her understanding of his character but that he, not having yet received full recognition for his novels, carried her letter about "like a talisman equally sovereign in mood of depression or exaltation. Everything you said delighted and uplifted me. I feel no one can ever have had a letter which was such a pure joy to receive."[11] The 1930s was a decade in which Bowen put talent and interest into her letters to others. After Cameron's death she openly confided her sense of vacancy to Hartley, he being one of her few friends who had appreciated Cameron.

Bowen was also drawn to the writing of Anthony Powell, becoming friends with him and his Anglo-Irish wife, Violet, when they moved to Regent's Park. She was interested in Violet, who had written a book she admired and reviewed, *The Irish Cousins*, about the kinship and the writing of Somerville and Ross, among her favorite authors. Powell said he was in the awkward position with her of recognizing that her books had considerable merit, but as a reviewer he found them extraordinarily tough to read. He was not alone in this difficulty. Bowen did, however, review three Powell novels, including *Venusberg*, and two novels from his later sequence, *A Dance to the Music of Time*, in 1952. She noted the change in his angle and manner from the 1930s novel to the later ones and admired the way in which he brought the past back. And with her visual acuteness, she noted his almost painted effect in his writings. *Dance to the Music of Time* was among the last volumes she read when ill in Hythe at the end of her life.

Bowen's life at White Lodge was low-key. She was writing her last novel, *Eva Trout*, and her cousin, Jessica Rathdonnell, was there to help with the typing. She remarked on Bowen's discipline, up early each morning to write. Bowen once explained her writing habits in an interview with the journalist, Raymond Bennett: arising early every morning to write, she explained that she carried the outline for a short story or a novel in her head, then wrote a dossier on each character, notes on home background, income, education and interests, and then went straight to the typewriter. She made three to five drafts of a work on average. Jessica Rathdonnell sketched Bowen then as a "tall, large woman, her hair pulled back, cigarette always in hand, and who put you at ease."[12] Importantly, said Jessica, she was loyal to her family that had taken charge of her after her mother's death. At that time, Bowen spent much time with her cousin, Veronica Colley, an unassuming companion who also loved literature, wrote stories, and worked at a local library in Buckinghamshire: both "bereft," according to Laetitia Lefroy, Veronica's daughter. Bowen was adrift without a stable home, struggling still with finances and not seeing much of Ritchie.

The Cost of Letters

Bowen was of the first generation of women writers to attempt to earn a living through writing. Throughout her life, she embraced popular culture not only because of her interest in a wider audience and new media but also because she needed money. In 1936, *The House in Paris* was chosen for the American Book of the Month Club, and she wrote to Humphry House that it brought in £1100, welcome because she had an appalling number of bills. She mentioned in the same letter that this had happened once before with her first novel, *The Hotel*, published in 1927, when she made "really pots of money over that" and did repairs at Bowen's Court.[13] And then *The Heat of the Day*, published in 1949, sold very well. The *Times*, wrote Rose Macaulay, "tells me it's going like hot cakes; so does Daniel George [her Cape editor]—And in America too; how lovely that an exquisite piece of work should be a hot cake too."[14]

Though partially supported by her husband before his death in 1952, she still had to earn money as there were more bills during the war, higher Irish taxes on Bowen's Court, and a need for cash to pay for war damages to her Regent's Park townhouse in 1944. She wrote to the Westminster Bank in Harpenden, telling them that Curtis Brown, her agent, would give them "a formal guarantee on the strength of £100 which I am to receive from Messrs. Jonathan Cape on the delivery of the final short story of a Collection […]. I ask this as I am anxious to settle a claim for £46 for Irish income tax and to pay out about £30 for expenses to do with repairs to this house. As you know, no compensation for war damage is to be settled in cash until after the war."[15] In 1946–1947, one-fourth of her income came from *Tatler* reviews: £525 out of her total earnings of £2164.[16] But, admittedly, she led a certain lifestyle, and in 1946 confessed after visiting the sumptuous apartment of Lord Gerald Berner, a wealthy and eccentric composer, "If you ask me, I hold that money can buy almost everything that is worth having."[17] Bowen loved to entertain generously and liked buying fine clothes, and so when asked how much income would need annually in a 1945 *Horizon* survey of writers, she replied £3500, compared to Plomer's and most other authors modest reply, £1100.[18]

In 1953, after Cameron's death, she wrote about reluctantly rejecting a remunerative *Holiday* magazine assignment on Princess Margaret's involvement with Peter Townsend as a matter of taste. Six years later, faced with the crisis of having to sell Bowen's Court, and having lost her husband's pension, she panicked and sold valuables and asked Ritchie if she could borrow £100. Fatigued with trying to finish *A Time in Rome*, she again noted financial strain. In 1959, she reported that her bank account was in an unhealthy state and the Vernons and the Blacks, close Irish friends, gave her a loan. Having to earn money interfered in her literary productivity and she agreed in 1962 to lecture at the University of Wisconsin for several months earning the handsome sum of $10,000. She said she would rather have spent the time finishing *The Little Girls*.

In the 1960s, after the sale of the house, she continued to write articles for *Holiday*, *Vogue*, and *Women's Day*, among others, alongside her stories and novels. Her agents at Curtis Brown aggressively marketed her writing, and the voluminous files document their efforts on her behalf. Spenser Curtis Brown urged chasing down the money, "Elizabeth is, as always, overdrawn and would therefore like you to collect the money [for *Eva Trout* rights] as soon as you can."[19] The files are replete with friendly and flattering memos from him, Allen Collins, and Emilie Jacobson to Bowen, editors, and publishers who pitched her stories to better-paying magazines: *The New Yorker*, *The Saturday Evening Post*, *Ladies Home Journal*, and *Vogue*. Bowen's versatility and range emerge in the popular articles she wrote over the decade, "How to Be Yourself but not Eccentric" and "Enemies of Charm" for *Vogue*; "The Beauty of Being Your Age" for *Harper's Bazaar*; "Mirrors are Magic" for *House & Garden*; "The Case for Summer Romance" for *Glamour*; "Elizabeth Bowen Talks about Writing" for *Mademoiselle*; "Whatever Became of Flirting" for *McCall's*; and "A Profile of Rome" for *The New York Times*. She would often earn $500 for an article in a women's magazine. There were print sales of short stories and fees for extracts, quotations, translations, and attempts at serialization during the time she was writing that paid well—*The Little Girls* and *Eva Trout*. A realization of the dramatic possibilities and screen-worthiness of Bowen's stories and novels also began to take off: lucrative options were offered for dramatic adaptations of *The Heat of the Day* and *The Death of the Heart*, and motion picture and television rights for *The House in Paris* by the producers, E. Mawby Green and Edward Allen Feibert who had unsuccessfully produced a dramatic version on Broadway in 1940. Drama and film options potentially paid $1000 a year and $20,000 purchase price. But though she earned some money, many of these projects did not come to fruition.

What also begins to filter into the Curtis Brown letters and memos toward the end of the 1960s is that Bowen's style is changing and going out of fashion. One editor wrote that though *Eva Trout* is impressive, it begins to seem too subtle or mannered for the women's magazine audience. When one of her most supportive agents, Emilie Jacobson, sent Bowen's autobiographical fragments for publication to her friend, William Maxwell at the *New Yorker*, he found her writing uneven and not of the moment. He "loved her books and loved her" but her gift was faltering.[20]

Disillusionment and fears about the future revealed a new vulnerability in Bowen but she was quick to develop a carapace, and increasingly relied on friends who invited her to stay in their homes for longer periods of time.

The Little Girls

She, nevertheless, finished *The Little Girls* in 1964, a novel shadowed by her childhood towns of Hythe and Folkstone. Its original title, *Race with Time*, reflects Bowen—now 65—circling around the topics of aging, memory, and past and present time. In the novel, three women in their fifties return to a place where they were schoolgirls and lived intensely in a conspiratorial friendship. Bowen investigates whether the return to childhood places as well as the objects and things of childhood can revive friendships and memory in adulthood. Critics praised the novel's sense of nostalgia—wrongly, according to Bowen; comedy, she asserted, is its core, a strain that continues into *Eva Trout*. She confessed to Ritchie that she often tied herself into knots over her writing, trying to conceal how "unguardedly silly" she was, but was casting off the mask in this novel.[21] Her publisher, Cape, found her tone and the ending of the novel, which she originally conceived of as a musical finale, problematic. She consulted with Plomer about revisions and was glad to receive his letter of advice about revision.

Bowen is drawn to the stories of female pre-adolescents and adolescents. She inhabits their sense of anger or dislocation caused by a mother or father's death that entails their being sent to a relative's home; those who have a touch of the demonic or "madness" or those who like to write diaries or letters that disrupt the hypocritical households they enter as in *The Little Girls*; She wrote of an unhappy orphans like Portia in *The Death of the Heart* who is sent to her half-brother's unwelcoming bourgeois home; or perky, rootless Henrietta in *The House in Paris* who feels as if she had been dropped down an emotional well on her way to her grandmother's; or aloof Theodora who is angry with hypocritical adults in *Friends and Relations*; or abandoned Eva Trout who is willfully destructive and angry with her narcissistic and neglectful father. And this leads to the conspiratorial secrets that young girls share with one another in *The Little Girls*.

This leads to little girls who conspiratorially entrust secrets to one another. Girls meet in the novel, *The Little Girls,* as grown-ups to reanimate their childhood memories and bonds. Recalling their secret world, they return to a particular location to find a coffer that they buried in the earth for posterity. They travel to their school, St. Agatha's, near a site with "a crooked swing," to unearth it, but time has passed, and when they find it, it is empty. They turn to the present and scrutinize what they have become as adult women. The most Proustian of Bowen's novels, the "voluntary" search for a memory through an object from the past summons a passage in Proust:

And so it is with our own past. It is a labour in vain to attempt to recapture it: all the efforts of our intellect must prove futile. The past is hidden somewhere outside the realm, beyond the reach of intellect, in some material object (in the sensation which that material object will give us) of which we have no inkling. And it depends on chance whether or not we come upon this object before we ourselves must die.[22]

The women's search for the coffer is "a labor in vain," as the material object that will summon memory is unknown. A "crooked swing" involuntarily sparks the past for Dinah as she prepares objects in a cave for someone to come upon in the future. Early in the novel *The Little Girls*, Dinah as an adult, in discussion with her friend, Frank, notes why she collects "things." They are, she says, "clues to reconstruct us from. Expressive objects. What really expresses people? The things—I'm sure—that they have obsessions about."[23] Dinah explains the sensory experience of the past that an object can arouse:

I've been having the most extraordinary sensation! Yes, and I still am, it's still going on! Because to remember something, all in a flash, so completely that it's not "then" but "now," surely is a sensation, isn't it. I do know it's far, far more than a mere memory! One's right back again into it, right in the middle. It's happening round one. Not only that but it never has not been happening.[24]

Dinah here offers a fair paraphrase of Proust's notion of how involuntary memory returns when an everyday sensation in the present triggers the taste of a madeleine or the memory of a swing. Dinah here blurs the distinction between time past and present: time past is always embodied in the present, and awareness of its reoccurrence creates a third time, that of realization. This is what Bowen in another context terms, "the enforced return."

In other stories about little girls, Bowen illuminates the defenses of adolescents who articulate or write in letters or diaries what they feel. Roger in "The Visitor" waits at his aunt Emery's house while his mother is dying: "here he was alone *enisled* with tragedy." Did Bowen's experience of being "next door" when her mother was dying in Hythe contribute to the feeling of the story? Her knack for an apt and unusual word choice, "enisled," to capture the boy's feeling of being stranded arrests our attention.[25] The boy in the story implores no one, but whispers "Let it not have to be," becoming hysterical in anticipation of his mother's death. When finally told of the death, he enters an emotionally surreal "blue empty space."

The notion of betrayal and abandonment of children by mothers—sometimes, voluntary and, sometimes, by death—is the nerve center of several of her works. In *The House in Paris*, the all-consuming Mme Fisher manipulates and betrays her daughter, Naomi, in regard to her fiancée, Max, with whom she, herself, is obsessed. Her maternal image hovers darkly not only over her daughter but shadows the young girls in her pension, the visiting Henrietta, and it haunts Max. Her three short taps on the ceiling for attention when bedridden has traces of a gothic presence. Another mother in the novel, Leopold's birth mother, Karen, promises to visit but never arrives. His young friend Henrietta, also motherless, witnesses his disappointment and hears him sobbing and reflects, "you only weep like that when a room hears." Bowen evokes vivid feelings when mothers menace or are absent in the lives of their children. This is reflected in the emotional barrenness of characters such as the young girl in "Coming Home," who returns to an empty house after school. The hollowness also figures in her motherless character Eva Trout, who experiences abandonment by her father: Eva is unable to receive love when it comes to her through her sympathetic teacher, and driven by blind needs, neglects her own son.

At other times, little girls are just oppositional toward the adult world. Bowen presents not only girls who are angry—colloquially, "mad"—but adolescent girls who conspire against and are "perverse" toward grown-ups. In "Charity," Rachel and Charity try to escape the adults around them by finding secret places to which they can retreat:

> They sat on the window-sill outside, told each other stories and listened to the rooks going to bed [...]. The happiness that she had been waiting for all day seemed to have something to do with the light behind the trees, the rooks, and the dry chintzy smell of the curtains when she leant back her head against them into the room. Also, there is something very heroic about dangling one's legs at a height.[26]

"The Jungle" is another story of an intense and secret relationship between adolescent girls. Their affection develops when they are away at a boarding school, where they discover life in "an absolutely neglected and wild place," physically and morally outside the school grounds and rules. Rachel desperately desires to share this secret place with her best friend, Elise.[27] When Rachel first enters this place, she "felt a funny lurch in her imagination as she entered [...] everything in it tumbled together, then shook apart again, a little altered in their relations to each other, a little changed." She longs to link arms with the elusive Elise, whose hair is cut short like a boy's and possesses a "quick, definite," and easy physicality. She wants to show her the secret place. Not a little girl anymore, Rachel is drawn to Elise's body, observing that Elise looks "just like a compact boy in tights." The sensuously described garden and jungle where they play is a setting for adolescent infatuation:

> It was early October, the day smelt of potting-sheds and scaly wet tree trunks. They had woken to find a mist like a sea round the house; now that was being drawn up and the sun came wavering through it. The white garden-gate was pale gold and the leave of the "hedges" twinkled. The mist was still clinging in sticky shreds, cobwebs, to the box-hedges, the yellow leaves on the espaliers, the lolling staggering clumps of Michaelmas daisies; like shreds of rag, Rachel thought, clinging to brambles.

Sexuality surfaces in this description but is accompanied by cold feelings of death. Rachel imagines finding in this lush jungle a "dead body, a girl's arm coming out of the bushes"; she also fears that she has committed the murder herself. This severed arm appearing in a bad dream at the beginning of the story turns out to be the real-life arm of the sleeping Elise. Rachel transforms the dream of death and awakens the sleeping girl to sexuality. It reveals both the sense of conspiracy and intimacy in girls' friendships, and their emerging female sexual identity and longings.[28]

Moving to Hythe

But there was always a place for Ritchie, even in her new home in Hythe. When visiting in September 1963 with Noreen, she bought, on impulse, a modest red brick house on Church Hill facing St. Leonard's Church (Figs. 11.1 and 11.2). The hill was steep with a footpath up to the house; from the back, it looked over Romney Marsh. She named it "Carbury" (later changed to "Carbery") after the demolished family estate of her mother's forebears in County Kildare. The cost, £4700, was more than covered by the sale of some of her papers to the Ransom Center at the University of Texas at Austin.[29] Work on the house began in January 1965, and in March of the same year, she wrote that she was glad to leave Oxford and move to Carbery. Visitors were welcome and stayed in town enjoying hospitality at the White Hart Hotel on High Street, run by Bowen's accommodating friend, Edna Strawson.

That summer, Bowen traveled again to a city she loved, New York, and painted a word picture: "August in NY is rather fascinating: a sort of miasma

Fig. 11.1   Carbery, Bowen's last home in Hythe, England. Rights holder and Courtesy of Sue Kewer

of heat and emptiness. Long stretching avenues really almost literally empty, pallid in the hazed over sun. And mile-long empty untrodden corridors even in the Plaza Hotel. New York should be painted now."[30] She was already working on a new play and a novel, *Eva Trout*.

The *Nativity Play*: Finding Common Ground

After the publication of *The Little Girls*, Bowen became engaged in a new venture, a collaborative project with Derek Hill to address the divisions in Irish society. In an ecumenical spirit, they produced *A Nativity Play* during a period of violent conflict between the Irish and the Black and Tans. Hill created the theatrical design and Bowen, the script, and it was first performed in a

Fig. 11.2   St. Leonard's Church. Rights holder and Courtesy of P. Laurence

Catholic church in Limerick in 1964. Another performance occurred at Christmas time in 1970 in a Protestant cathedral in Derry. Bowen considered it a great success because the Pope had lifted the ban against Roman Catholics entering Protestant churches, and people of different faiths attended. Another timely presentation of the play occurred in Londonderry Cathedral after Bloody Sunday in January 1972, the pivotal event at which 26 unarmed civilians were shot by British soldiers during a protest march in Derry, Northern Ireland. Many Anglicans and Catholics attended the sad but hopeful event that Bowen and Hill created in an attempt to find common social and religious ground. The play, when presented in the Londonderry Cathedral, was "almost certainly the last ecumenical event held in the cathedral" said Hill, "as the Troubles had already begun." The *Londonderry Sentinel*, in reviewing the Derry performance, noted that 1000 people attended, and it was the first time the cathedral had been used for an interdenominational purpose.[31] In this performance Jean Black, Bowen's friend, and Hill were the narrators. It might seem surprising for the Anglo-Irish Bowen to pen such a play to be performed in Derry where violence erupted daily, but her participation reveals her evolving commitment to the traditions of conciliation through religion. The *Nativity Play* uncovered her little-noted ability to write an accessible dramatic pageant that emphasizes the human element in religion. Bowen structures the pageant around three themes, the Annunciation, the responses of the three Kings, and the Adoration of the Shepherds and the Magi at the birth of Jesus. Interweaving traditional carols such as "Adeste Fideles" with both poetic and everyday language, Bowen writes in Act II, of "The Annunciation," "Young girls, friends of Mary, enter her chambers wondering where she has gone. One tampers with Mary's weaving; another places anemones in a water pot asking, "What is it that sets her apart?/From you and me."[32] In Act III, a shepherd waits for his fellows to come back from their flocks, and the narrator announces, "silence/Silence, As though the Earth were holding her breath." Later, the angel's prophecy is fulfilled: the babe is born to Mary in a stable in Bethlehem and visitors arrive to worship. Three children arrive bearing gifts of smooth multicolored pebbles, Bowen's poignant touch. One brings a shell, another a mouse, and the last one, nothing, as his father is a beggar. The play was an ecumenical and political venture for Bowen as she collaborated with Hill in a creative project to reconcile cultural divisions in Irish life that were exploding into violence around her.

Hill also evoked other aspects of Bowen's Anglo-Irish identity. Years earlier, she had squabbled with him about his insulting descriptions of the Anglo-Irish in his 1946 "Letter from Ireland," appearing in Connolly's *Horizon*. Attempting to define what he labeled "the class," Hill made sweeping assertions about "an old-world squirearchy now dying off," and about some Anglican references to Roman Catholicism as "'the religion below stairs,' whilst others still refuse to employ a Catholic interior staff," which, he said, "shows how isolated, and exceptional they have remained."[33] The Anglo-Irish, he said, represented "a more British than the British 'county' outlook," stereotyping their interest in hunting foxes rather than the pursuit of literary interests, which he stated had not flowered since the eighteenth century. He parodied the Anglo-Irish habits of wearing faded brocades, felt hats, and regimental brooches. Bowen attacked his description as "presumptuous" in *Horizon* and asserted her authority as an Anglo-Irish person by heredity, family relationships, and loyalty. Her tone was sharp: "The Anglo-Irish are a study in themselves, and you haven't had time to get round to them. I should think: they take up a lot of time and you're here in Ireland to paint; so what you say seems much less perceptive, more superficial and less near the mark than anything else you say. Also it is most awfully rude."[34] Hill prefigures Declan Kiberd's criticism of the "performance" of the gentry. Despite the ambivalence she felt, Bowen justified her Anglo-Irish culture, and though *Reports from Eire* offers a culturally ambivalent view, her family history, *Bowen's Court,* conveys her love of Ireland and the traditions of the Bowens the exploitation of land and labor upheld by Protestant nationalism. In *The Shelborne Hotel,* she again aestheticizes elite Ascendancy traditions in presenting its social history, a hotel that Isaiah Berlin stayed in en route to visiting Bowen. He observed its charm: "the people in the Smoking room of this hotel, with & without mad eyes or whiskers c[oul]d all occur in Turgenev short stories."[35] All of this attests to the complexity of Bowen's identity and the many strands in Anglo-Irish experience.

Bowen, proud of aspects of her culture, resented Hill's attack, and asserted Anglo-Irish contributions to Irish literature when she attended a West Sussex art festival event in December 1970. Though trumpeted as a nonpolitical event for "eccentrics," this festival was a celebration of nineteenth-century Anglo-Irish literature and a masquerade for a disappearing culture. Lady Birley hosted the discussion of Irish art and poetry, "The Long Table Irish Talk," inviting Bowen, Edith Somerville, and Violet Martin, authors of *The Real Charlotte,* and Connolly to give talks, along with other notables such as Raymond Mortimer and Maurice Collins. Hill also invited Bruce Arnold, who became his biographer. Arnold remembered his impression of Bowen at this event, somewhat formidable and opinionated in these last years of her life, but nevertheless "an elegant, elderly lady dressed in a summer frock, her shoulders slightly stooped, her eyes clear and bright, she watched everyone and seemed pleased as she recognized old friends."[36] In her talk, Bowen spoke of her own generation of writers and its struggle to find new forms of expression and noted her admiration for O'Faolain as "the most complete and abiding example Ireland has of the man of letters."[37] She added, seeking common ground and breaking the mood of Anglo-Irish homage, that O'Faolain was the son of an Irish constable and a devout Catholic mother. At the same event, Arnold observed that Bowen and Connolly were of the same Anglo-Irish class, altered by time and circumstance, and they knew each other well. They were neighbors, not only in sharing an Irish past but both having houses in Hythe after 1965. But Arnold also observed that Connolly, educated at Eton and Oxford and living in England, had erased most traces of Irishness, "appearing" English. Nevertheless, to Connolly's credit, his 1942 Irish issue of *Horizon* sought balance: to give a picture of contemporary Eire as seen by Irish writers living under the restrictions of neutrality. In his "Comment" on the issue, Connolly accepts the Irish suspicion of Britain and its bitterness about the ports that the British wanted to take back for defense. "No one could read any Anglo-Irish history without being convinced of the Irish case … our record in Ireland is one of seven centuries of cruelty, injustice, intolerance and exploitation."[38] "Our record" reveals Connolly's identification with the English. He bridled at the varieties of anti-British feeling in Ireland and supported those willing to take the risk and die in the war, not those who have "kept their calendar at 1938," alluding to Ireland's stance of neutrality. The *Horizon* issue is devoted to propaganda for the Irish, where he identifies Irish talent, beleaguered and isolated during neutrality. And despite cultural sparring with Patrick Kavanaugh in the same issue, he published part of Kavanaugh's neglected long poem, "The Great Hunger," bringing attention to Irish woe and the deprivations of the country; O'Faolain's "Yeats and the Younger Generation"; and Frank O'Connor's "The Future of Irish Literature."

Eva Trout

In 1966, Bowen's bouts of bronchitis were seriously beginning again and they interrupted work on her novel *Eva Trout*, as she related in letters to Veronica Wedgwood. She had two cases of the flu that winter, yet carried on with her story of a bold, alarming, and independent-minded woman. This novel reflects a marked change in Bowen's view of the world and narrative style. Set in the postwar years, *Eva Trout* reeks of abandonment, homelessness, and inhumanity, a climate generated by World War II and the Vietnam War. She is a monstrous character who verges on the grotesque and the comic, and veers into a realm of ugliness that does not appear in Bowen's earlier novels. Eva, having suffered the loss of her mother as a child, lives an estranged life under the shadow of her father's consuming passion for his lover, Constantine. "Displaced persons" whose lives and language are fractured raise her, influencing the development of her strange speech pattern. She is blighted by homelessness, always an important theme in Bowen, and remains itinerant throughout the novel, living an alienated life in an abandoned castle with a dying friend with whom she has a fragile lesbian relationship, and, later moving to a bombed-out house, symbol of the destruction and emptiness of her life. Yet she is consumed with longing for a home. "In some other life, Eva had been shown a knocked about doll house (had it not stood on a verandah somewhere?) and knelt down to look deeply into its dramatic rooms. She desired it."[39] And though welcomed into the home of her beloved teacher Mrs. Arable, she perversely sets out to destroy it. She is a shape-shifter and evokes horror as she lures her teacher's husband into a sexual liaison that destroys all their relationships. She is ruthless as she moves through others' lives and homes, shattering them with "the patient, abiding, encircling will of a monster." She lies to Mrs. Arable about being pregnant and bizarrely runs off to buy an American baby, who turns out to be a deaf-mute. She lives a lavish material life, finds romance, and is accidentally killed by her son.

And though Eva's body, like her character, is misshapen and evokes repulsion, the paradox is that she also excites fascination. She is a new subject for

Bowen, an independent woman who boldly lives her own life and openly seeks sexual relationships, but also seems, at times, to be a parody of a woman gone amok with liberation. Eva moves straight ahead through "changing scenes" (the book's subtitle) in a destructive whirl set during the women's movement. With her fractured language, outlandish behavior, and outsized body, Eva is a caricature bordering on the grotesque and humorous. Iris Murdoch responded to the macabre aspects of the novel upon publication: "What a splendid and delicious novel … I believed Eva so absolutely and cd [sic] have enjoyed going on and on, anywhere in her company! And the funny parts were so funny (the lunch, that school)."[40] Murdoch reveled in and shared Bowen's interest in absurdity and erotic adventure, a mixture found, for example, in her own novel *The Severed Head.*

Eva Trout is a novel of its time, revealing the toll the Vietnam war, the women's movements, and changing times exacted on people's minds and bodies. The novel's plot and style are more tortuous than those of her earlier novels, reflecting the turbulence of the 1960s and marking a shift in Bowen's sensibility and writing to a more menacing, violent, inarticulate, and ugly world. After Eva flees the Arables, she finds a house of her own, Cathay, in North Foreland, that has, like her life, been partially destroyed by a bomb, imaging the novel's traces of the effects of war. Houses, Bowen's continuing preoccupation in this novel, are often windowless, shuttered, sightless, and silent; people are disembodied, shadowed, submerged, and occult. And time, "inside Eva's mind, lay about like various pieces of a fragmented picture."[41] Her adopted deaf-mute son seems like a character who has wandered in from a Beckett play; however, Bowen had observed deafness in her Uncle George who lived nearby in Dublin, and was close to her in her childhood. Both characters expose language as ineffectual or manqué, traces of modernism, reflecting Bowen's loss of trust in words in her later years. The story "Look at All Those Roses," written a few years later, creates the same frightening atmosphere as in *Eva Trout*, in a house where an absent father has mysteriously injured a daughter who becomes an invalid. Like Eva, the damaged girl is "the core and nerve of the house" and exposes the hidden injuries of a father, a dysfunctional family, and a culture.[42] Eudora Welty and William Maxwell discussing this story puzzled over what the father had done to the girl's back— "did he do it while he was drunk?"—and was he buried under the rosebush? Welty concluded that he probably dropped the girl and was buried under the bush.[43]

John Bayley thought that the novel was a response to war: "Now, one feels the War is all." He sees that the loving relationship between Eva and her friend Elsinore when young, "their ambiance, so marvelously conveyed, turn[s] everything into a nightmare (in a sense) because nightmare is all there is. Other responses to the War reveal this absence of any alternative because the waif plays with matches not in a house but in a petrol dump." What he finds so intriguing, as had Murdoch, his wife, is the mixture of comedy and tears in the novel, but what is most stimulating to him is the "modernity: the sense of burning one's fingers with the present moment."[44] The novel won the James Tait Black Memorial Prize in 1969, one of the oldest prizes in England, and was shortlisted for the Booker Prize in 1970.

Bowen was venturing in new directions in this novel with a character longing for a home but destructive of it. It links her to other writers: Murdoch, for example, with her mixture of melodrama, humor, and grimness in a novel such as *The Bell*, and also a writer such as Ian McEwan in his alarming novel *Saturday*. A link among them can be found in Bowen's atmosphere of domestic terror not only in *Eva Trout* but in "The Move-In," the first chapter of an unfinished novel that she was writing at the end of her life.[45] This opening chapter generates again the menace of domestic crime and violence with the arrival of a group of young strangers at an isolated house inhabited by elderly people. The young punks prepare to invade the house. The violation of a home's safe space elicits the fear and terror of strangers committing crimes and causing havoc. Similarly, in Ian McEwan's *Saturday*, thugs enter the house of a distinguished neurosurgeon to terrorize his family during a politically troubled time after 9/11 and the impending war in Iraq. Bowen's theme of domestic terror rebounds from the horrors of the Vietnam War and reverberates in *Eva Trout*, but is also prescient of the domestic and global terror of today.

Bowen was also racing at this time to finish *Pictures and Conversations*, an autobiographical collage that she was developing with her agent, Curtis Brown, and hoping to complete by February 1971. She wrote at that time to Plomer of "the return of the wretched bronchitis," but she was resilient.[46] After publishing *Eva Trout*, her health failing, Bowen took up her last residency at Princeton University in September 1969, earning $6000 for the course. She met with student unrest and anti-Vietnam War protests, and her ire was piqued by what she termed the "hysterical Moratoriums" on the campus. She considered them "idiotic." Conservative and out of touch with the political energy in America, she sided with Nixon's silent majority in support of the war; she also was detached from the 1960s politics of Oxford's New Left.[47]

Bowen was at Princeton to teach creative writing for a term, September to December 1969, and she was inspirational, as always, with students. Sensitive to her surroundings, she described the campus, the curious physical atmosphere of Princeton: part suburban; part "coloured quarter" with gaily painted balconied houses with gardens; part decaying patches; and a distance away, the wealthy part, all sweeps and lawns. She described the eight undergraduates assigned to do advanced work with her "as mild as gazelles; and long may they remain so." One of them, Thomas Hyde, distinguished himself by becoming her protégé in the years after she left Princeton. She not only furthered his application to New College, one of the oldest in Oxford, but invited him to visit her at Hythe and at the Vernons' estate in Kinsale, despite her failing health.

About six months after her return to England in 1970, Bowen wrote to Plomer about "Poor Princeton": "To tell you the truth. I don't care two hoots about the Vietnamese, Northern or Southern: what I can't stand is that America should suffer. What I do feel is that these insane protests and demonstrations can only be doing more harm than good."[48] Showing her Tory colors, she revealed that she was cheered by the election of the Conservatives in England, having always admired Edward Heath: "the idea (up to last June) of a possible further five years of that dreary Labour government had become a nightmare." A few years earlier, she had also alluded to politics in America when John Kennedy beat the more traditional Henry Cabot Lodge in the senate race.[49] She again flaunted her conservative politics, siding with the Lodge dynasty, and felt "a curious sensation to have our lives gambled with by President Kennedy," who became part of the botched Bay of Pigs invasion of Cuba.

Illness

After her brave jaunt to Princeton in the spring of 1970, Bowen's acute bronchitis returned, as it would at increasingly short intervals. She spent time at the Vernons' home in September. Writing regularly to Veronica Wedgwood during this period, she related that she went to a nursing home for pneumonia in January 1971. But the next year was a busy one, attesting to her will to go on. In February she was at the Bear Hotel in Woodstock, an elegant thirteenth-century inn near Blenheim, to get away from the damp sea fog of Hythe that irritated her lungs. It was a hotel believed to be haunted, according to local legend, a feature that would have pleased Bowen. She also was receiving radium treatments at University College Hospital, London, and was yet determined to publish *Pictures and Conversations* before the end of the year. In the same year, from her theater of her bed, she was reading Pushkin and Iris Murdoch, and judging a Booker prize with Cyril Connolly and George Steiner. Bowen defied the observation of the feminist critic Carolyn Heilbrun that there is little overt triumph in the last years of a woman's life.[50] Molly Keane, one of her favorite Irish friends, captured their last meeting in a restaurant the year before Bowen died. Keane observed that men turned their heads when Bowen entered a room, as she had a striking presence and certain quality of "enchantment." On this occasion she wore a stiff white silk Viennese coat and talked about buying wigs. "She never dwindled," Keane said. "I wish Elizabeth were here."[51]

In 1955, after attending a Church of Ireland family funeral, Bowen was depressed, and ironically observed that Roman Catholic funerals were much gayer. Confirming her life-enhancing spirit, she announced to her Aunt Edie that she would like her own funeral to be "more like a wedding. I'd like to be followed to my grave by a string of beautiful girls carrying roses, each attended by a charming and ardent lover." She should hate, she added, "to be seen off by people who looked like hell and depressed each other."[52] In February 1973, Bowen was back in Hythe, and after a last visit to the site of Bowen's Court with a busload of nuns and acolytes, she entered the hospital again with pneumonia and a foot injury that never healed. Here she was surrounded by her closest companions: Audrey Fiennes, her favorite cousin; Isaiah Berlin and Cyril Connolly, longtime friends; Veronica Wedgwood and Ursula Vernon, close friends in later life; and Rosamond Lehmann, who was with her a great deal in her last years. The day after Bowen's death, Eudora Welty wrote to William Maxwell that she had meant to write not knowing Bowen was so ill, yet admiring always, and remembering "a grand time" they had a few years back on New Year's.

In these last weeks, Bowen lost her stutter and then, completely, her voice. Charles Ritchie spent the last two weeks of her life with her, visiting the hospital daily. He remembered, as Bowen did, the brilliant roses in Regent's Park that drew them together the day they met in 1941.[53] That garden, he said, "with its burning gaiety, stayed in both their minds like an apparition" that she later transformed into fiction. "'Hundreds of standard roses bloomed,' she would write in one of the wondrous word pictures in her story, 'over-charged with colour, as though this were their one hour. Crimson, coral, blue-pink, lemon and cold white, they disturbed with fragrance the dead air.'"[54] Ritchie re-experienced the garden through her sensibility as he had daily life through her imagination. One day Ritchie arrived at the hospital and uncorked a bottle of champagne with his usual élan, and they drank their last glass together.

After her death on February 22, 1973, her body was transported from University Hospital in London to Ireland for burial. Farahy locals went up to Cork airport to meet her coffin. In a final will, Bowen had written that she wanted to be buried in the Farahy churchyard. Eudora Welty observed that "her heart turned straight back to Ireland in this last year" and related Audrey Fiennes' [Bowen's cousin] description of the funeral: "It was beautiful and moving—the country people came in crowds with flowers—they looked—Audrey's word, "dedicated"—Charles was with her up to the last."[55] In a BBC 1999 Centennial Program, Fiona Shaw described again the funeral procession: "as her body came into Cork, the local people joined the funeral cortege holding scarce winter blossoms: snow was falling, and it was by torchlight that they brought the coffin up to the lonely Farahy churchyard, where her father, Henry Cole Bowen, and her husband, Alan Cameron, were buried."[56] The snow and the churchyard, evocative of one of Bowen's favorite passages in literature, was heard "falling faintly through the universe and faintly falling, like the descent of their last end, upon all the living and the dead."[57]

Post Script

When the issue of establishing a memorial to Bowen was discussed three years after her death, the reservoir of feeling in Eire about her espionage activities in Ireland at the beginning of the war, as well as the social position of her Anglo-Irish family, erupted again. In May 1976, the Reverend Robert Brian MacCarthy proposed the transfer of Farahy Church to commemorate the life and work of Elizabeth Bowen. He followed this with an appeal to Bowen's friend, Derek Hill, to help with the rescue of the church, as well as enlisting others to help financially in the preservation of the modest church that Bowen usually attended when at Bowen's Court. "I was horrified to find holes in the roof, window panes broken and a general air of post-atomic bomb about the place."[58] Would there be about 50 people, he queried, who would be prepared to subscribe to the project at £25 each? The initial absence of support for the project was glaring: from Bowen's family executor, Gilbert Butler, the bishop of Cork, Cork citizens, and the "trendy" Arts Council (which eventually donated). Gilbert Butler was in conflict with Hubert Butler and the preservation committee, which staunchly supported the proposal, and the diocese had complications about transferring the ownership of the unused church. According to Reverend MacCarthy, Gilbert protested MacCarthy's daring to erect a memorial plaque in the church with "Mrs. Cameron" inscribed on it when they had just "had an official biography done" of Bowen. (Presumably, he had commissioned Victoria Glendinning's biography.)[59] Reverend MacCarthy defended his passionate effort to save the church, as it was "the last physical reminder of the Bowens in Ireland" and Bowen's writings and the plaque was respectful of "its character as a place of worship, that being the role in which it occupies an important place in Bowen's writing."[60] His request to the diocesan secretary in Cork included the promise "that the church should be left very much as it is since it positively exudes that austere quality of Irish Anglicanism that Elizabeth Bowen has so well conveyed in Bowen's Court," and the altar a memorial to Bowen's mother and her uncle who died on the Titanic. But money was needed to repair holes in the roof and to prepare the vestry for assemblage photos, along with the use of Hill's painting *Bowen's Court*, then owned by the Colley family at Mill House, Dublin. Reverend MacCarthy reported on the progress of repairs on the site in 1978, finding "the one remaining protestant farmer engaged in mending the holes in the church roof," and he enlisted others to work for little or nothing. There were those who supported the project in a letter to the *Times*: Spencer Curtis Brown, Rosamond Lehmann, and Raymond Mortimer. But the *Irish Times* literary editor, Terence de Vere White, thinking the project impractical and Bowen, no moral model, warned that "hers is hardly a name that will draw many pilgrims."[61] MacCarthy noted that he was waiting for Hill's promised £300 contribution, and others: Ritchie, £100 plus an earlier gift; the Esme Mitchell Trust in Belfast, £500; the Arts Council, £100 (one-third of what was initially committed); and contributions from Southern Tourism, Georgian Society members, and friends such as the Blacks and the Vernons. The church was financially preserved, mainly by Bowen's friends in Anglo-Irish circles. MacCarthy concluded in a letter to Hill that the collection of funds for such a modest memorial "in any environment other than that of Southern Ireland … would be likely to present no insuperable obstacles." He implied to Hill," knowing the scene as you do," that he understood the hostility toward the Bowens, symbolic of Anglo-Irish exploitation in Ireland, and Bowen, the literary daughter, who, from their perspective, took sides against the Irish, investigating their "neutrality."[62] He also wryly added, "Heaven preserve us from the Protestant death-wish," implying that Gilbert Butler's resistance to this kind of memorial for Bowen would have ensured the disappearance of the memory of her and her ancestors in Farahy. MacCarthy, no stranger to controversy even in his opinions on the church in Ireland today, prevailed with the Preservation Committee and those who sustain it, Jane and Patrick Annesley. On October 18, 1979, in the repaired St. Colman's Church, a Bowen memorial plaque was unveiled by Gilbert Butler, along with memorial photos of Bowen's Court in the vestry (Fig. 11.3).

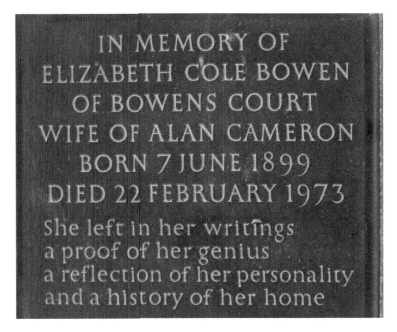

Fig. 11.3 St. Colman's Church, Farahy. Rights holder and Courtesy of P. Laurence

Bowen, one imagines, would have appreciated this memorial in her beloved Church, but would turn a gimlet eye upon the moniker, "wife of Alan Cameron," and the limited description of her writing. She would have understood much, though said little, about the people and the history surrounding this modest memorial, given her own "cloven-heart," split always among Irish, English, and European loves and loyalties.

Notes

1. *TR*, 64.
2. CR journal, October 20, 1970, *LCW*, 465.
3. EB to CR, Jan. 29, 1958. *LCW* 196.
4. *TR*, 4ff.
5. *Jean Santeuil*, 534.
6. EB to CR, October 26, 1947. *LCW*, 109–110.
7. *TR*, 74ff, 64.
8. EB to L.P. Hartley, June 7, 1961, JRUL, MS Letters.
9. L.P. Hartley to EB, April 3, 1955, HRC 11.5.
10. Fuller discussion of reviews in Hepburn, introduction, *WWF*, xv–xxxii.
11. L.P. Hartley to EB, August 12, 1935, HRC 11.5.

12. Jessica Rathdonnell, interview by PL, Dublin, June 2011.
13. EB to HH, May 28, 1936, HHC.
14. RM to EB, February 22, 1949. HRC 11.6.
15. EB to Westminster Bank, Harpenden, November 6, 1944, HRC 10.5.
16. Reported in *WWF*, xix (based on HRC 12.5–6).
17. EB to CR, November 6, 1946, *LCW*, 99.
18. Alexander, *William Plomer*, 265.
19. Curtis Brown Files, Folder 1.
20. Curtis Brown files, folder 1 and 2.
21. EB to CR, January 19, 1962, *LCW*, 382.
22. Proust, *Swann's Way*, 59–60.
23. *LG*, 10, 20, 130.
24. Ibid., 20, 130.
25. Audrey Fiennes reported that Bowen often used difficult words as a child.
26. Bowen, "Charity," *CS*, 195.
27. *CS*, 231, 234, 232.
28. See Renee C. Hoogland, "Technologies of Female Adolescence."
29. Editors' footnote, EB to CR, August 12, 1964, *LCW*, 425.
30. EB to DH, August 8, 1965, JRUL, MS Letters.
31. *Londonderry Sentinel*, January 13, 1971.
32. Bowen, *Nativity Play*, 130, 143.
33. Hill, "Letter from Ireland," 270.
34. Arnold, *Derek Hill*, 263.
35. IB to Cressida Bonham Carter, August 28, 1938, Berlin, *Flourishing*, 278.
36. Arnold, *Derek Hill*, 271.
37. Arnold, *Derek Hill*, 275ff., and Arnold interview.
38. Connolly, "Comment."
39. *ET*, 80, 95.
40. Iris Murdoch to EB, n.d. (ca. 1968), HRC 11.6.
41. *ET*, 80, 42.
42. Bowen, "Look at All Those Roses," *CS*, 515.
43. Welty, *What There is to Say....*, April 12, 1983.
44. John Bayley to EB, n.d., HRC 10.6.
45. Bowen, "The Move-In," *PC*, 67–76.
46. EB to WP, September 1, 1970, DUR 19.
47. EB to CR, September 22, 1969, *LCW*, 459.
48. EB to WP, September 1, 1970, DUR 19.
49. EB to C.V. Wedgwood, December 17, 1959, BOD, MS. C6289-41.
50. Carolyn Heilbrun, *The Last Gift of Time*.
51. Molly Keane, "Life with the Lid Off," September 28, 1989, panel, NSA.
52. EB to CR, September 1, 1955, *LCW*, 214.
53. CR journal, August 13, 1973, *LCW*, 472.
54. Bowen, "Look at All Those Roses," *CS*, 514.

55. Welty to William Maxwell, …., April 16, 1973, 302.
56. Fiona Shaw, "Sunday Feature: Radio 3," 1999 Commemoration of Bowen's Centennial, NSA.
57. Joyce, "The Dead," *Dubliners*, 124.
58. R.B. MacCarthy, letter to DH, August 22, 1975, PRONI D/4400/C/2/28.
59. Ibid., July 16, 1979.
60. Ibid., letter to the diocesan secretary, May 12, 1976.
61. Terence de Vere White to R. B. MacCarthy, November 19, 1975, PRONI D/6600/C/2/28.
62. R. B. MacCarthy to DH, July 16, 1979, PRONI D/4400/C/C/2/28.

Abbreviations

Abbreviations for Libraries and Collections[1]

BNA   British National Archives, Kew, London.

BOD   Oxford University, Bodleian Library, Oxford, England.

DUR   Durham University Library, Durham, England, William Plomer Collection.

HHC   Humphry House Collection. With permission of the Literary Estate of Humphry House, London.

HL   Huntington Library, Pasadena, CA. Papers of Elizabeth Bowen.

HRC   Harry Ransom Center, University of Texas at Austin, Elizabeth Bowen Collection: Correspondence (Incoming, Outgoing), Vertical File.

JRUL   John Rylands University Library, University of Manchester, Manchester, England, L.P. Hartley Collection.

KC   King's College Library, Cambridge University, Cambridge, England, Rosamond Nina Lehmann Collection.

LSU   Louisiana State University Archives, at the Mississippi Department of Archives and History, Jackson, Mississippi, Eudora Welty Papers.

NSA   National Sound Archives, BBC recordings, British Library, London.

NYPL   New York Public Library, Berg Collection, New York.

PRONI   Public Record Office of Northern Ireland, Belfast, Ireland, Derek Hill Collection.

SC   Smith College, Northampton, MA, Sophia Smith Collection, Mortimer Rare Book Room, Neilson Library.

SU   Sussex University Library, Sussex, England, Monk's House Papers of Virginia Woolf.

TC   Trinity College Library, Dublin, Ireland, Manuscript Division.

UCC   University College Cork Library, Cork, Ireland, Special Collections.

© The Author(s), under exclusive license to Springer Nature Switzerland AG 2021
P. Laurence, *Elizabeth Bowen*, Literary Lives, https://doi.org/10.1007/978-3-030-71360-7

Abbreviations for Names

CR   Charles Ritchie
DH   Derek Hill
EB   Elizabeth Bowen
EW   Eudora Welty
GR   Goronwy Rees
HH   Humphrey House
IB   Isaiah Berlin
MS   Manuscript
OM   Ottoline Morrell
PL   Patricia Laurence
RL   Rosamond Lehmann
SOF   Sean O'Faolain
SS   Stephen Spender
VW   Virginia Woolf
WP   William Plomer

Note

1. Abbreviations for frequently cited works by Bowen and secondary sources precede their entries in the bibliography.

Bibliography

Works by Elizabeth Bowen

"The Achievement of Virginia Woolf: Review of *The Writer's Diary*." *New York Times Book Review*, June 26, 1949, 1.

"The Artist in Society: Elizabeth Bowen, Graham Greene, V.S. Pritchett." July 8, 1948, NSA.

"Autobiograhical Note" for *Everywoman*. HRC 1.5, 2.

BC: Bowen's Court. New York: Ecco Press, 1979.

Castle Anna, 1948, unpublished.

CI: Collected Impressions. New York: Knopf, 1950.

CJ: The Cat Jumps and Other Stories. 1934. Reprint, London: Jonathan Cape, 1967.

CS: The Collected Stories of Elizabeth Bowen. Introduction by Angus Wilson. New York: Barnes and Noble, 1981.

"Coming to London." *MT*, 85–90.

"The Culture of Nostalgia." In Hepburn, ed., *Listening In*, 97–102.

"Daughters of Erin—Radio Review." BBC, *The World of Books*, M44 9R CI I. NSA, 1965.

"Dead Mabelle." *CS*, 276–85.

DH: The Death of the Heart. 1938. Reprint, New York: Anchor, 2000.

DL: The Demon Lover and Other Stories. New York: Chatto and Windus, 1945.

"Disloyalties." *MT*, 60–62.

ES: Early Stories: Encounters and Ann Lee's. New York: Knopf, 1951.

"*The Echoing Grove*—Review." *SW*, 218–22.

"Eire" *New Statesman and the Nation*, April 12, 1941, 382–83.

Elizabeth Bowen: More of Her Espionage Reports from Ireland to Winston Churchill. Cork, Ireland: Aubane Historical Society, 2009.

© The Author(s), under exclusive license to Springer Nature Switzerland AG 2021
P. Laurence, *Elizabeth Bowen*, Literary Lives, https://doi.org/10.1007/978-3-030-71360-7

"Enchanted Centenary of the Brothers Grimm." *New York Times Magazine*, September 8, 1963.

English Novelists. Britain in Pictures Series. 1942. Reprint, London: Collins, 1947.

ET: Eva Trout; or, Changing Scenes. 1968. Reprint, New York: Anchor, 2003.

FBMS: The Faber Book of Modern Stories. (Ed.) London: Faber and Faber, 1937.

FR: Friends and Relations. 1931. Reprint, New York: Penguin, 1986.

"Frankly Speaking." BBC with John Bowen, H.A.L. Craig, and W.N. Ewer. NSA, March 16, 1960.

The Good Tiger. New York: Knopf, 1965.

HD: The Heat of the Day. New York: Knopf, 1949.

The Hotel. 1927. Reprint, London: Penguin, 1943.

HP: The House in Paris. 1935. Reprint, Intro A.S. Byatt. New York: Anchor, 2002.

IGS: Ivy Gripped the Steps and Other Stories. New York: Knopf, 1946.

"Joyce, James. A Review." *The Bell*, 1.6, March 1941, 40–49. National Library of Ireland.

LG: The Little Girls. 1964. Reprint, New York: Anchor, 2004.

LS: The Last September. 1929. Reprint, New York: Anchor, 2000.

"Mainie Jellett." *PPT*, 115–20.

"Miss Bowen on Bowen." *New York Times Book Review*, March 5, 1949.

MT: The Mulberry Tree: Writings of Elizabeth Bowen, ed. Hermione Lee. New York: Harcourt, Brace Jovanovich, 1987.

Nativity Play. *PC*, 111–66.

"The 1938 Academy: An Unprofessional View." *PPT*, 28–31.

Notes on Eire: Espionage Reports to Winston Churchill, 1940–42. Ed. Brendan Clifford and Jack Lane. 3rd ed. Cork, Ireland: Aubane Historical Society, 1999.

"Notes on Writing a Novel." *PC*, 167–92.

"Notes on the Short Story," Vassar Course. MS HRC 7.3.

"Out of a Book." *MT*, 48–53.

"Paris Peace Conference: 1946—An Impression," "Some Impressions 1, 2, 3." *PPT*, 66–80.

PC: Pictures and Conversations. Foreword by Spencer Curtis Brown. New York: Knopf, 1975.

"The Poetic Element." 1950. MS HRC 7.3.

Preface to *Critics Who Have Influenced Taste*, *PPT*, 329–35.

Preface to *The Haven: Short Stories, Poems, and Aphorisms*, by Elizabeth Bibesco, 7–12. London: J. Barrie, 1951.

"Ray Strachey's *Our Freedom and Its Results*—Review." *New Statesman* (London), October 31, 1936.

"Regent's Park and St. John's Wood." In *Flower of Cities: A Book of London*, 149–58. London: Max Parrish, 1949. "A Ride South." *SW*, 165–88.

"The Roving Eye: The Search for a Story to Tell." *New York Times Book Review*, December 14, 1952.

"She Gave Him." In *Consequences: A Complete Story in the Manner of the Old Parlour Game*, by A.E. Coppard, Sean O'Faolin, et al. Beaconsfield, UK: Golden Cockerel Press, 1932.

The Shelbourne Hotel. New York: Knopf, 1951.

SIW: Elizabeth Bowen's Selected Irish Writings, ed. Eibhear Walshe. Cork, Ireland: Cork University Press, 2011, 77–98.

"Story of a Story." *Seashore* (Summer 1948): 1–3.

SW: Seven Winters and Afterthought: Pieces about Writing. London: Longmans, 1962.

"Telling." In *The Black Cap: New Stories of Murder and Mystery*, ed. Cynthia Asquith, 250. New York: Charles Scribner's Sons, 1928.

TR: A Time in Rome. New York: Knopf, 1960.

TST: These Simple Things: Some Small Joys Rediscovered. (Editor.) New York: Simon and Schuster, 1962.

TTN: To the North. 1932. Reprint, New York: Avon, 1979.

"The Unromantic Princess." In *The Princess Elizabeth Gift Book: In Aid of the Princess Elizabeth of York Hospital for Children*, ed. Cynthia Asquith, 83–99. London: Hodder and Stoughton, 1935.

"We Write Novels: An Interview with Walter Allen." *WWF*, 24–29.

"Women's Place in the Affairs of Men." *PPT*, 377–79.

WL: A World of Love. 1955. Reprint, New York: Avon, 1978.

Secondary Sources

Alexander, Peter. *William Plomer: A Biography*. Oxford: Oxford University Press, 1989.

Alexander, S. "A New Civilization? London Surveyed, 1928–1940s." *History Workshop* 64, no. 1 (2007): 297–320.

Alexandrian, Sarane. *Surrealist Art*. London: Thames and Hudson, 1970.

Andrew, Christopher. *Defend the Realm: The Authorized History of M15*. New York: Knopf, 2010.

Arnold, Bruce. "Bruce Arnold's People." *Sunday Press* (Dublin), July 4, 1971.

———. *Derek Hill*. London: Quartet Books, 2010.

———. *Mainie Jellett and the Modern Movement in Ireland*. New Haven: Yale University Press, 1992.

Avery, Gillian. *Oxford Dictionary of National Biography*, s.v. "Willis, Olive Margaret (1877–1964), a Headmistress." Oxford: Oxford University Press, 2004.

Bakhtin, M. M. "Discourse in the Novel." In *The Dialogic Imagination: Four Essays*, ed. Michael Holquist, 259–422. Austin: University of Texas Press, 1981.

Bance, Alan, ed., *The Cultural Legacy of the British Occupation in Germany*. London: Institute of Germanic Studies, University of London, 1997.

Banville, John. *The Sea*. London: Vintage, 2006.

Barber, Noel. *War of the Running Dogs: Malaya, 1945–1960*. London: Cassell, 2007.

Barnes, Julian. *Flaubert's Parrot*. London: Picador, 2002.

Barthes, Roland. *The Pleasure of the Text*. Trans. Richard Miller. New York: Hill and Wang, 1975.

Beckett, Samuel. "The New Object." *Modernism/Modernity* 18, no. 4 (2014): 873–77.

———. *Proust and Three Dialogues with George Duthuit*. London: Calder and Boyars, 1965.

Bedford, Sybil. "An Interview." *Paris Review*, Spring 1933, no. 126. https://www.theparisreview.org/miscellaneous/1963/an-interview-sybille-bedford. Accessed May 2016.

Bennett, Andrew, and Nicholas Royle. *Elizabeth Bowen and the Dissolution of the Novel*. New York: St. Martin's, 1995.

Bennett, Raymond. "A House That's Larger Than Life." *Housewife* 24 (April 1957).

Berlin, Isaiah. *Enlightening: Letters 1946–1960*, eds. Henry Hardy and Jennifer Holmes. London: Chatto & Windus, 2009.

———. *Flourishing: Letters 1928–1946*, ed. Henry Hardy. London: Chatto & Windus, 2004.

———. Interview by Michael Ignatieff, MI, Tape 13, 7 May 1991. http://berlin.wolf.ox.ac.uk/lists/interviews/ignatieff/biographical-interviews/transcripts.pdf, © The Trustees of the Isaiah Berlin Literary Trust 2017.

Berman, Marshall. *All That Is Solid Melts into Air: The Experience of Modernity*. New York: Penguin, 1988.

Betjeman, John. "The Executive" and "Inexpensive Progress." *Poet Hunter*. http://www.poemhunter.com/i/ebooks/pdf/sir_john_betjeman_2004_9.pdf. Accessed September 18 and 26, 2004.

———. "How Verse Saved the Poet from the IRA." *Guardian*, April 22, 2000. http://www.theguardian.com/uk/2000/apr/22/books.booksnew. Accessed March 2015.

———. *Letters*, vol. 1: 1926–1951, ed. Candida Lycett Green. London: Minerva, 1995.

"The Bigging Hill Aerodrome." *Wikipedia*. http://ramsgatehistory.com/zoomify/zeppelins_1915_viewer.htm. Accessed September 15, 2015.

Bloom, Emily C. *The Wireless Past: Anglo-Irish Writers and the BBC, 1931–1968*. Oxford: Oxford University Press, 2016

Bluemel, Kristin. *Intermodernism and the Literary Culture in Mid-Twentieth Century*. Edinburgh: Edinburgh University Press, 2008.

Bonce, Alan. *The Cultural Legacy of the British Occupation of Germany: The London Symposium*. Stuttgart: Verlag Hans-Dieter Heinz, Akademischer Verlag, 1957.

Boston, Ann, ed. *Wave Me Goodbye: Stories of the Second World War*. London: Penguin, 1988.

Bowen, Henry Cole. *Statutory Land Purchase in Ireland Prior to 1923*. Dublin: Falconer Press, 1928.

Bowra, Maurice. *Memories (1898–1939)*. Cambridge, MA: Harvard University Press, 1967.

Brooke, Jocelyn. *Elizabeth Bowen*. London: Longmans, Green, 1952.

Brown, Terrence. *The Literature of Ireland: Culture and Criticism*. Cambridge: Cambridge University Press, 2010.

Butler, Hubert. *Independent Spirit: Essays*. New York: Farrar, Straus, and Giroux, 1996.

Byatt, A. S. "Elizabeth Bowen: *The House in Paris*." In *The Passions of the Mind*, ed. A.S. Byatt. 241–49. London: Chatto and Windus, 1991.

———. Introduction to *The House in Paris* by Elizabeth Bowen, New York: Penguin Twentieth Century Classics, 1994.

Caestecker, Frank, and Bob Moore, eds. *Refugees from Nazi Germany and the Liberal European States*. New York: Berghahn, 2010.

Cameron, Alan C. *The Film in National Life*. London: Allen and Unwin, 1932.

Caron, Vicki. *Uneasy Asylum: France and the Jewish Refugee Crisis, 1933–1942*. Stanford: Stanford University Press, 1999.

Caws, MaryAnn. "Ladies Shot and Painted." In *The Female Body in Western Culture*, ed. Susan Suleiman, 261–69. Cambridge, MA: Harvard University Press, 1986.

———. *Surrealism and Women*. Cambridge, MA: MIT Press, 1991.

———. "Thinking North." *Raritan Review* 32, no. 3 (winter, 2013).

Corse, Edward. "British Propaganda in Neutral Eire after the Fall of France, 1940." *Contemporary British History* 22, issue 2, (May 2008): 163–180.

Chatterjee, Partha. *The Nation and Its Fragments: Colonial and Postcolonial Histories*. Princeton: Princeton University Press, 1993.

Cheyette, Bryan, and Laura Marcus. "Some Methodological Anxieties." *Modernity, Culture, and "the Jew,"* 29, no. 1 (1996): 1–20.

Collis, Rose. *A Trouser-Wearing Character: The Life and Times of Nancy Spain*. London: Cassell, 1979.

Conley, Katherine. *Surreal Ghostliness*. Lincoln: University of Nebraska Press, 2013.

Connolly, Cyril. "Comment." *Horizon* 6, no. 36 (December 1942): 9.

———. *Enemies of Promise*. 2nd ed. London: Penguin, 1948.

———. "It's Got Here at Last." Review. *New Statesman & Nation* (London), December 14, 1935.

———. "Missing Diplomats," *Sunday Times* (London), September 21 and 28, 1952.

Conradi, Peter. "The Guises of Love." *Iris Murdoch Review* 19, no. 5 (2015): 17–28.

Corcoran, Neil. *The Chosen Ground: Essays on the Contemporary Poets of Northern Ireland*. Bridgend, UK: Poetry Wales Press, 1995.

———. *Elizabeth Bowen: The Enforced Return*. Oxford: Clarendon Press, 2004.

Costello, John, and Oleg Tsarev. *Deadly Illusion: The KGB Orlov Dossier Reveals Stalin's Master Spy*. New York: Crown, 1993.

Coughlan, Patricia. "Women and Desire in the Work of Elizabeth Bowen." In *Sex, Nation, and Dissent*, ed. Eibhear Walshe, 103–34. Cork, Ireland: Cork University Press, 1996.

Craig, Patricia. *Elizabeth Bowen*. Harmondsworth: Penguin, 1986.

Cronin, Jim. *The Anglo-Irish Novel, 1900–1940*. Belfast: Apple Tree Press, 1990.

Cunningham, Valentine. *British Writers of the Thirties*. Oxford: Oxford University Press, 1988.

Curtis Brown Records. Bowen, Catalogued Correspondence. Box 3, Author files, Box 42 (3 folders), Columbia University, New York.

Dalgarno, Emily. *The Migrations of Language*. Cambridge: Cambridge University Press, 2011.

Darroch, Sandra Jobson. *Ottoline: The Life of Lady Ottoline Morrell*. New York: Coward, McCann, and Geoghegan, 1975.

Darwood, Nicola. *A World of Lost Innocence: The fiction of Elizabeth Bowen*. Newcastle: Cambridge Scholars Publications, 2012.

David, Deirdre. *Olivia Manning: A Woman at War*. Oxford: Oxford University Press, 2012.

Davis, Robert Murray. "Contributions to 'Night and Day' by Elizabeth Bowen, Graham Greene, and Anthony Powell." *Studies in the Novel* 3, no. 4 (1971): 401–4.

Davis, Rupert Hart, ed. *The Lyttleton Hart-Davis Letters*. 1978. Reprint, London: John Murray, 2003.

De-la-Noy, Michael. *Eddy: The Life of Edward Sackville-West*. London: Bodley Head, 1988.

De Lautréamont, Comte. *Les Chantes de Maldoror*. New York: New Directions, 1965.

Deer, Patrick. *Culture in Camouflage: War, Empire, and Modern British Literature*. Oxford: Oxford University Press, 2009.

Derrida, Jacques. *Archive Fever: A Freudian Impression*. Chicago: University of Chicago Press, 1998.

Devlin, Albert J., and Peggy Whitman-Prenshaw, eds. *Welty: A Life in Literature*. Jackson: University of Mississippi Press, 1987.

DeVries, Peter. "Touch and Go (With a Low Bow to Elizabeth Bowen)." *New Yorker*, January 26, 1952, 30–32.

DeWaal, Edmund. *The Hare with the Amber Eyes: A Family's Century of Art and Loss*. New York: Farrar, Straus, and Giroux, 2010.

DeWitt-Miller, R. "The Cure for Stammering." *Popular Mechanics* 74, no. 1 (1940).

Dictionary of National Biography, ed. Stephen, Leslie, Sidney Lee, and Christine Nicolls. 1885. Reprint, Oxford: Oxford University Press, 2004.

Donnelly, James S., Jr. "Big House Burnings in County Cork during the Irish Revolution, 1920–1921." *Eire-Ireland* 47, nos. 3 and 4 (2012): 141–97.

"Early Works by Modern Women Writers: Woolf, Bowen, Mansfield, Cather, and Stein." *Reference and Research Book News* 21, no. 3 (2006).

Eddington, Arthur Stanley. *The Nature of the Physical World*. London: Cambridge University Press, 1928.

Edgeworth, Maria. *Castle Rackrent*. 1832–33. Reprint, New York: Dover, 2005.

Ellmann, Maud. *Elizabeth Bowen: The Shadow across the Page*. Edinburgh: Edinburgh University Press, 2003.

Ellmann, Richard. *James Joyce*. New York: Oxford University Press, 1965.

Farrell, Marcia. *Elizabeth Bowen: A Comprehensive Bibliography*. Wilkes-Barre, PA: Humanities at Wilkes University, 2012.

Feigel, Lara. *The Bitter Taste of Victory: Life, Love, and Art in the Ruins of the Reich*. London: Bloomsbury, 2016.

———. *The Love Charm of Bombs: Restless Lives in the Second World War*. London: Bloomsbury, 2013.

Finkelstein, Haim. *Surrealism and the Crisis of the Object*. Ann Arbor, MI: UMI Research Press, 1979.

Fisk, Robert. *In Time of War: Ireland, Ulster, and the Price of Neutrality, 1939–1945*. 1983. Reprint, London: Gill and Macmillan, 2001.

———. "Turning Our Back on the Fire of Life." *Irish Times* (Dublin), October 19, 1999. https://www.irishtimes.com/culture/turning-our-backs-on-the-fire-of-life-1.240418.

Forster, E. M. "What I Believe." In Forster, *Two Cheers for Democracy*. 1951. Reprint, New York: Mariner Books, 1962.

Foster, Roy. *Modern Ireland: 1600–1972*. London: Penguin, 1988.

Fothergill, John, ed. *The Fothergill Omnibus, for Which Seventeen Eminent Authors Have Written Short Stories upon One and the Same Plot*. London: Eyre and Spottiswoode, 1931.

Foucault, Michel. *Discipline and Punish: The Birth of the Prison*. Trans. Alan Sheridan. New York: Pantheon, 1977.

Gilbert, Sandra, and Susan Gubar. *The Madwoman in the Attic: The Woman Writer and the Nineteenth-Century Literary Imagination*. New Haven: Yale University Press, 1979.

Gildersleeve, Jessica. *Elizabeth Bowen and the Writing of Trauma: The Ethics of Survival*. Amsterdam: Rodopi, 2014.

Gilligan, Carol. "Women's Voices," lecture, William Alanson White Institute, October 24, 2009.

Gilman, Sander. *The Jew's Body: Self-Hatred, Anti-Semitism, and the Hidden Language of the Jews*. New York: Routledge, 1991.

Giroux, Robert. "An Interview." *Paris Review* (Summer 2000), Interview Section.

Glendinning, Victoria. *Elizabeth Bowen: Portrait of a Writer*. 1977. Reprint, New York: Penguin, 1985.

———. Glendinning and Judith Robertson. Eds. *Love's Civil War: Elizabeth Bowen and Charles Ritchie, Letters and Diaries*, Toronto: McClelland and Stewart, 2008.

Gornick, Vivian. "Elizabeth Bowen in Love." *Raritan* 37, no.2 (Fall 2017), 109–118.

Gowrie, Grey. *Derek Hill: An Appreciation*. London: Quartet Books, 1987.

Green, Henry. *Loving; Living; Partygoing*. New York: Penguin Classics, 1993.

Greene, Graham. *Brighton Rock*. New York: Penguin, 1938.

Gula, Mariann. "Lost a Bob but Found a Tanner: From a Translator's Workshop." https://periodicos.ufsc.br/index.php/scientia/article/viewFile/1980-4237.2010n8p122/18129. Accessed September 5, 2016.

Hachey, Thomas E. "Nuanced Neutrality and Irish Identity: Idiosyncratic Legacy," in *Turning Points in Twentieth-Century Irish History*, 77–102. Dublin: Irish Academic Press, 2011.

———. "The Rhetoric and Reality of Irish Neutrality." *New Hibernia Review* 6, no. 4 (2002): 26–43.

———. ed. *Turning Points in Twentieth-Century Irish History*. Dublin: Irish Academic Press, 2011.

Hall, Radclyffe. *The Well of Loneliness*. 1928. Reprint, Ware, UK: Wordsworth Editions, 2014.

Halliday, Nigel Faux. *More than a Bookshop: Zwemmers and Art in the Twentieth Century*. London: Philip Wilson, 2003.

Hand, Derek. *The History of the Irish Novel*. Cambridge: Cambridge University Press, 2011.

Hanley, Lynn. *Writing War: Fiction, Gender, and Memory*. Amherst: University of Massachusetts Press, 1991.

Hardwick, Elizabeth. "Elizabeth Bowen's Fiction." *Partisan Review* 16 (1949): 114–21.

Hart-Davis, Rupert, ed. *The Lyttleton Hart-Davis Letters*. 1978. Reprint, London: John Murray, 2003.

Hastings, Selina. *Rosamond Lehmann: A Life*. London: Vintage, 2003.

Haughton, Hugh, and Bryan Radley. "Interview with John Banville." *Modernism/Modernity* (2011): 855–72.

Heaney, Seamus. *Sweeney Astray: A Version from the Irish*. New York: Farrar, Straus, and Giroux, 1984.

Heath, William Webster. *Elizabeth Bowen: An Introduction to Her Novels*. Madison, WI: University Microfilms, 1981.

Henty, G. A. *Boy Knight: A Tale of the Crusades*. Reprint, 1883. CreateSpace Independent Publisher, 2010.

———. *By Sheer Pluck: A Tale of the Ashanti War*. Reprint, 1897. CreateSpace Independent Publisher, 2016.

Henty, G. A., and Arthur Rackham. *Brains and Bravery, Being Stories*. Edinburgh: W. W. and R. Chambers, 1905.

Hepburn, Allan. ed. *The Bazaar and Other Stories by Elizabeth Bowen*. Edinburgh: Edinburgh University Press, 2008.

———. *Intrigue: Espionage and Culture*. New Haven: Yale University Press, 2005.

———. ed. *Listening In: Broadcasts, Speeches, and Interviews by Elizabeth Bowen*. Edinburgh: Edinburgh University Press, 2010.

———. ed. *People, Places and Things: Essays by Elizabeth Bowen*. Edinburgh: Edinburgh University Press, 2008.

———. "Trials and Errors: *The Heat of the Day* and Post-War Culpability." Ed. Bluemel, *Intermodernisms*, 131–49.

———. "War in the Archives." *Ransom Edition*, Spring 2008.

———. ed. *The Weight of a World of Feeling: Reviews and Essays by Elizabeth Bowen*. Evanston: Northwestern University Press, 2017.

Hewison, Robert. *Under Siege: Literary Life in London*. London: Weidenfeld and Nicolson, 1977.

Hill, Derek. "Letter from Ireland." *Horizon* 18 (1946): 270–74.

———. Hill-Bowen Correspondence. 1953–1971. PRONI. D4400/C/2/27.

Hillier, Bevis. *Betjeman: The Bonus of Laughter*. London: John Murray, 2004.

———. *John Betjeman: The Biography*. London: John Murray, 2006.

Hoogland, Renee C. *Elizabeth Bowen: A Reputation in Writing*. New York & London: NYU Press, 1994.

Horner, Avril, and Anne Rowe, eds. *Living on Paper: Letters from Iris Murdoch, 1934–1995*. Princeton: Princeton University Press, 2015.

Horowitz, Sara R. "Lovin' Me, Lovin' Jew: Gender, Intermarriage, and Metaphor," in *Anti-semitism and Philosemitism in the Twentieth and Twenty-First Centuries: Representing Jews, Jewishness, and Modern Culture*, ed. Phyllis Lassner and Lara Trubowitz, 196–216. Newark: University of Delaware Press, 2008.

Horsler, Val, and Jenny Kingsland. *Downe House: A Mystery and a Miracle*. London: Third Millennium, 2006.

House, John. Obituary. February 14, 2012. *The Guardian*. http://www.theguardian.com/education/2012/feb/14/john-house-obituary. Accessed March 2012.

Howard, Elizabeth Jane. *Slipstream: A Memoir*. London: Pan Macmillan, 2003.

Howard, Michael. *Jonathan Cape, Publisher*. London: Jonathan Cape, 1971.

Ignatieff, Michael. *Isaiah Berlin: A Life*. London: Chatto and Windus, 1998.

Igoe, Vivien. *A Literary Guide to Dublin*. London: Methuen, 2000.

Inglesby, Elizabeth. "Expressive Objects." *Modern Fiction Studies* 53, no. 2 (2007): 309.

Ingman, Heaather. *Irish Women's Fiction from Edgeworth to Enright*. Dublin: Irish Academic Press, 2013.

Jameson, Storm. *A Cup of Tea for Mr. Thorgill*. New York: Harper and Brothers, 1957.

———. *The Novel in Contemporary Life*. Boston: Writers Inc., 1938.

Jenkins, Elizabeth. Introduction to *Collected Reports of the Jane Austen Society, 1949–64*. Reprint, London: Wm. Dawson and Sons, 1967.

Joannou, Maroula. *Ladies, Please Don't Smash These Windows: Women's Writing, Feminist Consciousness, and Social Change, 1918–38*. Oxford: Berg, 1995.

Jordan, Heather Bryant. *How Will the Heart Endure: Elizabeth Bowen and the Landscape of War*. Ann Arbor: University of Michigan Press, 1992.

Joyce, James. *Dubliners*. New York: Viking Press, 1961.

———. *Ulysses*. New York: Modern Library, 1961.

Judt, Tony. "The Rehabilitation of Europe." In Judt, *Postwar: A History of Europe Since 1945*, 63–99. New York: Penguin, 1995.

Kavky, Samantha. "Max Ernst's Post–World War Studies in Hysteria." *The Space Between: Literature and Culture, 1914–1945* 8, no. 1 (2012): 37–63.

Keane, Molly. "Elizabeth of Bowen's Court," *The Irish Times*, March 20, 1985.

————. *Good Behaviour*. London: Virago Press, 2005.

Kelly, Marian. "The Power of the Past: Structural Nostalgia in Elizabeth Bowen's *The House in Paris* and *The Little Girls*." *Style* 36, no. 1 (2002): 1–18.

Kelly, Martin J. "The Last Days of the Colleys on Carbury Hill." *Journal of the County Kildare Archeological Society* 17, no. 1 (1987).

Kenney, Edwin J. *Elizabeth Bowen*. Lewisburg: Bucknell UP, 1975.

Kiberd, Declan. *Inventing Ireland: The Literature of a Modern Nation*. New York: Random House, 2009.

The King's Speech. Directed by Tom Hooper. 2010. New York: Weinstein Company, 2011. DVD.

Kopytoff, Igor. "The Cultural Biography of Things: Commoditization as Process." In *The Social Life of Things: Commodities in Cultural Perspective*, ed. Arjun Appadurai, 64–91. New York: Cambridge University Press, 1986.

Kochavi, Arieh J. "British Policy toward East European Refugees in Germany and Austria." Los Angeles: Museum of Tolerance: Simon Wiesenthal Center, 1945–47.

Kreilkamp, Vera. *The Anglo-Irish Novel and the Big House*. New York: Syracuse University Press, 1998.

————. "Bowen, Ascendancy Modernist." In Walshe, ed. *Elizabeth Bowen, Visions and Revisions*, 12–26.

Kreyling, Michael. "The Culminating Moment: *To the Lighthouse* and *The Optimist's Daughter*." In Kreyling, *Eudora Welty's Achievement of Order*, 153–173. Baton Rouge: Louisiana State University Press, 1980.

Landon, Lana Hartman, and Laurel Smith. *Early Works by Modern Women Writers: Woolf, Bowen, Mansfield, Cather, and Stein*. Lewiston, NY: Edwin Mellen Press, 2006.

Lane, Jack, and Brendan Clifford. "Elizabeth Bowen: A 'Debate' in *The Irish Examiner*. Cork, Ireland: Aubane Historical Society, May 2008.

———— eds. *North Cork Anthology*. Cork, Ireland: Aubane Historical Society, 1993.

Lassagne-Wells, Shannon. "'Disjected Snapshots': Photography in the Short Stories of Elizabeth Bowen." *Journal of the Short Story in English* 56 (2011): 39–48.

Lassner, Phyllis. *British Women Writers of World War II: Battlegrounds of Their Own*. London: Macmillan, 1998.

————. *Elizabeth Bowen* (Women Writers Series). New York: Rowman and Littlefield, 1990.

————. *Espionage and Exile: Fascism and Anti-Fascism in British Spy Fiction*. Edinburgh: Edinburgh UP, 2017.

————. "Out of the Shadows: The Newly Collected Elizabeth Bowen." Review. *Modernism/Modernity* 17, no. 3 (2010): 669–776.

Lassner, Phyllis, and Lara Trubowitz. *Antisemitism and Philosemitism in the Twentieth and Twenty-First Centuries: Representing Jews, Jewishness, and Modern Culture*. Newark, DE: University of Delaware Press, 2008.

Lassner, Phyllis, and Paula Derdiger. "Domestic Gothic, the Global Primitive, and Gender Relations in Elizabeth Bowen's *The Last September* and *The House in Paris*." In *Irish Modernism and the Global Primitive*, ed. Claire A. Culleton and Maria McGarrity, 195–214. New York: Palgrave Macmillan, 2008.

Laurence, Patricia. "The Reading and Writing of Silence." In Laurence, *The Reading of Silence: Virginia Woolf in the English Tradition*, 89–122. Stanford: Stanford University Press, 1991.

———. *Lily Briscoe's Chinese Eyes: Bloomsbury, Modernism and China*. Columbia: University of South Carolina Press, 2003.

———. Review, Allan Hepburn, *Listening In*. *Modernism/Modernity*. 19:3, 2012.

LCW: Love's Civil War: Elizabeth Bowen and Charles Ritchie, Letters and Diaries, ed. Victoria Glendinning and Judith Robertson. Toronto: McClelland and Stewart, 2008.

Leaska, Mitchell. *Granite and Rainbow: The Hidden Life of Virginia Woolf*. New York: Farrar, Straus, and Giroux, 1998.

Lee, Hermione, ed. *The Mulberry Tree: Writings of Elizabeth Bowen*. New York, San Diego, London: Harcourt, Brace Jovanovich, 1986.

———. *Elizabeth Bowen: An Estimation*. 1981. Reprint, London: Vintage, 1999.

LeFanu, J. Sheridan. *Carmilla*. Seattle: CreateSpace Independent Publishing Platform, 2012.

Lehmann, Rosamond. *The Echoing Grove*. New York: Harcourt Brace, 1953.

———. "Elizabeth Bowen—Obituary." *London Times*, February 26, 1973.

———. "Rosamond Lehmann—Interview: The Art of Fiction," by Shusha Guppy. *Paris Review* 88 (Summer 1985). https://www.theparisreview.org/interviews/2894/rosamond-lehmann-the-art-of-fiction-no-88-rosamond-lehmann. Accessed May 2011.

———. *Rosamond Lehmann's Album: With an W and Postscript by Rosamond Lehmann*. London: Chatto and Windus, 1985.

———. *The Swan in the Evening: Fragments of an Inner Life*. New York: Open Road Media, 2015.

Lewis, Jeremy. *Cyril Connolly: A Life*. London: Jonathan Cape, 1997.

Lloyd-Jones, Hugh, ed. *Maurice Bowra: A Celebration*. 1974. Reprint, Ann Arbor: University of Michigan Press, 2008.

London County Council School of Arts and Crafts. *Prospectus and Time Table, 1917–1918*.

London, Louise. *Whitehall and the Jews, 1933–1942*. Cambridge: Cambridge University Press, 2000.

Macaulay, Rose. Macaulay, Dame Rose: 9ALS, 2 APCS to EB, HRC. "The Virtue of Queenship." BBC Broadcast May 31, 1952. Bodleian Ms. 6829, #19.

MacNeice, Louis. "Neutrality," "Budgie" In *The Penguin New Writing*, ed. John Lehmann. 1943, 41.

Mahon, Derek. "MacNeice, the War and the BBC." Open Edition Books, Presses Universitaires deCaen. http://books.openedition.org/puc/544?lang=en%2D%2Don-line. Accessed January 2016.

Maloney, John J. "The Contemporary Feminine." *American Scholar* (1950): 110–30.

Manning, E. F. "The Oak Tree." *Blarney Magazine* 7 (1954): 22–27.

Marcus, Jane Connor, ed. *The Young Rebecca: Writings of Rebecca West, 1911–17.* Bloomington: Indiana University Press, 1983.

Marcus, Laura. *Dreams of Modernity: Psychoanalysis, Literature, Cinema.* Cambridge: Cambridge University Press, 2014.

Marrs, Suzanne. *Eudora Welty: A Biography.* New York: Mariner, 2006.

———. "Place and the Displaced in Eudora Welty's 'The Bride of Innisfallen.'" *Mississippi Quarterly* 50 (1977): 647–68.

Masters, Christopher. "John House—Obituary." *Guardian* (London), February 14, 2012, Education Section.

Maxwell, William. *So Long, See You Tomorrow.* New York: Vintage, 1996.

———. *What There is to Say We Have Said: The Correspondence of Eudora Welty & William Maxwell,* ed. Susanne Marrs. Houghton Mifflin Harcourt. Boston, New York, 2011.

McEwan, Ian. *Sweet Tooth.* New York: Doubleday, 2012.

McGuire, James, and James Quinn, eds. *Dictionary of Irish Biography.* Cambridge: Cambridge University Press, 2010.

McLaine, Ian. *Ministry of Morale: Home Front Morale and the Ministry of Information in World War II.* London: George Allen & Unwin, 1979.

McMahon, Paul. *British Spies and Irish Rebels: British Intelligence and Ireland, 1916–1945.* Woodbridge, UK: Boyardell Press, 2008.

McNeillie, Andrew. *Winter Moorings.* Manchester, UK: Carcanet Press, 2014.

McWhirter, David. "Eudora Welty Goes to the Movies: Modernism, Regionalism, Global Media." *Modern Fiction Studies* 55, no. 1 (2009): 68–91.

Maslen, Elizabeth. *Life in the Writings of Storm Jameson: A Biography.* Evanston, Illinois: Northwestern University Press, 2014.

Melchers, Christopher. "Bowen in Hythe." *Hythe Civic Society Newsletter* 147, April 2009, 2.

Miller, Jan. "Re-reading Elizabeth Bowen." *Raritan* 20 (2000): 17–31.

Mitchell, Leslie. *Maurice Bowra: A Life.* Oxford: Oxford University Press, 2009.

Monaghan, Charles. "Portrait of a Woman Reading." *Chicago Tribune Book World,* November 10, 1968, 80–83.

Morrell, Ottoline. *Lady Ottoline's Album: Snapshots and Portraits of Her Famous Contemporaries (and Herself),* ed. Caroline Heilbrun. New York: Knopf, 1976.

Morris, John, ed. *From the Third Programme: A Ten-Years' Anthology.* London: Nonesuch Press, 1956.

Moss, Howard. "Elizabeth Bowen: Intelligence at War." In Moss, *Writing against Time: Critical Essays and Reviews,* 214–19. New York: William Morrow, 1969.

———. "Heiress Is an Outsider." *New York Times,* October 13, 1968, Book Review, 1.

Murphy, Emily. "Regionalism and Nationalism in Elizabeth Bowen's Irish Writings." Master's thesis, University College, Cork, Ireland, November 1994.

Murphy, Tom. *Famine*. London: Methuen, 2001.

New Burlington Galleries Catalog. "The International Surrealist Exhibition, London," June 11–July 4, 1936.

Newell, Hilary. *Women Must Choose: The Position of Women in Europe Today*. London: Gollancz, 1937.

Nicolson, Nigel, and Joanne Trautmann, eds. *The Letters of Virginia Woolf*. Vols. 1–6. New York: Mariner Books, 1982.

Nicolson, Nigel, and Kenneth Clarke. "Exit Permit for Stephen Spender and Cyril Connolly to Visit Eire." 1941. London: British National Archives.

O'Brien, Edna. *Country Girl*. London: Little Brown, 2012.

O'Faolain, Sean, ed. *The Bell*, 1940–1946. Series. National Library of Ireland, Ir 05 b6. Dublin, Ireland. "Midsummer Night Madness." In *The Finest Stories of Sean O'Faolain*, ed. Elizabeth Bowen. Boston: Little, Brown, 1948.

———. "Reading and Remembrance of Elizabeth Bowen." *London Review of Books* 4, no. 4 (1982): 15–16.

———. *Vive Moi*. London: Sinclair-Stevenson, 1993.

O'Halpin, Eunan. *Spying on Ireland: British Intelligence and Neutrality During the Second World War*. Oxford: Oxford UP, 2008.

Oldfield, Sybil. *Women Against the Iron Fist*. Oxford: Blackwell, 1989.

O'Malley, Ernie. *On Another Man's Wound: A Personal History of Ireland's War of Independence*. Boulder, CO: Roberts Rinehart, 1936.

Osborn, Susan. *Elizabeth Bowen: New Critical Perspectives*. Cork, Ireland: Cork University Press, 2009.

———. "Reconsidering Elizabeth Bowen." *Modern Fiction Studies* 52, no. 1 (2006): 187–97.

Paxton, Robert, and Michael R. Marrus. *Vichy France and the Jews*. New York: Basic Books, 1985.

Phipps, Sally Keane. Molly Keane: A Life. London: Virago, 2018.

Pinter, Harold. *The Heat of the Day*. London: Faber and Faber, 1989. tratra

Plomer, William. *At Home*. London: Jonathan Cape, 1958.

———. *Double Lives & At Home: An Autobiography*. Afterword, Simon Noel Smith. London: Jonathan Cape, 1945.

———. *Electric Delights*, ed. Rupert Hart-Davis. Boston: Godine, 1978.

———. *Museum Pieces*. London: Jonathan Cape, 1952.

———. "Notes on a Visit to Ireland," in Peter Alexander. *William Plomer: A Biography*. Oxford: Oxford University Press, 1989.

———. *Selected Poems*. UK: Carcanet Press Ltd., 2017.

———. *Selected Stories*. Capetown: Africasouth, 1984.

"Polish Troops Hit Back at Danzig." *Evening Standard* (London), September 1, 1939, 1.

Porcelli, Stefania. "Careless Talk Costs Lives: War Propaganda and Wartime Fiction in Elizabeth Bowen's *The Heat of the Day*." In *Challenges for the Twenty-First Century: Dilemmas, Ambiguities, Directions*, ed. Spade Columba, Crisafulli, and Ruggieri. Rome: University of Rome Department of Comparative Literature, 2011.

———. "Elizabeth Bowen's Wavering Attitude towards World War II Propaganda." In *Propaganda and Rhetoric in Democracy: History, Theory, Analysis*, ed. Gae Lyn Henderson and Mary J. Braun, 96–117. Carbondale, IL: Southern Illinois University Press, 2016.

Poulet, Georges. *The Interior Distance*. Trans. Elliott Coleman. Baltimore: Johns Hopkins University Press, 1959.

Powell, Anthony. *The Age of Absurdity: Anthony Powell and Robert Vanderbilt, Letters, 1952–1963*, ed. John Smith and Jonathan Kooperstein. London: Maggs Brothers, 2011.

Powell, Violet. *The Constant Novelist: A Study of Margaret Kennedy*. London: Heinemann, 1983.

———. *The Irish Cousins: The Books and Backgrounds of Somerville and Ross*. London: Heinemann, 1970.

Powers, Bill. *White Knights, Dark Earls: The Rise and Fall of an Anglo-Irish Dynasty*. Cork, Ireland: Collins Press, 2000.

PPT: People, Places, Things: Essays by Elizabeth Bowen, ed. Allan Hepburn. Edinburgh: Edinburgh University Press, 2008.

Prenshaw, Peggy Whitman. "Conversations with Eudora Welty." In *Eudora Welty: A Life in Literature*, ed. Albert J. Devlin, Jackson: University of Mississippi Press, 1987.

Proust, Marcel. *In Search of Lost Time*, vol.1–6 (Swann's Way, Within a Budding Grove, The Guermantes Way, Sodom and Gomorrah, The Captive, The Fugitive, Time Regained). Trans. C.K. Scott Moncrieff, Terence Kilmartin; Revised, D.J. Enright, New York: Modern Library, 1992–1999.

———. *Jean Santeuil*. London: Penguin, 1994.

Quennell, Peter. *Customs and Characters*. London: Weidenfeld and Nicolson, 1982.

Quinlan, Kieran. *Strange Kin: Ireland and the American South*. 1995. Reprint, Baton Rouge: Louisiana State University Press, 2008.

Radden-Keefe, Patrick. "Where the Bodies Are Buried." *New Yorker*, March 16, 2015.

Radford, Jean. "Late Modernism and the Politics of History." In *Women Writers of the 1930s: Gender, Politics, and History*, ed. Maroula Jannou, 33–45. Edinburgh: Edinburgh University Press, 1999.

———. "The Woman and the Jew." *Modernity, Culture, and the Jews* 29, no. 1 (1996): 103.

Radice, Anthony. "Placing Elizabeth Bowen in the Canon." *Contemporary Review* 287 (2005): 115–16.

Rees, Jenny. *Looking for Mr. Nobody: The Secret Life of Goronwy Rees*. 1994. Reprint, Brunswick, NJ: Transaction, 2000.

Richards, Jeffrey. *The Age of the Dream Palace: Cinema and Society in 1930s Britain*. London: I.B. Tauris, 2010.

Ridler, A. B. *Olive Willis and Downe House: An Adventure in Education*. London: Murray, 1967.

Ritchie, Charles. *The Siren Years: A Canadian Diplomat Abroad, 1937–1945*. Toronto: McClelland and Stewart, 2001.

Robins, Joseph. *The Madman and the Fool: A History of the Insane in Ireland*. Dublin: Institute of Public Administration, 1986.

Rouda, Frank. Letter, March 1, 1946. Columbia University Rare Book Room, Box 1, HM52858.

Rowe, Ann, and Avril Horner, eds. *Living on Paper: The Letters of Iris Murdoch*. Princeton: Princeton University Press, 2016.

Rubens, Robert. "Elizabeth Bowen: A Woman of Wisdom." *Contemporary Review* 268 (1996): 304–7.

Saussure de, Ferdinand. *Course in General Linguistics*, ed. Charles Bally, Albert Sechehaye in collaboration with Albert Riedlinger. Trans. Wade Baskin. New York: McGraw Hill, 1966.

Sarton, May. *A Shower of Summer Days*. 1952. Reprint, New York: W.W. Norton, 1995.

———. *A World of Light: Portraits and Celebrations*. 1976. Reprint: New York: W.W. Norton, 1988.

Scott, Bonnie Kime, ed. *Selected Letters of Rebecca West*. New Haven: Yale University Press, 2000.

Sedgwick, Eve Kosofsky. "Paranoid Reading and Reparative Reading or You're So Paranoid You Probably Think This Essay Is About You." In Sedgwick, *Novel Gazing: Queer Readings in Fiction*, 123–51. Durham, NC: Duke University Press, 1997.

Seiler, Claire. "Immodernist Midcenturies." *Modernism/Modernity* 22, no. 4 (2015): 821–26.

Sellery, J'Nan M., and William O. Harris. *A Bibliography of Elizabeth Bowen*. Austin: Humanities Research Center, University of Texas, 1981.

Seymour, Miranda. *Ottoline Morrell: Life on the Grand Scale*. New York: Farrar, Straus, and Giroux, 1992.

Shakespeare, William. *Measure for Measure*. In *The Complete Works of Shakespeare*, ed. Hardin Craig. Chicago: Scott, Foresman, 1961.

Sheehan, Paul. *Modernism, Narrative, and Humanism*. Cambridge: Cambridge University Press, 2002.

Showalter, Elaine. *A Jury of Her Peers: American Women Writers from Anne Bradstreet to Annie Proulx*. New York: Knopf, 2009.

Smith, James. *British Writers and MI5 Surveillance, 1930–1960*. Cambridge: Cambridge University Press, 2013.

Smith, James M. *Ireland's Magdalene Laundries and the Nation's Architecture of Containment*. Notre Dame, IN: University of Notre Dame Press, 2007.

"Snowshill Manor." *National Trust*. http://www.nationaltrust.org.uk/snowshill-manor. Accessed January 13, 2014.

Somerville, Edith, and Martin Ross. *The Real Charlotte*. 1894. Reprint, Nashville, TN: J.S. Sanders, 1999.

Spencer, Elizabeth. *Landscapes of the Heart*. New York: Random House, 1998.

Spoo, Robert. *Without Copyrights: Piracy, Publishing, and the Public Domain*. London: Oxford University Press, 2014.

St. Gogarty, Oliver. *It Isn't This Time of Year at All! An Unpremeditated Autobiography*. New York: Doubleday, 1954.

"Stephen Gwynn—Obituary." *Columbian* (Dublin), July 1930.

Stonebridge, Lyndsey. "Creatures of an Impossible Time: Late Modernism, Human Rights, and Elizabeth Bowen." In *Judicial Imagination: Writing after Nuremberg*, ed. Lyndsey Stonebridge, 118–40. Edinburgh: Edinburgh University Press, 2011.

Stover, Justin. "War, Loyalty and Trauma in Ireland, 1914–1927." http://ak-militaergeschichte.de/stover_allegiances (accessed September 2020).

Sullivan, Walter. "A Sense of Place: Elizabeth Bowen and the Landscape of the Heart." *Sewanee Review* 84, no. 1 (1976): 142–49.

Summerson, John. *Georgian London*. Ed. Howard Colvin. London: Paul Mellon Centre, 2003.

Taylor, Elizabeth. *Mrs. Palfrey at the Claremont*. 1971, Reprint, London: Virago, 2006.

Teekell, Anna. "Elizabeth Bowen and Language at War." *New Hibernia Review* 15, no. 3 (2011): 61–79.

———. *Emergency Writing: Irish Literature, Neutrality, and the Second World War*. Evanston, Illinois: Northwestern University Press, 2018.

Toomey, Deirdre. Oxford *Dictionary of National Biography*, s.v. "Elizabeth Dorothea Cole Bowen," Oxford: Oxford University Press, 2004. www.oxforddnb.com. Accessed March 2007.

Trench, C. E. F. "Dermot Chenevix Trench and Haines of *Ulysses*." *James Joyce Quarterly* 13, no. 1 (1975): 39–48.

Trilling, Diana. "Fiction in Review." *The Nation*, February 26, 1949, 254–56.

Tweedsmuir, Susan. *A Winter's Bouquet*. London: Gerald Duckworth, 1954.

Van Haften, Julie. *Berenice Abbott, Photographer: A Modern Vision*. Forthcoming.

Waldron, Ann. *Eudora Welty: A Writer's Life*. New York: Doubleday, 1998.

Walkowitz, Rebecca. "Review of Mark Wollaeger's *Modernism, Media, and Propaganda*." *Modernism/Modernity* 15, no. 1 (January 2008).

Walshe, Eibhear, ed. *Elizabeth Bowen's Selected Irish Writings*. Cork: Cork University Press, 2011.

———, ed. *Elizabeth Bowen Remembered: Farahy Address*. Dublin: Farahy Courts Press, 1998.

———, ed. *Elizabeth Bowen: Visions and Revisions*. Sallins, Ireland: Irish Academic Press, 2009.

———, ed. *Sex, Nation and Dissent*. Cork, Ireland: Cork University Press, 1996.

Walshe, Keri. "Elizabeth Bowen, Surrealist." *Eire-Ireland* 42, nos. 3 and 4 (2007): 126–47.

Warren, Victoria. "Experience Means Nothing till It Repeats Itself: Elizabeth Bowen's *The Death of the* Heart and Jane Austen's *Emma*." *Modern Language Studies*, 29, no. 1 (September 1999):

Watanabe, Akiko. "The Cold War." *History in Focus*. http://www.history.ac.uk/ihr/Focus/cold/articles/watanabe.html. Accessed January 2015.

Wedgwood, C. V. *Montrose*. 1952. Reprint, New York: St. Martin's, 1998.

———. "The Value of Style in Historical Study." *London Times*, June 18, 1956.

Weininger, Otto. *Sex and Character*. 1903. Reprint, Bloomington: Indiana University Press, 2005.

Welty, Eudora. *The Bride of the Innisfallen, and Other Stories*. New York: Harcourt Brace Jovanovich, 1949.

———. *On Writing*. New York: Modern Library, 2002.

———. "Place in Fiction." In *The Eye of the Story: Selected Essays and Reviews*, 116–33. New York: Random House, 1970.

———. "Review of *Bowen's Court*, Photographs." *Eudora Welty Review* 8 (2016).

———. *What There is to Say We Have Said: The Correspondence of Eudora Welty & William Maxwell*, ed. Susanne Marrs. Houghton Mifflin Harcourt. Boston, New York, 2011.

West, Rebecca. "Mr. Setty and Mr. Hume," in West, *Train of Powder*, 165–232. 1955. Reprint, Lanham, MD: Ivan R. Dee, 2000.

"William Joyce." http://en.wikipedia.org/wiki/. Accessed July 14, 2014.

Wills, Clair. *That Neutral Island: A History of Ireland during the Second World War*. London: Faber and Faber, 2007.

Wilson Center History Project on the Cold War. "Marshall Plan of the Mind: The CIA Covert Book Program During the Cold War," broadcast, January 15, 2015.

Wohlleben, Peter. *The Hidden Life of Trees: What They Feel, How They Communicate—Discoveries from a Secret World*. Translated from German by Jane Billinghurst Greystone. Vancouver: David Suzuki Institute, 2016.

Wolf, Christa. *City of Angels: The Overcoat of Dr. Freud*. Trans. Damion Searl. New York: Farrar, Straus, and Giroux, 2014.

———. *The Quest for Christa T*. Trans. Christopher Middleton. New York: Noonday Press, Farrar, Straus, and Giroux, 1970.

Woolf, Virginia. *The Diary of Virginia Woolf*. Vols. 1–5, 1915–1941. Reprint, New York: Harcourt Brace Jovanovich, 1980.

———. *The Essays of Virginia Woolf*, Vols.1–6, 1904–1941. Vols.1–5, ed. Andrew McNeillie, Vol. 6, Stuart N. Clarke. London: Harcourt Brace Jovanovich, 1986–2011.

————. *The Letters of Virginia Woolf*. Vols. 1–6, 1888–1941. Ed. Nigel Nicolson and Joanne Trautmann. New York: Harcourt Brace Jovanovich, 1980.

————. "The Leaning Tower." In Woolf, *The Moment and Other Essays*. New York: Harcourt, Brace and Company, 1948.

————. "Modern Fiction." In Woolf, *The Common Reader, First Series*. 1925 Reprint, New York: Harcourt Brace Jovanovich, 1953.

————. "Mr. Bennett and Mrs. Brown." In Woolf, *The Second Common Reader*. New York: Harcourt Brace Jovanovich, 1932.

————. "The Narrow Bridge of Art." In Woolf, *Granite and Rainbow*. New York: Harcourt Brace Jovanovich, 1958.

————. Preface to *Orlando*, New York: Harcourt Brace Jovanovich, 1928.

————. *A Room of One's Own*. 1929. Reprint, New York: Harcourt, Brace & World, 1957.

————. *To the Lighthouse*. New York: Harcourt Brace Jovanovich, 1927.

Yeats, William Butler. *The Collected Poems of W.B. Yeats*. New York: Macmillan, 1956.

Young, Gwenda, ed. *Molly Keane: Essays in Contemporary Criticism*. Dublin: Four Courts Press, 2006.

Zwemmer Gallery. "Christmas Catalogue, London." 14 December–25 January, 1935.

Index[1]

---

[1] Note: Page numbers followed by 'n' refer to notes.